TRAVELLERS

TRAVELLERS

A Novel

HELON HABILA

HAMISH HAMILTON
an imprint of
PENGUIN BOOKS

HAMISH HAMILTON

UK | USA | Canada | Ireland | Australia
India | New Zealand | South Africa

Hamish Hamilton is part of the Penguin Random House group of companies
whose addresses can be found at global.penguinrandomhouse.com.

First published in the United States of America by
W. W. Norton and Company 2019
First published in Great Britain by Hamish Hamilton 2019
001

Permission granted by Ayebia for Helon Habila's quote from his poem 'Three
Seasons' from *Fathers & Daughters: An Anthology of Exploration* Ed. Ato Quayson
(2008): © Ayebia Clarke Publishing Limited, Banbury, Oxfordshire, UK.

Printed and bound in Great Britain by Clays Ltd, Elcograf S.p.A.

A CIP catalogue record for this book is available from the British Library

ISBN: 978–0–241–39450–2

www.greenpenguin.co.uk

MIX
Paper from
responsible sources
FSC® C018179

Penguin Random House is committed to a
sustainable future for our business, our readers
and our planet. This book is made from Forest
Stewardship Council® certified paper.

For Sharon, Adam and Edna

And for Sue

I cannot rest from travel . . .

ALFRED, LORD TENNYSON, 'ULYSSES'

It is part of morality not to be at home in one's home.

THEODORE ADORNO, *MINIMA MORALIA:*
REFLECTIONS FROM DAMAGED LIFE

Acknowledgements

My gratitude, first and foremost, to the voices whose stories animate this book – thanks for trusting me with your stories. In your travels, may you find the home you look for.

Thanks to my friends who made the time to read various versions of these stories and made suggestions, especially with the German language: Pascale Rondez, Branwen Okpako, Funmi Kogbe, Zainabu Jallo, Panashe Chigumadzi and Kai Hammer.

Johanna Meier, thanks for being my guide in Berlin.

Thanks to my agents, David Godwin and Ayesha Pande, for your undying support and encouragement, and for taking care of business. To my editors, Simon Prosser and Alane Mason, it's been a long journey over the years; thanks for making me a better writer.

The excellent *Tears of Salt: A Doctor's Story* by Pietro Bartolo and Lidia Tilotta was quite helpful in making me understand other dimensions of the refugee crisis in Europe.

The video installation referenced in Book 1 is by Branwen Okpako.

Thanks to the DAAD Fellowship for that magical year in Berlin. This book wouldn't have been possible without your support. To Flora Veit-Wild and Susanne Gherrmann at the Institute for Asian and African Studies, Humboldt University, Berlin, thanks for your friendship and support.

Finally, to those not mentioned here, you are always in my heart. Knowing you has changed me for ever.

TRAVELLERS

Book 1

ONE YEAR IN BERLIN

1

We came to Berlin in the fall of 2012, and at first everything was fine. We lived on Vogelstrasse, next to a park. Across the road was an *Apotheke*, and next to that a retirement home, and next to that a residential school for orphans. The school was once a home for single mothers, but eventually the mothers moved on and only the children were left. The school is made up of two cheerless structures – one noticeably newer than the other – behind waist-high cinder-block walls and giant fir trees. In the evenings the children ran in the park, jumping on trampolines and kicking around balls, their voices cutting through the frigid air clear as the bell ringing. In the mornings they sat in the courtyard behind the short fence to craft wooden animals and osier baskets under the watchful eyes of their minders. Once, out early with Gina, one of the boys, anywhere between the ages of eight and ten, sighted us and rushed to the low wall, he leaned over the top, almost vaulting over, his face lit up with smiles, all the while waving to us and shouting, '*Schokolade! Schokolade!*' I turned away, ignoring him. Gina stopped and waved back to him. 'Hello!' How his eyes grew and grew in his tiny face! Surprise mingled with pleasure as he ran back to his mates. He repeated this whenever he saw us, and Gina always indulged him, but I never got used to it. I never got used to the thin, eager voice, and how the other children, about a dozen or so, stopped and raised their eerily identical blond heads and blue eyes to watch him waving and calling '*Schocolade!*' as if his life depended on it.

•

I first met Mark when he came to the house with one of Gina's flyers in his hand. 'I am here for this,' he said, waving the yellow flyer. It said Gina was working on a series of portraits she called *Travellers*, and she was looking for real migrants to sit for her. Fifty euros a session, to be paid for by the fellowship. I pointed him to the guest room she had converted into a studio. Soon their voices carried to the living room, hers polite but firm, his questioning, arguing. He was being turned down, and I could have told him not to press, Gina would never change her mind. Later, when I asked her why, she said he wasn't right and didn't elaborate, but I guessed he looked too young, his face was too smooth and lacking the character only time and experience brings. Last week she had drawn a lady and her four-year-old daughter. I met the lady in the living room waiting for Gina to set up her easel, still wearing her outdoor coat, an old woollen affair, and when I asked her if she wanted me to take the coat she shook her head; I turned to the daughter, did she want a drink, she pulled the child closer to her. The week before that it was a man, Manu, who told me he was a doctor in his former life, now he worked as a bouncer in a nightclub, waiting for the result of his asylum application. His face was lined, prematurely old, and I knew Gina would love those lines, each one of them an eloquent testimony to what he had left behind, to the borders and rivers and deserts he had crossed to get to Berlin. She would also love the woman's hands that tightly clutched her daughter's arm, they were dry and scaly, the nails chipped, no doubt ruined while working in some hotel laundry room, or as a scullery maid.

Mark came out of the studio and stood by the living-room door, a wry smile on his face, his red jacket in one hand, still holding the yellow flyer in the other hand. Behind him Gina, in her paint-spattered overalls, was already back at her painting, dabbing away at the easel, her face scrunched up.

'I'll walk you to the bus stop,' I offered. I had been indoor all day reading, I needed to stretch my legs, or perhaps I felt sorry for him, coming all the way for nothing, or I might have sensed something intriguing about him, something unusual that maybe Gina had sensed as well, and for that reason had turned him away. That same thing that made her send him away had the opposite effect on me, it drew my attention. Right now he looked dejected, as if he had already made a budget for those fifty euros, which he was now realizing he would never see. I asked him if he had ever sat for a painter before. He hadn't. Who had, apart from professional models, but he thought what she needed were ordinary people, real people, and wasn't he real enough?

I walked ahead of Mark, down the stairs to the ground floor and out the door. My intention was to leave him at the bus stop and continue on across the road to the little lake where I sometimes went for a walk, but the bus was pulling away as we arrived and I decided to wait for the next bus with him, and when the bus failed to come on time he said he'd go by foot and on a whim I said, 'Let's walk.' It was spring and the sun lingered in the west, unwilling to set, its slanted rays falling unseasonably warm and bright. Perfect weather. We joined the flow of after-train crowd past the wurst stand, past the strawberry-coloured strawberry stand. Berliners sat alfresco eating ice cream beneath beach umbrellas, *Eis*, the sign said. Ahead of us a chubby diminutive lady in a red jacket was shouting into her phone, *Nein! Nein!* as she paced back and forth on the sidewalk, staring down passers-by. And the more people stared the higher her voice rose; for a moment she was famous. '*Nein! Ich weiss es nicht!*' she shouted, basking in the sunrays of her notoriety.

We passed a Roma couple on a bench next to a Kaiser's store, their dull, beady eyes focused on their daughter, who stood by the sidewalk with a pan in her hand. Mark walked with his head bowed, muttering to himself.

'It is a lovely day,' I said. He nodded. I'd walk with him, but it wasn't my duty to cheer him up. Two ladies walked just ahead of us, at the same pace as us, always a few steps ahead, and it was a pleasure to watch their slim and shapely bodies beneath their identical jean jackets, and their blonde hair bouncing with each step, hand in hand. They belonged to this day. One was older, in her forties perhaps, the other looked to be in her twenties; mother and daughter, or sisters, or friends, or lovers; there was a gentleness to their clasped hands, especially next to the rude screeching of tyres and the blaring of horns from the motor road.

On both sides of the road neon signs on storefronts blared out: *McFit, McPaper, McDonald's* – a very American top layer over the more traditional back streets and side streets and sleepy quarters that still throbbed on, timeless, like the tram tracks buried beneath the concrete and tarmac. In our first couple of months in Berlin, Gina and I had walked these back streets that led away from Kurfürstendamm and on and on and narrower and narrower to the front windows of artisans' workshops and soup kitchens and *Blumen* stores and family homes with children and parents seated at the table eating dinner. Just a few months ago these streets were empty and snow-covered, with garish Christmas lights strung from every leafless tree and storefront like charms to ward away winter's malevolent spirits. At George-Grosz-Platz the two women disappeared into a beauty store. Mark and I sat in the square and watched the yellow double-decker buses stop and start, and stop again, the people coming off and on. We sat, not talking, just enjoying the last sunrays of the day. Mark looked round at the people seated in front of the roadside cafés drinking coffee and smoking cigarettes and said, 'This could be Paris.' After about thirty minutes he sighed and stood up, waved and walked away with slow steps toward Adenauerplatz station. I wondered what his story was, if I'd see him again.

I continued to sit in the dying sunlight, wrapped up in my thoughts. A fat-jowled man ran awkwardly after a M29 bus, but he was too late. He stopped and waved his arms in frustration as the bus pulled away, his open trench coat flapping about him, but when he turned I saw it wasn't a man but a woman, her thick, porcine jowls clenched in annoyance. A young lady in high heels came off the M19 and sat on a bench next to me. She took out a lipstick and a mirror. When she returned the lipstick and mirror to her bag, she looked up and our eyes met, she smiled, and then she was gone, walking at that surprisingly fast clip people here have. I could have started a conversation, I could have said 'Hi', and we might have sat, and talked, elegant like Parisians. We might talk of George Grosz, after whom the square was named, painter, intellectual, rebel, who survived the First World War, and defied the Nazis in the Second, and fled to America only to be driven back to Berlin by nostalgia; he fell down a flight of stairs after an all-night bout of drinking.

'A beautiful death,' she might have said. But as I watched her go, I felt the already unbridgeable gap between me and this city widen. Even if I spoke her language, the language the city spoke, would she understand me? A month ago I had gone to the post office to post a letter, and the lady behind the counter, a flaxen-haired battleaxe, had stared at me, refusing to speak English, and we had stood glaring at each other as the line behind me grew and grew, she kept shouting German words at me, and I kept answering back in English, I wanted to buy stamps, I wanted to post my letter, till finally a lady from the back of the line stepped forward and interpreted. It was a tense standoff while it lasted, and I was sweating when I came out. A week later I started taking German classes.

2

'You must come, darling,' Gina said to me a year ago in our home in Arlington, 'I can't do it without you.' She had been offered the prestigious Berlin Zimmer Fellowship for the Arts. One year in Berlin. Perhaps this was what we needed, a break from our stagnating life and routine. Every year the Zimmer selected ten artists – writers and painters and movie directors and composers – from around the world, and this year Gina was one of two artists from the USA. She was an assistant professor at a local university, while I was teaching ESL to Korean immigrants in a back room in the local library. I was also a TA in my school, it paid for my tuition, but teaching was something I did with circumspection. Whenever I stood in front of the expectant young faces I felt like a fraud. Would they take everything I told them as the gospel truth, and what right did I have, what knowledge, what experience, to place myself before them as an authority? I was only thirty-five; perhaps if I were fifty, if I had travelled a little more, lived a little more . . .

'It is only a job, darling,' Gina, always pragmatic, told me. 'You are being overconscientious.'

Or maybe it was my fear of commitment – Gina mentioned this, referring not just to my uncompleted PhD dissertation, but also to the fact that we had promised to get married after graduating. She had graduated, I hadn't. We had lived together for three years in her tiny student apartment overlooking a parking lot. But no, I told her, it was only my immigrant's temperament, hoping for home and permanence in this new world, at the same time fearful of long-term entanglements and always hatching an exit plan.

But we did get married, and it was a good marriage, stable, we had our routines, like most married people, we woke up together, we went to work, in the evenings we sat on our narrow balcony overlooking the parking lot sharing a bottle of wine, sometimes we went to the movies, or to dinner, and perhaps that was why I hesitated to say yes to Berlin: What if we went and things changed between us? What if Berlin transformed us beyond where we wanted to go? It was obvious to me that part of the reason she applied for the Zimmer, apart from its prestige and its importance to her career, was because my dissertation was on nineteenth-century African history, on the 1884 Berlin Conference specifically, and what better way to encourage me to resume my research than by spending

a year in Berlin? Still I hesitated because I knew every departure is a death, every return a rebirth. Most changes happen
unplanned, and they always leave a scar.

Two months after our marriage Gina got pregnant. We
hadn't planned on that, and we certainly hadn't foreseen losing the pregnancy after just seven months. Devastating for
both of us, but something shifted in Gina. She stopped going
out; she cried all day; she stopped eating. There wasn't much
I could do; I sat by her side, held her hand, I reminded her we
were still young and there'd be opportunities to try again. I
read her poems, something I used to do a lot before we got
married. Her middle name was Margaret, and I would recite
Hopkins's 'Spring and Fall' to her: *Margaret, are you grieving / Over Goldengrove unleaving* . . . It always cheered her up,
and she'd smile and shake her head; but not this time. She
turned her face to the wall and curled into a ball, making
herself smaller, like a tiny foetus. Gina had always been strong,
maybe stronger than I was, certainly more resourceful than
me, and this was the first time I was seeing her so helpless.
How suddenly and unexpectedly everything had changed,
one moment we were a normal married couple, young, with
our future before us, the next moment we were stricken by
misfortune, prone and helpless.

One day she went to visit her parents in Takoma Park and
didn't come back; the next day her mother came and threw
Gina's things into a bag and said Gina needed to rest, to
recover, she added, her demeanour hinting that I was to blame
for her daughter's breakdown. I got along better with the
father, a retired professor who had spent a year in Nigeria on
a Fulbright scholarship in the 1980s, and who always looked

back to that year with great fondness. Alone in our two-room apartment, every morning I put in a call to Gina to see how she was doing, and to find out when she was coming back, and after that, with nothing more to do but sit and twiddle my thumbs in front of the TV, I began to drink. I drank in the nights at first, then in the afternoons, then in the mornings. I was sliding down a precipice, but I was unable to stop.

Gina stayed at her parents' for six months, and it was while she was there that she applied for the Zimmer. Exactly six months to the day she left, she walked into our tiny apartment, her eyes shining with hope and excitement as she showed me the Zimmer fellowship email. That night she didn't go back to her parents'. We lay in one another's arms all night long. Berlin. Maybe this was what we needed. A break from our breaking-apart life.

3

Even in Berlin I miss Berlin, Mark loved to say. He lived in Kreuzberg with his three friends, Stan, Eric and Uta, in an abandoned church building next to the river Spree. The church was tilted, as if a fingertip push could topple it, one of those crumbling buildings you occasionally saw around Berlin, spared by the war, and overlooked by the demolition ball, looking odd next to the newer structures. A baroque façade with a twisted spire faced the street behind a thick wire fence that cut off the building from the neighbouring houses and the passing cars. Most of the doors and windows were gone. In the courtyard the wind, like a restless spirit, drove pieces of paper and beer cans over the unruly grass in the driveway.

Mark and his friends had inherited the dwelling from another group of 'alternatives' who had moved on to Stockholm in search of stiffer anti-establishment challenges when Berlin grew too tame for them.

'I had to deconsecrate it when we moved in,' he said. 'There was a spirit living in the walls. I have a sense for these things.' It was one of his outlandish yet casually uttered comments that would have sounded crazy coming from another person, but from Mark it sounded normal, even reasonable. I met him again toward the end of spring, in a gallery. Gina was sleeping all day after working through the night – she wouldn't wake up till late afternoon when she'd emerge looking drawn and ethereal only to grab a sandwich from the fridge and go straight back to work – and I was left alone to stumble from place to place, mostly art galleries and libraries. I had learned about this particular exhibition from the emails sent to Gina by the Zimmer people. The gallery was exhibiting apartheid-era portraits by South African photographers. A young lady at the entrance handed me a pamphlet which proclaimed in bold Helvetica the bombastic title of the exhibition: *Apartheid, Exile and Proletarian Internationalism.* There were also photographs and video installations from local black artists. I drifted from room to room, reading the texts below the portraits – the photographs were mostly of South African exiles in East and West Berlin in the 1970s and 1980s. I looked at the unsmiling faces, thinking how ironic history was, that they'd come for succour here, escaping persecution and apartheid, this place that a few decades earlier had been roiling with its own brand of persecution under the Nazis. How did they cope with the food, the new language, with being visibly different, with the bone-chilling winter of exile? Most of them had returned to South Africa, those who had survived exile's bitterness, and were now their country's new leaders, replacing their white oppressors, most of whom had in turn been relegated to exile in the dark and dusty chapters of history.

I soon tired of viewing the identically grey and cheerless faces on the first floor and moved to the video installations in the basement. Apparently, I had the whole room to myself, and it felt a bit eerie, standing in the centre of the room, surrounded by multiple flickering TV monitors showing people opening and closing their mouths wordlessly. I sat in a booth nearby and put on the headphone and suddenly the mute faces became vocal. They were speaking German. I almost jumped when a hand touched mine. I turned. A figure had crystallized out of the dark space next to me. In the gloom his red jacket had coalesced with the red couch we were seated on and I had failed to see him. Now he was offering me his hand. The hand was slim and soft, and for a moment I thought it was a girl. He noticed my momentary disorientation and smiled, as if he was used to being mistaken for something he wasn't. His hand still in mine, he said, 'I am Mark.'

It was him, the would-be portrait sitter, turned down by Gina. He recognized me at about the same time. The silence lingered for a while, then I pointed at the TV monitors. 'What's this about?'

The TV monitors formed a triptych, one on our left with a woman on it, one on our right with a man on it, and one in front showing an old movie. The two faces on the left and right appeared to be discussing the movie in real time as it played. But it was all in German. 'The movie is *Whity*, by Rainer Werner Fassbinder. And these two are commenting on its handling of race.' I knew of Fassbinder, but I had not seen *Whity* before.

'The lady,' Mark said, pointing to the curly-haired woman, 'she made this installation. She is half-Nigerian.' Mark, I discovered later, was a film student, or used to be a film student – with Mark nothing was straightforward. We sat in the dark booth for a while, staring at the movie, the German words from the headphones bouncing around meaninglessly in my skull. Mark took off his headphone and offered to recap the movie plotline for me, I listened, impressed by his intensity. When he finished I thanked him and asked if he'd like a beer at the bar. He put down his headphone and put on his baseball cap. The bar was in the basement, next to the viewing room, and at the moment it was empty except for a couple seated by themselves on a couch in a corner. We ordered beers.

'Where are you from?' he asked.

'Originally, Nigeria.'

'Your wife is also Nigerian?'

'No, American.'

He was Malawian but had lived in Germany for over five years.

'Well, cheers,' I said, raising my glass.

'To Africa,' he said.

'To Africa.'

I tried to guess his age. He looked between twenty-five and thirty. The baseball cap covered the upper part of his face, and since he was shorter than me, I had to constantly lean down to make eye contact. He had lived a rather peripatetic life, moving from Stockholm, to Stuttgart, to Potsdam, and now Berlin. He loved Berlin most of all.

'Even in Berlin I miss Berlin,' he told me that day. He was only technically speaking a student, his registration had expired – something to do with school fees, and this had, or soon would, also affect his visa status – which was why he was squatting with friends in the old church in Kreuzberg. For pocket money he freelanced for crew.com, an organization for out-of-work actors and film technicians. But it had been a while since he had done anything for crew.com. He didn't tell me all this that day at the gallery, of course, but afterward, over several meetings. He looked a bit of a mess, almost feral, his black Converse sneakers were dirty and worn out, but there was an ease about him that I responded to.

'Come and meet my friends,' he said, after my second beer, his third, when I told him I had to go, 'we live close by.'

I followed him out of the bar and into the night. He walked with a swagger, at one point he casually stepped into the road and crossed to the other side, weaving between cars, raising his hand like a matador to halt a car that came close to hitting him, ignoring loud curses from incensed drivers. He stood at the other side, unperturbed, waving me over impatiently. I waited for the light to turn before crossing, not sure if I was impressed or alarmed by his reckless self-assurance.

'This is a church,' I said when he pushed open the little gate and waved me in. My comment was half question, half statement.

'We live here for the moment, yes. Temporarily.'

His three housemates were all there, Eric, Stan and Uta. I

nodded and sat down next to Mark. When Mark told them I was a 'fellow African', Uta immediately told me her mother was Cameroonian, her father German. She was lying on the couch, her legs in Stan's lap – he was half-seated, half-reclining next to her, his long dreadlocks falling over the back of the couch and over his shoulders. We were in what they called the living room, in the basement, which used to be a Sunday school classroom. There was a blackboard on one wall, and a wooden lectern in front of it. There were bottles of beer on a redwood table with scratched and grime-dulled wood grain. Mark opened a beer for me. Eric was holding a joint in one hand and browsing through a laptop with the other hand.

'So, what do you do?' Uta asked in her tentative English.

'I teach, back in the States. And here as well.' I gave English classes to some of the non-English-speaking Zimmer fellows, once a week. Uta was a student at the Free University and was currently working on a novel.

'A novel?'

'The novel is dead,' Mark declared. 'Cinema is the present and the future.'

'You think so?'

'The cinema does everything the novel does, but without being boring.'

I took a pull on the joint that had made its way into my hand. I felt light-headed.

The conversation drifted from subject to subject, lulling into a contemplative silence that never felt awkward, and then resuming, veering off in a totally new direction. Now Eric was talking about the last protest march they had participated in. They had been to Davos, and several G20 meetings all over the world.

'What are you protesting?' I asked.

They all stared at me, their faces showing their surprise at my question.

'Everything, man,' Stan said.

'Everything?'

'We believe there should be an alternative to the way the world is being run now,' Eric said.

'Too much money in too few hands,' Uta said.

'Millions exploited in sweatshops in Asia. Wars in Africa,' Stan said.

'This is the twenty-first century, no child should be dying from hunger or disease,' Uta said.

I nodded. I had met others like them here in Berlin, at readings, on the train, young men and women, in threadbare sweaters and tattered jeans, mostly living in communes in abandoned buildings, purveyors of an alternative way of life, often not agreeing on what exactly that alternative should be, just an alternative to the status quo, otherwise what was the point? I drank, and smoked, and listened. At one point Mark stood behind the altar and read from a passage from the Bible; his father was a preacher and he was mocking his father's preaching style. He stood with hands raised, eyes rolling, voice thundering: *The summer is ended, the harvest gathered, and still we are not saved . . .*

The others clapped. I looked on, uncertain if it wasn't self-mockery and even real pain in Mark's voice and face as he bowed to the applause before returning to his chair. They told me he had deconsecrated the church when he first moved in a month ago. 'The place was haunted. I could feel the spirits lurking all over.'

'How do you deconsecrate a church?' I asked.

'With alcohol. Pour alcohol in the corners and read secret passages from the Bible.'

Even in my tipsy, sedated state, I sensed how ephemeral this moment was. How long before they saw the world as it is, vile and cruel and indifferent, and there is really no changing it; how long before they moved out of their crumbling ivory tower and joined the rest of humanity swimming in what Flaubert described as a river of shit relentlessly washing away at the foundation of every ivory tower ever built? One day they'd start shaving and become bankers or middle managers and drive BMWs and Mercedes-Benzes; they'd start a family and surround themselves with the empty accoutrements of position and power, the same things they now derided. But now, right now, they were free and pure as morning dew on a petal, and something in me wanted to lean in and sniff the fragrance from that bud.

So I kept returning to that slanted, run-down church building in Kreuzberg. I kept returning even when I discovered they were a far cry from the downtrodden proletariats they so identified with: Uta's parents were both doctors from the former East Berlin; Stan was a PhD student at Humboldt, he grew up in Senegal where his father worked for a multinational food company, his mother was a painter. Nor were they

as young as they appeared. None of them was under thirty –
Mark was the youngest at exactly thirty, Uta was thirty-one
even though she looked twenty-five, Stan was thirty-two, and
Eric was thirty-five and married, though currently separated
from his wife, who lived with their daughter in Mannheim.

4

Then it was May. Mark and his friends invited me to the May Day demonstrations. 'You'll like it,' Mark said. The first of May protests were a tradition I had to experience, they told me, young men and women breaking down store doors and government buildings and flipping over cars on the high streets, sometimes setting them ablaze, denouncing the status quo.

That day in Kreuzberg, from Hermannplatz to Moritzplatz, the police began their patrol early. They came in riot gear and bulletproof vests, they cordoned off streets with their trucks and wagons, and only documented residents were allowed in or out. I arrived earlier at the church to avoid the cordon.

I found them by the door, all dressed up in boots and jeans and ready to go. Mark was talking to a girl I had never seen before. His girlfriend, Lorelle. I stopped myself from staring openly at the pins and rings in her lips and nostrils and cheeks and eyebrows, the stud in her tongue, making her face look like a pincushion. It must hurt. I imagined more piercings in hidden places beneath her lumpy sweatshirt. There was a mandala tattoo on her left cheek, in pink and blue colours, bringing her face alive like a neon light. Her hair, one side shaved off completely, was a mix of blue and pink over blonde roots. I shook her hand.

'Well, nice to meet you,' she said, 'I have heard so much about you from Mark.'

Her handshake was firm. Her voice was nothing like her appearance, it was warm, and soft, with a strong American accent. She was American, but born in Heidelberg. Her parents were military, now back in the US; but she had remained, preferring life here. She, like Mark, was a student at the film school.

We passed through parks and back streets, avoiding the cruising police vans and large congregations. Our destination was the Berlin-Turkish café, whose owner had been turning away black people, claiming they were all illegal immigrants and drug dealers. A surprisingly large crowd had already gathered in front of the café; young men and women in jeans and boots and sneakers, some with raised placards, others with raised phones recording the protest even as they chanted along to the songs. We joined them. We threw stones at the police who stood in front of the café to protect the owner, who was cowering inside. We marched in circles up and down the block, stopping traffic. By noon I was tired, and hungry, and beginning to feel bored. I could see Mark and Uta, she beautiful in her cutoff jeans and fiery red bandanna, side by side waving their placards like baits at the police. I decided to take a break. I crossed the road to a *Bäckerei* and ordered a sandwich and a coffee. I had two missed calls from Gina. When I left home at 6 a.m. she was still in her studio painting, and I hadn't told her where I was going. I called her back but there was no answer – she would be sleeping by now. Outside, the demonstration had almost doubled in size in the short time I had been in the *Bäckerei* and I could feel the tension rising all around. Time to go home. I edged into the crowd looking for Mark to let him know I was leaving, but soon I was carried by a tide of bodies making straight for the line of policemen standing behind their shields, their sticks raised. Stones and bottles and cans whizzed over our heads to crash against the policemen's shields. A shoulder knocked into me and I fell, knees hit my face as I tried to get up, shoes marched on my hands. Everyone was running, chased by the police. I kept trying to stagger up, but I kept falling back down under the ceaseless wave of knees and legs crashing into me. I stayed on the ground, mesmerized by a dully glowing square of brass embedded in the sidewalk – I had seen them before, *Stolpersteine*, they were called, meaning to stumble. There were names on them, entire histories, birthdays, transportation days, and the names of their final, terminal destinations. Four names, the Hartmanns: Elisabeth, Marcus, Lydia and Eduard. All ended up at Sobibór, all died the same day, 5 December 1944. I was blinded by the rusted glow of the brass, shocked by the brutal indifference of history, teary with tear gas, too winded to move. A hand was pulling me up, and for a moment I resisted, thinking it was the police, but it was Mark. He was smiling, an exhilarated look on his face. 'Are you okay?' he asked. I stood up. My palms were grazed and burning, my pants torn at the knees.

'I am fine.'

But he was already gone, hurling a stone toward the line of policemen. A tear gas canister landed next to me and I saw a wild-haired youth snatch it up and throw it back at the police, its arc of smoke hanging in the air like a dying thunderhead. To my right Lorelle was running straight at a row of policemen, using her ample bulk as battering ram against their shields. They knocked her down finally and hauled her away, screaming and kicking, to a police van. I stood there, disoriented by the tear gas, my eyes and nostrils streaming freely. I was alone on a tiny island, and all around me the sea was roiling and crashing with nameless rage.

'I have to go,' I said to Mark.

'No. Not yet. This is it. This is our moment,' Mark said. He was waving his arms as he talked. 'This is our Sharpeville, our Agincourt.'

I felt like laughing at his hyperbole. What moment, I wanted to ask, will this really change the minds of the so-called capitalists and racists and bring harmony and everlasting love to the world? And yet I couldn't help being impressed by it. I said, 'You don't want to get arrested, not with your expired visa. Come now.'

'Where are the others?' he asked.

'I don't know. I saw Lorelle being taken away. Come on.'

We walked away, taking random turns, till the sirens and

chants were a distant susurration on the wind. We sat in a bar and ordered two beers. My phone rang, it was Gina. I was too tired and too rattled to answer. We finished our beer, but Mark wasn't ready to go yet. He called for another.

'That's the way,' he said. He slammed his hand on the table. 'Resist the system.' We drank and ordered another round. I felt the edge coming off gradually. Outside, the smoky yellow streetlights were coming on as the sky darkened. The day had gone by already. A patrol car wailed past, its flashing blue lights mingling with the streetlight yellow.

'I should be going home.'

'Come on,' Mark said. 'Another drink, on me.' He looked drunk already. He called for a double shot of whisky.

'Not for me. Hurry up, I'll walk you home, then I am off.'

On the way Mark stopped at a currywurst stand to buy a sausage. A boy, his face red with drink, his girlfriend tugging at his arm, flopped into the bench next to us. He bent forward, his face in his hands. '*Scheisse*,' he kept muttering. The girl was dressed in a manga comic outfit, her face heavily made up, eyes slanted with kohl. Across the street a man in a hooded sweater stood in a dark doorway, whispering to passers-by, '*Alles gut?*', never fully making eye contact.

'Let's go, Mark.'

He couldn't walk straight, so I hefted his arm over my shoulder, bending awkwardly sideways since he was much shorter than me, and together we staggered toward the train station. At the abandoned church we found the door kicked off its hinges and lying on the floor just inside the threshold. The lights were on. The chairs were overturned, papers lay across tables and chairs.

'Fucking shit.'

'What happened?'

'I don't know. Looks like we've been raided.'

Mark went from room to room, picking up chairs and books from the floor. His room was at the end of a hall, next to the kitchen. His flimsy mattress was torn and almost cut in half. His backpack, which contained all his worldly possessions, lay open in the centre of the room.

'Motherfucking pigs. It's the police, they've been targeting us for a while.'

'Where are your friends?' I asked.

He looked at me and shrugged. 'I have no idea.'

'Well, what are you going to do, where are you going to sleep?'

He said, 'I'll be fine.' He didn't sound very convincing.

'Why don't you go over to your girlfriend's place?'

'Lorelle? Won't work. She has a flatmate. But hey, don't worry. I have places I can go to. I'll be fine.'

I left him standing there with his empty backpack in hand, swaying on his feet, assuring me he was going to be okay, and then I remembered that he couldn't have gone to Lorelle's anyway even if she didn't have a flatmate; Lorelle had been taken away by the police. I was tired, I was sore, and all I wanted was to get home, take a shower, and crawl into bed.

5

I didn't hear about Mark's arrest till a week later, when I stopped by the church. There was something different about the place, the door was back on its hinges, and the yard looked like someone had run a rake through it. A pile of trash was neatly packed under a tree, waiting to be bagged. I knocked, but there was no answer. I pushed the door and went in. The ratty couches and lamps were gone. The lectern was still there, and I remembered Mark standing behind it to read from the Bible, mocking his preacher father. I felt a bit sad, and a bit hurt – they had left without telling me. They had my phone number, at least Mark did, he could have called. But then, they lived an improvised and makeshift life, they had probably been chased out by the police and were even now holed up in another squat; they might get in touch after a week or so, after they had settled down. At least Mark might. I realized I missed them; I missed stopping by the church in the evenings when Gina was working and listening to them talk about everything, from global warming to despicable politicians to refugees, even when I secretly, arrogantly considered them naïve and hopelessly idealistic. Now I had to admit they were at least able to think of something, and others, apart from themselves, they were willing to throw stones at the police and even go to jail for their ideals – how many people could do that? Certainly not my self-centred, overambitious classmates back in graduate school, and definitely not Gina's oversensitive, even narcissistic fellow Zimmer artists we met regularly at dinners and openings and readings. Throughout the week I waited for Mark to call. Did he even have a phone? I couldn't remember. In the end it was Lorelle who called. She had been released from the police lockup a day after the demonstration. I said, 'Where's everyone? I went to the church and there was nobody.'

Mark's little group had disbanded, she told me. Stan had moved back to Mannheim, Eric to France, and Uta was back with her parents. The gap year from life has ended, the search for alternatives is over, I thought, the revolution lost. I felt a twinge of disappointment.

'And Mark?' I asked. Mark had been arrested, and that was why she was calling. She wanted to meet. She was waiting for me outside Neukölln U-Bahnhof, in a café across the street from the station. She called for a chai and I asked for a coffee.

She looked a bit different, more subdued, as if she hadn't been sleeping. Even the mandala on her cheek looked less fluorescent, the colours in her hair less celebratory.

'The last time I saw you,' I told her, raising my voice over the street noise, 'you were being hauled away by the police, kicking and screaming.'

'Oh God, I was so high that day. They released me the next morning. It is routine. One of the thrills of the struggle, you might say.'

'But what of Mark?'

A young man with hair falling to his shoulders and a long, mournful face loomed over our table and meekly whispered some words to Lorelle. He smelled of urine and faeces and old sweat. He smelled acidic. His thick battered boots were crusted with layers of dirt and grime. She shook her head. '*Ich habe keine.*' He turned to me. I looked away. He shuffled off to the next table.

It seemed after I left Mark that day at the church, he had gone out to get still more drunk, then he had returned to the church and started playing loud music, and that had attracted a cruising police car. They asked him why he was staying there, and if he had a place, and when he began to rail at them, they took him away. Things got more complicated when they discovered his visa was expired. Now it was a case for the immigration service.

'Well, where is he now?'

'In detention, at one of their centres. I was there yesterday and he told me to call you. He has no one. He needs help. They are going to send him back to Malawi – it is the worst thing that can happen to him. He cannot go back.'

How definitive she sounded: He *cannot go back* to Malawi. What did she mean by that?

'Well . . . what can I do?' I asked.

'He needs a lawyer.'

'What of those humanitarian NGOs – Amnesty International, can they help?'

'I have already talked to them, but this is not exactly their province. They gave me an address though, a lawyer. He belongs to another organization, they specialize in cases like this, and they work pro bono.'

'Have you called him?'

'Yes, he is happy to help, but he needs to pay for access to documents and for making copies, et cetera.'

'How much?'

'About two hundred euros. I don't have enough, I am afraid . . .'

'Of course, that is no problem.' I was relieved it was only two hundred. I'd hate to have to ask Gina for the money. The lawyer's office was somewhere in Mitte, a twenty-minute train ride from where Mark was being held. It was a small office, with two desks, one for the lawyer, one for his assistant, a prim and sour-faced lady. Her black skirt was well below the knees; her sky-blue blouse was buttoned up to the collar, with lacy ruffs fanning round her neck and holding up her head like a neck brace; on her chest was a name tag, *Frau Grosse*. There was only one chair for visitors, so I stood. The lawyer's name was Julius Maier, but just call me Julius, he said, rising out of his chair to shake hands. He was slight of frame, almost insubstantial next to the grave and heavily present Frau Grosse. His father was from Burkina Faso, he added, as if to establish his credentials, and his mother was German. Lorelle handed him the two hundred euros in an envelope. He counted it and gave it to Frau Grosse, who counted it again before returning it to the envelope and sliding the envelope into a drawer. I almost expected her to lock the drawer with a key attached to a chain hanging from her waist. She caught me looking at her and frowned; I turned away.

'First, your friend needs to prove he is not an illegal, and to do that, he needs to establish he is still a student.'

'He came here as a student, it is on record. Why don't they believe him?' I said.

'It is on record, yes. But it is not that simple. He is now out of status, so he has broken his visa conditions.'

'Is that very serious?'

'Very. He can be deported, or detained.' He waited for me to comment, and when I didn't, he went on, 'The best way to help is if he can show that he has applied for a visa extension. I have spoken to him, and he told me that he has not applied for an extension.'

'Well, can he do that now?'

'To do that, he will need a letter from the school, saying he is still a student – but that will not be easy. He told me he hasn't been in school for the past year. He was in another school in Potsdam before coming here. His scholarship has been stopped. He has almost graduated, all he needs is to fin-ish his final project.'

It was a bureaucratic conundrum straight out of Kafka – to get a hearing he must prove he had applied for a visa exten-sion (which he hadn't), but to apply for the visa extension he must prove he was still a student (which he was, technically, even though his tuition had lapsed and he had not set foot on campus in a year, and because he had changed schools a few times his paperwork trail was as tangled as Bob Marley's hair). Still, the lawyer looked optimistic. Lorelle looked sceptical. I must have looked puzzled.

'But really,' he said, 'it is simpler if he asks for asylum.'

'You mean like a refugee?'

'Yes.'

'He won't,' Lorelle said.

'Why not, if it will make it easier . . .'

'Well, he is not a refugee. He is a student.'

We took a train to the detention centre, a Brutalist edifice straight out of the Nazi architecture catalogue, where we were asked to fill out multiple forms. Julius filled them out and handed them to a lady, who looked like Frau Grosse's twin. She went over them line by line, running a thick finger over each line, before bringing out a rubber stamp and smashing it to the bottom of each page, making the table shake each time. She then looked at us and pointed – her hand rising with infinite slowness to hang in the air – to a row of chairs in a corner. We sat. I felt exhausted already. I felt like I was on trial for a crime and I would definitely be found guilty and hanged. I avoided the lady's glare and ran my eyes over the long, rectangular room. A row of square windows opened high up in one wall, with parallel iron bars blocking any hope of egress – if one were inclined to seek egress that way. A metal door to the side had a sign across it, *VERBOTEN*. A man came in and talked to Julius in German, and then turning to us he switched to English and asked us to follow him. We passed through many doors, each of which he opened with a key from a bundle of

keys in his hand, each door a different key, before finally asking us to sit in a sort of anteroom facing another door. A while
later, the door opened and Mark joined us, accompanied by a
guard who stood discreetly but visibly by the door. After the
fortress-like entrance, and the multiple doors, and the bureau-
cracy, I expected to see Mark in chains. He was dressed in his
usual red jacket and T-shirt. He looked subdued, and a bit lost
and vulnerable without his hat.

'Thanks,' Mark said to me.

'You'll be fine,' I said to him.

Lorelle sat tense and straight in her chair, her eyes fixed
on Mark, as if she wanted to cross over to him and hold him,
but she remained seated, smiling whenever their eyes met. As
it turned out, Julius's optimism was well founded. Mark was
released two days later. I got a call from the lawyer and we
met in his office. Mark was there, cap low over his head as
usual, his red jacket over his layers of shirt and T-shirt, in the
same Converse shoes and high-flying jeans. He was free, for
the time being. The school had issued a letter acknowledging he was a student, the visa application had been submitted;
Mark had been released into the supervision of the lawyer.

I shook Julius's hand, impressed.

'He has to be readily available if he is needed. He must not
travel outside Berlin. They needed an address, just for formality, you know. We gave your address, is that okay?'

'Of course,' I said. I did not ask him how he got my address.
'But where is he going to stay?'

'At the Heim,' Julius said, and when I looked blank he
added, 'The *Flüchtlingsheim*.'

Refugee camp. Where asylum seekers were kept pending

the result of their asylum application. I turned to Mark to see what he thought. He was looking out of the window at a tree branch.

'But he is not an asylum seeker,' I said.

Julius shrugged. 'It is a temporary arrangement.'

I said to Mark, 'You know what, come to my place, you can crash there for a day or two before moving on.'

Mark shrugged, wordless. Thank you would be nice, but then, he had been through a lot. Before we left, Julius took me aside. 'How well do you know him?'

'About two months now. Why?'

He shrugged. 'Well, I think you need to talk to him.' He looked as if he wanted to say more but wasn't sure if he should. He looked over at Mark, then back to me. 'Just talk to him. You know, to find out more . . . about himself.'

'Okay,' I said, puzzled. Was there something Mark was hiding from me? Surely he'd let me know if there was any danger to putting him up? We stopped at a bar and I bought Mark a beer to celebrate his freedom. 'My first in days,' he said. He was quiet most of the time. I wanted to bring up Julius's comment, but how did one broach such a subject? I decided I'd bring it up as tactfully as I could at an appropriate time. When we finished our drinks he looked up and said, 'I hope your wife won't be upset with you bringing home a foundling.'

'She'll be fine,' I said. I knew that by taking him home I was crossing a line after which it would be hard to turn back. He was now my responsibility. Whatever he did, whatever happened to him, would have a direct bearing on me and Gina.

6

I heard the voices as I unlocked the front door, and I remembered we were hosting today. Gina had completed her *Travellers* paintings and was having her sitters and a few people from the Zimmer over for drinks and a viewing, and I was supposed to get the drinks on my way back. 'Damn,' I muttered, thinking of a reasonable explanation.

'All good?' Mark asked, eyebrows raised. I smiled and waved him in.

Gina was standing in the middle of the room, a glass in one hand, talking to a man in a Ralph Lauren shirt, half-unbuttoned to show his hairy chest. She opened her mouth to speak, then stopped when she saw Mark. Her eyebrows arched, forming a question mark on her face. I went and kissed her on the cheek. 'Hi darling,' I said. There were two women out on the balcony, smoking, wineglass in hand. I waved to them and shook the man's hand.

'You are Gina's husband,' he said. 'I am Dante.' He sounded French, or Italian, or Spanish. I wondered if he was comfortable exposing his chest like that. I nodded and turned to Mark. 'This is Mark – a friend.' I waited to see if Gina would remember him, but she gave no sign she did.

'Mark, my wife, Gina.'

Gina looked from Mark to me, the question mark still evident, then she gave him her hand. Mark, in his baseball cap and jeans stopping at his ankles and backpack slung over one shoulder and the stench of detention on him, looked so out of place next to the elegantly bare-chested Dante that I felt embarrassed for him.

'Come,' I said to him. I took his backpack and led him to the bathroom to wash his hands; I also needed a minute to compose myself. But what I needed more than anything else was a drink. In the kitchen there were two bottles of wine on the counter, white and red, both open. As I looked in the drawer for a glass, Gina entered. She closed the door and stood with her back against the door, not coming in.

'I have been trying to reach you.'

I filled my glass with wine and drank it all in one go. Gina came and took the empty glass from my hand and placed it carefully in the sink. I picked it up and refilled it. A week after we got married two friends of hers had come to town on their way to Baltimore, and Gina had wanted to introduce me. She had cooked and I was supposed to grab the wine on my way home from the library, teaching my ESL students, but I had totally forgotten. The annoying thing was that I wasn't doing anything, I had just sat in the library, browsing through a novel, and by the time I remembered I was three hours late. She was in bed when I came home and she wouldn't talk to me the next day.

'I forgot we were hosting tonight. I am sorry.'

She looked radiant in her red dress, I told her.

'I kept calling. I left messages.'

'I can still get more wine, if it is not too late . . .'

'Of course it is too late. Dante brought a few bottles. And who is the kid? He looks familiar.'

'His name is Mark. He was here a while back.'

'What is he doing here?'

'He needs a place to crash.'

'To crash?'

'Yes. I'll explain later.'

'You can explain now.'

'Too complicated. Later.'

'Don't drink too much, please,' she said before she left. I finished a second glass, slowly this time. Facing the guests in the living room was the last thing I wanted to do; for that I needed some artificial cheer – and a change of shirt. As I walked down the corridor to the bedroom I saw the door to the studio was open. There were people in there, a man and a woman, talking in low voices. I stood at the door and cleared my voice. In the dim light I saw it was Manu, and the woman, the daughter was also there, standing in the shadows next to a canvas.

'Hi,' I said. They all turned and stared at me, silent, as if waiting for me to make an accusation. The woman moved a step closer to her daughter.

'I didn't know you were here,' I said, keeping my eyes on Manu. They continued to stare at me in silence, and as the awkwardness mounted I went on, 'I just came in. I was out to see a friend.' Still they said nothing, and after a while the woman took her daughter's hand and, keeping as far from me as possible, squeezed past me through the door to the living room. I looked again at Manu, and after the woman. 'I never got her name.'

'Bernita.'

'She doesn't talk much.'

'She is shy,' he said.

I stepped into the room and stood next to him, before one of the canvases. There were six in all, arranged in order of size, the biggest, a 60-by-50-inch, on the left, and the smallest, a 24-by-20-inch to the right. They were placed so that a single light from a lamp fell on them. Manu's portrait, the 60-by-50-inch stared back at us, thoughtful, a little tired, but filled with gravitas, like a defeated king amidst the ruins of his palace.

'A good likeness,' I said.

On the next canvas was the woman and her child. I was seeing the finished paintings for the first time. Gina hated to show her work in progress, even to me. The woman was seated with the child asleep in her lap.

'Like the Pietà,' Manu said. A woman holding her broken child, grieving as only a woman can. She was wearing the bulky winter jacket, her face staring down at the figure in her arms, the light falling on her covered head like a halo. Three small canvases carried sketches of the child alone – I moved closer. No, they were not the child – not the woman's child. It was a white child, the boy from the motherless children's home, standing over the fence, shouting *Schokolade!* And yet, it wasn't him in the next canvas. It was a more generic child, an everychild. Anyone's child. And the next one was even more generic, genderless, neither white nor black; what was clear, though, was the almost accusatory pain in its liquid eyes. I pulled back and turned to Manu. I wondered what he thought of it. He was bending forward, his face close to the canvas.

'There is so much sadness here,' he said. When I remained quiet, he went on, 'But perhaps it is only my interpretation.'

'Do you want a beer? I'll change my shirt and join you in a minute.'

Manu had a daughter, he told me. They lived in a Heim.

'Why didn't you bring her?'

'She has her German lesson today.'

I tried to guess his accent. 'Senegal?'

'No. Libya. My father came from Nigeria, originally.'

'Oh,' I said.

Mark was on the couch, a glass of wine in hand, flanked by the two women who had been smoking on the balcony. One was Ilse, the PR person for the Zimmer, the other one I had never met before. Mark was describing his ordeal at the hands of the immigration officials to the women. Dante and Gina drew closer, and now there was a little group around Mark, who seemed to be enjoying the attention. He spoke with his trademark braggadocio, making it all sound funny. As I listened I felt like I was also hearing it for the first time, as if I hadn't been there with him, and I couldn't help but admire his resiliency. The other lady, a brunette, in a blue dress that stopped mid-thigh, leaned toward Mark and asked, 'Are you going to seek asylum then? It will be easier for you, no?'

'Mark is a student,' I said, joining them.

'Oh, I see,' she said, looking up at me. She looked to be in her forties. A journalist, from Frankfurt, I found out later. Her name was Anna. I wondered where Gina found her, most likely through Ilse. The fellowship was tireless in promoting its fellows.

'Why,' Mark said, turning to me, a mischievous twinkle in his eye, 'do white people always assume every black person travelling is a refugee?'

'They don't,' Anna said. 'I don't,' she corrected herself. 'I cannot speak for every white person in this world, can I?'

I left the group and went to the kitchen to pour myself a glass of wine, by the time I came back the woman and child had left. I saw Manu standing a little apart from the group, near the door, a glass in his hand. He was staring at the group, and when I followed his eyes I saw he was looking at Gina, who was talking to Dante. 'Your wife is very talented,' he said.

'Come and join us,' I said, 'don't stand here by yourself.'

'I am afraid I have to go now. It is getting late.'

I gave him his coat, and when I rejoined the group Anna was asking Mark if he had experienced any racism in Berlin, surely Berlin was the most liberal and welcoming of all European cities, no? Mark, unfazed, smiled and said, 'I like it here. Even in Berlin I miss Berlin.'

'Ha ha ha,' Anna laughed, delighted. She had a rather unexpectedly loud laugh. 'I like that. Can I quote you?'

Mark raised a hand, his face flushed with wine. 'Before you

quote me, let me add . . . I have also noticed this, the women always hug their bags when I am in the vicinity, without fail. Like this.' He demonstrated. 'With both hands. I didn't notice it at first, but then it became so obvious I couldn't ignore it.'

Anna laughed, looking more guarded now. Gina threw me a look – Mark was my responsibility. He was making her guests uncomfortable. Dante, trying to salvage the situation, said, 'But the race situation in Europe is good, no? Better than America? I go there often, for exhibitions. And they disrespect Obama, is true, is because he is black.'

Gina said, 'Well, it is not perfect, but it is not that bad either. We have come a long way since the 1960s and the civil rights struggles.' She looked at me, but I had nothing to add.

'What is your experience, as an African in America?' Dante persisted, turning to me. I looked at his distressed jeans, his blue Polo shirt with his chest hairs springing out of the unbuttoned top, and I decided I didn't like him, but I smiled and told them about the first time I went to New York. I had approached a policeman at Penn Station to ask for directions, which is the logical thing to do anywhere in the world, and as I got closer to him I noticed his hand inching toward the gun at his waist. I had stopped and looked behind me, thinking surely it was someone else he was reaching his gun for, not me. Now he was gripping his gun tightly, but still I asked him for directions, my voice wavering, and he looked at me, unsmiling, and said, 'Keep moving.' When I told Gina that story a long time ago, she had been angered. She had called the police pigs and racists. She was fiery then, recently she had grown more tolerant, more oblivious of what was happening around her, her gaze focused only on her painting.

That night, after the guests had left, and Mark lay snoring on the couch in the living room, Gina said to me, 'How long is he staying?'

'A day or two.'

'How could you invite him without asking me first? If anything goes wrong . . .'

'What could go wrong?' I asked, and even as I said it I remembered the lawyer's worried expression as he asked me if I knew Mark well enough. I pushed the thought aside. 'Is he going to set the house on fire, rob the neighbours? Come on. He may look a bit . . . disjointed, but he is okay. He just needs a place for a day or two to get his act together.'

'What kind of trouble is he in?'

'You heard him earlier. He needs to sort out his papers. He is a student. A lawyer is working on it.'

I lay awake most of that night, listening to Gina's soft breathing. I wanted to ask her about the baby in the painting, and what it meant, but she was already asleep. She slept with her face to the wall, far away from me. I lay sleepless all night long till the morning birds started chirping outside. I opened the window and poked my head outside and gulped in the morning air. I was never fully awake till I smelled the fresh morning air and heard the cry of birds in the trees, even in winter. The leaves were turning reddish on the trees. Already, summer was ending. When we came last October the leaves were already variegated and falling. Late in October I had stood at the window and watched a single leaf still clinging to a twig, thinking that must be the last leaf left on a tree in the whole street, in the whole city, in the whole world, and it was there, outside my window. Fall was my favourite season; an in-between moment, neither winter nor summer, and so brief. I loved to watch the leaves swirl and circle and rise and fall, driven by the wind and the passing cars to pile up against the fence by the sidewalk. I loved to watch the children from across the road play with them, picking up armfuls and raining them down over each other's heads. They'd hold hands and scream and jump up and down on the red and brown and dry leaves, soothed and excited by the crunching and breaking sound they made under their feet, their pellucid laughter rising through the street, up into the leafless trees to startle the birds, up into the upstairs balconies and windows still open as if in defiance of the coming winter.

Mark was already awake, seated on the couch, looking at the open door leading to the balcony and the top of the poplar trees lining the street. He was wrapped to the neck in a blanket, and seated like this, not in constant motion, he looked vulnerable, almost childlike. He had been out on the balcony for a smoke, and the smell had trickled into the room. I told him Gina had to go out for an event.

'Yes, I saw her,' he said.

She hadn't said where she was going. Recently she seemed to be always coming in when I was going out the door, or going out when I was coming in; she was waking up when I was getting into bed. Yesterday in the morning we stood in the bathroom side by side, but we couldn't speak because our mouths were full of toothpaste, we only stared at each other in the mirror over the sink, a brief eye contact before she bent down to spit into the swirl of scummy water spiralling into the drain. I often thought of Gina in her studio, alone all day, battling with colours and lines and fear and hope, coaxing the brushstrokes into shapes, a limb, a face, hair, eyes, and sometimes despairing, as Plato once said, of ever capturing that ideal form she saw in her mind. When we first came to Berlin everything seemed to be working out fine, but now I knew she sometimes stayed in the studio just to get out of my way, just as I went out to visit Mark and his friends to avoid her. Sometimes, when she came out of the studio and found me in the living room reading or watching TV, she looked taken aback that I was there, that I was me, and she was her, husband and wife, in a house, together, and I couldn't tell when this awkwardness had started. I wanted to hold her and just sit quietly, like we used to do a long time ago, but it required so much energy to do that, more energy than I possessed. Instead I would put on my jacket and walk the lonely Berlin back streets, and there is no loneliness like the loneliness of a stranger in a strange city.

Mark asked, 'How did you two meet?'

'Let me get some tea first,' I said. 'Do you want some?'

'Coffee is better if you have it.'

'No problem.'

He was out of the blanket and already dressed when I returned with the beverages. I had met Gina at an Obama rally at the American University in Washington in March 2007. Obama had just declared for the presidency and Gina was a campaign volunteer. I noticed her standing next to me, with her friends, all of them volunteers, wearing campaign buttons, and she was simply the most beautiful thing I had ever seen. Twice our eyes met, and I could see she was conscious of me too – I hardly heard a word the candidate was saying, I was busy plotting how to talk to her, but they left to be introduced to the candidate before I could summon the courage to approach her.

'What were you doing in America?'

'I went there on a scholarship, in 2006 – I was doing my PhD in history. As fate would have it, she was also a student, in the same department. A week later I met her in the library and this time I did not hesitate. When I mentioned I was from Nigeria she told me her father had been a Fulbright scholar in Nigeria. That is how it started. Your turn,' I said.

'What do you want to know?'

'Tell me about Malawi. Do you have brothers and sisters?'

'Yes,' Mark said. 'Two of each, I am the middle child.' His voice was serious, the frivolous and evasive Mark had momentarily disappeared.

'Tell me about them, your family.'

'I . . . my father and I, we didn't see eye to eye. Did I mention he was a pastor?'

'Yes. What denomination?'

'It is a Pentecostal ministry, one of the few in Lilongwe. When I was a child he encouraged me to join the church drama group. I loved it. I had the flair, I guess, from very early. We'd dramatize stories from the Bible, mainly. I loved the performance, the power to make the congregation laugh with my goofiness, to bring them to tears sometimes, with

only words and gestures. I was always the lead. One day I'd
be the Prodigal Son, cast out, eating with the swine, and then
returning home to be welcomed home by my father, another
day I'd be Joseph, dumped in a well by my brothers. I can
understand why actors sometimes become schizophrenic. It is
easy to get carried away, and then coming back is a problem.
I really believed I was those characters. Even then I guess I
was trying to escape something, I don't know what. That was
my childhood, in the church, no outside interests. While my
friends were out there discovering sports and other interests,
I was in the church, always under my father's watchful eyes.
That's the sum of my childhood. When I finished secondary
school, I naturally wanted to study theatre at the university,
but my father would have none of that.'

'Why?' I asked.

He brought out a pack of cigarettes from his jacket pocket.
We stood side by side out on the balcony, smoking. 'Well,
it was okay to be an actor in church, but not outside the
church. It was living a lie, he said. Making believe for a living. Ungodly, he called it. But with my mother's support,
I was able to get in. I invited the whole family to my first
performance. I had the lead role in *Sizwe Banzi Is Dead*, by
Athol Fugard. I was nineteen. I had worked hard to master my
role, you know, the lines, the movements. But still, even there
onstage, I could see the disappointment on my father's face.'

'What exactly didn't he like?' I asked.

He dragged deeply on his cigarette, then he leaned over
the balcony and flicked away the stub. 'He said it would bring
disgrace to the church. He said it was too worldly. You have
to understand, my father lived in the church, in the Bible,

for him there was nothing else. Well, I was so disappointed, I stopped going home. During the holidays I'd stay with my friends and we'd perform in small theatres and nightclubs and in the streets. We made enough money to live on. I had fun. My mother came to see me, and she begged me to come home. But I didn't go back. When I graduated I moved to South Africa to stay with my uncle Stanley. He is my father's youngest brother. He is a lecturer at a university, and he is the direct opposite of my father. I never went back home again. It was he who suggested I should look into going abroad to study further. He linked me up with his friend at the Goethe Institute in Johannesburg. I registered for German-language classes, and applied for a scholarship to come here to study. Just like that, everything came together.'

'Have you ever thought of returning?' I asked. He shook his head and shrugged. 'Sometimes. I miss my mother. And my uncle, and his wife and kids, and my brothers and sisters. But I don't see myself going back. Not soon anyway.'

I wanted to bring up what the lawyer said, but Mark took me by surprise when he said he had to leave.

'Leave?'

'Listen, I am not sure your wife is happy with me being here. I could see it last night. And this morning she didn't reply when I said good morning.'

I said, 'I am sorry. But you really don't have to go. Gina's just preoccupied at the moment . . .'

'It's okay,' he said. 'Really. I appreciate all you have done for me.'

I felt like Judas walking Mark to the bus stop, at the same time I felt a relief, which I tried to suppress. He said he had friends who'd put him up, and if that didn't work out there was always the Heim. I reached out and gave him a hug, the Judas hug, and watched him run through a gap in the traffic, the wind lifting his ridiculous jacket behind him. He had lost some weight in the last few weeks. He caught the M400 bus and as it pulled away I saw him through a top-deck window, waving. I waved back, my hand leaden.

My chest was heavy and my legs dragged as I walked back. Everything was changing. The leaves in the trees, the display clothes in the shop windows. There was an almost imperceptible chill in the air. I thought of home and the harmattan in November, and how it always made me sick, my mother said it was my body adjusting to the change in seasons. Our bodies always want to continue with what they know, pulled along by inertia. I hadn't spoken to my mother in a while. When I first got to America I used to call her every Sunday, talking through five-dollar call cards, the phone being passed from her to my father, to my sister and my two brothers. The plan was for me to return after my PhD, but then I met Gina, and the days turned into months, and the months into years, and then I just stopped calling home. The last time I called, over a year ago, my mother's voice had sounded so distant she could be talking about the weather to a stranger. I had handed the phone to Gina, but my mother always found it hard to understand Gina's American accent, and the call had lasted only a few minutes. I thought of Gina before the pregnancy. We used to sit by the window in the evenings, drinking white wine, watching the empty parking lot across the street, kids step-pushing their skateboards on the concrete, roaring down the pavement, jumping high in the air with skates glued to their soles, falling, jumping up again, high-fiving after each success. I was so lost in thought I bumped into a woman looking into a display window, then immediately after into a man. I was on a strange street, I couldn't recognize the landmarks and the store names. The man was tall and fashionably dressed in a leather jacket. He held my arm by the elbow and shook it, jolting me out of my sleepwalk. 'Hey. Watch it.' I nodded and walked on.

As it turned out, my questions were answered one week after the day I walked Mark to the bus stop. It was the day of Gina's exhibition at the Zimmer Gallery, somewhere on Karl-Marx-Strasse. Gina hadn't commented that day when she came back and Mark was gone. Our life had reverted to its normal rhythm. We went out to dinners, and openings, and readings and performances by Gina's fellow artists. Today she looked happy as she guided visitors from painting to painting, answering questions about colour, technique, concept. There was a solemn instrumental music playing in the background, her fellow artists from the Zimmer were all there. It was going to be an all-day affair. I stood in a corner, trying to be helpful, chatting with Julia, the Zimmer director, a thin, tall, unassuming woman, with her partner, Klaus, a tall beefy man who kept downing glasses of Riesling like it was water. I had been there for three hours, and I was tired, and hungry, and I was thinking of where to go for a bite – I wanted something more substantial than the finger food on offer, I wanted to ask Gina if she'd come with me, and at that moment a man walked in. He looked familiar. He was with a group of three, and he saw me at the same time.

He left the group and came over. It took me a while to recognize him. It was the lawyer, Julius. He looked different in jeans and T-shirt. I told him it was my wife's exhibition. 'Oh,' he said, looking impressed. 'I heard about the exhibition from my girlfriend.' He pointed to one of the girls in jeans and bombardier jacket. 'You know, I was going to call you tomorrow. I need to get in touch with Mark. Is he still staying at your place?'

'Actually no. Is everything okay?'

'Well, I need to get in touch with him. It is regarding the visa renewal application.'

'He left my place a while back, but I can pass on a message . . . I am sure I can locate him if necessary.'

The lawyer hesitated, then making up his mind he said, 'Well, it is urgent . . . I just found out today that his application for visa renewal was declined. I am sorry.'

'Oh,' I said, 'I am sorry to hear that.'

'Can you let him know, please?'

'Of course.'

As he turned to go, he said, 'This is none of my business,

but . . . you know, his real name is Mary. But I guess you knew this already? After all you are very close.'

I looked blankly at him. Mary?

'He is a girl, or rather she is a girl. Mary Chinomba.'

Mark, a girl? 'Are you sure?' was all I could manage.

'Yes, of course I am sure. I saw the official documents. I see, you look surprised. You didn't know.'

10

My phone calls to Mark went straight to a voice who told me, in clipped German, to leave a message, *bitte*, and after a while it stopped taking messages. I called Lorelle. She also hadn't seen him in a while, but she had heard he was putting up at a Heim close to the Görlitzer Bahnhof. We met at the station and walked together to the Heim. We passed empty and decaying buildings with graffiti in blue and green and black running down the walls, and shops with their pull-down doors permanently shut; we passed seedy corner shops with drunk men coming out of the narrow doorway with six-packs of beer under their arms and their beer guts spilling out of untucked shirtfronts, and moustachioed Turkish men smoking from hookahs under beach umbrellas. We came out on a completely deserted street with a fence blocking the far end and long grass growing beneath the fence.

'Have you been here before?' I asked Lorelle. She shook her head.

We took a corner and entered another street, also deserted except for two men sitting on the pavement with their backs against the wall and their legs sticking out in front of them, still captive to whatever chemical was coursing in their blood-stream. They stared at us, their faces red and grimy, sucking greedily on their cans of beer, until we turned another corner. The Heim was an abandoned school building, most of its win-dows had no panes, and its yard was overgrown with grass and trash. The front gate opened into a driveway that led to the big grey building. On one side of the driveway was a smaller structure, which must have originally been the security post or an office building, now its windows were boarded up with plywood turned black and peeling from rain and sun. Four men, three black, one Asian, stood at the doorway, talking in whispers. They stared long at Lorelle's hair and piercings, before turning to me. One of the men, with a red, yellow, green and black Rasta man's beanie over his dreadlocks, nod-ded at me and I nodded back. At the main building's entrance, a huddle of men, dirty, unshaven, and visibly drunk, stood haggling over something. They looked up when they saw us, and one of them, the lone black man in the group, walked away. The smell hit us even before we entered the building: fetid and moist and revolting. Heim. Home. This was the most un-homely place I had ever seen.

'This is it?' I asked Lorelle. It was a four-storey building and from here I could hear voices and muted music coming from upstairs windows.

'This is it.'

By the first landing was a bathroom, its entrance faced the staircase, half-blocked by a pile of trash falling out of and partially burying a trash can. A man came out of the bathroom, stepping carefully over the trash, a towel around his waist, his scrawny chest bare, his hair still wet.

'Hi,' I said. 'We are looking for a friend. Mark Chinomba.'

His glance switched from Lorelle to me. He shook his head. 'Where he come from?'

'Malawi,' Lorelle said. '*Sprechen sie Deutsch?*' she switched to German, sensing the man's wavering English. He shrugged his scrawny shoulders. 'Check upstairs.'

Stuck to the walls by the stairs were handbills screaming slogans, *No to Borders! No to Illegal Detention! Asylum Is a Right!* They ran all the way along the staircase, some announcing events, in English and French, but mostly in German: drama group meetings, church group meetings, social worker schedules. We met no one on the second-floor landing, so we turned right into a double doorway that led into a long and dark corridor littered with old bicycles and broken tables and chairs and more trash. A row of doors faced us, most of them half-open, showing bunk beds with tattered mattresses on them in which men slept with their legs hanging over the sides.

I knocked on one of the doors and entered. A man stood in front of a small stove with a pot on it, in his hand was half a chicken, in the other hand a knife. The sight of Lorelle behind me seemed to startle him – obviously women didn't frequent this part of the Heim. He put down the chicken on the table next to a pile of freshly cut peppers and onions and, wiping his hands on his pants, turned fully to us. No, he had never heard of Mark Chinomba. 'From Malawi? No, he cannot be here. This room is Senegal.'

Another man sat on his bed, watching a TV screen on a table next to the bed – it was an old TV, with the convex protrusion behind it. He didn't look up as we conversed with the man with the chicken; he continued to stare fixedly at the screen whose light illuminated his face, his expression swiftly changing with the images. There were shoes and more mattresses on the floor, cluttering the passage between the beds. A rancid smell hung over the room, rising from the cooking and the shoes and the unwashed bodies.

'Where are the Nigerians?' I asked, curious.

He pointed up, shaking his head. 'You can't find Nigeria now. If you want Nigeria you come back in nighttime. Most of them sleep now.'

I stopped at the foot of the stairs. I felt tired, depleted. I said to Lorelle, 'I think I've seen enough.'

She looked at me. 'Don't you want to find Mark?'

On the next floor the door opened into a room much larger than the last one, a small hall, with all the mattresses on the floor. Most of the men appeared to be Asian, most likely Syrians, or Pakistanis or Bangladeshis, or Afghans, with a few black men, all with the same furtive, calculating look, all quick to shake their heads when we asked after Mark Chinomba. A few lay on their mattresses, fiddling with their cell phones, some sat around a table in the centre of the room, playing a card game, their voices raised in dispute. As we passed in front of more open doorways and stepped over more piles of trash – almost fainting from the stink – nodding at the men congregated in groups on the balcony or standing idly by the windows, I seemed to be passing through some region of Dante's *Inferno*. None of them had heard of Mark. The top-most floor was the women's floor, and from the stairs we could hear a voice trying to calm down a screaming child. Its shrill, piercing cries brought me to a stop.

'Do you think he'd be there, with the women?'

She shook her head. 'No. Never.'

We left.

The next day Lorelle called. 'There's a film showing this evening, at the Neue Kino, it is a documentary about Mumia Abu-Jamal. A friend mentioned it. Mark is a big fan of Abu-Jamal,' she said.

I had no idea who Mumia Abu-Jamal was, but I took down the directions she gave me. After the movie we sat in a little café next to the tiny cinema house. There were people seated at neighbouring tables, still talking about the searing documentary we had just seen. Mark and Lorelle sat on a couch, holding hands, Lorelle gazing at Mark with a tender-ness that looked alien on her hard, pierced face. She hadn't seen Mark in almost a month. Earlier, when we came in and saw him by the concession stand talking to the barman, they had thrown themselves at each other and locked lips, and the people nearby had cheered while I stood and watched them, absently thinking it must be painful for Lorelle to kiss with all the rings on her lips, but touched like everyone else by the performance.

'I had never heard of Abu-Jamal before.'

'But how could you have?' Mark said, laughing. He looked

upbeat. 'You live in a big house, with a beautiful wife. You live in America where everybody is a movie star and drives a big car.'

'You make it sound like it is a sin or a disease to live in a big house.'

'Well, I wouldn't go to see movies about men in big houses. I wouldn't make movies about them either.'

'Quite a manifesto. What kind of movies would you make?' I said.

'Let me tell you the kind of movie I'd make. It is about a man in a tunnel. A long and endless tunnel, at the end there is his lover waiting for him, but he begins to realize that also, next to his lover, there is death waiting. But we never see him reach the lover, or death, just a single continuous shot of him in the tunnel, nothing more. The journey is the thing, the monsters that leap at him from the dark are all in his mind.'

I nodded. 'Nice allegory about the human condition. Beauty and death, side by side. We are all in a tunnel, pulled forward by love, but love is actually death in disguise. To desire is to die.'

'Yes, and not to love is also to die,' he said. He let go of Lorelle's hand and leaned toward me. 'When I make my movie, it will be edgy. It will be Marechera. Dostoevsky. Caravaggio. Knut Hamsun. So edgy it will cut your heart to watch it. What is the point of art if it is not to resist?'

'To resist what?'

'Just to resist, period. On principle.'

'That's the kind of films you want to make?'

'That's the life I want to live. Where art and life become one.'

'Wait till you are older, and married with kids, with bills to pay.'

He laughed and shrugged. 'Maybe that will never happen.'

Lorelle listened, her head on his shoulder, smoking a cigarette. She leaned forward and said, 'Mark's made a short, it won an award.'

Mark made a movie? My surprise must have shown on my face. Mark laughed and waved her away. 'A short short. Thirty minutes long. Something I did for a school project two years ago.'

'But it won a directing award, here in Berlin.'

'Nice,' I said. 'About a man in a tunnel?'

'You have to see it. I have a copy I can lend you,' she said.

I wanted to talk to him about his options now that his visa application had been rejected, but he didn't appear to be interested in talking about it, and perhaps this wasn't the place.

'Try and call that lawyer. Today if possible. Julius. He has been trying to reach you.' He nodded, and immediately changed the subject. 'Hey, are you free next week? There's a vinyl record store you have to see. It is humongous, the biggest in Berlin, maybe in all of Europe.'

'I am free.'

'Good. We'll go, the three of us. We can have lunch afterward. Hang out.'

'Great idea, but you must promise not to disappear again,' I said.

Mark raised his beer and, laughing, quoted from Shakespeare, '*When shall we three meet again, in thunder, lightning, or in rain . . .*'

He looked happy, and that was how I'd always remember him, leaning forward to clink glasses, with Lorelle beside him, because as it turned out that was the last time the three of us were ever together again.

'*When the hurly-burly is done / When the battle's lost and won,*' I completed automatically.

A day after our meeting at the Kino, the refugee riots, as the papers later dubbed it, happened. The inmates at the Heim woke up to find the building surrounded by policemen, their vans and cars blocking all the exits to the streets. Next to the police vans were buses provided by the local council, long double-decker buses. A police spokesman, talking through a megaphone, told the inmates to pack their belongings and vacate the building – they had six hours. The neighbours, it appeared, had complained to the council, they felt threatened, their daughters and sons were not safe on the streets where refugees sold drugs, and got drunk and fought; the aliens had turned the entire street into a dumpster, trash everywhere. Six hours to move out. The buses were there to take them to another Heim outside the city, meanwhile no one was allowed to go in or out. To hurry them along, the lights and water were cut off. But soon activists in the city heard of the blockade and descended upon the street, forming a human chain around the block, chanting in solidarity with the inmates, shouting at the police to leave.

'Mark texted me about it. Tension was high when I got there. Already the police were throwing tear gas at the activists, warning them to keep away. They wouldn't let us go beyond their perimeter,' Lorelle said.

'Where exactly were they being taken?'

'Nowhere. It is a trick they like to play. They pile migrants into buses, promising to resettle them, and then dump them outside the city, in the middle of nowhere.' She sipped her tea, as if to wash the bitter taste away. 'It is a cruel thing to do to helpless people. You know what is written on the buses?'

'What?'

'*Fahren macht Spass.*'

'Riding is fun?'

'That, accompanied by images of happy families holding hands – children and parents and even dogs. It is cruel.'

'What happened to Mark?' I asked.

'I kept trying his number, but he never answered, and I began to hope that maybe he had managed to slip out.'

She laughed and shook her head. 'It was wishful thinking. Mark wouldn't do that. He loved such standoffs with authority. "This is our moment", he would say, "this is our Sharpeville, our Agincourt." He was in there, barricaded with the rest. They had locked the doors from inside, blocking them with iron beds and tables so the police couldn't break in. We could see them at the doors and windows, waving their shirts and holding hands. The police said they were ready to wait for as long as it took. It took three days.'

'But, it wasn't even in the news . . .'

'The news covers what it wants to cover,' she said, her voice flat. 'I was there. Go online, look for alternative news sources, you'll read all about it. On the third day, when the police got tired of the standoff and threatened to break in and drag them out, the migrants soaked their mattresses, bedding and floors in kerosene, they promised to set the building and themselves aflame. Some went to the roof and threatened to jump. Mark was there, on the roof. I recognized his jacket.'

'What happened?'

'I saw his red jacket. I saw him fall, from the roof to the concrete pavement.'

'He . . . he jumped?' I asked, waiting for a twist in the story. But there was no twist.

She said, 'Afterward, I saw his body in the police car headlights before they took him away.'

I said nothing. I continued to stare at her. We were seated outside a café we had often visited with Mark and Uta and Stan and Eric. Across the road was the church, looking more abandoned than ever. Mark was dead.

'They say he jumped.'

'Well?'

'He wouldn't. He loved life too much. Others say he was pushed. I believe them.' She lowered her head, her face was filled with the heaviest agony.

'Pushed? Why?'

'Because he was different, and even in that moment, that desperate moment, they couldn't forget that. Anyway, what does it matter now? He is dead.'

Mary Chinomba. A preacher's daughter who loved to dress in drag, who loved to perform male roles onstage, who wasn't interested in the nice boys nudged in her direction by her parents. Who ran away from home to stay with her uncle, the only one who must have known and sympathized with what or who Mary was. The scholarship to Germany must have been the perfect solution for everyone involved, a godsend, literally.

'Once, you told me that Mark could not go back to Malawi. What did you mean?' I asked.

'A year after her arrival in Germany, Mary wrote her uncle a letter, pretending it was from her friend. The letter said Mary had died in an accident, and that the body had been cremated because nobody came to claim it. She signed the letter "Mark". That was the day Mary died.'

'Did the uncle believe him . . . her?' I asked.

'The letter wasn't for the uncle, really, it was for the father, the family. She figured it was best for everyone concerned. Mark dropped out of her first university in Hamburg and became a nomad. He didn't want to be traced by accident. I asked him if he would go back home someday, and he always said, Maybe.'

We sat down, watching our food go cold. None of us had the will to stand up and say goodbye.

'Tell me,' I said, 'how did you meet her?'

'Him,' she said.

'Him. How did you meet him?'

Lorelle got married at twenty-two, against her parents'

will. The parents had been redeployed back to the US and wanted her to go with them, but she refused. After a few years, her husband, a DJ she had met at a party in a converted bunker, had turned abusive. 'He beat me. I tried to leave him a few times but he threatened to harm me if I did. I eventually ran away to Berlin; I enrolled at the university. I met Mark, on the very first day. We became friends, much later we became lovers. A weird couple around campus, the cross-dresser from Africa and the freak from the US. Mark gave me the courage to ask Thomas, my husband, for a divorce. I grew up. Because of Mark.'

I took her hand. 'I am so sorry.'

She nodded.

'So, you are going back to America?'

'I've been thinking about it for a while, now this . . . I feel as if things have lost their focus for me here. I want to see my parents, get to know them again. What about you?'

'I am not sure yet.'

'Well, good luck. And when you come back to the States, give me a call.'

•

I got off the bus at the stop next to the *Apotheke*. I walked past the retirement home, my head bowed in thought, and as I passed the school for the homeless children I saw him running to the fence, waving, chased by his eagerness, his face alight just as in Gina's painting. '*Schokolade!*' I averted my face and walked faster, but then I stopped and turned to him. I had to admire his persistence. I raised my hand and waved back. He stood with both hands on the top of the wall, just like in the painting, his shock turning to delight as I called back, 'Hello.'

Slowly his hands dropped and he turned and walked back to his friends. I walked on beneath the poplar trees, my mind still churning.

The summer is ended, the harvest gathered, and still we are not saved. The line ran in my mind. I could see Mark standing behind the lectern, thumping his fist on the baize surface, his eyes flicking over his imaginary congregation, imitating his father.

'I am not going back,' I said to Gina. I had not thought about it, but as soon as I said it I knew I had decided long before today. I would stay in Berlin, for a while. I could support myself for a few months teaching ESL while I decided what to do next. I could also do some work on my long-neglected dissertation. Gina was seated on the couch, a book in her hand. She didn't look surprised. I thought of our home in Arlington. The parking lot across the road, and us sitting on the balcony, watching the kids skating. That seemed like another life now; recently I couldn't find myself in that picture, next to Gina. She was sitting alone.

'We used to be so happy,' she said. And I knew she meant before the miscarriage. 'I thought if we came to Berlin, together, away from everything . . . I thought Berlin would heal us.'

She sighed. The silenced lengthened, broken occasionally by birdcalls. Perhaps that was what we needed, silence. A little time apart. She looked directly into my eyes, and nodded. Somewhere, in the trees outside, a cuckoo's unmistakable call. I went to the window and looked up. A chittering, a flash of wings, grey and white and dappled. Then it was gone.

Book 2

CHECKPOINT CHARLIE

Manu walks up the driveway, then back, flexing his fingers and stamping his feet to keep the circulation going. It is almost midnight, two more hours to the end of his shift. His thick army surplus coat and the layer of woollen sweater under it feel useless against the cold claws of Berlin winter tearing into him. He is so hungry he feels weak. Stay awake, he whispers, stay alert, that's all you have to do for two more hours. He forces himself to imagine the clients staggering out, flush with drink and dancing. Part of his job is to hold the door for them as they come out trying to orient their senses to the cold, sometimes he helps them find their car if they can't find it by themselves. In the one month he has been working here he's never had to lead a lady to her car, there is always an eager and muscular young man with the ladies as they come out, laughing and listing on their high-heeled boots. To be escorted home afterward by young men is why most of them come to the Sahara Nightclub, after all. Mostly white and older ladies, mostly black and younger men.

The Sahara sits like an island amidst the parked cars, its brash neon sign reflecting in red and green off the cars' shiny bodies. Both sides of the sidewalk are covered in snow, heaped up like sand at a construction site. He shivers again and takes another drag on his cigarette. He is not a smoker, he got this from his partner, the Turk, but neither is he a doorman, or a bouncer, or a Berliner, but here he is, holding the door, bouncing, smoking cigarettes, in Berlin. Two more hours. He curses the cold again but quickly catches himself; he is lucky to have a job at all given his status. His daughter needs new shoes now that she'll be starting school, new clothes, new underwear, including training bras – she gave him a list. She will be twelve in May. Bras. What does he know about bras, apart from how annoying they can be to take off when one is in a hurry! Ah, the cold, the blasted European winter. Perhaps, if he has some form of distraction, apart from smoking and listening to his talkative partner, the job, the bouncing, may be less tedious. Sometimes the clients come out to catch a quick cigarette, or spliff. He mostly ignores them. Keep it professional, the manager told him on his first day. Keep it professional or you are out. Gruff-looking, gruff-talking redhead, incessantly smoking. She wore jeans that were too tight at the thighs and calves, emphasizing her short, chunky legs, her hair was piled high on her head, as if to give her extra inches. She looked up at him when he stood in her narrow office and told her he had heard of an opening. The office was dark and filled with cigarette smoke; on the walls were photographs of musicians and actors, some of them in the outlandish costumes of their art, some of them posing with the manager, there were bold, ostentatious signatures across the face of each picture. Next to the pictures was an old poster from the movie *Mandingo*. 'Aren't you a bit too old for this job?' She blew smoke at him. He was only forty, he wanted to protest, and he might look a bit tired, but every muscle on him is real, earned in the strawberry and grape fields of Greece where he spent last season picking fruit, sleeping on hard floors, escaping the police and the neo-Nazis, and making sure Rachida was safe. The manager reluctantly nodded, acknowledging his lean, imposing presence, and said he could start tomorrow.

•

They come out, they smoke, they make small talk, and they go back inside to the loud dance music. Mostly young, mostly muscular, most likely West African. He wonders if they have wives back home, children, waiting to join them here in Europe, or waiting for them to come back rich and with all the right papers, the all-important papers that would open up life's cornucopia. He wonders what his wife would think if she saw him now, a bouncer at the Sahara. She'd understand, surely. Rachida needs a new jacket for the winter, new underwear. Just for the winter, in spring he'll find something somewhere, cleaning, construction, dishwashing. All temporary, till he gets his papers.

•

He recognizes the green jacket as the woman staggers out as if pushed by the loud dance music that follows her from inside the hall. He helped her with it earlier when she came. She arrived after 11 p.m., and she is leaving already. Maybe she doesn't like the music. Maybe she doesn't like the men. She staggers a little, pulling the jacket tight around her, looking around slowly. As he turns to her, mouthing 'Alles gut?' and smiling, always smiling, trying to look as harmless as possible, she casts a contemplative stare at him, up and then down. The light falls directly on her and he notices her eyes are clear, probably not that drunk, just a bit disoriented, the brash lights and the cold do that to you coming out. His partner, Ahmad the Turk, pushes him aside and starts talking to her in his overfriendly, overeager way. She hugs herself beneath her jacket and, ignoring Ahmad, looks directly at Manu and says, 'Can you help me find my car? It is somewhere out there.' She points.

He takes the keys and goes out among the cars, pressing the beeper on the fob. The cold gets worse the further away he goes from the building. Ah, a Mercedes-Benz. Tucked away between a wall and a tree at the edge of the parking lot, as if she doesn't want it to be seen. New to the Sahara, most likely. He gets in and turns the key; loud music from the radio startles him, and he almost hits his head on the roof as he pulls back, then, relieved, he laughs at himself. He turns down the volume. The car smells of vanilla and sandalwood. Basma smells like that in the mornings, fresh, dressed for work. He leans back in the plush leather, he closes his eyes and lets the music wash over him like balm. It carries him away and he is home, Rachida is two again and he is putting her to bed, she can't go to sleep without her favourite lullaby playing softly in the background. A loud knock on the passenger-side window jolts him back to the present. Where is he? Green jacket. He wipes the moistness from his eyes before leaning over and opening the door for her. She gets in.

'Hallo,' she says.

'Nice car. Scared I'd run off with it?'

She looks surprised by the question. Of course, she wouldn't expect small talk from the bouncer, only he isn't a bouncer, not really. 'Well . . .' he mutters, and begins to step out, but her leather-gloved hand on his right arm stops him.

'Stay, please,' she says. She removes her hand from his arm and begins to take off her gloves, a finger at a time. As she removes the jacket he notices for the first time the luxurious fur at the collar. She smells of perfume, rich, musky. The music comes to a stop, another tune starts.

She puts her hands over the air vent, turning them over slowly like meat on a grill.

'I have to get back to work. Will you be okay?'

She shakes her head and gives a small laugh. 'I . . .' she begins, 'I am no good when I've had more than two drinks. Can you drive me home, please? My place is not far.'

'I can drive, but I am working.'

'I asked your partner, he said it is okay. He says he will cover for you.'

He looks at her, he looks outside at the pile of snow glowing in the dark. 'Okay,' he says.

•

They drive in silence. She sits with her head uptilted, her eyes closed. He enjoys the silence, the dreamlike ride in the deserted night streets. On a narrow back street a homeless man staggers into the road, looking like something out of Dickens with his overcoat blowing in the wind behind him, his long beard, his wild, baleful eyes caught briefly in the headlights, then he is gone. Manu follows her directions, conscious of her form, her smell, her swan neck illuminated by the streetlamps and the headlights of the cars they pass, and he knows she is conscious of him too for she sits half-facing him, expecting him to say something. She lives in Grunewald. He follows her finger down a quiet and dark street and eases the car into the narrow driveway, the tyres loudly crunching the gravel on the cobblestones. He turns off the engine and they sit in the dark for a while, then she stirs, and he stirs. She points him in the direction of the U-Bahn and hands him a fifty-euro note. He hesitates, then he shakes his head. 'No.'

'Well, *gute Nacht.*'

•

They leave the Heim early as they do every Sunday. Sunday is a good day, he and Basma were married on a Sunday, and Rachida was born on a Sunday. If she is going to be there waiting for them with the boy, if a miracle is going to happen to them, it is most likely going to be on a Sunday. And so, every Sunday, for the past one year since they arrived in Berlin, he and the girl have taken the train from the station near the Heim to Kochstrasse U-Bahn, and from there they walk across Oranienstrasse to Checkpoint Charlie.

He is glad the trains are mostly empty today. He hates the

weekdays and the rush hours and having to stand face-to-face with other passengers, breathing in the smell of stale beer and sausage and cheese, listening to their loud, unrestrained chatter on their cell phones.

They sit side by side, away from the cold wind that blows in every time the doors open. At a station an official appears before him and demands to see his pass. He always maintains a month's pass for the two of them, no need to take chances. After the ticket check he feels Rachida tugging at his arm. 'Father.' He is muttering to himself again. He clasps her hand. She looks at his face, anxious. Recently it is happening more regularly. The sallow-faced young man next to them leans over to lock lips with his even sallower-faced girlfriend. His hair stands in a ridge on his head, held up by gel. The girl wears a biker jacket and knee-length boots. Manu looks out the window, willing Rachida to look away. As they get off the train they face a billboard with a completely naked man seated on a stool, leering into the camera, his crotch barely covered by his hands clasped over it. A few months ago Manu would have stepped in front of his daughter to block her view, but now he simply turns his gaze away. It is a new world, another culture. She'll get inured to it. Beside the naked man's picture is another of a starving, fly-specked black child, looking out plaintively at the passengers, asking to be saved from whatever hell the viewer imagines is lurking in the shadows behind her. What does Rachida think of it all? He looks down at her walking quietly next to him, her face set, trying to avoid the pedestrians, trying to keep up. She needs her mother.

As they come out of the U-Bahn and join a body of pedestrians waiting for the light to change, he feels a familiar mix of hope and dread. Two weeks back, as they waited right here to cross, in this very spot, he thought he saw her in the distance, holding a toddler, the same height and hair shape as Omar. He pointed and they ran, ignoring the cars, pushing through the cluster of tourists on the sidewalk, past the mock MPs, one black, one white, standing in front of the guard hut on the median, hoisting the American flag, posing for pictures with tourists at two euros per picture. A child in a blue jacket momentarily separated from its parents stood in their path, alone on the sidewalk, looking about, trying not to panic. They turned left into Zimmerstrasse and hurried past the Stasi Museum, past the ancient Lada cars parked by the sidewalk, past the giant balloon waiting to take up its passengers for a lofty view of Berlin. Then they turned back, breathless, toward Stadtmitte U-Bahn.

'Where are they?' Rachida cried. There were tears in her eyes. The woman had disappeared, her black jacket swallowed by a sea of black jackets, then she reappeared crossing the road, hand in hand with the child. She was like a swimmer dipping and surfacing in a choppy sea.

'There,' he shouted.

'Mother!' Rachida shouted.

They waited at the crossing, watching the pair receding further into the crowd. The light changed, they ran. He felt a clutch of pain in his chest, he needed to exercise. He realized he was pulling Rachida too hard, her hand almost slipping out of his moist grip. But they were catching up to the woman and the boy, who had just entered a souvenir shop. Why was she not looking around, searching for them like they were searching?

Later, he sat on a bench by the roadside, his hands shaking, trying to console Rachida as she covered her face with her hands, her shoulders shaking. The memory of the woman's surprised, then frightened face as he grabbed her hand shamed him. Her gaze went from him to Rachida, two demented faces in the middle of the souvenir store, he shouting 'Basma, darling!' and the girl shouting 'Mother!' Passers-by looked casually at them and he wondered what they saw: a tired-looking man and a crying girl by the roadside, clearly foreigners, in their old and ill-fitting winter jackets – mostly, though, they didn't see you at all.

•

The lights change and they cross, he takes Rachida's hand at a crossing, pretending to guide her through the crush of bodies, but really just wanting something to hold on to. They loiter around the souvenir shops and then they turn back and head toward Stadtmitte U-Bahn. Their legs are used to these routes by now, rising and falling and turning automatically, only the eyes are on full alert, head swivelling, searching for the beloved faces. Hours later, when the girl's legs begin to drag, he stops and they enter a McDonald's. She orders a chicken sandwich. Again, he is reminded that only last year she was ordering the Happy Meal: six chicken nuggets, fries and a drink. He tries to make small talk as she eats. He feels her eyes on him, full of questions, and he quickly smiles and touches her cornrows. 'Your hair looks different. When did you do it?'

Her eyes light up as she runs her hand over the imbricated, dovetailing rows. 'Hannah did it, last night while we were waiting for you to return.'

Last night. While he sat in the car with the lady in the

green jacket, yearning to put his hand over hers, his lips against her neck.

'It's beautiful. We must thank Hannah when we get back. Maybe we'll pick up something for her.'

They hang around till the crowd has thinned, and the doner kebab and imbiss stands by the roadside have closed and the tourists are replaced by another kind of crowd, younger, louder, walking hand in hand, and then they head back to the trains.

•

At the Heim, Hannah is waiting for them in what the inmates refer to as the garden. A barren and gravelled space at the back of the huge and charmless building. It is littered with cans and plastic bags clinging to the base of the building, vestigial rosebush stalks, and iron benches presenting a windswept and dismal tableau. The inmates, especially those with children, come out on warmer days to sit on the benches and gaze at the slate-grey skies, enjoying a moment of quiet, pretending they are somewhere else, not at a Heim in a strange city thousands of miles from home.

Hannah turns her kindly, questioning eyes on him and he smiles briefly in response, saying nothing. Is that a flicker of relief on her face? He feels a spark of anger at her. He knows what she is thinking: for another week they will remain a make-believe family, till next Sunday when he and the girl go back on their search. They met in Greece and for one year they travelled together, almost a family, he and Hannah and Rachida, in the manner he has seen many people do on the road, childless women falling in with motherless children, wifeless husbands with husbandless wives, proxy partners for as long as it lasts – then they parted when she came to Berlin ahead of them, and now they are together again. Sometimes he wonders what she wants from him. Love? Friendship? Protection? For almost two years she has never asked for anything that he wouldn't have offered without being asked. Protection, yes, friendship, certainly, but not love. She is a beautiful woman, and even in these circumstances she manages to look pretty, with long silken hair framing a face from which the joy and light are fading. She sometimes mentions a daughter and a husband back in Eritrea. She never offers more details, and he never asks for more. Details have a way of piling up, layer upon seductive layer, making you think you know the person, until one day you realize you don't. Stories are made up and traded as currency among homeless, rootless people, offered like a handshake, something to disarm you with. He has long stopped wanting to know – he knows better than to get too close. They are here for a new start, not to re-create or hold on to the past. The water they all crossed to come here has dissolved the past. But, he can't give up on Checkpoint Charlie. Because she is alive. He knows. If she isn't he'd know, and if she is alive she'd never rest until she finds them.

•

His partner, the sour-tongued, sour-tempered Ahmad, says, 'What these young men want is power. When they fuck these women they think they own the world. By fucking them in the ass or the mouth or wherever, they feel they are fucking the whole of Germany. I swear, that's what they think. Haha. What do you think, Ghaddafi?'

'I don't know, Ahmad.'

'You should know. You are educated. You must have an opinion.'

'You are right, I guess.'

'You are right I am right, Libya.' He pauses, dragging on his cigarette. 'Tell me, if you are Libyan, why are you so black?'

'My father is originally from Nigeria. He settled in Libya before I was born.'

He never considered himself different from any Libyan till after the fall of the dictator when ordinary citizens, including his neighbours, some of them his patients, began attacking whomever they thought looked different, foreign. He doesn't tell the Turk this. He shrugs. 'There are many like me.'

The Turk is an ex-boxer. Ahmad the Turk, they called him in the ring. Once, he was a contender for the heavyweight title for the region of Bavaria, but he broke a wrist in the fifth round, he didn't even know his wrist was fractured till the next round. He just couldn't feel his hand any more.

They stand side by side in the little alcove next to the entrance, sheltering from the cold, smoking furiously to keep away the cold. Ahmad is given to hyperbole, especially on nights like this when the cold is most bitter, and the women and young men that pass before them seem to be having all the fun in the world. He knew the Klitschko brothers, he claims. Once, he was a sparring partner for both brothers, three years back, when they came to Heidelberg and he got to stay with them in the Hotel Europäischer Hof Heidelberg, the most expensive hotel in town. Sometimes he gets overcome by nostalgia for his fighting days, usually when the weather dips too far below freezing, and the Sahara is deserted, then he'll smoke cigarette after cigarette while doing a little shadowboxing, his fighter's muscles rippling under his jacket, and when he gets tired of that, he'll step into the bar to refill his hip flask with vodka.

'Muammar,' he says, sipping his vodka, 'these women come for company, a little fun, and our job is to help them get it. Right?'

'Right.'

'One day, one of them asked me to walk her to her car, just like it happened to you that day. Hold my hand, she said, and we went. Beautiful. Young. Tits this big. I walk her to her car and she pulls me inside and begs me not to let her go home alone. I swear to Allah, Libya. Now we are holding each other in that car, and we go at it, giving no quarter, boom, I go at her, and she comes back, pow, she scratches my back until I bleed, I pound into her, she pushes up, I push down and now the car is rocking with our movement, and still we go at it.'

He assumes a boxer's crouch, fists forward and raised. 'Now we are locked together, like this, swaying together. She is a tigress. And all the while that woman Fairuz is playing on the car radio. Now we both fall back into the car seat, locked together, breathing heavily in each other's face. She holds me, like this, two hands around my neck, as if scared of falling off a cliff, harder, she says, harder, and then, I can't hold back any more, my body shakes, I am down. I am out.' He leans against the wall, panting in recollection. 'Ah, Ghaddafi. Those were the crazy nights . . .'

Then he straightens up, looking past Manu into the night. 'Hey, look who's here.'

For two weeks the club had been shut down. A mysterious fire had started behind the bar, some say it was a jealous husband who had followed his wife to the club. Not much damage was done.

In those two weeks, as he walked the streets of Berlin looking for casual employment, and even on Sundays at Checkpoint Charlie, he thought about her, attracted and guilty at the same time. He remembers her hand on his arm, a brief electricity, a frisson, and her mouth near his ear as she whispered, 'Gute Nacht.'

Now he watches her approach. The cold has intensified over the last few days. As she approaches, swathed in her green jacket, he feels like turning and walking away in the other direction, into the cold night. She ducks into the tight alcove next to him and takes out a cigarette.

'How can you stand this cold?' she says. He hands her a light, saying nothing. She takes a drag and passes him the cigarette. They smoke, not talking.

'You should go in,' he says. 'It is warmer.'

'I am okay here,' she says. 'I am not a very good dancer.'

'Then why do you come here?'

'Maybe I need the company,' she says. She turns and looks at him directly. The Turk slips into the bar and returns with a bottle of vodka. 'I can't drink,' she says. 'I have to drive back.'

'I can drive you,' Manu says. The Turk winks at him and makes a shadowboxing motion with his fists.

'That will be nice,' she says. She takes the open bottle and sips.

Later, in the car, he asks, 'What is your name?'

'Angela.'

'Like the chancellor,' he says. At her house, they sit in the car for a while, listening to a piano concerto on the radio. The night is quiet, all the windows are dark. A cat slinks across the balcony and into a garden.

'What do you do?' She turns, facing him. 'I mean, before you came to Berlin.'

He says, 'I was a doctor. A surgeon.'

She takes his hands and looks at them, as if by so doing to divine the truth of his claim.

'I knew there was something different about you when I first saw you that night. You looked out of place standing there, helping people to their cars. What happened? Where's your family?' When he says nothing, she rubs his hand in hers. 'You have very good hands.'

'Thanks.'

'Your partner told me you are from Libya. Do you miss your country?'

'I have no country.'

'Come inside.'

He looks out the car window at the house, quiet, the darkness settled around it like a mist. 'Perhaps not,' he says gently.

'Come on, have a cup of tea before you go. I live alone.'

He follows her into a big hall. He can tell it is a big house even though she doesn't bother to turn on the lights. A baby grand piano stands near a window in the living room, which connects to the kitchen in an open plan. A silver shaft of light comes in through the kitchen window, falling on the silver refrigerator and stove. She opens the fridge and takes out a bottle of gin, then she leads him through the living room, into a corridor, and then into a bedroom. She leaves him there, standing in the middle of the room, the bottle of gin and two glasses on the table next to him, and disappears into the bathroom. Soon he hears the shower running. He looks around the dark room, feeling his way to a light switch. The overhead light comes on, transfixing him in its glare, he quickly turns it off and turns on the night lamp. He sits on an ottoman by the window, and takes off his thick boots. The boots are worn at the heels. He has been wearing them for two years now. When she comes out of the bathroom, wrapped in a flimsy robe, he continues to sit, motionless. She drops the robe.

'I have a wife,' he says. His voice is hoarse, his eyes fixed to her voluptuous body.

She sits next to him on the ottoman, the heat from her body rising toward him. 'And I have a husband. But we are separated.' She takes his hand and places it on her breast, all the time looking into his face. Slowly she helps him take off his jacket, dropping it on the floor. He stands up, conscious of the bulge in his trousers. 'I'll take a bath.'

In the bathroom, still warm, the mirrors still covered in steam, he fills the tub with hot water. The heating at the Heim has broken down and bathing for the past month is simply turning on the freezing shower over his head and standing under it for as long as he can endure before dashing out of the bathroom. He dips his leg into the very hot water, and then the other leg, then slowly lowers his body; the hot water on his skin is a benediction and he almost cries out with pleasure. He sinks in to his chin and closes his eyes.

The sun coming in through the blinds wakes him up in the morning, and he sits up momentarily disoriented. Where is he? He is in a strange room, in a strange bed, and there is something important he has forgotten. When he sees the

naked woman next to him he gets out of bed and begins to
dress. It is Sunday.

'Where are you going?' she asks, reaching out an arm
toward him. He continues to dress, hurriedly, almost desperately. 'My daughter will be waiting for me,' he says finally.

'What is her name?' she asks.

'Rachida.'

'Bring her, one of these days. I'd love to see her. I have
horses, she could ride them.'

•

Each time he goes back to Grunewald she asks him to bring
Rachida, and each time he promises he will. He goes on
weekdays when he isn't working, and on Saturdays before
going to work at the Sahara. Occasionally he stays overnight,
but never on Saturdays. He makes up excuses for that: he
has to take Rachida to the park, he has German-language
lessons – which he does, though not on Sundays. To Hannah
and Rachida, he says he is out job hunting in Grunewald, and
he tries to salve his conscience by getting them little presents,
things he can afford, scarves for Hannah, sweets and trin-
kets for Rachida. Sometimes Angela hands him a grocery bag
stuffed with packets of sugar, tea, fruit. 'For your daughter.'
Hannah takes the bag each time, saying nothing, but her eyes
are always filled with questions, which he avoids.

'Where are we going, Father?' Rachida asks. Her appre-
hension shows in the way she clutches his hand as they get
off the train at Grunewald, she walks close to him, staring
at the gated houses with vines running over the walls and
fences. This is far from Kreuzberg and the Heim, far from

the touristy bustle and noise of Checkpoint Charlie, far from anything she has experienced since they came to Berlin.

'We are going to see a friend. She has horses and she might let you ride one.'

She looks up at him, surprise and doubt on her face. How will she behave with Angela? he wonders. It will be fine. Angela is charming, easy to talk to, and surely she will be great with children. With her he can talk about the past. Lying in bed naked, post-coitus, the words come easily, gently coaxed by her attentive face, the right questions, and on each visit he tells her more. 'Tell me about Libya,' she always begins. He told her how the students at Rachida's school began to disappear, one by one. 'What happened to all my friends?' Rachida had asked him. 'They don't come to school any more.' The school population dwindled as the violence grew, the NTC rebels gradually took over town after town, those who could afford it left, till only the children of the poor remained. The worst part was when the teachers started to leave. By the end of 2010, almost all the schools in the area were closed.

'Every day I woke up, I took the kids to school, I went to work, I pretended that things would soon get back to normal. I was the only doctor left for miles around, when eventually even the sick stopped coming to the clinic for fear of the violence on the streets, I told my wife to take the children and leave. She refused, she wouldn't go without me. Then one day, I took the kids to school as usual and the gate was closed, not even the guard was there, that was when I knew it was time to go. When we came home, my wife was ready, unknown to me she had packed weeks before, and just waiting for me to come to my senses. And still I was reluctant to go. "But if we go, who will take care of the sick and the wounded?" I asked. "Let the politicians take care of them," she said.

'We decided to come to Berlin, that's where everybody was going. Also, I had an old school friend here, Abdul Gani. We had no plan, nothing. The most important plan was to get out of Tripoli alive. Also, I told her, "If anything happens on the way and we are separated, continue on to Berlin. Look for me at Checkpoint Charlie. I'll wait there, every Sunday."'

'Why Checkpoint Charlie?' Angela asked.

He shrugged. 'I had read about it in books. It seemed as good a spot as any.' Then he added, almost shyly, 'In the movies lovers always meet at a prominent landmark, like the Empire State Building, or the Eiffel Tower.'

'You must love your wife very much.'

'Yes,' he said.

'So, did you meet your friend, Abdul?'

'Unfortunately no. By the time we got here he had moved on. He now lives in America, in San Diego.'

•

He wonders if Rachida can sense his nervousness, how his steps falter as they approach the front door, how his hand takes an infinitesimally long time to rise to the doorbell. The door opens and a man stands at the door, a man with a thin, unsmiling face, his hair greying. Manu can tell he isn't that old, mid-fifties. He looks at Manu, then the girl, then back to Manu.

'Who are you looking for?' His voice is challenging, his posture, one hand on his hip, is aggressive. Manu turns to Rachida, unable to hide his confusion, he looks at the house number again, 47, then he says to the man, 'I think we have the wrong house. Sorry to disturb you.'

He pulls her hand and they turn to go. As they cross the road he hears Angela's voice calling, 'Manu! Hey, Manu. Come back.'

They take off their muddy shoes by the door. The man is seated behind the piano, running his fingers aimlessly over the keys. He doesn't look up when they enter.

'Joachim, this is Manu, a friend. And this is Rachida, his daughter,' Angela says. She comes forward and frames Rachida's face in her hands, pulling it close, running a hand through her hair. 'She is so beautiful, Manu.'

'Hello, Joachim,' Manu says.

Joachim remains bowed over the piano, his back curved over the keyboard until it seems he is going to tip forward, then he raises his hands and a tune rings out. It rises and falls, repetitive, rising and falling.

Angela leads the girl away. 'My, you are so cold, come to the kitchen, I'll make you a cocoa. And you, Manu, I'll get you a coffee.'

The man keeps playing, his head lowered, his eyes closed. Manu sits, feeling the awkwardness of the moment. Joachim is the husband. Angela has mentioned the name several times. He wonders what he is doing, why he is back. His eyes run over the familiar room, every surface is redolent of him and Angela caught in blind passion, panting and sightless and naked. The piano. She, bent over, her hair dripping into the keyboard, he behind her, his hands on her waist, together banging out a sweet and strange tune. He begins to stand up, and just then Joachim turns and says, 'Charles Mingus.'

'What?' Manu asks, smiling. He takes a deep breath to regain his poise, always smiling to show he is harmless.

' "Take the A Train", by Charles Mingus. You know it?'

'No. I am not a musical person, unfortunately. I am a doctor.' He adds the last with a squaring of his shoulders.

But the man interrupts him. 'Did Angela tell you I am a musician, jazz?'

'I believe she must have.'

He continues before Manu can answer, 'Jazz is like life. You have to trust in chance, sometimes it will work, sometimes it will not work. It is like sex. When it does work, it is magic. Tell me, does it work like that for you?'

'I am not a jazz person myself,' Manu says.

'I don't mean jazz. With my wife. The sex, is it magic, is it chemistry?' He has been playing as he talks, but now he stops. Manu turns to the kitchen, hoping Angela will appear. He can hear laughter from the yard outside, coming through the open back door. He hasn't heard Rachida laugh like this in a long time. He stands up. 'Let me see how my daughter is doing . . .'

And just then Angela enters, a cup of coffee in her hand. She hands him the cup. She looks from him to Joachim, who has gone back to picking at the piano keys.

'What are you two talking about?'

Joachim continues to play, turning fully to face Angela. Manu stands up and heads for the kitchen and the back door leading to the courtyard. Rachida is in the barn, feeding a piebald mare an apple. She turns and sees him, her face alight with wonder. She hands him the apple. 'You can feed her, Father. Isn't she pretty?'

'Yes.'

He can see into the living room from where he stands. They are shouting at each other. Joachim is trying to take her arm, but she shakes him off angrily and walks away to the kitchen. Joachim follows her, she leaves the kitchen and heads into the corridor to the bedroom.

'Come, we have to go now.'

'The horse, Father, what of the horse?' she asks. She is wearing a pair of Angela's boots. He hugs her tightly, 'I am so sorry, child. This was all a mistake. We have to go.'

'But . . .'

'Hurry, Rachida, hurry.'

As they pass through the living room, a door opens and Angela comes out. Manu whispers, 'Sorry, we have to go now. Thanks for everything.'

'You don't have to go.' She goes to Rachida and takes her hand.

'I am sorry,' he says, looking into her eyes. 'This was a mistake.'

Rachida looks with perplexity from her father to the woman.

'Come, Rachida,' he says. Their feet landing on the hard snow makes hollow crunching noises as they leave.

•

'She says she can't go today. She is not feeling well.'

Hannah stands by the door, a tense smile on her face. She is wearing a quilted housecoat that reaches below her knees.

'Well, it is Sunday. Please go in and remind her. It is Sunday.'

'What happened yesterday? She came back distraught.'

He searches her face, most of it covered by her hair falling forward like a veil. He wonders how much Rachida has told her. It is Sunday, he wants to repeat, but says instead, 'Can I see her?'

He steps forward, trying to go around her into the women's section. The women and children occupy the top floor of the Heim, and although it is not forbidden, the men consider the women's section off-limits. If they want to see a woman, they stand at the entrance and send for her. Hannah remains static.

'Come,' she says, 'let's go to the garden.'

In the deserted garden a plastic bag flies in the wind around the square space, and ends up stuck on the leg of the bench they are seated on, side by side. Hannah says, 'I heard from my lawyer today. The review board has approved my asylum application.'

He looks at her, speechless. Finally, he says, 'Well, that is great news, Hannah. I am so happy for you.'

She nods. 'I have been allocated a place, a small place. One bedroom, and a living room. A bath, a kitchen.'

'When do you leave?'

'No date yet, but soon.'

'Rachida will miss you.'

She nods again, silent. He adds softly. 'We will miss you.'

'You two can come with me.'

'But we can't,' he says.

'Why not?'

When he gives no answer she lays a hand over his. 'You don't have to answer now. Think about it. Rachida is like my daughter now. I want to know she is okay. I want to watch her grow into a woman.'

A light snow is falling, turning the sidewalk white. He exits the train station and walks toward Checkpoint Charlie, alone. The mock MPs are at it again, posing with tourists. The wind in his face brings tears to his eyes. The diehards brave the bone-chilling cold, drifting like windblown paper from one display to the next, their faces barely visible pink splotches under scarves and hats. He continues on Friedrichstrasse till he sees the blue *U* sign in front of Stadtmitte U-Bahn. The lighted sign sucks him forward like a fly, and soon he is on the train, not caring where he is going. He changes trains a few times, from U-Bahn to S-Bahn and back again. Once, he starts and looks around, fearing he has forgotten something. 'Rachida,' he mutters. As he gets out of a station he notices the train tracks running in multiple directions: at times they look like fault lines separating sections of the city; other times they are stitches, holding the city together. Now he is walking by the Spree, alone, and where is everybody, the summer crowd sitting in the grass watching the tourists in boats gliding by. Lumps of dirty snow from the last snowfall litter the dry brown grass. He stands staring at the water.

He can hear Hannah's voice, rising from the water, 'Why don't you take a break today?' And his voice, sounding horrified, 'You know I can't. What if she comes today, the very day I decide not to go? I won't forgive myself . . .'

'Maybe it is time to let go, Manu.'

'What are you saying?'

'Rachida . . . She knows her mother is never coming. She is doing this just to please you.'

'What?'

'Listen . . . my husband . . . he is not coming either. He died, killed in front of my eyes.'

'But you said he was coming, you are waiting for him.' She was lying to him. Why was she doing that? But she went on, gentle yet still insistent, 'We say things sometimes to keep our sanity. Your wife, she died, didn't she? And the boy, and you blame yourself.'

'Shh. Stop. You know nothing about me.'

He left her and ran out into the street, clutching at the hot molten pain in his chest, till he got to the train station. Now his face in the Spree stares back at him – tired lines on his forehead and around his eyes, deep like a freshly ploughed field. His hair, when did it turn so white, so thin at the top? The wind blows over the water surface; ripples, waves rise, tall and towering like horses rearing up to attack, and everywhere he turns there are bodies floating, people screaming. He holds on to Rachida, he is a good swimmer, but Basma, where is she, she has the boy, he can't see them anywhere. Bobbing and sinking. Flotsam everywhere. But he won't give up. He will go to Checkpoint Charlie every Sunday. Rachida will come with him. They will walk past the souvenir shops and ice cream stalls, together. If they keep their memories alive, then nothing has to die.

Book 3

BASEL

1

A drive of twenty minutes outside the city toward Liestal and a confusion of intersections led to the tiny town where the woman lived. Katharina, that was her name. They'd left the autoroute and taken a narrower road that rose gently into the hills through little towns with cars bearing ski equipment clamped to their roofs parked in front of houses and hotels. Skiers getting ready to go off to the mountains, the taxi driver explained, he pointed ahead, French border. The border was even closer than Basel, which was still visible behind them, its tall buildings and communication masts rising into the cloudy sky. The house was tiny, separated from its neighbours by fir trees and grass hedges. Portia told the driver to wait. She got down and stood before the door and peered into the glass panel before ringing the bell. A woman opened the door halfway, sticking only her head out in the crack between door and frame.

'Katharina?' Portia asked.

'Yes.'

'I am Portia. David's sister. We spoke on the phone.'

The woman nodded and opened the door wider. Portia paid the driver and followed the woman into the house.

'Welcome in Basel,' Katharina smiled. She ran her hands through her hair, twisting it into a knot at the back. *To*, Portia found herself correcting mentally. It was the same in Berlin. *Welcome in Berlin*, they'd tell her. It was a direct translation from the German, she knew, but she corrected them anyway, mentally. Welcome *to* Basel.

'Sorry, it is a very small house,' Katharina said. Her hair was raven black and tousled. A beauty, Portia noted grudgingly, if you like the petite type – she stood just over five feet tall. Part of the reason she was here was to see this woman whom her brother chose, to try to understand why he chose her. What was the attraction? She was an educated woman, a former lecturer at a university, a PhD. Was that part of the attraction, an intelligent person he could talk to, look up to, or was it the beauty? That would be a good place to start, an instant icebreaker. Why do you think my brother chose you? Unless of course if it was she who did the choosing. The house was a veritable dollhouse, the living room already felt crammed with only two of them standing in the middle. Two bedrooms at most. An open door led into a kitchen adjoining the living room. A square patch of tartan rug covered the floor, on the edges of the rug were a couch, two armchairs, and a circular dining table by the window. A glass flower vase with a single red rose in it rested on the window ledge – it was a large window, almost taking up the whole wall, and it gave the small room an illusion of space. Next to the window was a bookshelf. Everything in its place, a tidy mind.

'It is a beautiful house,' she said.

'Thank you,' Katharina said, and, out of modesty or a stubborn determination not to concede the point about how unimpressive the house was, she pointed at the wood beams in the roof, thick and long and tubular. 'It is an old house, my aunt built it. Long ago. Maybe twenty years now.'

They sat down, the ice still unbroken. Katharina took out a picture of her aunt from the desk drawer and showed it to Portia. A large, stern-faced woman, hair tied at the back of her head, her back straight and her chest thrust out like a drill sergeant at a parade. She had died a few years back, at the age of eighty – an independent, strong-willed woman, who lived in a time when such attributes were considered unwomanly. She grew up poor, she never married, worked various jobs all her life: laundry maid, nanny, cook, bus driver, all the time saving her money, driven by one desire, to build her own place. And she did, saving every penny. She taught herself carpentry and some of the wooden furniture, like the bookshelves and dining table and chairs, she made herself. Katharina was her only niece, and they were close, and she left her the house when she died.

'Sometimes I feel sad. She didn't enjoy life, she saved and economized, and now she is dead. She should have enjoyed more, you know.' As Katharina talked her eyes kept straying to the passage leading to the door next to the kitchen, and a minute later the door opened and a man came out. Average height, about forty, leading a bull terrier on a leash. He was dressed in boots and a windbreaker, ready for the outdoors.

'This is Sven.'

He shook hands with Portia.

The dog went over to Portia and she let it sniff her hands and her feet, circling her, before returning to Sven. He pulled at the leash, heading for the door, speaking softly to the dog in German. Katharina spoke to him in German and he nodded. '*Ja, ja.*' His eyes behind his glasses blinked weakly as he smiled and said, 'I am taking Rex for a walk. It is good to see you.'

'Bye, Rex,' Portia said.

Man and dog reappeared in the path outside the window, heading for the faraway tree line. Sven leaned down and scratched Rex behind the ears before taking off its leash. Rex bounded forward and the man followed till they disappeared into the trees. On the horizon a dense black cloud swarmed up over the fir and spruce forest, it changed into a storm of birds, a murmuration of starlings, shape-shifting, now a funnel, now a wave, now a sphere, now a sickle, rising and falling, breaking up and reconfiguring, fast and evasive and then it was gone.

Katharina said, 'Sven and I grew up together. At one time we were engaged, we were going to be married.'

'Oh,' Portia said. 'And?'

'It was a long time ago. Before I met your brother.'

Portia waited, but Katharina didn't offer more, her eyes were fixed on the distant line of trees where man and dog had disappeared.

'What happened?' Portia pressed.

Katharina shrugged. 'I talk about Sven if you like. But he is not too important for this, yes? Not concerned. My father and his father, they went to university together. Sven, he is a professor.'

'So, it was expected then, that you two would marry?'

'Well, not really, not like arranged marriage. He was my first boyfriend and we like each other, and everyone thought we were going to get married. Yes. Is there anything more you want to know about him?'

Portia shook her head, surprised by the directness and abruptness of the question. So much for breaking the ice. She wasn't the one who brought up Sven – but she sensed the woman was merely circling, sniffing her up, two strange dogs meeting. Portia smiled brightly, this was going to be a chess game. 'How old is he?'

'He is forty now. Five years older than me.'

'So you were about thirty when you met my brother?'

'I was twenty-nine. Your brother was thirty.' She stood up. 'I'll get some tea. You want?'

'Yes. Any green tea will do.'

Portia went to the bookshelf and looked at the titles: Bertolt Brecht, Goethe, Kierkegaard, Spinoza, all in German. Katharina had studied philosophy or something in that line. She wondered what they discussed, she and her brother, at night. She wondered why she was here, what purpose this visit would serve, after all, her brother was dead, gone. *Lycidas.* That poem had been running on her mind all day, driving her crazy – *For Lycidas is dead, dead ere his prime.* Three years dead. This inquisition, this raising up of the past, of what good was it? But she was here, and Katharina was here, so she might as well get on with it. Outside, the fog was steaming off the grass, rising to cover the trees.

As soon as she came back with the tea, Katharina jumped into her story without further preamble. They had met at the Basler Fasnacht festival in Basel. 'You know the Fasnacht? No? It is famous ceremony here. People dance and sing, mostly folk songs and political songs. People come from many countries to watch. That night, me and my friends, we were following the singers, they walk in the streets with their lanterns, dressed in traditional clothes. I was in final year for my PhD, and I was happy and carefree.' She paused, her eyes wistful, perhaps reliving the moment of her past happiness.

'Was David there to watch as well?'

'He was there with his wife, this he told me later. They were having some argument, I think. She left and went home. And he was alone . . .'

'My brother had another wife, before you?' she asked, putting down her tea. Katharina smiled, her cup held in both hands. She nodded, amused at Portia's reaction.

'Yes, he had a wife. Her name is Brigitte. And his name it was not David. It was Moussa. When your brother first came in Switzerland he was staying in a refugee hostel outside town. It is old building near a farming village, nobody was staying in the building so they give it for refugees. It is remote, far from town, and the refugees were not allowed to go anywhere, not church, or library, or public buildings. It was a new law. The government was trying to control immigration, too many new people coming in, and all over the country people are not sure how to treat them. There was suspicion.

The government even started paying refugees to return to their countries. About a thousand francs per person, I think.

'But Moussa didn't want to go back. He applied for asylum. They were allowed to work on farms, helping the farmers and also making some pocket money. When they first met, he was working on Brigitte's father's chicken farm and she had come to visit from the city. Her father and mother liked him very much because he is very nice, and sometimes he stayed for dinner after they work on the farm and they talk about things, what he planned to do. They even wanted to get lawyer for him to help him with his asylum application. But this day the daughter, Brigitte, she came with her two-year-old daughter. Brigitte was divorced. She was surprised to see him. Her parents have already told her about him, but she didn't know what to expect. He told me at first she was very hostile to him, she thought he was trying to take advantage of her parents. They were old, in their seventies. But later they became friends. Your brother, he was easy to talk to, yes? Very charming.'

Portia caught the faint cynicism in Katharina's voice. It was understandable, for despite all that had happened, Brigitte had been the first wife and still a rival, even if only after the fact. She went on, 'Very soon she was taking him to her place in Basel for weekends, and before a few months they were talking of marriage.'

'And did you meet her, this Brigitte?' Portia prompted when Katharina paused for a long time, her eyes on the teacup, which she held before her chest in a meditative pose.

'I have met her. I don't want to sound mean, but she is a common person, not very educated, you know, she was an assistant in a store. But she was lonely and just coming out of a divorce, and I think she loved him and her daughter liked him – he was very good with children. So why not, they try to get married quickly. And I think he told her that was the best way he can get his papers, and she wanted to help. So they went to the registry, but at registry they meet more problem. Instead of getting married he was detained for many days and finally he was deported back to Mali.'

Moussa. Portia was hearing that name for the first time. She had a lot of catching up to do. David had left home fifteen years ago, she was nine then, and he was nineteen. All she remembered was a long-legged kid who played soccer with his friends in the backyard, who was protective of her, and whom she idolized. She remembered one morning, walking her to school, he had told her he was going away for a long time and she might never see him again, but he would write to her and he would always love her. He left the next day, to South Africa, she later found out, illegally. He had spent a year in prison there. He came back home, and when it appeared he had finally settled down and was ready to return to school, he left again one year later, this time on a boat to West Africa; from there he planned to cross the desert to Europe.

She imagined his deportation. In England, when she was doing her MA, a classmate from Kenya had told her about an uncle who had been deported but had somehow found his way back. He told her it always happened at night. She imagined her brother, alone or with other deportees, handcuffed, led by immigration officials through a deserted terminal, *at night*, to a waiting plane chartered specially for the purpose. It would be a long and interminable flight. Once, on a plane to

Frankfurt on her way to Zambia, an Arab family had boarded, man, woman, two children, escorted by immigration officials. 'Why?' the man kept shouting, looking into the faces of the passengers as he passed through the aisle. 'Is it because I am Muslim, because I am not white? You send me back to die? My blood on your head.' In his seat, he banged his head repeatedly against the headrest and the armrest. 'I kill myself before I go back.' The children and the wife screamed with him, loud and sorrowful, delaying takeoff, till finally the pilot came out of his cockpit and spoke to the agents and the crying screaming family was led off the plane. She remembered the man, a portly, middle-aged man, in fishnet singlet and jeans – he must have been surprised by the agents as he watched TV or ate dinner with his family – and the quiet, tearful wife holding the two children, one on each arm. Did her brother also scream and beg to remain, and when they got to Mali, was he simply dumped at the airport with nothing but the clothes on his back, and who was at the airport to receive him? What do deportees feel: relief, shame, anger? Surely, they must feel relief to be away from all that European suspicion and alienation? And yet, some of them, no sooner do they arrive than they begin to plot their return. It is as if some homing device, focused toward Europe, is implanted in their brains and it never stops humming till their feet are on European soil.

'Why was he deported to Mali, why not to Zambia?' she asked.

Katharina looked at her and shrugged. 'Because he told everyone he was from Mali. That his family is there. Even me. I didn't know his family is from Zambia till much later.'

'What happened after the deportation? How did he return to Switzerland?' Portia asked.

'Brigitte, she promised she'd get him back. She got a lawyer who told her the only way he can come back is if they get married. So, she got on a plane and went to Mali and they got married.'

Despite herself, Portia was impressed by Brigitte's tenacity. What was it about her brother that attracted these women? She took a sip of her tea – it was cold. What is it about black men that acts like a super-magnet to these white women: curiosity, the exotic factor, love, or is it pity? What is it about white women that black men can't keep away from?

'She must have really loved him,' she said.

Katharina laughed. 'Yes. Like a movie, yes? Very romantic. And also, very foolish.'

'Foolish?'

'Well, it didn't last. They got married in a court in Mali, they came back, husband and wife. He got his papers, he started working at the rail station, everything was going well, then they were fighting. They live together less than two years only. He told me she wanted too much to be in charge, all the time, and his life became hell. He said his life was better when he was living in the refugee camp.'

'And that was when he met you?'

'It was love at first sight. For both of us. After that night at the bar, it was only one month later he left her and he started to stay with me.'

'Well, if you were so in love, why did you kill him? Why did you kill my brother? Can you make me understand that?' Portia asked. Katharina put down her cup, she went to the table and pulled out a drawer and took out a cigarette packet. She opened the window and blew the smoke outside. 'So, finally you ask your real question. This is the reason why you came. I wondered when you were going to ask.'

Portia sighed. At last, the ice was truly broken.

•

In the taxi going back to her hotel, Portia watched the raindrops hitting the window and she imagined heaven and earth conjoined by pillars of rain. Rainy Basel. *He must not float upon his watery bier / Unwept, and welter to the parching wind.* It had been raining yesterday when they arrived in Basel. A wet welcome. It felt like it was raining in every town and village and hamlet all over Switzerland. It had been raining at the Hauptbahnhof in Berlin when they boarded the train, and it rained all the eight hours the train ride lasted. She closed her eyes, exhausted by the bad weather, by her session with Katharina. In her mind she played over and over again Katharina's words, her halting English, the hand gestures, the direct, combative stare, till toward the end when she ended the conversation abruptly. She was too tired, she said, the memories were too disturbing, she didn't know they would be so strong, could they continue tomorrow? She would call, she had Portia's hotel number.

•

He had insisted on taking a room with two separate beds. To give her some space, he said. Or, to give himself space. He was a married man, separated, but still married. He liked her, she could tell, otherwise he wouldn't have said yes to her invitation. Come with me, to Basel. She had surprised herself. She hadn't known she was going to make the invitation till she did it; in her defence, she had been drunk at the time. Two days ago she hadn't even known who he was, and now here they were, in Basel, together, even if in separate beds. She loved having him here, she felt excited every time she turned in her bed and saw him in the next bed, mere metres away, a book in his hand, and he'd sense her looking at him and he'd give her his easy smile and ask if she was okay. She had wanted to go to Katharina's with him, but he had advised against it. 'We don't want to spook her.' He was right. His presence would have been a distraction.

He was not in when she entered the room, perhaps out for a walk. She decided to take a bath before he got back. The room was bare, almost utilitarian. A flat-screen TV was hooked to the wall, the table was wooden, the chairs plastic, she liked the spaciousness and the austereness. The beds were firm and comfortable. She had found the hotel on the internet, attracted by its proximity to the train station, and booked it hours before they left Berlin. She loved the view of a wide, grassy fen with willow trees and the fog hanging over it. Beyond it was what looked like a river, or a lake. *Watery bier.* She imagined drowned bodies floating in the water. She shivered. This was part of the old city, nearby was the university and many excellent restaurants, according to the pamphlet given to them by the receptionist when they checked in last night.

2

She had always wanted to see Berlin and had decided to stop over for a day or two before passing on to Basel. Luckily, she met a couple online who offered her a place to stay; they were out of town, somewhere in Denmark, and she had the use of their place for two days. She spent the first day indoors, sleeping. She had had to wake up at 4 a.m. to catch her Ryanair flight from Gatwick. She was reluctant to go out, even though she had a long list of attractions to visit – the wide, cold and wet Berlin streets were intimidating, and if only she spoke some German. All morning she watched American movies and sitcoms on television. Mostly old movies. Denzel Washington in *Training Day* sounding very fluent in *Deutsch*. They reminded her of the Hong Kong kung fu films David had been so fond of, and how they'd laugh at the off-sync between the English voice-over and the actors' moving mouth. The Germans, however, were not so sloppy, the asymmetry between lip movement and voice-over lasted only a syllable, a half-syllable, and you had to be assiduously watching for it. She amused herself watching for it, giving herself one point whenever she caught one; an idle game to pass an idle rainy day. By midday she was tired of watching TV and beginning to feel like a prisoner, so she explored the flat.

There were pictures of Hans and Ina, her absent hosts, on the mantelpiece, hiking, biking, camping, in different countries, mostly tropical, maybe even Africa. She had spent the night on the couch in the living room; she felt like she was camping here. There were two bedrooms, the one next to the living room was the guest room, mostly bare, with a bed neatly made up and a table and chair by the window. She had gone there only to get the duvet and return to the couch and the TV. Everything was in place, ordered, organized, they must have cleaned before they left. In the morning she got an email from Hans, he gave her their hotel phone number and wanted to know if she was fine? He had forgotten to tell her there was food in the fridge, eggs and bread and cheese, she was free to use that.

The rain stopped by midday and the sun came out. Furniture was being moved in the next apartment, somebody was moving in, or out. She had to go out. She had no excuse, the sun was shining, she had a map, and she had only a day left in Berlin before she moved on to Basel. This, after all, was why she decided to stop in Berlin, to see the city and the historic places she had read about in books: the museums, the famous streets, the WWII memorials.

She took a shower and changed into a pair of jeans and a T-shirt; as she stepped out into the corridor she noticed the door to the next apartment was open, in the doorway was a man on a ladder, a black man, and when he turned and looked at her, she knew he was African. What are the odds, she thought, as he returned her surprised gaze. She stood in the passage before the door, staring at him; she couldn't help herself. She had been starved of human contact for two days, black human contact, apart from the German-speaking Denzel Washington, and now right in front of her was a black man, an African, looking down at her from his ladder. But what if he wasn't African, what if he was one of those rare Afro-Germans she had heard about, who had lost all memory of Africa, who spoke nothing but *Deutsch*?

He was stepping down from the ladder now, a picture frame in his hand, his head tilted, mirroring the way her head was tilted to look up at him. She straightened her head. And then they spoke at the same time. 'Excuse me . . .' she began.

'Can I help . . . ?' he asked. In English. Not German then. The accent was West African, probably Nigerian. Nigerians were everywhere. She had met many in Zambia.

'I am sorry,' she said, blushing mentally.

'Can I help?' he said again. He was good-looking, not the sweet and lyrical Denzel Washington kind, but subtler, especially when he smiled just now. He had stubble, he looked like he hadn't been sleeping well.

'I was wondering . . . I am looking for directions.'

'Okay.'

They stood side by side over her map.

She followed his directions to the Museumsinsel, and it wasn't as hard as she had feared. She wanted to see the Egyptian collection, but when she got there she couldn't get in because of the long line. It'd take hours. The line looped and curved in on itself. The Museum Island was like a fair, with determined-looking tourists coming and going – a group of red-faced young men came riding past her on a contraption that looked like a bicycle, with five or six riders facing each other in a circle, all of them pedalling on the multiple pedals, a huge barrel of beer on the flat board in their middle from which all were sucking through giant straws.

She loafed around for a while, browsing through the books and DVDs for sale, then she joined a sidewalk procession toward the Brandenburger Tor, bumping into bodies and muttering excuses, and when she finally got tired of loitering and taking pictures at the gate, she took a bus and returned home. A wasted day. She should have purchased the museum ticket online before coming, she should have bought it the day before, she remonstrated with herself as she sat on the bus. She was usually well-prepared, and to be caught this flat-footed annoyed her.

•

The neighbour's door was closed. Maybe he didn't live there, most likely a moving man hired to move things. But no, he didn't look like a moving man, something about the way he looked and spoke. She was surprised at how sharply disappointed she felt. She paused briefly before the door and listened, hoping to hear the sound of lifting, or music, or feet, but all was quiet. It was almost 4 p.m. She opened her door and turned on the TV, she couldn't wait for tomorrow to come so she'd be on her way to Basel. Berlin had been a disappointment, her fault, not the city's.

But now the TV failed to occupy her and she wandered the apartment, from room to room, opened cabinets in the kitchen, read the labels on the wine bottles in the pantry. There was half a crate of red, and a full crate of white. She picked out a Bordeaux. She'd knock herself out and wake up tomorrow. She searched in drawers and cabinets for the corkscrew, but she couldn't find one. And, not until much later, after she had gone and knocked on the neighbour's door and, flashing her best smile, asked to borrow a corkscrew, please, and laughingly invited him to join her for a drink if he wanted and he said yes, why not, give me five minutes, and they were seated at her hosts' circular, three-seater dining table, raising glasses in cheers, not till then did she admit to herself that she could have drunk the Chablis with the screw cap but she had decided to drink the corked red as a pretext to go talk to and perhaps invite the neighbour for a drink. But, she had a good excuse; she had many good excuses: she was alone in a strange city and he was a fellow African and she was going stir-crazy.

'Portia,' he said. 'Very Shakespearean.'

Her name was a cross she had borne all her life. But he wasn't making fun of her as the perplexed kids at school had done, he wasn't puzzled as the lecturers at university had been. In England, at postgraduate school, a classmate had asked her if it was a traditional African name.

'My father was a fan,' she told him.

'So, how long have you lived here?' he asked.

'I don't live, here. I am couch-surfing.'

'Couch-surfing?'

'Couchsurfing.com. Never heard of it?'

'Sounds like a porn site.'

She laughed. Nice sense of humour. But what if he was dangerous, a rapist, an opportunistic ripper? Clearly he knew about porn sites. Well, too late now. Her mother would read all about it in the Zambian papers tomorrow. Hopefully, the circular glass table between them would offer her a minute-or-two head start before he reached her.

'It is a site that connects travellers with hosts, people willing to offer their couches to perfect strangers who might someday return the favour.'

'I feel bad that you didn't get to see the museum, and you are leaving tomorrow. Do you want to go out? Grab something to eat?' he asked. A rapist wouldn't be asking her to go out, unless he was the brazen kind that gets his kick out of doing it out in public. A flasher-rapist.

'I want African food,' she said. She hadn't eaten properly in over a day.

He thought for a minute. 'The closest I can offer is Asian, but it is about twenty minutes away by train. It is good, promise.'

She was still dressed from her outing, so she freshened up in the bathroom, picked up her handbag, and they left after a glass each of the wine. Restorative, the wine proved. She wasn't aware she had been tired from her first venture into the city. They took the train and sat side by side, but they couldn't speak for the din, so they smiled silently at each other whenever their eyes met. Two musicians, one a chubby child with an accordion, the other a man-and-woman duo with a music box, vied with one another to see who'd break the noise barrier first. She watched the stoic Berliners absorbing the abuse, their faces impassively turned to the view outside the train window. A *Mots* vendor tried unsuccessfully to get her to purchase his newspaper but she had no change. He handed the vendor a euro coin and took a copy even though, he told her when they got off, he couldn't really read German. 'You looked like you needed rescuing.'

She thanked him. Was that the vibe she gave off, like she needed rescuing?

'This way,' he said. They were on a busy side street, and almost every second or third store was a secondhand bookstore displaying English and German books in the window. Sandwiched between the bookstores and record stores were Asian restaurants: Thai, Vietnamese, Indian – people sat at tables on the sidewalk, reading menus, looking bored as Roma minstrels played popular tunes on their accordions and trumpets. Another bookstore. Inside a woman in a hat sat behind a desk, facing the street. She caught Portia's eyes and smiled, waving them in. Portia grabbed his hand. 'Come, let's look at books.' The interior of the store was a thicket of books, falling out of shelves, spilling out of cartons on the floor. It was hard to find a path around the room without stepping on books and magazines. Now Portia realized it was actually a man wearing a wig under the hat and a flowery red dress. Two men, actually, one in a blue shirt, youngish, sat further inside the store, half-hidden by a bookshelf. On the table before them were two glasses of red wine and a half-empty bottle.

'He is the real deal. He is Barack Obama before the celebrity,' the man in the blue shirt was saying.

'Oh, you are a Cory Booker fan too,' the man in the red dress said. 'How good to know. I love that man. He is my mayor. I am from Newark, you know.'

Americans, rolling their *r*'s and flattening their *a*'s. Portia pulled out books at random. They were used copies, 'for rent or for sale', a sign glued to the shelf said. There was a whole section dedicated to Graham Greene. She ran her hand over the spines, reading the titles. Her father was a fan, he had sent her Greene's memoirs, *Ways of Escape* and *A Sort of Life*, on her nineteenth birthday. She found the writing a bit too macho, a bit too Hemingwayesque.

The store appeared to be an apartment doubling as a bookstore. This was the living room, she could see the kitchen through a half-open door with dishes in the sink and a packet of what looked like cat food on a shelf. A closed door next to a shelf probably led into the bedroom, half-blocking the door were more boxes of books, some opened with books spilling out of them, some not yet opened. It was like a hoarder's haven here. She felt stymied by clutter, hamstrung. She waded back to the entrance where the man in the wig and hat and his friend were still talking about Cory Booker.

'They have Achebe here,' he said to her. She joined him. A whole section dedicated to African authors of the earlier generation, Alan Paton, Mazisi Kunene, Naguib Mahfouz. He flipped through a copy of *Things Fall Apart*. It was an early edition, with a folkloric sketch of Okonkwo's face upside down on the cover, and Introduction by Aigboje Higo. Inside were more folkloric sketches at the start of each chapter.

'I'll take this,' he said to the men at the table, 'how much?'

But they were laughing so hard they didn't hear. Tears formed runnels down the face of the man in the red dress, cracking his makeup.

' . . . that is so preposterous,' the other man kept saying. He banged his hand on the table and sipped his wine, all the time laughing. 'Preposterous!'

Portia picked out a book and handed it to him. He looked at the title: *Prison Dialogues*, by James Kariku. 'I remember this book. I had to study it for my secondary school finals.'

'My father,' she said.

'Your father is James Kariku?'

She nodded. She looked defensive, she had had this conversation many times before and was weary of it.

'No way,' he said. He looked at her, then at the book, as if trying to determine if she was joking.

'I am Portia Kariku. If you want, I can show you my ID,' she said, and turned away from him.

'Of course, I believe you, it's just . . . so unexpected. Okay. I'll take it and you'll sign it for me.'

'You buy it if you want, but I can't sign it for you. I am not my father.' Her voice had grown cold. He paid for the book and they left. What a clutter. Her skin crawled retroactively at the cat hair on the carpet and the spiderwebs on the roof and the dirty plates in the kitchen sink. How incongruous it all was, with the fancy storekeeper by the entrance, drinking red wine in his wig and la-di-da hat next to all that grime.

When they came out after eating, the very last sunrays of the day glistened on the wet cobblestones. It was an Indian summer day; the golden sunrays poured on the buildings and trees and sidewalks like honey. They took a train back to Mitte. 'Let's get off here,' he said.

'This isn't our station.'

'Yes. But it is a beautiful day. Let's walk,' he said. She followed him along a line of stones marking where the Berlin Wall once stood, and soon they were in a throng of young people, all moving in the same direction. She looked at him, questioning.

'They are coming from the park over there, Mauerpark. Come.' He took her hand and pulled her away from the crowd. She liked the feel of his hand in hers.

'I'll buy you a drink,' he said.

They entered a tiny bar, its entrance almost invisible from the street. Inside was dark and empty save for the barman, who was standing behind the bar, his back turned to the empty room, staring at a TV screen over the shelf of bottles on the wall. One part of the wall was lined with cigarette and pinball machines. A door led into yet another section of the bar, perhaps the restaurant, from which they could hear loud voices and laughter. They sat down, and eventually the barman came over.

'Two shots of vodka for me,' Portia said before he could speak.

He shrugged at the barman. 'Same for me.'

They downed the vodka in one gulp and then asked for a glass of wine each, red for him, white for her. 'So,' he said, 'what do you do?'

'I teach,' she said. 'My mother has a school in Lusaka, I work for her.'

'Do you like it?'

'I didn't at first, but it grows on you. The kids are adorable.'

An old woman in a white faux-fur jacket, its collar raised up around her neck, entered, in her hand a bunch of flowers. The front-door light in her red hair was a brush fire at night. She shook the rain off her jacket as she looked around the empty room, then she limped over to them. She picked out a pink rose and held it out to Portia. The woman had a ring on every finger, including her thumbs. Portia shook her head.

'Take it,' he said. He gave the woman a few coins. Portia held the red rose to her nose, then she placed it on the table next to her glass. 'Thanks.'

The old woman shuffled over to the bar and handed the barman the coins, she sat on a stool with her bunch of flowers on the counter in front of her.

'What are you doing in Berlin?'

'I came with my wife, over a year ago.'

'Oh,' she said. She pushed the flower further away. 'Where's she now, your wife? Of course, you don't have to answer . . . forget the question.'

Of course, she had seen the ring impression on his finger, but she hadn't given it any thought. They were two strangers in a strange city, soon they'd part and perhaps never see each other again.

'My wife left for America a few months ago. We used to live in a different part of town, in Charlottenburg. I moved here when my wife left.'

'Who lives here?'

'A friend, who I met through another friend. Her name is

Lorelle. She and her roommate . . . they left for America. I am helping them take apart the furniture and get it into storage, in exchange I get to stay for a few months, rent-free.'

'What do you do afterward?'

'Move on, I guess. I have to go back to the States and finish my PhD, eventually.'

'Oh, what are you working on?'

'The Berlin Conference of 1884 . . . though I discovered that here in Berlin they call it the Congo Conference.'

'That's an interesting topic. What's the title of your dissertation?'

'You really want to know?'

'Yes, really. I just finished my MA and I am thinking of going back for a PhD, eventually.'

'You should. My title is, "The Berlin Conference: Imaginary Borders and the Scramble for Africa". What do you think?'

'I like it.'

'Good. Now, your turn.'

'Yes, my turn. Give me a minute.'

She stood up and went to the barman, they talked and the barman led her to the cigarette machine and she came back with a packet of Marlboro. She opened it and handed him one.

'I don't smoke,' he said.

'Me neither, but I feel like a cigarette right now.'

They lit up and dragged in the smoke tentatively, coughing, their eyes watering.

'So, my turn. I am going to Basel. My brother used to live there. I am going to meet his wife.'

'Basel. Switzerland. Where does he live now?'

'He died. I am going to meet his Swiss wife, Katharina. I have never met her before.'

'Why do you want to see her now?'

'My mother wants to know how he died. The papers didn't say much. And Katharina was in prison for killing him, so we couldn't reach her.'

'His wife killed him?'

'Yes.'

A laying down of the ghosts. After her father died last year her mother had started talking about David more and more. Where did she go wrong, and why did he feel he had to go away? He had been so obsessed with emigrating. A month ago, when Portia was getting ready to go back to London to submit her MA thesis, her mother said to her, 'I want you to go and see her when you finish with London. Talk to her. I want to know what happened, why he left us for her, what he was looking for.' She handed Portia a photograph. The photograph, the one on the nightstand by her mother's bed. In the picture her brother was standing next to Katharina, looking at the camera with no expression. What was he thinking? The photo had come five years ago with a letter, the only letter he ever wrote since he left home. In it, he said he was fine, he was now in Switzerland, married to the lady in the picture, and they shouldn't worry about him. The next time they heard about him, he was dead.

Portia looked at her, shaking her head. 'Mama, it will not bring him back. He had made his choices.'

'But I want to know. I was a good mother, wasn't I, and a good wife?' And because all her life all she wanted to do was to please her mother, to make her happy, Portia said yes.

Her father had also left, long before David did, but her father did come back. He came back irreparably damaged by exile, and it could be said that the return was what ultimately killed him. She didn't tell him all this, though she wanted to. She felt she could tell him even the most intimate things and he'd respond with respect and full attention. She wondered what his story was. There was something lost and dreamy about him, as if he was waiting for something, or someone. What was he doing in Berlin, all by himself, his wife thousands of miles away in America?

She picked up the rose, sniffed it again, and said, 'So, do you give every woman you meet a rose? What would your wife think?'

'That poor lady looked like she needed the money,' he said. The lady was bent over the bar now, a cigarette in one hand, her drink in the other hand, the flowers on the counter next to her. She was staring up at the TV screen, discussing what was showing with the barman.

'That's a good reason. Well, thank you. I'll put it in a vase when we get back.'

After a while she said, suddenly, 'My birthday is next week.'

'Well, happy birthday in advance. How old?'

'You first. How old are you?'

'Old,' he said. 'Thirty-five.'

'I am twenty-five.'

'You are so young.'

'You sound disappointed.'

'I am not. I just feel . . . old at the moment. Superannuated. What is your wish, for your birthday?'

She shrugged. 'Joy, happiness, wisdom. What more can

one wish for? And, talking about happiness, I must mention you do look a bit solemn.'

He shrugged. 'I guess I have been indoors and alone too long. I have forgotten how to compose my features in company.'

'Compose your features, that's an interesting way of putting it. Why are you unhappy?'

'Is happiness very important to you?'

'Well, isn't it, to everyone?'

'To some, yes. In Dostoevsky's *The Brothers Karamazov*, Father Zosima says the purpose of human existence is happiness. God Himself wants us to be happy. Creation is fulfilled when God sees us happy. We are only unhappy if our mind is not very clean, if we sin.'

'Sounds like a rather convenient argument for the church.'

'It does.'

'Dostoevsky doesn't sound like he understood very well how life works. Happiness is important, but I wouldn't say it is the main purpose of human existence.'

When they got back to the apartment they stood by her door. She wasn't ready for the night to end. She dreaded going into the empty apartment by herself, so she waited, playing with the key on the key chain. He said, 'I'd invite you for a nightcap, but my place is a mess. The dust alone will give you an infection.'

'In that case, come to mine. We still have some wine left.' She hoped she didn't sound too forward, too shameless.

'Good. Let me get my phone. I left it when we went out. Ten minutes?'

Before he came back, she changed into a skirt and a fresh T-shirt. He walked around the room, stopping to look at the record collection.

'Mahler, Beethoven, Bach. Snooty folk, huh?'

He turned to the pictures on the wall. 'Turner. Kandinsky. Prints.'

'You know painting?'

'Only by association. My wife paints.'

He joined her on the couch. She handed him a glass of red wine.

'What if your friends walked in now? How would you explain my presence?'

'Is there anything to explain? We aren't breaking the furniture. At least not yet.' She looked contemplatively at him.

He said, 'You have nothing to fear from me.'

She liked that he said that seriously, that he could tell she wanted to be reassured.

'Tell me something about yourself. Anything.'

He told her about his friends, Stan, Mark, Uta, Eric, who used to live in an abandoned church. She listened. His voice grew sad as he described Mark's death. He stood up. 'Let's play some music. I don't want to depress you.' He slotted a CD into the Bose player.

'What song?'

'David Bowie. "Heroes",' he said.

She shook her head. 'Nice, but . . .'

'But . . .'

'Too white for me. I am a lover of the blues. My father had a stack of them, records with brilliant album-cover artwork. Billie Holiday. Robert Johnson. Muddy Waters.'

She went to the kitchen, her glass of wine in her hand. He stood up and followed her. The kitchen was long and narrow, a window opened into a courtyard with a gnarled and twisted

ash tree in its centre. He stood by the window. 'I have the
same view from my kitchen.'

'What of love?' she asked, coming forward to stand next to
him. She could feel the drink, making her light-headed, but
she didn't care. She leaned into him and pressed her lips on his
briefly. 'What does Dostoevsky have to say about love?'

He put one arm around her waist, saying nothing. She
pulled away and began cutting a block of cheese into cubes
onto a plate. She opened a tin and poured out cashew nuts
and almonds beside the cheese. They faced each other, he still
by the window, leaning against the sill; she resting her hips
against the sink, her head tilted. She picked up the bowl and
returned to the living room. He came and sat next to her,
saying nothing. She wondered if they were about to cross a
certain line, a certain border. She felt happy, expectant. She
got up and sat on the floor before the TV, the remote in her
hand, flipping through channels.

'You look beautiful, sitting there, like a TV fairy.'

She turned and looked at him, still flipping through channels. She stopped at a channel showing a western, in German.
'Do you speak German?'

'*Ein bisschen*,' he said. 'A little bit.'

She fell asleep before the movie ended. When she opened
her eyes he was still seated on the couch, the light from the
screen playing on his face. She smiled up at him.

'I am putting you to bed, then I am off.' He picked her up
and carried her to the guest room, putting her down gently
on the narrow twin bed.

'Don't go,' she said.

'It is one a.m.'

'If you go I can't sleep. I've been sleeping badly.'

'These people, the owners, what will they think?'

'They won't be back for a few more days,' she said, then added, sleepily, 'Come with me, to Basel. I don't want to go by myself.'

3

You've been humming that word for a while now. Lycidas.'

They were in their beds, waiting for their room service meal, neither of them feeling like going out in the rain. He had her father's book of poems in his hand. He was seated, his back against the headboard, she was lying on her stomach, her face turned to him. Outside the grey cumulus clouds hung low in the sky, over the trees and roofs, and the deluge seemed to be rising from the marshy bog itself.

'It is a poem, by Milton. An elegy for a friend who died in a boating accident. All day it has been in my head and won't go away. Perhaps it is the rain. It is making me sad.' She went to the window and stared out into the night.

'Were you close to your brother?'

She shrugged, not turning. 'He left when I was very young. I was around ten when I last saw him.'

'Fifteen years ago.'

She nodded. 'Yes. My father was in Europe then, trying to be an exile.'

'Trying?'

'He could have returned home anytime he wanted, but he refused.'

'Why did he leave?'

She returned to the bed and sat down, facing him. The room was dim, only the light from the TV flickered weakly against the blue wall, the rays soaking into the walls, like water on sponge. 'He got into trouble with the government because of his writings, not just his poems, but articles as well, in the newspapers. He was something of a rising star, I guess. Some people saw him as a possible future candidate for the presidency. He was young, smart and fearless, or foolish, depending on how you look at it. He belonged to that nation-alist era in African politics that produced young idealistic men by the bucketful, and then promptly threw them behind bars or killed them – the lucky ones like my father escaped into exile to spend the rest of their lives in limbo.'

'What did he write about?'

'Well, you have read his poems. His articles and essays accused the government of corruption, among many other things. He was part of a university-based group of intellectu-als agitating for multiparty democracy, they wanted Kaunda to resign. And they had a good following, and also supporters in America and Europe, which made them more threatening to the government, plus, they had a case, the economy was bad, people wanted a new beginning. I heard about it mostly from my mother, the rest I learned from history books.

'My mother met my father at university, just after independence in the sixties, they became lecturers at the same university, in the seventies. She was in the history department. He was in English. He was in prison for two years, then he was released and held under house arrest. While in prison he wrote his book of poetry, it brought him international attention when it was published by the Heinemann African Writers Series. He became an international celebrity – PEN awarded him the Freedom to Write Award, Wole Soyinka and Harold Pinter held a joint reading from his book in London. He was offered fellowships and visiting lecturer positions in England and America, but he didn't want to go. He wanted to stay in Zambia. Yet, despite numerous appeals and pleas, he never got his job back. My mother persuaded him to leave the country. She had just given birth to my brother and all she wanted was to be somewhere safe. They left in 1980, with the help of my father's foreign friends. They were in exile in England for ten years. My mother said it was the best years of their marriage, but she only saw that in hindsight. It wasn't a bad life, he had a job at the University of Leeds, teaching African literature, but while he was becoming more and more settled in exile, she was pining for home. Kaunda's dictatorship was over anyway. So, when she got pregnant with me she decided to come back to Zambia. My father told her to go on ahead, he'd join her in a few months. So, she took my brother and left. She returned home and managed to make a life for herself. She started an elementary school. But my father didn't go back. By then he had developed a taste for exile.'

Her voice was flat, bitter. She lay on her back, directing her words at the ceiling.

'How long did he stay back after your mother had left?'

'Seventeen, eighteen years. I never saw my father till I was eight, for me he was always a photograph on the wall, a wedding photograph with my mother, he in a suit, my mother in a wedding dress with yards of tulle flowing behind her. I saw him for the first time when we visited him in Copenhagen, Denmark, he was doing a fellowship there. We stayed with him for a year. I remember that year. It was cold, and my mother had no friends, she was always sitting by the fireplace, waiting for my father to return from some outing with his friends. Famous authors would stop by the house, all of them exiles, Soyinka, Mahmoud Darwish, Breyten Breytenbach – of course I didn't know who they were then, till later when my mother told me – and they'd talk poetry far into the night, about their countries, and exile, and they'd read poems they were working on or had just published.

'There was a little yard in the back, with a magnolia tree in the centre, and when the weather was good I would ride my bike round the tree, round and round and round till it got dark and my mother would shout for me to come in. I think my mother hoped my father would come back to Zambia with us after the Danish fellowship, but he didn't. He had become something of a professional exile. He went from fellowship to fellowship, from asylum city to asylum city. All over Europe. And they loved him, even though he hadn't written a book in over twenty years. He gave comments after every coup in Africa, on every civil war that broke out, every uprising, every plane crash. He was the Africa expert. He wrote fiery opinion pieces in newspapers attacking the government in Zambia, even though by now the government and most of the country had forgotten who he was. But in Europe he was a hero, telling truth to power. They called him the conscience of Africa. My father ate it up.'

Her voice died down with a sigh. Their food came, they ate in silence. She ate in bed, sitting up, her plate in her lap, he moved to the chair by the window, flipping through the book of poetry as he ate. She watched, and gradually her expression darkened. Why was he keeping so far away from her? Why did he come? And why were they in separate beds? In Berlin she had kissed him, and she thought he would kiss her back, but he hadn't. Perhaps he was here because he thought she needed protection, just as he thought she needed rescue. Her sullen mood persisted and she didn't answer when he asked her if she was okay. She went to the bathroom and brushed her teeth, she got into bed and pulled the sheet over her head. He came over and pulled back the sheet. He lay down next to her.

'I can't sleep,' she said. He held her, not saying anything.

'You mustn't be bitter against your father,' he said. 'Sometimes poets have to be imperfect so their poetry can be perfect. Reading him has taken me back to my school days.'

It was the most profound thing anyone had ever said to her about her father, and she felt grateful. Her mood lightened. He kissed her head. Like a brother, she thought. She closed her eyes. 'Tell me a story.'

'What kind of story?'

'Any kind.'

He told her about a rich young man who was addicted to palm wine. One day his father dies, and many days after, his palm-wine tapster who draws his palm wine from the palm trees falls from a tall palm tree and dies. The rich young man misses his supply of palm wine, and his friends no longer come to visit. He grows despondent. So, he decides to go to the Dead's Town to find his tapster. It is a long and hazardous journey. It leads him from his town to various parts of the bush, places outside civilization, inhabited by all sorts of inhuman creatures. Thus begin his many adventures. He stays with a man who promises to give him directions to the Dead's Town, but he must first rescue his daughter, who has been attracted to a Handsome Gentleman and followed him into the bush. The Gentleman, it turns out, is not really a person but a wild creature of the bush. He had returned with his young bride to the bush, and as he entered, he gave back each bodily part that he had rented from a human being, until he was nothing but a skull; he then held the young woman captive. The rich young man searches for the host's daughter, finds her, and the two escape the bush . . .

She fell asleep listening to him, her head on his shoulder. When he stopped talking, she opened her eyes.

'I know that story. Amos Tutuola. My MA is in post-colonial literature, remember. But go on, did he get what he wanted? Did he get his tapster back?'

'He got more than that. He gained wisdom, he also got a magic egg with a never-ending supply of palm wine.'

She drifted off, half-awake, half-dreaming, half-remembering;

she saw her father getting off the plane at Lusaka International Airport. He was home, finally. She could feel her mother's nervous excitement as they watched him at the customs counter, presenting his passport to be stamped. Her mother was wearing her best dress, her best jewellery. It was the happiest Portia had seen her in a long time. He, on the other hand, looked perplexed. He was in his black suit, with a white shirt and his best Oxford shoes.

'Where are the secret police?' he whispered, he looked disappointed. He was expecting to be arrested, to be whisked away in a black car by security agents. In the car he kept asking about old friends, why weren't they there to receive him at the airport, surely they must have read in the papers he was coming back? He had written about it in the English papers. Her mother told him most of the old friends had retired, returned to the village. Many were dead.

As the days passed alarming signs began to show, he appeared disoriented, unsure where he was, or what day it was. He'd go to the window and peek outside at passing cars, expecting the house to be stormed by agents looking for him. He tried writing. He was working on a volume on exile, he intimated, but he couldn't make headway, the lines came out dull and uninspired. Soon he started talking about going back. He had been home just two months, but already he felt stifled. He couldn't work here, he complained. Once, they found him seated in the yard, under the cashew tree, in the pouring rain. Portia took him inside, even as he fought her all the way. Then one day, they came back from work at her mother's school, and he was gone. He had left a one-line note on the table: he was going back to England. When had he planned this, when did he buy the plane ticket? They rushed to the airport, and when they got there they found him seated meekly on a bench in the departure lounge. He hadn't been allowed on the plane because he had no visa.

He thought he could just walk into the plane with no documents.

A month later he tried to leave again. An official, who happened to be her mother's cousin, called to tell them he was at the airport. He had attacked the immigration official who stopped him from boarding the plane. His passport had expired, and he still had no visa for the UK. This time her mother didn't go to the airport with her. When Portia got there, she saw him through the glass door, dressed in his best suit and white shirt, his carry-on bag in his hand, ranting as he paced up and down, waving his passport, and when she entered she heard him, in his careful professorial British English, asking them if they knew who he was. 'James Kariku. You can look me up. Google my name. I am a poet. This country doesn't appreciate talent. In Europe they will roll out the red carpet for me. You think I am lying, go ahead, google my name!'

She stood at the door, too embarrassed to go in, though the three officials at whom he was ranting could see her standing there. Finally, she took a deep breath and went in. She whispered 'sorry' to the officials and led her father to the car. In the car she broke down in tears and turned to him, asking, 'Why don't you want to stay with us, Baba? Why do you want to leave?' He remained quiet, hunched against the car door, staring out at the line of jacaranda trees with their fire-red flowers looking ghostly against the night sky.

He kept to his room, and from behind the door they could hear the sound of his typewriter, banging furiously. When he died two months later, they found a pile of paper covered in gibberish, only one line was clear, repeated over and over again, 'Down with the dictatorship.' He was a resistance poet, it was all he knew, just like exile was all he knew. He had been home less than one year. Her mother said, 'I made a mistake. I shouldn't have pressed him to return. Exile was his life. The return killed him.'

•

'Think of him happy,' he said. Her father had been happy in Denmark, drinking and arguing all night long with other poets. And she remembered the time she saw him in London. She had not seen him since that trip to Denmark, when she was eight. 'I saw him in London, he had flown in from The Hague, where he had been living as a writer-in-residence. I was doing my MA at SOAS, it was my first year there, and it was a bad year. I was homesick. It was winter, wet and dark and cold, typical London winter. I couldn't read, I couldn't think, I'd spend days in my room, sleeping, only coming out to get supplies. I was diagnosed with depression due to the weather and the doctor told me to install bright fluorescent tubes in my room, to compensate for the gloom. Anyway, my father came to town. My mother called me from Zambia and gave me his hotel address and his number. I went to his hotel and they made me wait in the lobby. He was still sleeping, they said, but they would let him know I was there. I didn't tell them he was my father, I just gave my name.

'Then he came down. There were two people with him. I

hadn't seen him in a long time, but I recognized him, he still had his beard even though it was all salt-and-pepper now. I was sitting in a corner in the lobby – and he almost passed me. It seemed he had forgotten I was there. Then he saw me. "Portia. You look exactly like your mother."

'He gave me a hug. He introduced me to his friends, "My daughter." He looked happy to see me. But it was awkward. I didn't know how to be a daughter, and clearly, he had forgotten how to be a father. Plus, I didn't know what to call him, Dad, or Father, or Baba. I followed them to the reading, I even remember the title of the event: Poetry, Exile and Resistance. But the truth is that he had long ceased to be a poet, and most of the resistance was imaginary. But the people there, they loved it. They didn't care. They didn't even know where Zambia was on the map of Africa. As far as they were concerned, all of Africa was one huge Gulag archipelago, and every African poet or writer living outside Africa has to be in exile from dictatorship. My father knew his audience and their expectation, he gave them what they wanted. He was dressed for the occasion, the beard, the austere dashiki. He read. He vituperated. He narrated his prison experience that had happened decades ago as if it were just happening now. The audience, they ate it up. They clapped. They cried. They bought books. I guess I also felt a bit proud. My father was a star, a minor one, but still a star.

'I followed them to dinner and spent almost two hours listening to him hold forth about African nationalism, pan-Africanism. What did it all mean? Ideas that at sometime, long ago, meant something but are now empty as any political jargon, something to whip out and flash before the masses, or in textbooks. I hate politics, what it makes people do, what it does to people. One of the ladies with him was his translator, she was nice. She was the only one who tried to make conversation with me. Her name was May and it turned out she was a lecturer at SOAS, she had translated my father into Greek, and I could tell there was something between them. She asked me about my studies, about my mother, but all I wanted was to talk to my father, alone, for just a few minutes, I wanted to ask him when he was coming home, if he missed my mother and my brother and me. I waited, but he wouldn't stop talking. So, I left. I told them I was going to the bathroom, I didn't return. I slipped out and returned to my room.

'The next day I left for Zambia, abandoning my studies. I knew if I stayed a day more I'd lose my mind. I did go back to finish my studies, eventually, but that year was my worst, ever. When I told my mother about the meeting she said, "Something is wrong with us. Our men keep deserting us." But I told her it was not us, it was them. There was something they wanted, something just beyond the horizon, something outside their grasp, they would keep searching for it till they died. He stayed on in London for about seven months, with his translator girlfriend, then he came home and that was the end of it.'

4

'Was she upset yesterday?'

Katharina had phoned early in the morning to say she wasn't available to meet today as planned. Portia stood at the foot of the bed, her expression switching between perplexed to annoyed. She was already dressed up and ready to go out when the call came. He was also up, still in his striped pyjamas, by the window with a laptop in his hand.

'Not really. She was a bit defensive, which is normal. I mean, she just came out of prison, I expected her to be a bit reticent, and even erratic, but I thought because I am his sister she'd want to talk to me about this.'

She dropped her bag and sat down on the bed, her face

downcast. Her flight back to London was tomorrow. In London she'd catch a connecting flight to Lusaka. She imagined the disappointment on her mother's face.

He said, 'Give her a call later, to see if she changes her mind.'

They went out for a walk. The rain had stopped; the sun was out. They ate an early lunch in a roadside restaurant. When they came back to the hotel the receptionist handed Portia a note. 'Miss, you got a call.'

She took the note and read it. 'The bitch. So whimsical. She is coming. She is having dinner with us. This evening.'

•

Paintings of dinner scenes covered the restaurant walls, rising all the way to the ceiling. Corpulent gentlemen and thick-waisted women, reaching into plates piled high with all sorts of meat – huge-thighed chicken, enormous slabs of ham, gigantic shanks of lamb – their mouths bulging with food, glasses raised and dripping with blood-red wine. The rest of the wall was taken up by colourful frescoes of flowers and birds, giving a warm and cheerful ambience to the room. The painting looked like an epicurean Last Supper, a bacchanalia, with Jesus left out, perhaps hiding out of sight, horrified by the gluttony. Gormandize, Portia thought. Her secondary school principal, Mrs Joyce Bisika, used the word often in her speech at Assembly, as in, 'Girls gormandizing in the cafeteria, asking for extra portions. So unladylike,' or, 'Girls gormandizing on life with their shameless, unladylike behaviour.'

Katharina saw Portia looking at the paintings. 'I hate them. They say it has been here even before the restaurant started. This used to be some kind of school cafeteria.'

Katharina had arrived at exactly 4 p.m., alone. Portia had expected her to come with Sven, but there she was, by herself, waiting for them in the lobby, looking subdued and almost formal in a black knee-length dress. She said nothing when she saw Portia was not alone. She said she had made a reservation for them for 5 p.m. and the restaurant wasn't far from the hotel, so they walked. They walked through quaint, constricted streets, cobbled and sloping, and as they came down the hill they could see right into compounds below, most of them with open courtyards in which stood tall, leafy trees, and then they were in an open street.

'This is a shopping area, very touristy,' Katharina said. Today she was friendly, even charming, at one point she took Portia by the hand as they walked, and Portia could see how a man would easily fall for her. The streets were crisscrossed with tram rails making the walk confusing, and not knowing where to look when crossing, they had to trust Katharina as they now dashed, now waited, now strolled through the wide, winding streets. They were not far from the university, and most of the people on the streets looked like students. They took a narrow alley and came out on another wide street. She pointed across the road at an imposing red stone building. 'That is the *Rathaus*, the city council chamber.' They crossed over.

'It is beautiful,' Portia said. In the centre of the courtyard, facing the street, was a sculpture of two gargantuan men, their arms and torsos impossibly twisted around one another in a silent, frozen combat, pulling at each other in strife and opposition, and yet balanced and equally matched. There was something elemental, almost mythic about them. Katharina took them to an imposing cathedral, from the cobbled courtyard they could view the Rhine below, and across the water in the distance the city itself. They looked down into the sluggish, frigid water, and Katharina, now enjoying the role of tour guide, told them how in the summer young men and women would dive into the water and drift downstream, their clothes tied in a waterproof bag which they also used for flotation.

She looked at her watch. 'Time for dinner,' she said. The restaurant was next to the Jean Tinguely Fountain, a little basin populated by curiously shaped sculptures and wheels and scoops, all playful, all lighthearted, but now all frozen and trapped by winter's breath.

'So, you go back tomorrow,' Katharina said. They had finished their meal and were finishing off a bottle of wine. Katharina had looked amused when Portia said she didn't eat meat and ordered a fillet of sea bass. 'But your brother loved meat. In fact, all the Africans we met really liked meat. You are the first African I am meeting who doesn't like meat.'

Portia opened her mouth, then closed it again. To Katharina's credit she shook her head and immediately apologized for her comment. 'I am sorry. That sounded so silly.'

'Tell me more about him,' Portia said. But Katharina shook her head firmly. 'We make deal. Today, I am your host. I show you Basel. We eat, nothing serious. You come to my house tomorrow and we talk about your brother. I feel happy today. Nothing sad.'

•

They checked out of the hotel early in the morning. Her flight was in the evening, from Basel to London, from there to Lusaka through South Africa. He would take the train back to Berlin.

'Why?' she asked Katharina as they sat down at the circular table by the window. They were alone, the men had gone out with the dog.

Katharina nodded and smiled. 'Maybe I ask you the same: Why do you want to meet someone who killed your brother? And if you had followed the trial you know I didn't plead guilty. I said I didn't kill him.'

'But you were found guilty, and sent away for three years. Very lenient. In most countries you'd hang.'

Again, Katharina nodded and smiled. 'Okay. You are his sister. You deserve to know. I tell you everything.'

'Not everything. You can skip the sentimental stuff, the romantic meeting and "love at first sight". '

'But what if it is true, the sentiments as you call it, the romance, even the love?'

'Well, convince me. That it was all true, that you loved him, that he wasn't a victim.'

'Victim how? Of what?'

'Of your anger and jealousy. Of the whole system, of Europe.'

'No. Moussa was never a victim. He knew what he wanted, and how to get it. That night, after the dance, my friends wanted me to go, but no, I said. I stayed talking with him till the bar closed at midnight. I was in love.'

That was the day they met, at the twilight of his first marriage. After that night, after that dance, she told Sven their engagement was not going to work. 'I didn't love him. He was a good, decent guy, but I wanted more at that time.' She shrugged. 'I was not so young any more. Time was passing for me. I wanted more . . . excitement.'

She looked out the window at the distant figures in the mist, dog, men, and Portia wondered what she was thinking.

'Exactly two weeks after that meeting, he left his wife and moved in with me. I was staying in a little place near the campus, one bedroom and a kitchen. Twice Brigitte came to shout at him and beg him to go back, but he said no, he wanted divorce. She didn't give him the divorce till after one year.'

'And your family?'

'Well, that is another story. My father is a theologian, you know. I am the only child. He is a good man, he didn't object to my relationship, but he didn't say yes. Every year we used to go on a retreat, we go with my family and the people in my father's church, and I wanted to bring Moussa, but my father said no. I either come alone, or I should not come at all. It was the most painful thing. I realized also how serious all this was. I talked to my mother, I begged them to talk to Moussa, to try to understand him. We had a big fight. I told them I was sorry to be source of embarrassment for them. Everything they had taught me was a lie then. They said we should love strangers, we should never judge people by how they look. It was the most disappointing time of my life. I was very close to my father, you know. I looked up to him. I asked him, What if he turned up in your church, would you turn him away?

'We got married. Just the two of us. I did not invite my family. My mother wanted to come but I told her no, I had no family. After the wedding we went to Mali. I took some time off from my studies, and he got time off from the railway where he worked. He had told me a lot about his father in Mali, and his brothers and sisters, and I wanted to see them. He never mentioned that they are not his real family. I only knew what he told me, that he was from Mali.'

Portia bowed her head and shrugged. 'I guess he was ashamed of his real family.' She wanted to know what this other family was like, the one he chose over his real family, over his mother and his sister and his father.

'In Mali we stayed in a hotel in Bamako. It was my first time in Africa and it was different than what I expected. It was big, and noisy, and everybody was busy. I thought it would be a bit like India, I was in India once, in Goa. But it was different. The house was on the outside of the city. Our first night he left me at the hotel and went to greet the family alone. I was surprised, but he told me that was the tradition. The next morning, we went together to greet his father and his mothers, there were four wives of the father. He is an Islamic teacher and there were many children learning with him. He received us in a little room, just outside the main house, and he was seated on a mat and we sat next to him, I had to cover my head because women were not allowed into the room with open head. Moussa had warned me about that before, so it was not a problem.

'The father was old, with a white beard, but very active. Also, he spoke good French, and I also know French, so we were able to communicate. He welcomed me, and he said Moussa was a good and dutiful son and he hoped we would have a happy life. Then he begin to tell me how Moussa came to him from the sea. He said it was God who told him to go to the sea that day, and he found Moussa and two other young men at the waterfront, they had just arrived and they didn't know where to go next. He brought them home. He said from that day Moussa became his son. I listened. I was confused. This is the first time I am hearing that the man is not Moussa's real father. But I didn't say anything there. I keep quiet and I pretend as if I know. After telling me the story of how Moussa became his adopted son, the old man prayed for us. Next, we went into the house to meet the women. It was a big compound behind a mud wall, with different sections for the wives and their children. There were many children and they all came to touch my hand, my hair, my nose. They were very excited by the visit. They ran out to invite their friends to come and touch me. We sat in the senior wife's living room, this is Moussa's mother, his adoptive mother now I know, and all the other wives joined us. They giggle when I speak. They find everything I do funny because it was the first time they were seeing someone like me in their house. We gave them a little money and the presents we brought, mostly clothes for the children, and for the wives. Finally, we went back to the hotel. For me, the holiday was already spoiled because of what I learned. I ask him, Why didn't you tell me about your real family? What kind of marriage is this when I don't even know where you really come from, your real family? He said he was planning to tell me. But when? I asked him. I say to myself, What other things is he keeping from me? I think like that in my mind. I make him promise to write to his mother, his real mother, and to tell her about me, about our marriage, with a picture of us, me and him. We didn't stay long in Mali. We had planned to stay one week in the hotel but we had to leave after three days.'

'Why?'

'Why? Because now I am angry with him. I feel I don't know him any more. Also, people kept coming to see us, his friends, more family, they'd knock on the door as early as six a.m. They will bring food, and they'll sit for hours and they won't go. It was impossible. Every day. I mean, this was supposed to be our honeymoon. So, we left to spend the remaining three days in Senegal. Things were better there. We met a German couple, tourists, Ingrid and Hermann, they said they came to Senegal for bird-watching. They wanted to see the African grey owl. Moussa went with them once, but I was not interested. By that time, I was tired, I wanted to come back.'

'A very short visit then,' Portia said.

'Well, that was our honeymoon. We came back with many plans. Moussa wanted to go to university, because he didn't finish his education, you know that. He also wanted us to make peace with my parents. He talked about parents and how important they are. When he talked like that, I find it confusing, because he himself was not at peace with his real parents, and he never told me why. Now maybe you can tell me.'

'I . . . wish I could tell you. He wanted another father, I guess, another family,' Portia said, turning away to the window.

'Why, what is wrong with his real father, your father?'

'My father . . . he left us. He was a poet, a political poet. He lived in exile all his life. He died recently.'

'I didn't know that. I am sorry for your loss.'

They sat without speaking for a moment, then Katharina took a deep breath and continued, 'Anyway, my plan when we came back from Mali was to finish my PhD, and maybe one day, to have children. Well, it was not easy. Moussa didn't have many friends, and some of my friends now started to avoid us. It was interesting. I would call, and they'd be busy, or they wouldn't answer the call. At my graduation only my husband and his one friend from the railway came, everybody else have their family there, and friends, we only three of us.

'After my graduation we decided to move to Geneva. It was becoming too lonely here in Basel. We had only two friends, a Nigerian woman, Obi, and her Swiss husband, Alfred. Geneva was more international. There were more mixed families, and we became part of that community. There were also many international cultural events . . . at one point our social life revolved only around international events, at embassies, at cultural festivals, at weddings, well, this is Switzerland, after all. Very international.

'I knew what I was going into when I married an African. But, still . . . The most painful was my parents. It was over one year before we finally made peace with them. It was Moussa who said to me, Let us go and meet them. He said he felt guilty, that it was because of him that my family left me. Well, we went. We knocked on the door and my father opened the door. He looked surprised when he saw us there. He wasn't expecting us. I felt sad when we all sat there, in the living room, with my parents, as if we are strangers, and my mother asking us if she can make tea for us. I wanted to say to her, Mother, I am your daughter, I have not changed. Why do you talk to me like this? And my father . . . ah, it was so painful because I used to be so close to my father, you know. But funny enough, they started talking, my father and Moussa. My father said he had a funeral service to attend the next day. And Moussa said his father oversees so many funerals in Mali. My father was interested when he learned that his father was an imam. And so they started talking about religion. My mother and I moved to the kitchen to talk. She wanted to know if I needed anything, if he was treating me well. I said I needed nothing, that I was fine. That I just missed her and my father. So, for a while things were back to normal with my parents.

'I started work in Geneva. Teaching at a research institute affiliated to the university, as a junior faculty member. I was making some money, but we needed more. He still worked for the railway, the plan was for him to go back to school, but he always made excuses. The truth is, he couldn't afford to go back because he was sending all his money back home to Mali, I discovered that later. I had to pay for everything. Sometimes he was supposed to pay the bills, but he wouldn't, he will forget, instead he will send the money to Mali. I discovered also that he had taken credits from the bank, just to send to his father. I saw the letter from the bank, reminding him to make payment. I was disturbed. He said he sent the money because his father was dying, and I said why didn't he tell me. He had told me about his father being sick, but I didn't know it was so serious, that he was dying. He said I didn't listen to him any more anyway. Ah, it was so frustrating to talk with him. I never talked about this to anyone before, not even my mother, but you are his sister, so I am telling you everything.

'He started accusing me of not wanting to have children, and I said I couldn't take care of two children, him and our baby. And he lost his temper, he said I was calling him a child. He said I was disrespectful, and that I was racist like all my friends. He had changed. We had those fights, but we always make up. But one day, it got so bad. He was praying, on a mat . . .'

'He was very religious then?'

'He didn't use to be, but suddenly he became religious and will pray five times a day on a mat. He will fast during the fasting time. And he even said that I must change my religion, that a wife must have her husband's religion. I said religion was not very important to me, and we started to argue. But anyway, that day it got so bad. I had just come back from work and right there in the mail was another bill I thought we had paid. He was going to pay, it was water, or electricity, I can't remember. I had a bad day at the office, the students, you know, they make you angry sometimes and I was beginning to think maybe teaching was not the best thing for me. It seems every decision I have made so far have been bad decisions, and then there was this bill. I couldn't take it any more.

'He was in the living room, praying on a mat. I couldn't wait for him to finish. I started waving the letters at him, I threw them in front of him, but he ignored me. I went to the kitchen and made tea. In the kitchen drawer I saw more bills, and I saw a Western Union receipt, he had sent almost a thousand francs to his family and here we were, our light bill unpaid, and also we were already behind on rent. When he finished praying we started arguing, and I pushed him in the chest and I said I had had enough of the marriage, I said I was leaving. That was when he took a knife, a kitchen knife, and pointed it at me. He said he would kill me and then he'd kill himself. I had never seen him like that before. He was shouting and banging on the table, and he put the knife on my chest, right here. It was late at night and the neighbours called the police. But by the time they came he had calmed down. But I didn't sleep there that night, I ran to a friend's house. And that was it, that was the end of our marriage. Two years of marriage, three years since we first met in that bar on Basler Fasnacht, and it was over.

'I was exhausted. I called Sven and he came with me to the house to get my things. Moussa couldn't believe I was really leaving. After all, we had fought and made up before, but this time I was afraid, for my life. Maybe I was overreacting, maybe it was all in my mind, but I kept seeing him with that knife, and he had changed: I was afraid. He begged me, but Sven said he'd call the police if he interfered, so he just sat there with tears in his eyes as I took my things. I was crying too. I think I still loved him. A little bit, but I couldn't trust him any more. I left my job and moved back to Basel.

'I had a little breakdown at that time. Everything for me had ended. At this time my former friends came back. And I am shocked at all the nasty things they say. They think they are trying to make me happy. They will say, You are lucky you didn't have any children with him. Or they ask, What did you guys talk about all the time? Did he even know how to use fork and knife? I told them that's it. Leave me alone, don't ever come back. What right did they have to judge him? What have they ever stood up for in their whole life? I told them I was ashamed to be their friend. I am sorry. He is your brother, but I have to tell you the truth. Some people here are very racist. I don't want to upset you.'

'Do I look upset?' Portia asked. A woman had once screamed in her face in the Tube in London, dementedly shouting, 'Fucking foreigner!' Foreigner, for some reason, was the worst form of insult the woman could think of. She had read in the papers about people being thrown out of moving trains by skinheads for being black.

'Don't worry about upsetting me,' she said. 'Just go on with your story.'

But still, she was touched. She had misjudged Katharina. Despite everything that happened, she had been truly courageous, going against her family and friends, standing up for love.

'Did you see him again, I mean, before the last time?'

'Yes. I'll tell you, but first, I go out for a cigarette.'

They went out together and stood by the door, smoking.

'I saw him. He also moved back to Basel. I couldn't stop him, he had the right to do that. But we didn't meet. We made contact only through my lawyers. I needed a lawyer because I didn't feel safe. Of course I sometimes see him at the station where he worked, at the Hauptbahnhof. And he will wave to me and I will pretend I didn't see him. And then, I don't know what happened, I came back one day and I found him waiting for me here. I don't know how he found my address, maybe through one of our old friends, maybe he followed me, I don't know. But he was waiting for me outside the door, and he waited for me until I had opened the door, then he came and said we should go in and talk. He said he was going back to Mali. I didn't believe him and I said he should leave. He left. Just like that. He just looked at me sadly and he shake his head and he left. I was surprised.

'Then the next day, I got off the train, and there he was. It was late in the evening, on a Sunday. The platform was almost empty. I think he came on the same train with me. I am not sure, but I think he followed me. I turn and he was there, coming toward me. I stood there, I was terrified. He looked so serious. You understand, I was not thinking clearly at this time. My aunt had just died, and then all the pressure from him. I stood there, paralysed. I wanted to scream for help, but I just stood there, watching him still approaching, and the place was deserted, just me and him. He said nothing, he came and hugged me. I remember a train was coming in then. It honked, very loud, and that added to my panic, and at that moment the train lights flashed into my eyes and it was as if I was released from chains. I . . . pushed him with all my might. I thought he was going to kill me. I am sorry. You know what happen next. There was the trial. At first, I didn't want to defend myself, I wanted to die, to be punished. I caused his death. I kept seeing his body, cut into pieces. But my father said, What is the use? Best to tell the truth and fight for my freedom. We got a lawyer and, you know the rest. They gave me three years, not for murder, but for what we call *Totschlag*, manslaughter.'

•

The community cemetery was located on a hillside populated by pine trees. It looked like a park, peaceful, the sort of place one would want to be buried in. They were the only people there, Sven was in the car, waiting for them.

'I have never been here before,' Katharina said, 'I was in detention when they buried him.'

It was one of the few community burial grounds in Basel that had a section for Muslims. They found his grave next

to a tree, tucked away at the back of the neat rows of head-
stones, all ritually positioned to face the east. It was raining
again. They clustered solemnly under one umbrella over the
headstone, speaking in whispers as if scared they'd disturb the
dead. Portia felt the tears fill her eyes. It was hard to believe
that under this stone lay her brother's remains. What drove
him, what did he seek, so far away from where he was born,
why so restless, and was he finally at rest, here, in this foreign
place? No wonder philosophers and poets always describe life
as a fever, a burning raging fever from which we all seek
relief. Her father had sought his in his activism and exilic
delusions. Her brother had left home and taken a boat to Mali,
and he had ended up in the home of the preacher who became
his father, but the fever had still raged, driving him to Europe,
and she wondered if it was all worth it. He had died at thirty-
three, so young. Would his soul fly back to Africa, back to
where he was born? She had started thinking more and more
about death, since her father died. And she, what did she seek,
what was her fever and how did she seek relief from it? She
wanted to make her mother happy. She wanted to find out
more about her brother – but she could hardly call that a fever.
And what was the use blaming it all on their father – he was
a shitty father, of course, but ultimately we all make our way,
driven by our own appetites and predilection.

On the way to the airport they passed people standing at
bus stops waiting for the next bus, it was wet and watery and
windy, somehow that was how she always imagined Europe
to be. Katharina sat silently in front, next to Sven, looking
at the passing landscape. Earlier, in the cemetery Portia had
asked her what her plans were. 'I am not sure,' Katharina

said with a shrug. 'For me I cannot stay in Basel again, not in Switzerland. I have lost my friends. Maybe I go to another country, maybe Germany. I have my education. Of course I come back to Basel once in a while since I have my house, but I have to find a new life somewhere.'

When they got out of the car Katharina stood in front of Portia, her eyes wet. 'I have nothing more to say, but I want you to know I am sorry and I really loved your brother. But there was so much problem between us and it was never going to work. It is life.' She rejoined Sven in the car, walking away without looking back, her shoulders heaving violently.

Now there were just the two of them, sitting on a bench, not talking much. Her mind was here, and also in Lusaka. She was walking down a tree-bordered path toward a modest brick house in front of which her mother was standing, waiting for her. She still wasn't sure what she'd tell her mother, she wasn't sure if the journey had been a success or a failure, but she was glad she came. She mentioned this to him. 'I didn't want to come, you know. I told my mother, What is the point? Plus, he is already dead. But this has been worth it. I met you.'

'I am also glad I came.'

She wrote down her number and her email. 'Call me, or write. I am also on Facebook. Will you?' He held her tight for a long time, then they parted. Walking toward her gate, she imagined him watching her until she disappeared. She refused to turn back, if she did she'd break down and run back to him and say, 'Come to Lusaka with me.' He had said yes to her once, why not a second time? But, she had no claim on him. When she asked him drunkenly that night to come to Basel with her, she had been surprised when he said yes. Perhaps he also needed to get away, deferring a final decision by aimless motion. Now he had a train to catch, he had to return to Berlin, back to the house in Mitte, cluttered with boxes that he had to put in storage. His mind was in between places. Eventually, she was sure, he would make the right decision. Maybe he would go back to his wife. She hoped he wouldn't, she hoped he would write, she hoped they would meet again. She came up on the escalator and there, through the glass, she saw a plane on a runway speeding for takeoff. She watched, impressed by the certainty, the power, every bolt, every screw, every drop of liquid focused on that takeoff. Nothing tentative or hesitant. It was amazing, and beautiful.

Book 4

THE INTERPRETERS

It was fortuitous that I bought a ticket for the French TGV train instead of the Deutsche Bahn, which, it turned out, was on strike today. It meant I had to go through Zurich to transfer to a Berlin train. I passed through a line of disappointed Deutsche Bahn customers waiting for answers regarding their travel. As the train pulled away from the glum faces on the platform, I tried to suppress a smug feeling of false prescience we all get when things work out for us and don't work out for others in the same situation. It was three hours to Zurich, so I closed my eyes as soon as we got under way. I jerked awake as the train came to a stop at the Zurich station. I stood up and ran to my next train, I felt sluggish, slowed down by sleep, but I made it before the doors closed. I put my head down and slept off again. The next time I woke up a border policewoman was standing over me. We were at the German border, the train had come to a stop and the police were going around the train, checking documents. There were two officers in the carriage, the other, a man, was talking to another passenger a few seats away from me. I couldn't help but notice that the other passenger was also African, with the tall thin frame and curly hair common to some East Africans. A Somali, most likely; with him was a boy of about twelve.

I handed the officer my passport.

'Nigerian,' she said. She looked at the picture in the passport and then at me in that way immigration officers always do, then she asked me if I had bought any watches or jewellery in Switzerland. I wasn't worried about my documents, my German visa still had two more months on it, and I'd be long out of Europe before it expired. The other passenger seemed to be involved in a long discussion with the officer who had now taken his document, a piece of A4 paper, and was consulting with the female officer. They went back to the Somalian and asked him a few more questions before returning the document to him. Our eyes locked and he nodded at me, I nodded back. I closed my eyes, but I couldn't return to sleep. When the train stopped at the next station and I opened my eyes, I saw he was sitting opposite me. 'This seat is free, yes? You don't mind if we sit with you?' he asked. We were the only black people in the carriage, and it was natural for him to assume some solidarity, a closing of ranks, the same way some black people would carefully avoid talking to another

black person in a room full of white people. Obviously he was
starving for company. I nodded. 'Please.'

He looked to be in his middle to late fifties, but when he
smiled he had a twinkle in his eyes and it took away five years
from his face. 'I see you from there, you look sad. That's why
I join you.'

'I look sad?'

'Is about a girl, maybe?' he said, leaning forward, eyes
twinkling. I thought of Portia on the plane. I smiled, saying
nothing. He pressed on, 'This girl, she is your wife maybe?'

'No, not my wife.'

'I see. I understand. But you love her.'

'Why do you say that?' I asked, not sure if I should be
offended by his persistence or not.

'I see in your eyes. I travel a lot and I see many things. I
know love when I see love. You tell this girl you love her?'

I laughed at his intensity.

'Are you travelling in Europe?' he asked. I caught the odd
phrasing. Of course I was travelling in Europe, but I understood he meant something else; he wanted to know the
nature of my relationship to Europe, if I was passing through
or if I had a more permanent and legal claim to Europe. A
black person's relationship with Europe would always need
qualification – he or she couldn't simply be native European,
there had to be an origin explanation. I told him I had been
to Basel with a friend, and I was now going back to Berlin
via Frankfurt.

He said, 'I live in Munich. Two years now in Munich. I
take this train to Munich.' He had the hoarse voice of the
cigarette addict, with the accompanying phlegmy cough and

nicotine-stained teeth. I turned to the boy, who was staring at the passing landscape where the day was slowly evanescing into night. He had a vacant look on his face.

'What's your name?' I asked. He looked from me to his father, then he turned back to staring out at the landscape.

'His name is Mahmoud. He don't like to talk. He is shy of strangers,' the man answered. The boy looked at him, the annoyance briefly flashing in his eyes the way all kids at that age are always annoyed at their parents. He said something to the boy, and I asked him, 'Is that Somali you are speaking?'

'No, that is Turkish.'

'Ah, you are from Turkey!'

'No, Somalia. But we lived in Turkey long time. He speaks Bulgarian as well, and Arabic, and some German, and English.'

'Wow. A walking Rosetta stone,' I said.

'Stone?' He looked puzzled.

'How did he learn to speak so many languages? He is so young.'

'My son, he have very small school education. He learn everything from travel.'

'I see.'

'We have been to many countries, but now we live in Germany. This boy, he has been travelling since he is four years, now he is fifteen.'

'So, you are going back to Munich?' I asked. Clearly, he wanted to talk. I wasn't particularly in the mood for talking but I was intrigued by the boy, who sat silent, looking out at the passing landscape – rather quiet for someone who spoke so many languages. I wanted to hear him speak, I wanted to test him.

'Tell me something in Bulgarian,' I said. He didn't even turn from the window.

'We go to Munich first, then maybe we go to Bulgaria,' the father said.

'You are going to Bulgaria today?'

'Yes, maybe, but first we go to Munich. Listen, is a long journey, many hours before we come to Frankfurt. If you want, I tell you my story. To kill time. It is long story, but interesting, and is all true. I swear, by Allah, it is all true.'

The offer was made matter-of-factly, it sounded reasonable, we had a long trip ahead of us, what better way to shorten the trip? I leaned back in my seat. 'Go ahead.' I could always feign sleepiness if it got boring.

•

His name was Karim Al-Bashir and he was born in Somalia, long before the tribal wars and internecine killings started. His father was not ethnic Somali, he came from North Sudan as a young man and settled in Mogadishu, the Somali capital. The father, Al-Bashir, married into a good and moderately well-to-do family of traders, he was hardworking, and lucky, he prospered. His father-in-law gave him a loan and he started his own business, selling provisions in a corner store. His first son, Karim, was born one year after the marriage. Al-Bashir died in a car accident when Karim was only twelve years old, and suddenly the young Karim had to assume the responsibilities of an adult. With support from his uncles he was able to continue his father's business, buying and selling. He got married at twenty and had his first daughter before he turned twenty-two. And then gradually things began to change. In 1990 President Siad Barre died and overnight Somalia descended into political chaos. Time passed. Factions organized around family ties and tribal loyalty divided the country into fiefs overseen by tribal warlords. And thus began Karim's personal nightmare.

In his phlegmy voice he said, 'One day a young man come to my shop and says he wants to marry my daughter, Aisha. She is only ten. She is too young, and I want her to finish school. But I am afraid of telling him no. This is a powerful man, the son of the local warlord, even though he is young, everyone knows him. His name is Abdel-Latif. He go around with a group of bad boys, all with guns, and they can shoot you, just like that. So, I go and tell my in-laws. My mother-in-law she knows about this man Latif and she tell me, Be careful. She say I must not give any answer now, we wait and see, maybe he lose interest and go. But every day this man he come to the shop. He will sit and his friends will take a few things and not pay, cigarette and biscuit and Coca-Cola, small things, and I will smile and smile, and he will remind me that he wants to marry my daughter. He begin to call me his father-in-law, just like that. One day he say, "Why you don't want me to marry your daughter, you think I am not good enough? Are people from where you come better than us Somalis?"

'And now I know. It is not only about my daughter, Aisha. He wants to destroy me because my father is not originally from Somalia. That day, we have a family meeting, my wife's two brothers, Mustafa and Abu-Bakr, and my wife and her mother and father. I can see in their eyes that they have no hope for me. My father-in-law, he say, "We will go to Abdel-

Latif's father, I know him very well, he is my namesake, Muhammad. We grew up together, if his son will listen to anyone, he will listen to his father." It is our only hope. The only other choice is to run away to another town far away, but even that is not hundred per cent safe, because these people they can have friends and family in different towns and they can get you. That night we go to see his father, Muhammad, who is namesake of my father-in-law. He is an important man, he live in a big house and there are many people all waiting to see him. Many cars are parked outside the house. It is in the evening, after the Maghrib prayer. We sit on a mat in the outside room, four of us, me and my father-in-law and Mustafa and Abu-Bakr, my wife brothers. Soon he come in and people greeted him. Though others are there before us, the moment he see my father-in-law he invite him forward. "Muhammad," he say, "what a surprise, what a pleasure to see you here in my home." They go aside and they talked. When they come back, I can see there isn't much hope on my in-law's face. But we don't leave immediately, food is brought in by two young girls, their head covered in hijab. Plenty food, because he is an important man. Rice and chicken. We eat together, from the same bowl using our fingers. Then we left.

' "He'll talk to his son," my father-in-law say. "He'll reason with him."

'That night, I go to sleep full of hope. Since the whole thing start, I cannot sleep very well, both me and my wife. The country has changed. People shooting guns every day on the streets. People go about in fear. Women are punished for very small reasons, like not covering their heads, or not marrying the person the mullahs say they must marry. Well, we

wait to see what will happen after the promise from Muhammad. Our answer come two days later. Latif and his friends
came to my shop. My shop is not big, just a small room in
front of the house, facing the road in a quiet part of town.
Suddenly we hear gunfire, ta-ta-ta, they fire gun on the door
of my shop. I thought I was dead. Bullet everywhere. My
eldest boy, Fadel, he is just seven years, he always stay with me
in the shop, he run into the house, me I lay on the floor waiting for them to come in and kill me. They come in, three of
them, Latif is leading. They stand over me where I am lying
on the ground. "Stand up," he say to me. I stand up, and as I
look into his eyes I know it is going to be my last day. It is not
the eyes of a normal man. His senses have been turned by the
terrible plant they eat, kwat. You know kwat? It is like drug.
They eat it from morning to night and is very bad. It make
you go crazy. He is chewing like this, in handfuls.

'He look at me and he say, "So you think my father can
save you from me?" My hand and my leg start shaking, and
all I can do is to pray in my mind that they kill me quickly
and that they don't touch my wife and children. He tell me to
go into the house and to bring my daughter and her mother.
He say he want to hear from their mouth that they have no
objection to this marriage propose.'

'Proposal,' I said.

'Yes, proposal. So, I go in, but the house is empty. My wife
when she hear the gun, and she see Fadel running inside, she
take the children and they run to her father house. I come back
and tell him that they have heard the gun and they are afraid,
they run and I don't know where they are. I am sorry. "Okay,"
he say. "Just prepare your daughter for the wedding. It take

place next Friday, five days from today." This talk is happening
on a Sunday, I remember everything as if is today. I tell him
I have no problem with that. I only have one request. More
time, please. One month maybe, so I can buy my daughter
new clothes and pots and other things for the marriage, I am
poor man and I need time to get the money together. "Two
weeks," he say, and they left. I sit there, too afraid to go out.
I can't believe I am still alive. When I see the gun I think my
last day has come. As soon as my legs become strong to walk,
I go to my in-laws' house and tell them what happened. We
have another meeting.

'My father-in-law, he say, "You have two choice here. You
can stay and let him marry your daughter, or you can leave
town. You decide." "No," my wife said. All these time she
have been quiet and left all the decision to me, but now she
speak, very strong. "That man will never marry my daughter.
What son-in-law is this? He is crazy man and one day he will
kill my daughter. My daughter will never sleep in the same
room with that man. Never."

'And that is how we leave our country Somalia. First my
wife and children leave for Hargeisa to stay with her aunt,
my mother-in-law's sister. I stay behind and continue to open
the shop, to pretend everything is okay and normal. Latif and
his boys sometimes stop in front of the shop to ask me if I am
getting ready for the wedding, and I always say, Yes, insha
Allah, when they ask me where is Aisha I make excuse, I tell
them she have gone to school, or she have gone to the market with her mother. They will take a few cigarette and small
small things from the shop and they will go. I wait, and one
day before the wedding, I leave town. I follow my wife to

Hargeisa. I leave everything we own, everything, including the goods in my shop. I tell my in-laws to sell everything they can sell and send us the money after. This is the beginning of our life on the road.'

'What year was this?' I asked.

'2002, is twelve years now. I feel sad to leave Mogadishu. I feel in my heart as if I will never see Mogadishu again. I feel sad for my family also. I have three children at the time, Aisha, who is only ten, and Fadel who is seven, and this one, Mahmoud, who is only four when we leave, and his mother was pregnant that time. Now Mahmoud is fifteen, almost sixteen. I leave Mogadishu with three children, now I have five children. Two were born on the road.'

The boy, Mahmoud, who had been quiet all this while, his face glued to the window, gazing at the small towns and countryside and farms outside, now turned and whispered to his father, the father nodded. The boy stood up and headed for the toilet at the end of the carriage. He had a limp, perhaps even worse than it appeared because he walked self-consciously, trying to minimize the limp with a stylish roll of his body. Karim saw me staring after the boy and he said, 'He is a good boy. He speaks four languages, and all he learn on his own. His brother speak five language. I speak three.'

'What happened to his leg, was he born like that?'

'No, no, he wasn't born like this. He get accident. It happen in Yemen. I tell you my story, I tell you everything. It is a sad story, but still, we thank God we are alive together and we are healthy. I have seen people who suffer more than me. I have seen people die in the forest, trying to cross the border. Once, me and my boys, when we are leaving Turkey through forest, we saw a woman and her daughter in the bush. They are looking around, and I ask her can I help you, are you in trouble? She say she was looking for her husband grave. He died when they tried to cross into Bulgaria with human smugglers. He just fall down and died. The smugglers help her quickly bury him in the sand. That was many days ago, but she came back because she kept thinking of him. "You come back to do what?" I ask her. She say she come to say *du'a* for him, to pray for his dead body, she and her son, the son is maybe five, maybe six years old, she say only if she pray for her dead husband can she be able to go forward. Now they look for the grave and she can't find it, it was over a week since they buried him and everything look different. She go from one little place that look like grave, then she begin to pray, then she go to another pile of sand, about four times I see her go from one sand to another. Sometimes while praying she forget what she is doing and she begin to fall asleep because she is so tired and she didn't sleep for many days, then she will start again, then she will forget the words and she will start to cry. We leave her there, she and her son. I tell you, I have seen so many suffering. My story also is sad, but I have seen more sad stories in my travelling. My boy, he broke his leg in Yemen. And you know all his dream is he wants to be a football player. He wants to grow up and play for the Turkish club, Galatasaray.'

'How did it happen?' I asked.

Now we were in Cologne. The noise made by passengers coming in and going out, the sound of their laughter and their German words formed the background to our talk. The boy was back from the toilet. He looked glum, too serious for a kid. His father turned to him and said something in Turkish and the boy looked at me, then he turned back to the window. After a while he stood up and took some money from his father to go to the canteen. At the table to our left a German family was staring pointedly at us, their faces impassive, making no attempt to disguise their curiosity.

'Life in Yemen was not easy at first. But good thing is that we are safe and we are together as a family, this is the most important blessing. We register with the United Nation refugee service, and they give us small money every month, not much, about fifty dollars each. That is not enough for food and house, but things cheap in Yemen. And soon my in-law was able to send us small money from what they sell of my property back in Somalia. We rent a small place, just two rooms and a little kitchen. The children in one room, me and my wife in another room. Sana'a, the capital of Yemen, is a small city. The buildings is not much different from Mogadishu. Large families live in large compounds, with many children and the women wearing their veil and people walking on the narrow streets, just like Mogadishu. There isn't much work to do, but soon I meet some Somalis and one of them, Othman, he invite me to work with them. We buy cigarette and small small things we can buy cheap in Yemen and we take it to Somalia and make some profit, not much, but enough to survive.'

'Was it dangerous?'

Karim laughed and shrugged. 'Well, what we are doing is smuggling, you know. I don't ask too much question. My partner is young Othman. There are many Somalis like him in Yemen, they live in the refugee camps, with no wives or children. I don't even think they are real refugees, just businesspeople. He sometimes talk that his brothers are Somali pirates and they kidnap big ships on the sea and make big money, but something happen and his brother die and they stop doing pirate work. He doesn't say more than that. Now they smuggle people from Somalia to Yemen and other countries. And then they take back cigarette and other small things to sell in Somalia. Me, I did not join in smuggling people, but I join in buying and selling cigarette. Still, my wife, she was not happy. She said I can't do this kind of business. But I tell her, What can I do? We can't live on fifty dollars every month. We will die.

'Well, everything is good for a time. Everything go fine. We are happy. My children start going to school and we can eat good. My wife give birth and we move to a bigger house, not too bigger than the last one, but with three rooms. This is our first year in Yemen. The Somali community is very small then, but soon things start to change. More people start to come, then Othman start doing more people smuggling, and he want me to join him. I will not lie to you, I did join him for a time, and the money was good. Then my wife become unhappy, she say, "Why you do this? Are we not managing okay, what if you get arrested, what if you die, then what will happen to us? Now we are in this strange land, you can't break any law." I say I will think about it. And that day, as I go to meet Othman to tell him I can't do people smuggling any more, they tell me Othman is dead. He died in a boat on the sea. His people were sitting in the room and they are crying and I quietly left them. That same day my son fell from the veranda. Because we are on the fifth floor, in our new house, it is cheaper to rent the

fifth floor, the ground floor is more expensive because no elevator or anything and everybody want ground floor, and there
is a little garden in the yard. Well, my son was playing with his
brother, Fadel, and he is leaning on the rail and it broke, he fell
and thank God he survived without any major broken bone,
but he broke something in his kneecap and from that day he
was limping like this. At first we didn't know that his kneecap
broke. But after a while we see that as he grow, his left leg is
not growing like the right leg.'

'Did you take him to the hospital?'

'Yes, but in Yemen, there is nothing they can do. Yemen is
small country, and poor. They tell me the only place you can
get help is in Europe, Germany, or France. I look at my son
who all his life wants to play football and I promise myself
that I will bring him to Germany or France as long as I am
alive.'

They were three years in Yemen, from there they moved
to Syria. The family continued to grow. There were five children now, three girls and two boys. They got to Syria in
2005. In Damascus their life improved almost immediately.
There they'd spend the best seven years of their lives since
they left home. The economy was good, Karim was able to
get a job with no difficulty, as a kitchen assistant in a hotel he
described as the best hotel in all of Syria. His face lit up as he
remembered. 'Food is not a problem. I get plenty food from
the hotel. Food they want to throw away, good food, the best
food in the world because this is a very big hotel. I tell them
no, I will take it. That way I didn't have to spend my money
on food. No more fighting with the wife, and the kids all go
back to school. My oldest son, Fadel, he is now ten, and my

daughter Aisha is almost fourteen; she was only ten when we left Mogadishu. My wife have not seen her mother or her father for over three years.

'In Damascus we decide we will not get in touch with the Somali community. The last experience with Othman was not good. But we are able to keep in touch with our family back home. They tell us things in Somalia are getting worse every day. Every day Shabaab is growing bigger, now there are bombs on the street. Some of my wife people and my uncles have now moved to refugee camps in Kenya. We hear that Abdel-Latif, the evil young man who caused us to leave home, is now one of the most powerful men in all the country. Seven years in Syria, and we would have stayed even longer but for two reasons, one is my son's leg, we have to get to Europe, and second reason, every day Syria is becoming like Somalia. War has started everywhere and even the Syrians are running away from the cities to the countryside, some are leaving the country. And so my wife said, "We have to go, we are not safe here with our children." We left Syria in 2012, we follow a group that is leaving for Istanbul in Turkey.'

Karim fell quiet, and before he turned to the window I saw his eyes fill up with tears. The boy was asleep, his head resting against his father's shoulder. Outside, night had leaped onto the landscape, and we could be anywhere, Turkey, Syria, Yemen, Germany, it didn't matter. What mattered was to hear what happened next. I wanted to know what happened in Turkey, why was it only him and the boy on the train, where was the rest of the family, Fadel, the girls, the mother . . . ?

'In Turkey things very difficult. My wife almost left me. We have only one room and a parlour for me, my wife, and the children. We are always fighting and the children couldn't even go to school. When we live in Syria my wife and daughter are able to get work, sometimes cleaning, sometimes cooking, and in the hotel there was always food, leftovers, chicken, rice, fish, and we were never hungry, we eat rich-people food. But in Turkey, all the foreigners are treated bad. I only get the worst job, in a furniture company, we carry furniture to people houses, sometimes we repair furniture, and as you finish one job, another one is coming. You have to work many hours, for very little money, they just force you to work overtime with no pay, whether you like or not. If you complain, they say okay, go, other people want your job. You work like slave. My wife say, We can't continue like this. If we continue like this, we will die. We have to decide. We have to go to Europe now.

'Every day I worry: how we get money to travel, where do we stay in Europe? I was afraid, I was tired, I miss my home and I miss Mogadishu and my shop and my simple life selling little things with my family. I know if I enter Europe, I may never come back to my country for ever. So, me and my wife, we agree, I say, I will take the three older children with me, she will stay with the two young ones. I go first, if everything work out fine, she will come after me. But my wife, she say, No, take the two boys, I stay with the girls, Aisha who is nineteen and Fatima who is eight and the youngest, Khadija, who is only three. She say girls must stay with their mother because they are women and they need their mother. I agree.

'The next big problem is, how to go to Europe? My son, this one, he say, "Baba, can we not take our hundred euro that we get from the refugee service people and fly to Europe?" We laugh. It is not so easy. Our two choice to travel is to go through Greece, and directly to Western Europe, but if we go through Greece we have to fly and we have to have papers and do registration and fingerprint and so many things, the other one is to go from Istanbul, which is near the border, then we walk across the border into Bulgaria, which is East Europe, but it is still Europe because Bulgaria just join the EU. Finally, we decide we will go by foot to Bulgaria.

'So, we say goodbye to my wife and my daughters. That night we did not sleep. All of us, we cry all night. I didn't know if I will see my little girls again, and my wife. But we have to go, there is no choice. In Istanbul we meet the people who will help us across the border to Bulgaria. Ten hours we walk with my two boys, in night, from nine p.m. to seven a.m., always hiding. Ten hours and we have to hurry all the time because of danger and we have to stay with the other people in the group and the smugglers who are guiding us. My boy, this one, with his leg, he get tired and he cannot walk any more, and he start to cry. I tell him we are doing this so we can get medicine for his leg. He said no, he doesn't want it any more, he say he only want to go back home. He is tired. Me and his older brother we carry him, under the arm, like this. That is when we saw the woman and her son who are looking for the grave of her husband to say the *du'a* for his soul. It is long time ago, but I feel sad and scared every time when I think about it. That woman alone in the forest with her son, not knowing whether to go forward to Europe or to go back, because her husband died. What can she do, where can she go?

'As we got to the Bulgarian border the border police come out and arrest us. We are happy to be arrest, I tell you. As they put us in line, one lady come, she is not Bulgarian, she come from France or Belgium, I think, she say to me, "Are you together with these boys?" I say, "Yes, they are my children." She say, "In that case you are lucky, because we treat family different. We will keep you together and you will get a better room and food and everything will be fine. Just always remember to join the family line." We very happy, me and my children. We think, this is the end of our journey, our suffering is over. But we don't know this was just the beginning of our bad luck.'

I said, 'What do you mean? You had made it to Europe at last, with your kids, and the nice lady had promised to assist.'

Karim shook his head. 'Ah, she is nice, but the Bulgarians are different. They are not like real Europeans, I tell you, they are more like Asians, and they just join the EU, they are not very friendly.'

'What do you mean?'

'I'll tell you. They bring truck to take us to town, and because of what the lady said, I take my boys and join the family line, but a man come and say to me, "Hey, you can't join this line, this is only for women and girls, are you a woman?" I say, "No, but I am with my children. The lady say I am to stay with family because I am together with my young children." The man say, "Where is your wife?" I say, "My wife is not here, only me and the boys." The man say, "Okay, join the men."

'I want to argue more, but I can see they are getting angry. They say to me, "Hey, we don't care who you are." This is after I show them my refugee protection paper from UNHCR in Yemen, they say as far as we are concerned, you have no right here. You enter this country illegal and you are a criminal. So just shut up. Now I see my boys are beginning to cry and people are staring at us. Everybody is tired and I don't want trouble, so I join the men in the line and we enter big truck, like military truck. We drive far and we can't see outside because we are sitting on the floor inside this truck and there are many men, many from Morocco, Algeria, Eritrea, Nigeria, Ghana, Mali, Afghanistan, Syria . . . everyone speaking different language. When we get to the home, which is actually a prison . . .'

'What do you mean prison?' I interrupted.

'This place used to be an actual prison, but now is empty so they use it for refugee but it is really prison. Very big stone building with iron bars and many floors, with women and family on one side and the rest for men, all packed into small tiny rooms. As we are coming down from the truck to be registered, we see the woman again and I quickly run to her. "You," she say. "Where did you go? Why are you not with the families?" I told her what happened. She turned and talk angrily to the man who say I cannot join the family. They argue, then she say to me, "Don't worry, from now on, I talk directly to his boss. You will be fine. Just finish registering and I will see you inside." She was angry. We register and we go inside and all the time I keep looking for her, but I didn't see her again. They begin to take us to the rooms, and I tell you this is a bad bad prison. As we go to our rooms the refugees who are there already, they stand by the door and shout at us and spit at us. My children they are crying now. "Where are we, Baba?" they ask me. They have never seen anything like this before. I tell the official, "But you can't do this, you can't put my small children in the same place with all these men. It is not right. Look at my youngest boy, he only seven, how he stay in the same room with all these men?" I touch his hand when I talk and now he is angry. He push me away and call me illegal alien. He say, "If you don't like our accommodation, you can go back to your country." Still I try. I say, "But I am a United Nation protected refugee, see my paper here. You can't do this to us." He say he does not care about any rights and protection, and I can wait when I go Western Europe. Here is Eastern Europe, they don't care about this. Still, we are a bit lucky, they put us not in the long big room with dozens of men, but in a smaller room with four other people, with my children we are seven in the room. There are bunk beds, and my boys are able to get the top bunk bed, one on top of my bed, the other on the next bed. We stay in that place for one year. It is a bad place, a prison. There are guards everywhere, these guards they work with prisoners before, so they still treat us like prisoners. The food also was bad. We all have to eat in the cafeteria, and even if you are not hungry you cannot take your food to your room, not even bread. It was hard for the young boy because we eat at five p.m. and by eight to nine before we sleep he is hungry again and he will be crying.'

He was quiet for a while, looking out of the window. The boy was still sleeping. The father gently ran his hand on the boy's head, his eyes faraway. The memories of that grim place, the prison as he so bitterly called it, had darkened his face, and yet, when he looked at the boy, his eyes softened and he sighed and turned back to me.

'It was not all bad, you know. We are lucky to be in that little room away from others. It is only seven of us in our room, in the other rooms there are twenty, thirty people. And most rooms are doing segregation, the people stay together in one corner according to their country or colour or religion. The Algerians and Pakistanis and Syrians, they stay together. Our room is black people, African. But I tell you, after a few days, the Algerians and Moroccans, these people who didn't want to stay with us, they run away from their room and come to our room because they say, Hey we African too. They say the other rooms are too much fanatics. Too much argument and fighting over religion and Arab Spring and little little things. Our room is called TV room because everybody like to come and watch TV in our room, even though they also have TV in their room. Any chance they get, they come to our room. The TV room is more fun. If you see any refugee who was in Bulgaria, ask them about TV room and they tell you. It was popular place. People everywhere, some playing cards, some eating, some listen to music, some fighting!'

Was that nostalgia in his voice? Did he perhaps in some little corner of that recollected room etch his name in the wall: 'Karim Was Here'? Why do people do that only in places of bitterness and suffering and sweat: prisons, locker rooms, grimy toilets; but never in fancy hotels or restaurants or churches? Is it to affirm their existence in those places that try to diminish the human in them, a cry against extinction? Karim sighed and went on, 'And sometimes they call my children to interpret for them. Sometimes when there is argument and two people can't talk to one another, because one speak English and the other is only speak Arabic and maybe the other Turkish and even Bulgarian, it is my children who help them talk. This is a good thing for us, because everybody in the prison now know Fadel and Mahmoud. One day, the big overall prison guard, his name is Bogdan, but everybody call him Boss Bogdan, he come to the TV room. He stand by the door like this and say, "Who is Fadel?" At first I fear, I think, what has my son done now? Is he in trouble? But my boy he stand up and he say, "I am Fadel." The officer enter the room and he speak to Fadel in Bulgarian, but Fadel his Bulgarian is not very good yet. Boss Bogdan speak in English, now they talk, and they laugh. Then Bogdan switch to Turkish. The younger one, Mahmoud, he jump in, because his Turkish is a bit better, and the officer turn to me and he say, "Interesting family." Boss Bogdan he say, "Okay, come quick quick, we go to my office." A lawyer is having meeting with one refugee in his office, and the lawyer speak only Bulgarian and English, the refugee he speak only Arabic. Many of the refugee they only speak Arabic and nothing else. Fadel he go and he translate for them. Boss Bogdan is very impress. And suddenly he become friends with my boys. Sometimes he ask them to come to his office and read a letter for him, or just to talk and to watch TV, like his own children. When he go on inspection around the prison, they go with him. They walk with him from floor to floor, talking to the prisoners, my boys they translating for him what the prisoners are saying. He give them extra food and little little present. From that day, many refugees who want to talk to their lawyer, they come to look for Fadel and Mahmoud. Many of them want to leave Bulgaria immediately and they need lawyer so my children have to interpret for them all the time. If Fadel is busy, then Mahmoud will translate. For that they respect us and they always tell me, These children are very smart, you must take them to school. And even though they say it as a praise for me, I still feel sad because of the life we are living. I always think, what if we are back in Somalia, and everything is okay, and we are living in our small house with our shop. My daughter, Aisha, who is almost nineteen now, she would have been married, and maybe I will be a grandfather. Fadel would have started taking over my little business by now, and maybe we will have another shop by now. But here we are in this place and we don't know what will happen to us today or tomorrow.

'One day, Boss Bogdan he call me and say, "These boys, they are very intelligent, they should be in school, not in a prison like this. We will see what we can do for you." I tell my boys and they dance and jump. I look at them and I begin to cry. Fadel who was big and strong in Syria, he is now so thin his eyes are big in his head. And Mahmoud, he doesn't like the prison food and he has been having stomach problem since we came here, his back is all covered with rashes and we have no doctor, no health workers. People die in their rooms from sickness and there is nothing anyone can do for them. Every day they take out dead bodies. Mahmoud, as he is growing taller the limp in his leg is becoming bigger. Whenever we talk to the mother she ask, "Are you really in Europe, how soon can we come and join you? The girls are getting bigger every day, and they miss their brothers. The youngest one is always asking for you, because you used to play and carry her, now she cries and ask for Baba."

'One day a woman, her name is Sonia, she come and say Boss Bogdan send her and she is going to help us. She belong to a charity that work with refugees. She say she have find us a place to stay, but it is outside town, not too far, but it is cheap. It is a little house in a big bloc of houses, they all look the same, with one room and one living room and a kitchen, but for us it is like a palace. We can cook and take shower and have a little privacy. Sonia, she pay the first rent, and she say after this I have to find work and continue to pay my own rent.

'So finally we leave that prison. We leave TV room and everybody is sad. But it is not easy to get work. Me I have no training, I am a shopkeeper, and also, Bulgaria is not a rich country. Even the people of Bulgaria they can't find work, they want to leave Bulgaria and move to France and Germany, just like me. But I keep trying, every day I take the bus and I go to town to look for work, I go from hotel to hotel from shop to shop, anything I can find, and sometimes I don't come back home till night. Sonia keep coming every day. She try to help. But nothing. Soon however a bigger problem begin. Every day the Jehovah people come to our house to preach to us.'

'You mean the Jehovah's Witnesses?' I asked. He pronounced it *Yehova*.

A family of five in the seats behind ours, mother, father, girls and boy, were talking at the top of their voices, one of the girls kept trying to sing in a shrill voice. Karim had to raise his voice to be heard. 'Yes, these people are not good people. They are like the Al-Qaeda.' There was so much anger in his voice.

'Why do you say that?'

'I tell you why. When they come first time, I tell them, me I am not Christian, I am not even a very good Muslim, all I want is to take care of my children and for my family to be safe, just leave us alone. Please, please, don't come again. Leave us alone. Then one day, I come home from looking for work, and Fadel is not around. I ask his brother, "Where is Fadel?" He say to me, "Fadel he go out with the Jehovah people." I say, "When did this thing start?" He say, "For many days now. One day the Jehovah people come when you are not around and they become friends with Fadel. They come every day and talk to him and he begin to follow them."

'When Fadel come back I just look at him and I can't speak. I ask him, "Why you do this, Fadel? What you want with these people?" He stand there, he say nothing, just looking at me. I look at him, and I see that my boy has grown up. He is already a man. He has a little moustache already. Some beard is already on his chin. I tell him, "Look, I don't care what religion you follow, you can be Catholic or Protestant Christian, but not this people. They will break our family. They are like cult." He say nothing, and I know it is too late already. I search his room and I find a Bible that the Jehovah people give him. The next day I did not go to look for work. I stay at home to watch him. They did not come that day, but in the night, Fadel he ran away from home to stay with these people. They have plan it long time. Now, I don't know what to do. I go look for Sonia to ask her to help me, but when I see her, she tell me, the social service people they want to speak with me. Fadel has told them that his father, me, Karim Al-Bashir, is a religious fanatic, and I am forcing him not to be Christian. I go with her in her small car to the office. Fadel is waiting for me with the Jehovah people, three of them. Two men and one woman. That day, I cry. I stand there in the office and I look at my boy, sitting with these people, the Jehovah people, and me sitting there, and I don't know what to say. I wanted to go away and let him do what he want. But then I think of his mother, I think of him when he was a little boy, when he was playing with Mahmoud and he fell from the balcony and how he was crying and saying sorry, it is his fault, and how he didn't eat food for two days because of his sadness for his brother. I say no, I will not give up my first son so easy. I will fight these people.

'Sonia say the only thing I can do is talk to the Muslim Council of Bulgaria. I didn't even know there is a Muslim Council. She tell me, Yes, there is Muslim Council in Bulgaria, they are mostly from Turkey, but they have been in Bulgaria many years and they are very strong, they even have like thirty per cent in parliament. Maybe they can help and talk to the government and government can help me get my boy back. So, I go to these people. I meet one of them in mosque, during evening prayer, and after he take me to his house. I tell him everything that happen with my son. Well, he is angry when he hear everything, he say it is not right to break family because of religion, and he say he will help me. We try to meet Fadel, but he will not meet with us. We only meet the Jehovah people and they say Fadel doesn't want to see us. Every time we try to set up meeting, he will not come. His brother say they sometimes see him walking with the Jehovah people, dressed like them in black jacket, and they go from house to house to preach. The Muslim Council, they get a lawyer and the lawyer say I must say that the boy is young, and he has to stay with me. So, we have another meeting at the social office, and they say he say I am religious fanatic and he is afraid to stay with me. But I say he is my son and he too young . . . and he is . . .'

'Underage.'

'Yes, he is underage, so they can't take him from me. But the social people say okay, they will keep him and when he is eighteen he can decide what he want. In a few months, he will be eighteen. Now, I don't know what to do. Finally, I begin to give up. What can I do? I am a poor man, this is not even my country. I say to the Muslim people, I give up. I have to leave here, I can't stay here any more, we have to go to Germany. Because I think of all we have come through, from Somalia to Yemen to Syria and Turkey and Bulgaria, and I say, Well, we are lucky we are still alive. I think of that woman and her son in the forest trying to pray on her husband grave. And I say to myself, I don't want to lose my other son. They say no, you must stay, we will put Mahmoud in Islamic school and he can become good Muslim and we will keep fighting for the other one. But I don't want to be trap in religion and fighting over religion. I am tired, and I still have no job, and life in Bulgaria is too hard. If Fadel want to see me one day, he know we are going to be in Germany. So, we put together all our money and we get some help from the Muslim Council and we come to Munich.'

'How has it been in Munich?' I asked.

His face looked drawn in the poor light of the train carriage. The family of five had finally quieted down and we didn't have to shout. He shrugged. 'Sonia, she connect us with another charity in Munich, a church. They give us place to stay, me and Mahmoud. I have a lawyer, he help me apply for asylum and I have document to stay in Germany for five years. He say we will fight my case and we will win. We will get paper for my wife and my daughters to join us. He say the German government care very much about family and education, and they will not send us back to Somalia because no school there for the children, and maybe my son will soon have his operation. I am happy for that.'

'What of your wife, have you been in touch?' I asked.

He lowered his head. 'I talk to my wife. I say soon maybe now she can join us, because the lawyer say it is now possible to get them to come. I have not seen my daughters in almost three years and I don't know how they look now. You know women grow fast and their face change. My wife say Aisha now has a boyfriend, and he want to marry her, but Aisha say no. She say she will not leave her mother alone.' He looked at me, his expression an alloy of sadness and pride and despair. He said, 'Why God give me such good daughter and such bad son? Why? When I tell my wife about Fadel she get angry. She start to cry, all the time on the phone. She say I lost her son. She say is my fault. She say she will never join me in Germany if I don't find Fadel. So, every day I call Bulgaria, I ask Sonia if she hear about Fadel and she say she hear he has move to Switzerland, to another Jehovah people. Switzerland, how possible? Well, I go to Basel in Switzerland, two days ago. We stay with friends Sonia introduce to us, and we ask everywhere, all the Jehovah people, but no Fadel. We can't find him. I don't know what to do. Maybe I go back to Bulgaria. Maybe I wait. Maybe my wife will change her mind.'

His eyes searched mine in the gloomy carriage, and I saw

the hunger on his face. He was hungry for hope, hungry for
a break. He shouldn't feel down, I told him. He had come a
long way from Somalia. His boy would be fine. I patted the
sleeping boy gently on the head before leaving them. We were
in Frankfurt and I had to change for my connection to Berlin.
I waved goodbye to them, my mind already moving on to the
next thing. I had an hour to kill, and it wasn't till I sat down
in the empty food court with a cup of coffee before me that
I realized I had left my bag on the train. The bag in my hand
was Karim's – it was similar to mine, a black leather valise,
but a bit older, more tattered. I jumped up and ran down to
the platform, foolishly hoping the train would still be there,
but the platform was empty, and was this the right platform to
begin with, it was a big station, and the platforms all looked
the same, with the German signs incomprehensible to my
fatigued eyes. I stopped the first uniformed person I saw. He
shrugged. He couldn't help. He looked at my ticket and spoke
into his phone, he pointed up, I had to go to the information
office upstairs, maybe they could help. But, as I dragged my
feet toward the escalator, an ominous feeling descended over
me, I felt I had dreamt this scenario before and I knew how
it was going to unfold. Everything was in that bag, including
my passport and my green card.

At the office I stood in line, lost in thought.

'*Nächste*,' the lady behind the counter barked at me. When
I didn't move she snapped louder, '*Nächste, bitte!*' her German sense of order ruffled. The man behind me gave me
an impatient nudge, muttering angrily in German, and still
I hesitated. What would I tell the woman, even now my
bag was flying away in the night, would Karim get down

at the next station and report the bag? He didn't have my address or number, and would he even notice he had the wrong bag before he got to his destination? I could follow him to Munich and try to locate him, but he said he might soon be leaving for Bulgaria. I needed to keep calm, I was tired, sleep-deprived, I decided to go on to Berlin, to think things through on the train. I had my ticket at least. I left and went back to the platform.

I saw the same officer, standing on the platform. He looked at me suspiciously when I asked him for the train to Berlin. 'You find your bag?' he asked. Just then a train pulled into the station, and I saw a face at the window, it was Karim – he was back, looking for me. I ran toward the train. The officer called after me, trying to tell me something, but I was already entering the train. Through a window I saw the officer waving urgently at me, but I made my way down the aisle, toward that face at the window, and why was the train so dark, it felt like a continuation of the darkness that had settled over me since I discovered my bag was missing. The train jerked forward, almost throwing me into the lap of the person sleeping in the aisle seat next to me. I groped my way to an empty seat at the back, one row next to Karim, who even as I sat down I realized was not Karim, and flopped down by the window, looking at the receding platform dotted with sleepy passengers holding their tickets in one hand and their bags in the other.

I sat, tense and alert – I'd get off at the next station and catch any train to Berlin. But the next station came and passed, and the next one, and still the train didn't slow down. I fought to keep my eyes open, I couldn't work up the strength to turn to not-Karim, to ask what train this was. The sense of doom

settled more firmly over me like a blanket. Soon the lights and
buildings gave way to monotonous open country. I jumped
to my feet and rushed up the aisle looking for an official to
ask when the next stop was. I passed through the carriages,
eyes glowed at me from the seats, faint reflection of the light
outside rose from dark faces; there were no officials to see. I
dropped into a seat, exhausted, and immediately fell into a
deep stupor. A baby was crying in my sleep and when I woke
up it was still crying. Perhaps it was the crying that woke me
up. We were pulling into a station, and I got up, trying to see
the name of the station, definitely not Berlin Hauptbahnhof,
my destination.

More people were coming on, there was a commotion by
the door, curses and shouts, a man fell and then stood up
again. There were guards, holding guns, forcing more people
onto the train. Now I noticed the people being forced on
were mostly women and children. Mostly Asian and African.

'What train is this? Where are we?' I asked the man next
to me.

He shrugged. 'We are at the border.'

'What border?'

'Italy. That guard was speaking Italian. I speak the language.' He said the last with pride.

The train started to move again.

'Italy?' I asked, flummoxed. Perhaps I hadn't heard right. 'I
am going to Berlin.'

'You are on the wrong train, my friend,' he said, and started
to laugh. Another man joined in the laughter. I looked around
the dark train. 'What train is this?'

'We are being deported, don't you know?' the man asked.

His words were gentle, chiding almost, as if he were talking to a slow child. The exhaustion redoubled heavily on my shoulders. The train grew darker, the way the light fades as day ends abruptly in winter. I stood up. If only the baby would stop crying. I wanted to go and talk to the mother, to tell her to feed him, to do anything to shut him up, but suddenly my willpower left me and I sat down again, my brain simply shutting down, and I couldn't keep my eyes open. When I woke up we were being led off the train to buses waiting by the kerb outside the station. It was a small station, with a single track passing through it and a single exit on either side of the track. I hurried over to the soldier.

'There's a terrible mistake. I got on the wrong train.'

I showed him my ticket to Berlin. He called to another soldier and they conversed for a while, the other soldier shrugged and turned away. I felt my heart sink.

'I cannot help you here. You make complaint when you get to camp,' the soldier said, gently turning the barrel of his gun toward me. The weak morning sun splashed itself over the trees and concrete buildings as we came out of the station and into the buses. I couldn't read the signs, they were in Italian, probably. We followed the direction of the sun, meandering and climbing through sleepy villages and hamlets and endless olive farms.

The bus was worse than the train. At least in the train there was more space and more air. In the bus the press of bodies and the cries of babies and the cursing of men intensified. The crying baby was in the same bus, and the mother's cooing continued, trying to calm it down, until suddenly it stopped. I could understand how it must have lost its will to cry any more, the same way the energy had drained out of me earlier. I waited for the cry to resume, but it didn't. We were in some countryside, and suddenly we could smell it, the sea. The smell was unmistakable, salty, minerally, and then we could hear the distant rush of water against the coastline. Somehow I wanted the baby to cry again, to articulate the feeling inside me, a deep, confused cry.

Book 5

THE SEA

As he drove down the sloping road to the camp he caught a glimpse of the sea below. The southern Italian sun was gleaming on the waves and for a moment it all came back, the woman lying half-covered in the foaming waves on the beach, and he running toward her. At first he thought she was dead. The camp sat on the slope of a hill by the sea. Today the sea was restless, roiling and snapping at the foot of the hill, spouting foam like an enraged leviathan. This hilly landscape, which in his childhood had looked postcard-idyllic with its view of the endless blue Mediterranean below, was now ruined by the slapdash red-brick structures and white tents covering it, and the smell, the unbearable smell.

His late uncle, who had been in a prisoner-of-war camp in
WWII, said the smell was unmistakable, it was more than
human effluence and trash, it was the smell of misery and
despair. The tents were more recent; the brick structures
had been there since the 1920s as offices and temporary staff
accommodations when the hill was mined for copper, when
the copper veins ran out in the 1940s the mine was turned
into a military camp, and when the war ended the site was
abandoned to wild goats and rodents, and for decades its
brick structures and iron roofs rusted away in the humid,
acidic sea air. When, a decade ago, the refugees started coming and the small island started running out of space to keep
them, the town council voted to salvage the rotting structures and turn the place into a refugee centre. The migrants
were brought here as soon as they arrived in their boats, to
be examined by the doctors, to be deloused, to be registered,
and officially welcomed to Europe. As Matteo drove past
the sign that said *Welcome Centre*, he couldn't help grinning
at the lack of irony by whoever had proposed the name.
A bored-looking guard nodded at him and he parked his
motorbike under a tree and climbed the four concrete steps
to the camp director's office. He wondered why the man
had sent for him. They had been together last week – a body
had washed up on the beach in front of his house, and he
had called the director to come pick it up. It was not the
first time. Twice, a leaky boat with shivering, terrified and
surprised-to-be-alive families had beached on his property
and he had driven them in his truck to the refugee centre.
All except the woman and the child.

   North, they all want to go north, the director shouted into

the phone as Matteo entered the tiny office. The man caught his eye and nodded.

Yes, Germany, France, England. This is not a prison, you understand, they are free to go if they want. He put down the phone and stood up and shook Matteo's hand. American reporter. He wants to know if this is some sort of detention centre. Whatever gave him that idea.

Perhaps he wants to borrow my truck, Matteo thought. The refugee centre was badly underfunded, and the director was often asking for help, which Matteo was always willing to offer. Most of the town's inhabitants, men women children, had at one time or another volunteered at the camp.

Come, the director said, I have something to show you.

They descended the steps and followed the path leading to yet another gate which opened into the camp proper. The ground underneath was hard and pebbly; this stark, ugly land-scape was somehow offset by the sea, white foam turning to soft aquamarine. Between the hill and the sea was the camp. A central structure dominated the entire camp – rectangular and unremittingly utilitarian, its aluminium roof arched over the concrete building, square windows cut into the concrete at precise, regular intervals. This was the medical centre where all newcomers were examined by doctors, nurses and other volunteers. Matteo had volunteered here before, more than once. On busy days it looked like a marketplace, men and women and children dehydrated from their long ordeal on the sea were stretched out on cots and hooked to drips for rehydration – it was never a pretty sight: some had feet rotting in their wet shoes, some had shit and vomit caked to their skin and hair, some were delirious with fright from being trapped between dead bodies for days in the boat – pregnant women had to be checked to see if the baby was still alive, or not, in which case emergency caesarean sections were performed right there on the floor, more serious emergencies were flown out by helicopter to bigger and better-equipped facilities in Palermo and nearby cities.

Matteo hadn't been to the centre in over a month, but nothing had changed, it was overcrowded as usual, it was meant to hold five hundred people, but it always had over two thousand migrants, some just arriving and waiting to be processed, some leaving. Toilets had been converted into sleeping spaces, it was either that or leave women and children exposed to the weather. As they descended further into the camp he saw them coming from all directions, men and women and children, in their hands were bowls they presented at a table where two men stood behind three huge aluminium basins from which they ladled out food, which the inmates began to wolf down immediately without waiting to sit.

The director, still not explaining where they were going, said, There are more in those tents. Some are too sick to come out.

They came to a tall fence facing the sea. Matteo was about to ask what exactly they were looking for when he noticed the line of bodies standing or sitting, men and women and children, all facing the sea, their faces pressed against the fence. They were not talking, just facing the sea, away from the kitchen and the diners. Nearby a woman sat on the hard pebbly ground, moaning softly, all the time knocking her head against the fence. They did not turn when Matteo and the director approached.

What are they doing here? he asked.

The director pointed at the woman and whispered, They say she sits here every day to listen to the voices of her children who drowned.

Matteo imagined the voices rising from the impassive depths, woven into the wind and waves, faint and then dying, snuffed by the wet air, but since they say sound never really dies, the voices must continue, diminished, inaudible to ordinary ears, but still detectable with the right listening device, like a mother's ears. The director came to a stop abruptly. His voice still at a confidential pitch, he said, A week ago a man hanged himself in one of the bathrooms. Another woman went crazy and started screaming for no reason around the camp, she was subdued, but that night she stabbed herself to death. Another man managed to scale this fence and threw himself into the waves, he drowned immediately.

In the distance a fishing boat, or a ferry, rose and dipped, leaving a contrail of churning sea behind it. Coast guards, most likely, on patrol. In the sky a Frontex helicopter circled in long and widening loops as it searched the inscrutable waters.

I don't understand . . . Matteo tried to hide his impatience. The director raised a hand, urging him toward a man standing alone by the fence, also staring into the water, quiet and motionless. The day was dying and soon the mild Mediterranean sun would dip into the sea, its last rays slanting over the water and the coastline, turning the skyline and the white sands and the rooftops russet, and the aquamarine water black.

Who is he? Matteo found himself whispering, not sure why. He has been here for a month now. He has been passed from camp to camp. He is very sick and I fear he cannot last much longer.

Now Matteo noticed how frail the man looked, with the wind flapping his baggy shirt and pants, threatening to sweep him over the fence and into the sea. He was of average height, his clothes hung on his gaunt frame and a beard covered his chin. The director was staring at the man with a regretful look on his face. Matteo wondered why the man was important, why his case differed from the other hundreds around him.

The director turned to him. He was brought here with a bunch of others, deported from the north. This has been happening more and more often, migrants rounded up and dumped into trains and sent back to their first European country of entry, usually Italy or Greece. They want to send them back to their countries, or at least to Libya or Egypt, but the government often forgets about them. After a while most of them simply walk out and return to the north. This one, he came to my office two weeks ago. He was not a refugee, he said. His documents went missing and he ended up on the train by accident. I didn't believe him of course. You get such stories every day. Once, a woman from Togo told me she was a queen in her hometown, she had been chased out by rivals and should therefore be given automatic Italian citizenship, not even asylum, citizenship. She demanded to be taken to the king of Italy.

What did you tell her?

I told her we had no king. I get all kinds of stories here. But this guy, he persisted, and I agreed to take him to the US consulate in Palermo. We went and he placed his complaint, but they said there was nothing they could do about his green card. They said they'd flag it if it ever appears anywhere and let him know. He can apply for a replacement only in America or in his home country, Nigeria, meanwhile, he can apply for a visitor's visa, but he needs his Nigerian passport to do even that. They gave him some forms to fill out.

If he is not a refugee, then he shouldn't be here, Matteo said.

Yes, I told him the same thing. But it appears he has nowhere to go, or nowhere he wants to go. I also suspect he doesn't have the means to go anywhere . . . but most important, he doesn't appear to want to go anywhere.

Doesn't he have family, a wife?

He mentioned a wife, but I got the feeling he doesn't want to call her. The director sighed and with a last look at the man turned and started uphill back to his office.

You believe him? Matteo called after him. The man hadn't once looked at them.

I retire next week. This is my last week here. I can't sleep at night. I see dead babies and drowning mothers. The director's face was gaunt as he stared at Matteo, his eyes hollow with sleeplessness. I don't want to leave any loose ends, you understand.

How does that involve me? Matteo asked, even though he was beginning to suspect just how. Giuseppe, the director, was a childhood friend. They had grown up in cottages next to each other, their fathers, fishermen, and sons to fishermen, and grandchildren to fishermen, co-owned a fishing boat, till Giuseppe's father died five years ago, drowned on a fishing expedition off the Tunisian coast. Unlike Matteo, who had never left the island, Giuseppe had studied at the university in Palermo before returning to the island. He had been the camp director for three years now.

This man will die if I don't get him help.

Suicide?

No, he doesn't look suicidal. But he seems to have lost all will to live. I have seen it happen before. When I told him that he was free to go, that this was not a prison, you know what he told me? He said he was thinking about it. About his next move. Go back to Germany, I told him, get in touch with your friends. But he said no, not Germany.

Maybe he wants to go to his country, Nigeria, Matteo suggested.

Maybe, but he has been here over one month now. He is ill. You see how he looks. I have seen people like that. They grow apathetic, they withdraw, they neglect their health, and they die.

And why do you believe I can help him if even he doesn't want to help himself? That's why you called me, isn't it?

Well, he came from Berlin. He has lived there for over a year. I thought that might interest you.

•

I stand by the fence till the sun sets. This is the best spot to watch the water change colour with the dying sun. I don't want to go back inside. Last night the man, boy really, on the bed next to mine was screaming in his sleep, and this morning he refused to get up, he lay there, staring at the ceiling. He is not more than twenty, and usually he is very chatty, always talking about his journey across the desert and his prospects in Europe. England is his ultimate destination, he and everyone else. If not, he would settle for Germany. And should we travel together, do I have any money, and how long have I been in this camp. Then the lapse yesterday. I have seen many like him, the high spirits alternating with depressed silences. This is my third camp. The first was Lampedusa, then Greece, then this island. Every camp is different, and yet the same.

I spend my time staring at the water. If you stare at it long enough you notice the gradations of colour, the minute shifting spectrum between green and blue and indigo. Once, the director came and stood next to me, this was a day after we had gone to the American consulate in Palermo, he asked me what I looked for in the water. Nothing, I told him. I have always been fascinated by water. I was born in a landlocked town, with no rivers or lakes, the streams were seasonal, formed by flash floods of the rainy season. As kids, after it rained, we stood on the banks to watch the moving mix of water and mud and tree limbs and dead birds and the occasional goat or dog and marvel at the power of water. Rainfalls were the most spectacular events, magical, and anything seemed possible, giants could fall from the sky, trees could be uprooted and tossed about like twigs, humans could wash up by the roadside, sometimes chunks of ice fell, making holes in the roof and shattering car windshields and windowpanes. Hail. After the rains, vultures sat for hours on baobab trees, their cinereous wings soaked and useless, waiting for the sun to come out. It was the most pathetic sight, these huge ungainly creatures, yet still birds, still built for flight, and yet, for this moment, before they dry out, stuck on tree branches, wingless.

Try to get out of here, the director urged, if you stay here, you will die. I have seen too many die here. Healthy, normal people. The next day they fall ill and the next day they are dead. I listened. I nodded. I thought, Who is to say if I am not dead already, the people around me could be shadows, wraiths, like me. If I am alive, then I am barely alive. Barely walking, mostly standing and staring at the water.

I feel his gaze, he and the other man, a new face, a reporter, perhaps, but he has no notebook, no bag for his recorder, and he doesn't have that hungry, vulpine look reporters have. Just another islander, a church member perhaps, another attempt to save me, to get me out of this camp. He was quitting, he told me. He seems desperate to save me. No man can save his brother, or pay his brother's debt – or something to that effect. Some poet said that. I pretend not to see them, and finally they turn and they leave. I am thinking, I wanted to tell him. I have all the time in the world. I have nothing to do but stare at the water and think. I am trying to decide if I want to go out there, to live, or to wait here and embrace whatever comes. No, I am not a fatalist, I am not reckless, but I feel if I wait here long enough, presently something would be revealed to me, someone would step up to me, a familiar face, or a total stranger, a child, a man, a woman, and they would say, Listen. And they would tell me a story, a fable, a secret, something so pithy, so profound, that it is worth the wait. Listen, they would say, listen carefully.

•

The next day the man comes back alone and offers to take me into town, if I have time. Time. He is mocking me, perhaps. Time is all I have. He introduces himself, Matteo. A friend to the director, and perhaps like the director he also suffers from a saviour complex. But I indulge him. All I have is time, after all. I have been here one month, and I have never been into the village. We go in his small car, up the hill, past a line of trees, and we are in the town centre. It is a small town, its narrow stone-cobbled streets meandering between white-painted houses and a central church facing a square with a water fountain with the statue of a lion rampant in its middle.

We park by the fountain and walk around the quiet town. Sleepy old men and women sit in front of cafés under umbrellas and awnings, drinking coffee in the hot afternoon sun. We come upon a busy street leading away from the fountain, a street market is in session; we pass a butcher's stand displaying haunches and sides of sheep hanging on hooks.

I grew up here, Matteo says, waving at a familiar face. I know literally everyone in this town.

After the market is a line of stores selling clothes and ladies' bags and shoes. The clothes on display make me self-conscious about my own tattered clothes; I have been wearing the same thing for weeks now and I must look like a scarecrow. More and more I notice in front of hotels and pensions African and Asian men sitting in little groups on steps and on benches, talking in whispers. Their faces have a speculative, haunted look, as if weighing how long they could stay in this small town before wearing out their welcome.

Come, let's have coffee, Matteo says.

We sit outside one of the cafés and order coffee. From here the sea is visible in the distance. There are a few men and women sitting at nearby tables, most of them stare curiously at me as we sit down. A group of young men at the next café stare pointedly at me and whisper among themselves. The waitress refuses to look at me and addresses herself all the time to Matteo. I order tea. When she comes back she slaps the tea-cup in front of me and stands there waiting for payment. Matteo says something sharply to her and hands her some money. She gives him change and walks away.

I am sorry, he says. There is anger in this town. Half of the population has left.

Why? I ask.

The economy is bad. People blame that on the refugees. In the last five years the refugee population has almost surpassed the population of the locals, and so more and more locals leave. As he speaks an African woman drifts into view, she is wearing a colourful print dress and leading a child by the arm. She walks slowly, meditatively, and she could be in her hometown, going on a visit to the neighbours'. More brown faces pass as we sit, Indians, Arabs, Africans. I drink my tea. The bell at the church tolls the hour. From where we sit the church steeple is visible, pointing forlornly into the glaucous air. Matteo says in the Middle Ages anyone who broke the law would be hoisted up in a cage in front of the church and left exposed to the elements till they died. It was useful as a crime deterrent.

The director told me you used to live in Berlin.

Yes, I reply. I want to thank you for the coffee, and for this. I wave my hand.

We can do this again tomorrow if you like, he says.

He has something to tell me, or to ask me, I can tell, but he is waiting, sizing me up. We go back to the camp as the sun is going down. He comes again the next day, at the same time,

and we go back to the same café. The same waitress brings me
my tea, with croissants, avoiding my eyes as she places down
the tray. I watch the Africans pass, and in the distance the
blustery sea is bluer today.

I'll tell you a story, Matteo says. He sips his espresso and
lights a cigarette. He has an angular face, his skin is sunburnt.
He is a housepainter, he tells me, he used to be a fisherman,
like most men in the town. His hands are covered with streaks
of green paint. It is about a woman, he says. Think of it as a
fairy tale.

•

*Once upon a time a man came upon a woman lying on the seashore,
half-covered by the foaming waves. A mermaid, he thought. Her lower
body was in the water, her wet hair falling over her face, her clothes
wave-torn. He stood over her, the waves crashed and receded and
crashed back again, she appeared dead. Then he saw the child some
distance away from her, struggling to rise, tied to a life buoy with a
piece of red cloth. He ran over and scooped up the child. It was a boy,
about one year old, with seaweed tangled in his hair and water pouring out of his mouth and nostrils. The woman was moving, raising a
hand toward him, trying to speak, her voice weak. He ran back to her
and brought his ear close to her. Help, she croaked, pointing at the boy.
Please. He tried not to panic, he looked around, seeking help, but the
beach was empty. Only the waves washed against the sand and rocks
of the narrow bay. He pulled the woman away from the waves. He
took off his shirt and covered her naked chest.*

Can you stand?

*She tried to stand but her legs kept giving out under her. He put
an arm under her shoulder and, the child in one hand, he led her to*

his house not too far away from the beach. He lived with his old father, Pietro, in a house that had once been full of the voices of his brothers, but his brothers had all left for the city, and three years ago his mother had died. Only he and his seventy-year-old father lived in the big house, which was now crumbling as houses tend to do in this weather.

For two days mother and child slept, side by side, on the queen bed in one of the bedrooms. The man sat on a chair and watched them, scared they might be slowly dying from some secret injury, an internal haemorrhage or infection contracted in the water. He watched the woman turn and kick and roil in her sleep, re-creating the motions of the sea that had recently disgorged her. The child whimpered and held on tightly to the arm of the woman. All night long he watched, sleepless and anxious, sometimes raising his hands as if to still the restless motions of the sleeping pair, then retracting them. Fancying the couple were too still, he placed a hand on the woman's chest to feel the heaving, up down, up down, of her breathing, then he placed a moist finger under the child's nostrils to feel the draught of its breath.

Come, his father, Pietro, said, go and rest. There is nothing you can do. I'll watch over them and I'll call you as soon as she wakes up.

The woman woke up that night. She stared at the old man dozing in a chair by the window and she looked neither surprised nor alarmed. Her first action was to reach over and cradle the sleeping boy in her arms. The old man brought her a bowl of soup and watched her as she drank.

•

They say I collapsed while standing by the fence, watching the water as I always do. I have no recollection. I wake up and a doctor in white is crouching over me, shining a flashlight into my eyes. I am in the medical centre.

Can you hear me? the doctor asks.

I close my eyes and turn away from the light.

How do you feel, any headaches? he asks.

No, I reply, well, a little bit.

I try to sit up but the doctor pushes me back to the cot. I have seen the doctor before, there are two of them, him and a woman, they take turns, each dropping in about twice a week. He is not up to forty, about my age, with a receding hairline and a permanent frown of worry on his face. He sits on a chair by the cot, the frown deepening.

You are dehydrated and malnourished. We are going to keep you here for a few days and give you saline solution.

In the morning the director comes, and he sits down on the same chair the doctor sat in and shakes my hand, as if congratulating me on something I have achieved. You are leaving, he says. It is all settled. The man, your friend, Matteo, he is taking you with him. You can stay with him till you get better.

I want to protest that Matteo is not really my friend. I hardly know him, or when and how this was all settled, but I don't want to sound ungrateful. Matteo looks harmless, polite, ready to listen, I am sure I will get along with him. Still, I don't want to be in someone's house, I don't want to be obligated to anyone. But I am too tired to argue. Back in my corner, I get my things together. I don't have much. A toothbrush given to us by the camp, a comb, a change of underwear, a sock, my slippers – I put them all in a polythene bag and I sit to wait for Matteo.

The room is empty. The bunk next to mine has a new

occupant. The young man has left a few days back. He wanted me to go with him, he said we'd make a good team. He was from a small town in Nigeria, he told me, not mentioning the town or the state. He was poor and felt he stood no chance in his hometown of ever achieving the good life, so his mother sold their land and gave him the money to pay his way across the Mediterranean. I imagine him on a train, or in the back of a truck, or walking on a bush trail, going north. I admire his optimism, which, inevitably, will get shattered, it is impossible that it won't, but still I admire it. In a corner of the tent I hear a radio, BBC, the announcer's voice interrupted by static. I used to listen to BBC a lot as a child. Another voice is on the phone, always on the phone, the ubiquitous cell phone, the only link to the world left behind.

I am in Italy. Everything is good. Everything is working fine. Soon I go to Germany. Yes, insha Allah.

I think of Karim and his son Mahmoud, and how he chose the wilderness of exile over home. I remember the pain in his voice when he said he knew he might never see Somalia again. Once upon a time, to be away from the known world was exile, and exile was death. Through the tent entrance I see a group of young men, about four of them, they always gather there, by the hillock, talking earnestly, they keep to themselves, sometimes it appears they are arguing. They make phone calls. They are planning their route, their forward path. They talk bravely, boldly turning their back on all they know, embracing change and chaos, and yet, sometimes I catch the nervous note in a laugh, I imagine them back in their tents, on their cots, pining for home. I hear their voices heading toward the gate, going into town, to try to earn some money, or to make connections, to hustle. Endlessly hustle.

•

The first day she was able to stand up, she followed a door, which led into a larger room, and then into another room. Some of the windows were broken; the walls had cracks in them. An air of decay and forgetfulness pervaded the entire house, and even in her semi-somnambulistic state she could tell there was no woman's touch anywhere, and that, for some reason, made her sad. She stood in a room between a kitchen and another room, a dining room perhaps, and looked around, lost. It was some sort of storeroom; there were boxes under wooden shelves, and cans of paint piled on top of each other, there were brushes on a table, the paint dry on the bristles, some of the paint had run down on the table, making lines, now dry and multicoloured. Then the old man entered.

My son is not here, he has gone to work. Do you want something? I want to go outside. Please.

He looked closely at her for a while, then he nodded. He led her by the hand through a side door, then down a flight of half a dozen lichened stone steps, down a vine-hedged path, and they were in a garden. This used to be a beautiful park and people would come from the village just to sit here and look at the roses, he said. As they approached a fountain, the smell of dead leaves in the water rose in the air. Nearby a nymph held a cracked vase, in her abdomen and shoulders were what looked like bullet holes. He led her to a bench facing the sea.

This is where my son found you, Pietro said, pointing. And suddenly she was agitated again. He reached out and took her hand, she looked at him without recognition. The children, she cried. She wrung her hands. Where are the children? He took her back inside, and they passed through the many doorways until they came to the bedroom. The boy was there, sleeping. The worry and panic left her face, she sat on the bed and folded the boy in her arms, burying her face in his chest, all the time whispering to him.

She looked up and the old man had gone, in his place the younger man was standing there. How much time had passed, she had lost track.

What is his name? he asked.

Omar.

What is your name?

She shook her head. At night she dreamt of fire and loud explosions in the sky. There was a man, and a girl. And there was water, so much water, and she was swimming in it, kept afloat by the orange life buoy around her middle, she and the child. She dreamt the same dream in a loop, over and over, and the dream always ended with the man standing over her, telling her it was all right, she was safe.

He whispered again, What is your name?

She shook her head, desperately now.

Come.

He led her to the bathroom and stood her before the mirror. Toothbrushes with flat, chewed bristles stood in a cup over the sink. The mirror was stained by soap suds and dirt, there were cracks in it, a long diagonal crack ran from bottom to top, cutting her face in two. Her hand flew up to her face, as if in reaction to the cut in the mirror. She ran her fingers through her hair; she touched her cheeks and her lips and her eyelids, as if touching the face of another.

I am sorry. I don't know.

Behind her in the mirror he smiled in encouragement. He said, It will all come back to you. Take a bath, then rest. He left. Alone in the bathroom the woman looked at her face in the mirror, she saw the grime, the sand and sea salt in her hair, and try hard as she might, she couldn't remember who she was or where she came from. All she could remember was the sea. She undressed and ran her hand slowly over the caesarean scar on her abdomen.

•

This is my house. It is not much, but here you are safe, the man said gently.

She looked up at him, the word 'safe' registering in her sea-muddled mind. Her eyes at first questioned him, then they trusted him, and could that be the moment that he fell for her, for her eyes, so huge, so beautiful. He fell and it was a long and bottomless fall.

She was scared of the dark, she told him. She slept with the lights on, and sometimes he heard her screaming in her sleep. At those times he'd sit on the chair till she slept, sometimes he knew she only pretended to be sleeping, like a child, her eyes closed, listening to him breathe and move in the chair, but he knew she found his presence reassuring. Once she woke up when the lights were off. She raised a hand and pointed to the window. Light, she said. Please. She remembered the dark boat; all she wanted as they rode the waves up and down was a ray of light to touch her skin. Please, she repeated.

Once she had overcome her fear of waking up in this strange place, she loved to take walks in the mornings, while the boy still slept, to walk in the park and sit on the bench and stare at the water in the distance. The man watched her from the house, through the kitchen window. A week ago she wasn't here, a week ago he didn't know her, now here she was and all he could think about was her. She was a mother, a wife, perhaps greatly loved by a husband who was now probably dead in the water, his corpse beached and half-buried on some European shore. Of course he might not be dead, he might

be somewhere, ahead, or behind, sitting with his cell phone in hand,
waiting for a word from her. The man was surprised by the quick
jealousy he felt at the thought of a husband waiting for her.

She could stay here, he said to his father.

Why not. She had no memory of a past, or a destination; sending
her to the camp would be cruel. With a child. This would be a new
beginning for her, for them. He could give her that. He would give her
that. But he had to take it slow. He didn't want to scare her.

•

We used to be fishermen, Matteo told him, but not any more.

Why did you stop fishing? the man asked.

Fishing became too painful, Matteo said, and he did not
elaborate. He went on, I taught myself how to paint. The
painter left the island, so I am in some demand at the moment.

He had been a week in the house now, and already the
memory of the camp was fading from his mind. He remembered the woman who sat by the fence and said she could
hear her children's voices from the depths of the sea. And
the camp director, Giuseppe, who must have retired by now.
Every morning he took a walk on the beach, for about thirty
minutes. The doctor ordered it.

It is up to you if you want to recover or not. You are young,
nothing is really wrong with you. Your malaise is really in
your mind. Of course your body is weak, due to poor diet and
other minor infections. But it is in your power to get better.
Eat well, exercise. It is the best medicine I can prescribe for
you, the doctor told him.

The doctor was an old man, a childhood friend to Pietro.
He had sat on the chair next to the bed, the very bed the mer-

maid must have lain in, and he wondered if the doctor had also attended to her when she lay here, lost and sick with fear. He was wearing a white doctor's coat, as if he were in a hospital making his rounds, his doctor's bag by his side.

Tell me, the doctor asked, are you married?

Yes, he nodded.

Don't you miss your wife, don't you want to be with her?

Did he miss Gina? He thought of home before he met Gina. He had two sisters whom he hadn't seen in over ten years. They were much older, married with grown-up children, and when he was a child they never really had time for him, and apart from the occasional phone call, they hardly met. His father was a retired government contractor and he had been born when his father was in his fifties, too old and too tired to take much interest in him after the initial joy of having the much-desired male child. Once, during his early months in America, he missed his mother so much he felt embarrassed by how much he missed her, but after a while he got over that. Gina had replaced his family, and he was not lonely any more. He missed Gina, he missed her so much it felt like there was a hole in his chest, but he knew with time her memory would get blurry and it would be like a dream, recollected vaguely at unexpected moments. He felt scared when he thought of that. He didn't want to forget her. He wanted to call her a thousand times every day, but for what purpose? He had avoided calling her so far, he felt ashamed at the way they parted. Time would fill up the void in their hearts left by the other, fill it up like an empty well gradually filled up with household junk till people have forgotten that it was once a well. Those who dug it would die, those who knew it was a

well and even drank from it would move on, and its time as a
well would be forgotten.

Twice the doctor came back to see him, and he always
stayed for dinner. Meat, and vegetables, and pasta, but never
fish. They sat, the three of them, eating and watching the sea
through the window, in the distance a boat circled the water.
Pietro's dog lay in the corner, its eyes closed. Coast guards,
Matteo said; no, that is the *carabinieri*, the police, the doctor
argued; wrong, Pietro said, squinting his old eyes, it is a private boat, one of the rescue volunteers.

Matteo told him the doctor's story: he had left the village to go to Rome to study medicine, he had married there,
making a good living, but he missed home, he missed the
sea, and when in 2013 he saw in the news, with the rest of
the world, the bodies of over three hundred migrants fished
out of the Mediterranean in the nearby island of Lampedusa,
he had gone there to volunteer, and he had never returned to
Rome since then. He moved back to the island and opened his
own practice. He volunteered at the refugee camp, and old as
he was, he went out with the rescue boats daily to search for
capsized migrant boats.

Before leaving, the doctor ordered him to rest, he still
wasn't as strong as he thought he was, it would take time for
his body to recover. He tried to read after his walks. There
were books in the house, on bookshelves in the living room,
all in Italian, except for one in English, translated from the
Italian, *The Leopard*, by di Lampedusa. Matteo asked him if
he wanted to go out on the boat with them, they were going
round the island, he and Pietro – the island was so small you
could go round it a dozen times in a day – and at first he said

no, but once they were on the water he liked it, until he grew seasick and started to vomit and had to be helped out of the boat to his room when they got back.

•

He said, You have been here six months now. Tell me, what do you remember?

She said to the man: Omar is my son, I know that, instinctively, but I don't remember his birth date, or his favorite colour. I know I am a good mother. I will do anything for him, I will give my life for him, willingly.

But there was more she was not saying, recently she had started to dream of other faces, a man, a girl, and when she woke up her head ached from trying to follow those images. All day the headaches persisted, a dull blunt pain at her temples. Other images came up unbidden, street names, faces, she remembered a car number. 1980. She saw herself walking down a street and into a white house with a date palm tree in front of it, with two children holding on to her hands. A boy and a girl. It was a happy place, but she couldn't get past the doorway, she always stood by the door, and when she opened the door everything was blank.

She said, There's a man. There is a house, white. We live there, I am sure. It is burning. There are gunshots and buildings are crumbling about us. That is all I can see, the man, the house.

He said gently, sadly, Don't think about the past. You are safe here. I'll take care of you both.

•

We are in the kitchen. I stand in the corner watching Matteo cook. He throws a slab of red, bloody meat on a skillet. Next to it long stems of asparagus are steaming in an open pot. He cooks well, self-sufficiently, waving me away with a napkin whenever I offer to help. I stand by the open window, feeling inadequate. From somewhere in the house a radio is playing, a woman's voice singing a sad opera tune. I pass him the salt, I clear the table of onion skin, and when I run out of things to do, I engage him in small talk: why does he live alone with his father in this big house, where's the rest of his family? It is hard to tell if he is young or old, his face is indeterminate, sometimes when he sits facing me in the room, bent forward in his chair, he looks old and wise and tired. He must have witnessed a lot of things thrown up by the waves in front of his door. I have seen some myself since I have been here, pieces of clothing, children's toys, a shoe, a cell phone case, when walking on the beach.

We have settled into a routine, I wake up, I walk on the beach, when I get back I wash the dishes if there are any to be washed, then the rest of the day I sit in the park facing the water. Sometimes staring at the beach, I see the old man appear out of the distance, with his dog, and then I'll join him and we'll walk together quietly, the waves lapping at our feet, the distant roar rising and falling, soothing, and at such moments I almost forget how malevolent and predatory the sea can be. I feel indolent, and for the first time in a long while I have started thinking about what to do, where to go. But, when I bring this up with Matteo at dinner, he shakes his head. You are not fit. You think you are, but you are not. The doctor said you need at least a month before you can even think of travelling.

And to take my mind off my restless thoughts he takes me for a walk into the town. We go past the water fountain, past the church, past the café. He points, There is the telecommunication store. It does more business than all the other stores in town.

There is a line of dark-skinned men in front of the store, they are buying SIM cards and call credit, they will call home and let their family know they are alive, they have made it to Europe. As we pass them some of them turn and stare at us curiously, I look back trying to see if I can recognize a face from the camp. I wonder, are they disappointed yet, is this what they expected, these empty, cold and wet cobbled streets, the deserted hotels, the crumbling aged houses? Behind the square is the museum – Matteo says it used to be a fortress, long ago, in the time of Garibaldi, and in front of it is a statue of a soldier on a horse, wielding a sword. The fortress juts out of the rocky ground and over the water, defiantly facing the African shore in the distance. It is surrounded by a wall bearing gun towers at intervals, each tower has a rusty cannon facing outward, ready for the enemy to emerge, spectral, from the sea mist.

We go from room to room in the museum, starting from the ground floor – the entire museum is dedicated to military history. The artefacts are curated to start from the earliest and most rudimentary weapons, spears, lances, bayonets, with drawings of ancient knights dressed in chain-link body armour, on foot and on horses, charging into the fray, and then progressing to rooms showing more sophisticated and contemporary weapons, guns, pistols, muskets, rifles, cannons and machine guns. There are pouches of gunpowder, grenades, rockets. Here is a history of a militarized Europe, of war and conquest and devastation.

Back in my room, I stare out into the park, the dying

light has thrown dappled shadows of the tree leaves onto the flowers. Somewhere behind the house Matteo has shown me a tilled patch of ground where the mermaid in his story had tried to make a small garden last spring before she left. It isn't big, just a practical, workable portion, which she tried to bring alive, pulling out the weeds, crushing the hard lumpy clay with a shovel and soaking it with buckets of water, transferring some of the living roses from the flower beds in the park and planting them in a row. It was tough making plants grow in the acidic, saturated sea air, yet she persisted, daily, doggedly, and at a point he realized she was not really convinced she could make anything grow, really, she was just killing time. She was sowing her fears, her doubts into the ground – who was she, where was this place, who were these people she was staying with? – and hoping some answers would sprout, magically, out of the soil. Matteo would watch from the window, and he saw how she sometimes forgot where she was, squatting and staring at the soil absently for minutes, muttering to herself. Then she caught herself, she looked around guiltily, she sat on one of the iron benches, her head bowed, and he knew the tears were running down her face as she stared out to sea. He came out, casually, as if he were just passing by, taking a walk on the beach, he sat next to her, pretending he didn't notice her covertly wiping her eyes, and he talked disconnectedly, trying to take her mind off her troubles. When she appeared exhausted, when he saw her attention wavering, her eyes turning to the water, he stopped talking and led her back to the house. He'd sit and watch her sing to the child a nursery song in a strange language.

•

She was conscious of him staring at her from the house. Soon he would come out and ask her, anxiously, if she remembered anything at all. They would sit for hours, hardly talking. Once, he pointed at the tall stone building near the water and said it used to be a fortress before it was converted to a museum. A fortress with moats and drawbridge – the moat was now dry, the drawbridge broken. Then he turned to her and whispered suddenly, Sophia.

Sophia? she asked.

You don't remember?

She repeated the name over and over in her mind, trying to see if it resonated, if it struck a chord. Should I know the name? she asked, her face beginning to look confused.

It is your name, he said.

The words came of their own will. He hadn't planned it, but as he spoke it all made sense. At first he thought with time she'd forget who or what she was looking for, where she was going, and settle down. This would be home. She'd get used to the sea, and the house, and him, show him some love. But she had been here for months now and he couldn't wait any longer. And now that he had started talking he couldn't stop. And as he spoke he also believed what he was saying. Every word rang true. Because he wished them to be true.

We were lovers, many years ago. I visited your country. We met. We fell in love.

She turned to him. She ran a nervous hand through her hair. Then what happened, did we break up?

No. We couldn't get married because your parents . . . well, they had another man they wanted you to marry. And I left. I had to come back home. I was heartbroken.

Then what happened?

You promised you would never forget me. You promised you would come find me someday, no matter how long it took.

And you, you waited for me?

Yes, I promised I would never leave my island, I'd wait for you. Time passed, I had almost given up. Then there you were, in the water. You came like you promised.

She wanted to believe him, she wanted her days to have meaning, she wanted the headaches to stop. She believed him. She said, I am sorry. You must have suffered, waiting for me. She took his hand. He leaned forward and kissed her on the lips.

You came, that is all that matters.

That night she tried to make up for the pain she had cost him as she lay under him, her arms and legs locked around him. In the other room the child slept alone for the first time.

•

Carefully they dressed up in the new clothes he had bought for them. She wore white, and over that a red spring jacket. The child wore a blue jacket and khaki pants. The man wore a black suit, a white shirt and a blue tie. They drove in the tiny car to the town centre, the boy sat with his face pressed to the window, following the backward swirl of the lampposts and the narrow streets that receded and convoluted and rose and fell. They got down at the square. The boy watched a family, a man, a woman and their daughter, throw bread crumbs to dun-coloured pigeons that fluttered and settled and fluttered again as people passed. They sat on a bench before the fountain, the man and the woman. They watched the boy join a group of children dipping their hands in the fountain. The town hall was a few metres from the fountain, and the registrar was waiting for them. The registrar asked if

the woman wanted to freshen up in the restroom before the ceremony,
she said no.

Good, he said. Please, come this way.

Afterward, the family of three had lunch in a Greek restaurant,
then they entered the car and drove back home.

•

In the evenings he took her on a drive around the town. It became
their routine. Far from the town centre, on the road that followed the
coastline, with a clear view of the water, half-circling the town. He
drove fast, trying to outrun something behind, some memory, some
history that doggedly followed in their wake. They drove, his eyes on
the strip of empty road ahead, her eyes on the ineffable view of the
sea and sand. They came upon a ghostly housing development of vil-
las and apartments, grand and untenanted. They passed courtyards
and gardens that had started to run to seed, over roads eaten away by
neglect and weather. The waves' whoosh was a lover's lament of lone-
liness. They drove round and round, through some developer's failed
dream of sand and sea that came up against harsh economic reality,
and not a single human being was in sight. The streets between the
villas and apartments were named after famous cities, Naples, Paris,
Milan, Barcelona, Berlin, Frankfurt, Athens, Florence, Vienna, each
one deserted.

•

And then one day she woke up suddenly, it was midnight, but the
moon was shining into the room, and she could see everything, clear
as day. He sensed her movement and asked, Is everything all right?

She turned to him, and he saw that something had changed in her
eyes. She said, My name is not Sophia.

What did you say? He sat up and moved to the opposite side of the bed. She was looking out into the garden, the light on her face, her back to him.

My name is not Sophia. She turned to the man. Calm.

Well, what is your name?

She shook her head, overwhelmed by the memories racing into her head, a flash flood carrying so many things in its stream. He waited, his breath coming out with difficulty. He had seen this before. Soon would come the panic, the tears. He waited.

I have a husband.

I am your husband.

She raised a hand, and in the movement there was a sadness he had never seen before. Please, don't say that. I remember everything.

She looked at him, her eyes bitter.

Well, what is your name?

Basma, she said, and repeated the name slowly, savouring it, like the name of a newborn, uttered for the first time, Basma. I have two children, Omar and his sister, Rachida.

The man stood up. He was naked. He quickly put on his clothes and sat with his head in his hands, saying nothing, not looking at her. That day she moved out of his bedroom and into the guest room with her son. She didn't come out all day, and all day the man stayed in his room, and she could hear him through the wall, pacing up and down, she could hear his father knocking on his door, but he didn't open it. At night she lay awake, and her mind was like a churning sea, throwing out to shore bits and pieces of floating memory.

As he paced his room he asked himself why he was surprised, surely he knew this day would come, his father had cautioned him about it. He loved her, he loved her like he had never loved anything before. He felt like dying.

Be brave, his father said through the door, maybe she loves you too. But she has a child, and a husband. Let her decide what she wants to do.

When she finally came out, she was dressed to leave. She had a little plastic bag with a single change of clothing in it, the boy was dressed in his blue suit. Father and son were seated at the dining table, she went to them and sat, and they could have been a family at dinner, except there was no food in front of them. Finally, he said, Please don't go.

How she had changed. Already he could see the resolute, confident woman she must have been. Where was Sophia, the woman who had flailed about, plucking at plants in the garden, singing soft lullabies to the boy?

She said, her eyes staring neither at him nor at the old man, We were the last to get out. We made our way to the coast and paid five thousand American dollars each to get on a boat. I was scared, I didn't want all four of us on the same boat. What if something went wrong? I told him, go on ahead, find a place and come back for us later. But he wouldn't hear of it. Without you and the children, I die, he said. So we left, all of us. They shot at our boat as we left the coast. I don't know what happened, or why. There was confusion, the screams began and never stopped. Have you ever been on a refugee boat? Pray you never do. Pray your country never breaks up into civil strife and war, that you are never chased out of your home. The boat was really nothing but a death trap, an old, rickety fishing trawler that should have been retired a long time ago. Because we paid five thousand each we got to sit on the upper deck where we could get a bit of fresh air. Some, who were down below in the hold, stacked on top of each other, died within hours of our departure – the children and the pregnant women died first. We saw them bring up the bodies and throw them in the water. Our engine was on fire, the captain wanted to turn back, but we begged him to go on. We would rather die in the water than go back. There was nothing to go back to. My husband tried to save us as the boat sank. He is a great swimmer. He held me and the boy and I held the girl and for an hour we floated, clinging to a raft. A helicopter appeared overhead, and we thought finally we were safe, but after circling for a few minutes it left. I told my husband to let me go, to save the children, but he wouldn't. We decided that he would take the girl, and I would take the boy because he was smaller. He gave us the life jacket. We drifted. I tied the boy to my back. Something, a log, rose out of the water and hit me in the head, and I must have fainted. When I woke up you were standing over me, and I couldn't remember a thing. I guess my mind didn't want to remember. After a while I stopped trying to remember, it was easier to listen to your stories. Sophia. How badly I must have wanted to believe I was Sophia, and that this place is my home and I have not lost a husband, or a child.

He stood up and went over to her. Is there no way I can convince you to stay? You are making a mistake.

Was there really a Sophia?

He went back and sat next to his father, he stared out the window. The sky was low and darkening; it was setting to rain. Seagulls flew over the water in cycles, making weak and shallow dives. He lowered his head, his elbows rested on the table.

Yes, there was a Sophia, but that was a long time ago. Someone I knew as a kid.

She stood up and took the boy's hand. He stood up and followed them to the door. You don't have to go today.

She turned and looked at him. I have to go. I thank you for saving my life. But I am angry at you for lying to me. I have a husband and another child, I belong to them.

You don't know if they are alive. You don't know where to find them. Stay. I can help you find out where he is.

I know where he will be. In Berlin. We agreed, if we ever got separated, to wait there. In Berlin. He has a friend there. Every Sunday we promised to go to a spot and wait, Checkpoint Charlie.

The man followed her out of the house, down the lichened stone steps. She stopped briefly in the garden and looked at the roses that had started to sprout, now wilting in the autumn chill. He took them in the small car to the ferry depot to catch a ferry to the mainland, the first stop in their uncertain journey. As she got out of the car he handed her an envelope.

Take this, he said. Our marriage certificate, you will need it. You can't travel without some form of documentation. You'll also need money. Here. Please take it.

She began to shake her head, opening her mouth to utter no, but he pressed the papers into her hand. You can destroy it as soon as you get to your destination. He stood by the car and watched her and the boy join the line of passengers waiting to get onto the ferry.

•

Finally, the story has come to an end. We are in the park, sitting on the bench on which he and the woman must have sat so many times before, nearby is the patch of ground where she attempted to start a garden.

Basma, I say. Is that why you helped me, why you brought me to your house, in the hope that I might have some knowledge, some information about her?

He shrugs. His eyes are dark, hooded, and for the first time I see how withered and tired he looks.

He says, I am like a man drowning, and I must grasp at

every straw. Have you ever been in love? Surely your wife, or another?

I think of Gina, and I wonder where she might be now. In America, probably, right now she'd be in a studio, in her overalls, painting, trying to capture on canvas something elusive, something even she can't put a name to. Our story is over, the ink has dried, each of us must move on now and it will be as if we had never met, never loved, and never dreamt together.

Maybe not your wife, Matteo says shrewdly, reading my face. Maybe another.

I think of Portia, and I feel light and breathless with longing. I would like to see her again. You are right, I say to Matteo, there is someone else, but I doubt I will ever see her again.

Why did you let her go?

I didn't let her go. Circumstances got in the way.

Far away we can see old Pietro staring at the water, next to him the dog chases seagulls as they skip and flutter over the waves. He looks like he belongs here, megalithic, one with the rocks and sand and waves that throw themselves at his feet like supplicants. The dog yelps, then retreats and returns in a playful dance with the waves and the gulls.

Did you go after her, Basma? Did you try to find her, to convince her to come back?

He says, I went to Berlin, twice, but I just sat in my hotel room and watched the streets through the window all day, then I came back. Twice. I didn't have the will to go into the streets looking for her. I thought, what if I saw her with her husband, her children, and what if they were happy together? I couldn't bear it. So I took the train and I came back. I promised myself to forget her, but then, when the director told me

you were from Germany, from Berlin, and since you have
been among the refugees, I thought, perhaps you might know
something, anything.

I say, What of her husband, what of her children?

He says, What of me? What of love? His voice is at once
pleading and also defiant. I can't sleep. I think of her all the
time. I want to know if she is okay, and the boy.

So I tell him of Manu, the doctor turned bouncer, who
sat for Gina, who went every Sunday to Checkpoint Charlie hoping to see his wife and son there. As I tell him I see
his countenance fall and his eyes grow more hooded. He is a
good man, even if a little unusual, and I owe my life to him.
We continue to sit as the sun goes down, turning the water
and the sand purple and pink. The iodine smell of the sea is in
the air. In the distance the old man appears, heading for the
house, the dog by his side, in the sea a rescue boat rises and
dips on the water, searching for distressed migrant boats.

That evening we leave in the boat as if we were going fishing, then we head south and keep going. I watch the coast
recede and shrink – somewhere out there is the refugee welcome camp on its hilly perch, and I imagine the inmates seated
against the fence watching the water and the distant African
coast hidden in the mist. I imagine the Syrian woman, knocking her head against the fence and moaning the name of her
vanished children, and of her destroyed hometown over and
over, Aleppo.

We will be a few hours, Matteo says, you should go down
and get some rest.

Earlier, before we set out, he asked me if this was what
I wanted, if I wasn't better off staying on in Europe, going

back to Berlin, or even staying on the island with him and the old man. I lie on the bunk downstairs, using the tiny backpack Matteo gave me for a pillow. All my worldly possessions are in there, a pair of pants, some underwear, the book *The Leopard* by Tomasi di Lampedusa. I close my eyes but I can't sleep, under the engine sound I hear the susurration of the wind on the water, and soon I am on the deck, standing by the rail watching the water. It is dark, the fog lies thickly over the water and there is nothing to be seen but the inky black. I feel as if there is no deck under me – I am standing over the water, and when I bend down I see my reflection glowing up at me, my forehead glistens with sweat. I am . . . I look terrified. A restless, writhing motion fills the water. Fish. A school of them in a feeding frenzy, but when I bend closer, my face almost touching the water, I see they are not fish, they are human. Bodies floating face-up, limbs thrashing, tiny hands reaching up to me. Hundreds of tiny hands, thousands of faces, until the surface of the water is filled with silent ghostly eyes like lamps shining at me, and arms reaching up to be grasped; they float amidst a debris of personal belongings, toys, shoes, shirts, and family pictures all slowly sinking into a bottomless Mediterranean. I drift past, and they drift past, and God drifts past, paring His nails. I pull back, tears on my face. *I had not thought death had undone so many.* I repeat the line over and over, rolling it over my tongue like a prayer, till my whisper turns to a scream. A hand on my shoulder is shaking me.

Wake up, Matteo says, we are here.

I sit up and grab my bag, discombobulated from my vivid dream, and follow him up to the deck. At first I don't see anything, then gradually over the bow a finger of light appears. Then more lights. Faint, wavering needlepoints of light.

Tunisia, he says, we can't get any closer than this, I am afraid.

We drop the tiny, inflatable dinghy into the water and using a small rope ladder I lower myself into it. I look up at the face looking down at me anxiously. The dinghy wobbles and rises and falls with the waves, then I begin to paddle. I feel like a man treading water, then I begin to pull away, carried by the flood tide, and soon the coastline is rushing at me. With a mighty heave the water spews me onto land and I am on all fours, my eyes and ears and mouth filled with briny seawater, but underneath me is the firm African soil. I grasp a handful and feel the emotions overwhelm me. I stagger to my feet and look back to sea, but there is nothing to see, only mist and black rushing water.

Book 6

HUNGER

When I got her email saying she'd be in London in July, and if I happened to be in the neighbourhood she'd love to see me, I packed my bag and got ready to travel. The invitation came at a good time – I had completed my dissertation defence back in Virginia and I was contemplating whether to return to Nigeria or to stay on in the US. Her father's English mistress, who was also his translator, had died and her son had discovered a box full of her father's things, including unpublished manuscripts, and she was going to London to pick it up. The flat was in a high-rise on Boswell Street, a narrow back road tucked away in the warren of roads behind Russell Square. There were similar buildings on both sides of the road housing boutique hotels and one or two art galleries, others were council flats with balconies littered with satellite dishes and children's toys – plastic cars and bikes too big to store indoors and too new to throw away, blocking the space between the doors and the stairs, a veritable fire hazard. Not too far away was a park, a rectangle of green enclosed in a chain-link fence, where workers from nearby offices sat during their lunch break to catch half an hour of air and sunshine. The offices were mostly hospitals and labs that seemed to be concentrated in the neighbourhood, over three hospitals within a radius of a few blocks, there were also pubs and cafés. The park soon became our favourite spot, and in the first week we spent hours there every day, mostly in the late afternoon when the workers had left, watching the pedestrians pass, sometimes staying till the lazy summer sun finally dimmed at around 8 p.m.

I had never been to London so she sent me a careful description: *Take the Piccadilly Line and you don't get off till you get to Russell Square station, I will be in a red shirt holding a 'Welcome to London' sign.* As promised, she was standing at the station entrance, unaffected by the stream of passengers coming in and going out through the turnstile, the wind pulling at her long skirt and red button-down shirt, and as promised she had a *Welcome to London* sign which she held stiffly in front of her with both hands. She actually had a sign.

I waited for her with my bag next to a phone booth as she dashed into the Tesco opposite the station to grab a packet of tea and sugar and a bottle of wine. Later, she confessed she hadn't recognized me at the station till I stood in front of her and whispered, –Hi Portia.

In the bathroom I stared at my reflection in the mirror: my hair had thinned and turned white at the sides. Friends in Nigeria and in the US had looked at me once, twice, sometimes thrice before uttering my name, with a question mark, unsure if it was really me. My bones showed at the collar, my cheeks were sunken, but I liked to think the fire still blazed in my eyes.

–What happened? she asked.

–I am fine, I said.

The flat was small, large enough for two, an end unit on the third floor with a single bedroom, a living room and a kitchenette. From the stairwells and behind doorways came voices of children and mothers trying to be heard over the drone of the TV. May, the late owner of the flat, was a lecturer at SOAS, she had lived here with Portia's father before he finally moved back to Zambia. She retired four years ago, the year he moved to Zambia, and she died a year ago, three years after him. She was a pretty woman, even in old age: her picture next to the TV showed a steady kindly gaze, with deep laugh lines around the mouth and eyes. She had married once, early in life, and had a son from that marriage, he now lived in Australia, an accountant with a tidy bookkeeper's mind, and it was he who wrote to Portia's mother about the box belonging to her late husband; he said Portia could stay in the empty apartment while she was in London, the flat was paid for till autumn when he'd come and clear away whatever was left before turning over the flat to the landlord. Here the two aged lovers, the exiled writer and the retired lecturer, had spent their days and nights, alone save for occasional outings to readings and theatres and perhaps dinner with old friends:

retired teachers, editors, writers – some of them exiles living anonymous exilic lives in the big, grey city.

We did not sleep early that first night – it had been two years since we last met, and then for less than a week. I had thought I would never see Portia again, and to have heard from her, and now to actually be with her, left me speechless. I tried to tell her how I felt, but lacking words I simply held her and kissed her slowly on her lips and all over her face before leading her to the bed. Afterward we opened the bottle of wine and sat staring at each other, smiling wordlessly. What were we to one another, lovers, friends, strangers? We sat by the window and talked till the weak, watery sun inched its way over the trees and the morning birds began to chirp. I hadn't talked to anyone like this in a long time. It felt good. I told her about my time at the refugee camp, and about Matteo and his father. When I finished the tears ran down her face.

–I am so sorry, she said.

–Why, sorry for what? I tried to sound cheerful, lighthearted.

Later, when we crawled back into bed, she showed me a picture on her phone. Me and her, standing in the courtyard of the cathedral in Basel, overlooking the Rhine.

–Do you remember? she asked.

It seemed a lifetime ago. I looked different then. I said, –I feel like the guy in the John Donne poem.

–Which poem?

–I don't remember the title, but it is about a lover who left on a long trip. Before leaving he hands his girlfriend his picture so she would remember how he looked in case he returns all worn out and changed by time.

−I know the poem, she said. You really haven't changed that much.

She put her head on my shoulder, running her hand over my chest. −You are the same inside. And that's what matters.

•

When I woke up Portia was hunched over a rugged, much-travelled red Echolac suitcase with combination locks, taking out binders and notebooks, one item at a time. She took out a moleskin diary and flipped through the pages. I went to the kitchen and filled the kettle with water to make tea. My mornings never came into focus till I had a cup of tea in my hand. I made two cups and placed one on the table beside her.

−Thanks, she said.

−What's that? I asked.

−My father's notebooks. There are at least five of these. I am not sure what to do with them.

−What's in them? I asked, taking it from her.

−All sorts of things. Poems, diaries, essays, articles.

She held her tea mug in both hands. She looked around the room. She had been here four days before my arrival.

−Do you think they were happy here? she asked, staring at May's picture, almost glaring at it. There was an unuttered subtext to her question. Was he happier with this woman than he had been with my mother? she was asking.

−Who can tell? Remember, he left her and went back to Malawi to be with your mother. That says lot.

Portia too had changed. Physically she was the same, a bit softer around the eyes, a little fuller around the hips, but the quick clever girl had turned into a quieter, more patient woman. I liked her this way. She was now a mother, she said, almost casually. She showed me a picture on her phone. A curly-haired, twinkle-eyed boy, with a smile like his mother's. She had married the German in whose apartment I first met her in Berlin, couch-surfing. He had turned up in Lusaka three years ago, and he needed a couch to sleep on. That was how it started. He had broken up with his girlfriend, Ina. He was on an assignment, a film company was making a documentary on the 1884–1915 German genocides on the Herero in neighbouring Namibia, and he was writing the script. He didn't need to be in Zambia, actually, but he remembered she lived there and he wanted to see her. He stayed for two weeks, and every night he took her and her mother out, to dinner, to dance, to the cinema, and on the final day before he left he told her he loved her, he wanted to marry her. Her mother liked him, she thought he was a gentleman.

—By then, Portia said, I had given up hope of ever seeing you again. When we parted in Basel, you were supposed to get in touch. I gave you my email, I didn't have yours. When you didn't write I guessed it was because you didn't want to.

She didn't give Hans an answer right away, she held out for six months, till one day her mother said to her, —What do you want, my child? Does this person – this Nigerian – even know you are waiting for him?

And so she called Hans in Germany and said yes. He flew back and they got married in a small church in Lusaka and they moved back to Berlin, back to that same apartment where we first met, and every time she passed my door, where she first saw me standing on a ladder, she'd linger, hoping the door would open and I would step out and say, —Hi, can I help? Finally, she couldn't bear it any more, she told Hans she couldn't live in that house, she told him it was because of the pregnancy, she didn't like climbing the stairs daily, she wanted to live near a park. They moved, out of the city toward Wannsee, but even then she felt Berlin closing in on her, daily, slowly. She fell ill constantly, she was sick for home, sick for something she didn't know. She stayed indoors and cried all day. Hans thought it was the pregnancy, the hormones, and he said yes when she decided to move back to Zambia, ostensibly to give birth at home, to be with her mother.

—I felt myself descending into depression, I was losing track of time, of my mind, and I feared I'd harm myself, she said. Hans didn't come to Zambia with her, he sensed that something had ended. The marriage had lasted less than a year.

—What's the baby's name? I asked.

—David, she said, we named him after my brother. My mother did.

Hans came to visit after the baby was born, twice, he tried to convince her to return to Berlin, but she said no. Her stay in Berlin was over, and going back wouldn't be fair to him. She didn't know how to tell him it had been a mistake. She told him she wanted to raise her child in Africa, surrounded by family. Some days she woke up in the night to scour Facebook, trying to find me. Several times, she called my Berlin number and listened to the German voice telling her the subscriber didn't exist. That was when she decided to write to Gina to ask for my email.

—It was the only way I knew how to contact you. I remember you mentioned she was a Zimmer fellow, so I wrote to them asking for her contact details, I told them it was about a painting. They were helpful. I wrote to her and she wrote back.

–Yes, Gina forwarded the email to me.

•

Of the three of us, Gina had perhaps changed the most. Since Berlin she had become something of a world traveller, when I arrived in Virginia a year ago to complete my PhD she was just returning from a six-month stint in Paris, and was on her way to Venice for the Biennale. She had visited Germany again, many times, had been back to Berlin, and once she spent a month in Dresden. We met in a restaurant in Chantilly not too far away from Dulles Airport, she had an hour to spare before her flight to Rome. I was staying in a drab hotel off Highway 66 in Manassas, and each morning I'd pick up the phone to call her, then put it back again, and when I finally called she told me it was fortunate I called that day, she was on her way to the airport. She sounded happy to hear from me. She looked different, she had a red scarf around her neck, its colour reflected against her skin, making her cheeks and her eyes glow.

–You look great, I said when I sat down.

–You don't look well. What happened? Why didn't you call? How long have you been in the States? Why are you staying in a hotel?

–Which question do you want me to answer first? I asked, raising my hand.

–All of them.

So I told her of Italy, of the refugee camps, of the two months I spent in Tunisia trying to convince the Nigerian embassy I was Nigerian. Finally, they put me on a plane with over a hundred deportees and dumped us at the airport in Lagos.

–Where is your American wife? my mother asked me when I got home. I explained to her that we were separated, but each time people came to see me, she would tell them, 'He came back alone, but his American wife is coming soon to join him.' I could hear the shame in her voice, her son who had gone to America had returned poorer and thinner than he had left. I left as soon as I recovered my health. My father cleared his bank account and gave it all to me; he wanted me gone to spare my mother the pain of having me there, of having to explain to people why my American wife still hadn't arrived.

Our tiny apartment was still there if I needed it, Gina said. She wasn't staying there. It felt too big for her alone so she had moved in with her parents and used it only occasionally to paint. The light there was always good in the afternoon.

–It belongs to you as much as it does to me. How long are you here for?

–I don't know. I am meeting my supervisor tomorrow. I'll leave as soon as I defend my dissertation, maybe six months, maybe a year.

–I'll be away for over a year, she said.

The waiter was standing over us, a smile on his face, his pencil poised. Gina ordered a salad, I ordered the sea bass with asparagus.

–You look weird with your hair all white, she said. She

reached over and touched my hair, as if to confirm the white was real.

–Tell me about your travels, I said.

She told me about Dresden. She had spent a winter month there, painting, and sightseeing. Their guide told them Dresden was the most bombarded city in the Second World War, if not in all of history, 3,900 tons of bombs dropped by Allied bombers, destroying up to 90 per cent of the town, and then, after the war, when the town had a chance to rebuild, they decided to re-create most of the buildings exactly as they had been before the bombardment. Their guide took them to the Altstadt to see the rebuilt cathedral, the Frauenkirche, which took almost ten years to reconstruct, with architects using 3-D computer technology to analyse old photographs and every piece of rubble that had been kept.

–They had the choice to do something new, make a clean break from the past, but they decided to rebuild the city like it was.

–Nostalgia, I said, they were homesick for their past.

She looked disapproving. –Not all of us have that luxury, of a past. My history doesn't offer me much in that respect. Once I go past Martin Luther King and Rosa Parks, there is nothing else but the plantation and after that the insurmountable Atlantic. So, I have learned to look forward, to embrace the new and to shape my future. I find it weird, this clinging to the past.

Gina, I realized, was saying goodbye to me. I felt sad, and proud all at once: I liked what she had become. I was a part of her past, therefore I had contributed to her present. I reached across the table and took her hand. And we sat like that, holding hands, not talking, till at last she looked at her watch and said, –Time to go.

–Have a safe flight. And . . . take care of yourself.

•

–Did you see her when you went to the US? Portia asked.

–Yes, I said.

She was sitting with her head bowed, doing her nails. Her voice sounded remote, almost cold.

–Did you stay with her?

Portia had these dark moments. This morning I woke up and found her crying into her pillow, when I asked her what was wrong she told me about a girl she saw when we were in Basel.

–I didn't tell you at the time, but I saw this girl, a school-girl, a black girl, about six or seven years old. Her hair was nicely braided. The whole class was going somewhere, walking in a neat file, their teachers walking beside them. The black girl was alone at the back of the line. All the other kids were chatting and laughing, except the black girl. I saw her nice braids, and her little red barrette, and I thought of her poor mother, she'd be anxious all day think-ing of her little daughter, the only black girl in the class in that strange, cold country.

•

I told her about my stay in the US – I stayed for exactly one year, and I never saw Gina again after that goodbye in the res-taurant. It was strange being by myself in our small apartment overlooking the empty parking lot, in the evenings I almost expected the door to open and for Gina to walk in, back from work. In the closet she had neatly stacked my clothes and books and binders in a corner.

Our photos still hung on the walls and on the stand next to the TV. In the wedding picture I looked so young and happy, in a black suit, Gina was smiling into my face in her white wedding gown, a bouquet of flowers in one arm, and around us were the faces of her family and our friends. Some of the faces I now couldn't put names to.

The year passed by quickly. I worked on my thesis at night, in the day I walked around the city, I rode the train to the end of the line, I went to the National Mall and walked with the polyglot crowd at the Cherry Blossom Festival. I stood under the Washington Monument and watched parents and children pulling and running after kites, I passed the Tidal Basin to the new Martin Luther King monument and read the wise quotations on the wall. Once, I went to the public library near the apartment and walked between the aisles, running my hand on the book spines. I sat and read the papers, hoping someone would recognize me – this was where I used to teach ESL classes and had formed a nodding acquaintance with most of the staff – but no one did. I passed in front of the information desk, the lady manning the desk was called Jill, and I had often stood there and exchanged small talk with her, but now she smiled vacantly at me and asked if I needed help finding a book.

Gina called me on Thanksgiving Eve from Venice, Italy, and asked if I had any plans for Thanksgiving. I didn't. She said she hoped I was not planning to sit in the apartment alone. She had told her parents I was around and they were expecting me for dinner. The next day I dressed carefully and bought a bottle of wine and got into a taxi to go to her parents' in Takoma Park. Her whole family would be there, cousins, nephews and nieces, uncles and aunts – I was particularly fond of Uncle Keith. On my first Thanksgiving with them before we got married, before dinner the whole family had gone to a nearby park to play football. It was something of a family tradition, Gina told me. I knew nothing about football, but I was conscious they were all sizing me up, trying to see what kind of in-law I'd make. I gamely chased the ball with them, I endured being knocked down multiple times by Gina's six-foot-four, two-hundred-pound knucklehead cousin, Ruben, who was playing football at college. Finally, when I could do so without loss of face, I left the players and joined the old folk cheering from the sidelines. I stood next to Gina's father, who nodded at me encouragingly, and Uncle Keith, who looked at me and said, –That was an awful performance. Clearly you know nothing about football.

I nodded, trying not to appear miffed. My knees were scraped, my ribs were sore from collisions. I thought I had handled myself well under the circumstances.

–Yes. I am more of a soccer person, I admitted.

Uncle Keith, it turned out, was a former football player, now a coach. He walked with a limp, which he got when he broke his leg playing. –Listen, all sports are essentially the same. Decisive victory is the aim of every game, just as it is in war, because all competitive games are descended from warfare. Remember that.

Now my taxi was in Takoma Park and almost at the house. Suddenly I knew I couldn't face them. I couldn't imagine

myself seated there, trying to appear cheerful, trying not to
have to explain to the whole assembly why my marriage to
their daughter, niece, sister, cousin, was no more. I couldn't.
I told the driver to stop. I paid him and told him to keep the
wine. I got down and went into a restaurant and ate by myself,
then I returned to the apartment and sat in front of the TV
till I fell asleep.

On my last day in the apartment, before leaving for the
airport, I signed the divorce papers which Gina's lawyer had
sent over by courier. I sat in front of the computer and tried
to compose a short, sincere email to her: *Thanks for the past
we shared, and good luck with the future*, but it felt inadequate. I
deleted it, turned off the computer, and left.

−No. I didn't stay with her. She was out of the country. It is
over between me and her. I signed the divorce papers.

−Well, what next? You have your PhD. Are you going back
to the US, to become an American, or back to Nigeria?

−I haven't decided.

She went back to her nails. After a long while she said,
−Come with me?

−Where? Basel? Again?

She laughed and shook her head. The dark cloud had
lifted. −No, not Basel. To Lusaka. If you want. And, I can
offer you a job. My mother is retiring, so I will be running the
school. You can work with me.

−I have never been to Zambia. I don't know what to
expect.

−Oh, you will love it. She put down the nail polish. Her

face lit up, her voice became eager, joyful. The kids are great, you will love them. And, it is quiet, peaceful. You will have time to think while you decide what to do next. You can expect to stay with me and my mom. Plus . . .

She held my gaze, a wicked smile on her lips.

–Plus what?

–All of these. She stood up and gestured at her body, shaking her full, braless breasts and her curvy hips. –Think about it.

•

Portia and I sometimes walked from Boswell Street all the way to the British Library. She used to live not far from the library when she was at SOAS, she said. She pointed out a Pret a Manger. She said she and her roommate used to have lunch there every day for a whole term, the roommate's boyfriend worked there.

–This roommate of yours, was her name Portia? I teased.

–You are jealous. Some emotion, at last.

–What do you mean? I can be emotional. I am emotional.

Sometimes we took the opposite route, toward Holborn station and on to the British Museum, or to Covent Garden to mingle with the tourists watching the painted jugglers and magicians. Once we stumbled on a pop-up street market selling food from every corner of the globe. We joined a line at a Thai stand, then we sat and ate in the open air, tears running down our eyes from the spice. It was getting dark when we came back. A crowd was standing in front of our building, some of them holding placards.

–A protest, Portia said.

There were actually two protests, the one in front of our building entrance, and another one across the road, on both sides men and women held up signs, the two groups appeared to be in opposition to one another. Two police cars were parked by the kerb at a distance, their lights flashing.

–What is happening? Portia asked a lady next to her. The lady was wearing a tracksuit, as if out for a jog, except she was pushing a child in a stroller – the child looked contented, swaddled in blankets and sucking its thumb. It appeared a man was hiding in our building, the lady told us breathlessly, an asylum seeker, being sheltered by a humanitarian organiza-tion. She pointed vaguely to a window, –Up there.

At that moment a bus cruised by, and as it passed the crowd before our entrance gave a loud cheer. I looked at the bus puzzled, till I saw what they were cheering. On the side of the bus, in huge black letters were the words: *Foreigners Out!* The other group shouted jeers and threw water bottles at the bus. The bus disappeared at the end of the street, and as we stood there it came back again from the direction where it first appeared, eliciting the same response from the two groups as before. I wondered how long it had been circling the block, round and round, slowly, like a shark circling a drowning swimmer.

–He is Nigerian. His name is Juma. We were back in the room and Portia was on her laptop. I went over and sat next to her. An organization, calling itself 'The Guardians', appeared to have been hiding the escaped asylum seeker for weeks now, moving him from one safe house to another, evading the police and immigration officials. His asylum application had failed and he was about to be deported when he escaped with the help of the group, who claimed the deportation order was illegal since they had an appeal pending. Nativists had finally traced him to our building, and what we saw downstairs was a standoff between them and the anti-nativists.

–It says here he has been on hunger strike for months, and he swears he'd rather die than be deported.

Juma appeared to be quite popular, there were dozens of articles and opinion pieces about him in the papers, some supporting him, others calling for his arrest and deportation. The home secretary had vowed to deport him. There was a photo of him under one of the articles, a gaunt, pensive, yet defiant face, staring unblinking at the camera.

The next morning, I woke up and went to the window almost expecting to see the demonstrators still there, and the bus with its ominous sign circling the block. Had there really been a large red bus circling the block, or was it all a dream? And the police car by the kerb, and the woman with her child in a pram, breathlessly describing to Portia what was going on. The wind blew dead leaves and pieces of paper down the deserted street. Only plastic water bottles trapped by the kerb and a few discarded placards on the grass bore testament to last night's protest. It was only 6 a.m. on a Sunday, the streets were empty, the city was still asleep, recovering from the weekend's endless parties and drinking, getting ready for Monday.

As I sat on the windowsill, looking out, enjoying the quiet, waiting for Portia to wake up, I became aware of voices coming from the hallway outside. The voices had been there for a while, quietly buzzing, and now they seemed to be coming from right outside the door, arguing in lowered tones, as if afraid of being heard, or of disturbing the still-sleeping neighbours. I opened the door and poked out my head. A door down the hall near the stairs stood half-open, the voices were coming from there. I put on my shoes and went over to the door and knocked, the voices stopped, when no one came to the door I stepped in, not sure what I was doing, or what I was going to say. A young man, dressed casually in tracksuit top and jeans, was standing in the middle of the room, alone, and didn't appear surprised to see me. Where was the other voice?

–I'll be with you in a moment, he said, and he went back to his phone, furiously typing a message with his thumbs. Behind him was a table loaded with cartons stuffed with folders from which pieces of paper were falling out. The room was sparsely furnished, a table by the wall, a couch in a corner. I wandered over to a window which opened to the street and looked out at the same view as the one from my room. Now I could hear movement from another room, the sound of things being dismantled, books taken off shelves and put into boxes – that must be the other voice. A windowpane behind the table was broken where a brick had sailed through it last night. I had no doubt this was where Juma was being kept. But where was he? I waited for the young man to look up from his phone, but he kept fiddling with it, sending out texts and staring at the screen, waiting for the ding of the answer. Just then the owner of the second voice came out from the inner room, carrying a carton filled with books.

–You look like you are moving out, I said.

He stopped, carton in hand, and looked from me to the phone-obsessed young man, not sure what to make of me. He ran his hand in his hair and looked around the empty room. He must have been in his twenties.

–The landlord wants us out by the end of the week. You saw the damn fascists throwing rocks at us yesterday. Who are you?

I said, –I live down the hall. I heard the commotion yesterday, and I wonder if everything is okay?

The other young man finally looked away from his phone and said, –You are not from the *Metro*? I thought you were from the *Metro*.

–The *Metro*? I said blankly.

–They were sending a reporter for an interview . . . forget it. What do you want? Now he looked suspicious, turning to the open door as if expecting more people to come in. He went and closed the door.

–I am your neighbour. I heard all the noise last night. And, I am Nigerian, like Juma. If I can be of help . . .

He ran his fingers through his hair, a thoughtful look on his face, weighing me. The other young man dropped the box on the table and stretched out his hand to me. –I am Josh, this is Liam.

We shook hands. Liam appeared to relax.

–Well, Josh said, I have to head out. Nice to have met you.

He left and now it was just me and Liam in the half-empty room.

–Listen, I began, I hope I am not disturbing you or . . .

–Come, Liam interrupted, let me show you something.

I followed him to another room that looked like a study, with bookshelves against one wall. He stood in the middle, staring at me. This was where they must have kept Juma. It looked like a monk's cell, with a narrow cot in a corner, a bare redwood table with a single book on it, a chair; a naked lightbulb hanging from the ceiling threw a dull yellow spray of light on everything. I picked up the book. It was *Hunger*, by Knut Hamsun.

—He read that over and over, as if he was preparing for some exam, Liam said. His voice was low, almost reverential. I opened the pages idly. I could understand why a starving man would read a book about food, but not why he'd read a book about a starving writer. It seemed masochistic.

—Is it true, I asked, that he has fasted for seventy days?

He started to answer but we heard a knock on the door and he hurried out. The reporter, most likely. I put down the book and followed him. A man in a shabby rain jacket and a backpack slung over one shoulder was talking to Liam. I nodded to the newcomer and headed for the door.

—Well, good talking to you . . .

Liam stepped toward me, almost blocking my path, and said, —Listen . . . I was wondering . . . you are Nigerian, right?

—Yes. I am Nigerian.

He lowered his voice. —Can he call you? It'd be lovely for him to have someone to talk to, someone from home.

—Where is he?

He glanced at the reporter, who had gone over to the table and was taking out a notebook from his backpack. —Well, we don't know.

—You don't know?

—Last night, when those fascists started gathering outside, we smuggled him out, through the back entrance. Molly took him to a café near the square to wait out the protest. He gave her the slip. He went to the bathroom and he never came back.

—Who is Molly?

—My colleague, one of the volunteers.

I said, —I am in flat number 20 down the hall. If there is anything I can do . . .

On impulse, which I would soon after regret, I gave him my number. Perhaps I felt the unfairness of it, the crowd with their placards, like a lynch mob, and the bus like a shark circling the block, while the gaunt, terrified Juma lurked in his room, unsure what his fate was going to be. I couldn't help but be in solidarity with him; I had known so many like him along the way, I had been one of them.

Portia noticed me checking my phone.

—You are not listening to me, she said. She was telling me about a cousin in South London. Her mother had called and wanted her to go see him.

—I am sorry, I said, and told her of my meeting with Liam, of the tiny, empty room a few doors down the hallway.

—And they don't know where he is? The Guardians don't sound very professional to me. Who are they?

—Well, I met only two of them, both are young. And there is a third, a lady, but she wasn't with them.

When the phone rang it was almost 10 p.m. The voice was low and apologetic, they were outside and could they come in for a few minutes? We were already in bed. Portia, tired of poring over her father's notebooks, was watching another episode of *Doctor Who* on her laptop, she watched the show addictively, sometimes I watched with her – a Dalek had the doctor trapped, and this time it looked like there would be no intergalactic escape through the trusty phone booth.

–They want to come here? Right now? Portia asked, tearing her eyes away from the screen. It is late.

–They are at the door.

–Bloody hell, she muttered. I changed and went to the living room. Portia cleared the empty teacups from the table while I removed the wine bottle and opener from the windowsill. The doorbell rang. I went and opened the door. There were two of them: Liam, still wearing the track-top and the jeans, followed by a tall, sturdy young lady. She was strikingly tall with a ponytail severely twisted at the back of her head – she looked capable, ready to take charge. Like a nurse, I thought.

–I am Molly, she said. Her grip was firm, and she was a nurse, as it turned out.

I pointed to the couch. –Sit, please.

Liam began to apologize for the unexpected visit, and for the late hour, but I told him it was fine.

–We couldn't come earlier because they are out there again.

We had seen them through the window, arrayed in the same formation as yesterday, including the big red bus.

–Have you found him yet?

–No, Liam said. The worry lines were pronounced on his face. Molly, on the other hand looked calm, unflappable.

–He is fine, I am sure, she said.

–How can you be so sure? Liam snapped.

–If he had been found, if something had happened to him, it would be on the news by now.

Liam and Molly had met Juma at the hospital where Molly worked. He had been brought there from the detention centre after he had started his hunger strike and his health was failing. The officials wanted to force-feed him, pushing tubes down his throat. Molly was the nurse assigned to him, and she was horrified by what she saw. When she was alone with him she asked him about himself and gradually he opened up to her. Liam, her boyfriend, had also been following Juma's story in the news, and together they decided to intervene. One day, Juma tried to escape. Molly met him in the hallway, he was barefooted, his bedsheet wrapped over his hospital gown, he looked confused, searching for the exit. She led him, protesting, back to his room and told him she could help. —You can't make it this way, she told him. I have a plan.

The next day she brought a pair of sturdy boots, a jacket with a hood, sunglasses and a pair of jeans. She hid them in the men's toilet and as soon as the guard was out of the way she led Juma to the toilet where he changed, and then to her car in the underground garage. It was easy, easier than she had hoped. She took him to her one-bedroom apartment, which she shared with Liam. That was how it began.

—Why? I asked. You could lose your job, or go to jail.

—I have lost my job already, she said calmly, and I don't care if I go to jail. I just couldn't sit and watch them try to force-feed him with those tubes, it is horrible, inhumane. It is illegal.

—So, who else is in your organization? I asked.

—Well, we are a small organization, Liam said, looking at Molly.

—How small? You must need a lot of logistics to keep ahead of the immigration officials.

—Well, there are only three of us. Me and Molly and Josh.

–Just three of you? Portia asked, giving voice to my surprise.

–Well, we have done well so far, Liam said defensively.

Liam was a postgraduate student at the University of East Anglia, Josh was a schoolteacher, both were passionate advocates for migrants' rights. Molly was passionate about health care and justice in general. They had made up the name, The Guardians, to make themselves look professional, but there were only three of them. How did they manage it? It hadn't been easy, and as they spoke I could hear the stress reflected in their voices. The organization was born when Juma stayed in their little flat, sleeping on the floor in the living room, then, when they got a tip-off that officials were coming, they moved out. In the past few months they had moved Juma to five different locations, mostly the houses of friends, some of whom didn't even know who Juma was or what exactly was going on. Others knew and were willing to help on principle. All the time they had kept the media involved, sending detailed information about Juma's hunger strike, about the government's efforts to arrest him even though his case was under appeal. They were excited when Josh told them they could bring Juma to this place – the flat belonged to his uncle, a banker who had been posted to Spain and left the flat in Josh's care. I tried to hide my disappointment. The whole plan sounded shockingly rickety, and it was just a matter of time before everything came crashing around their heads. I was not so sure I wanted to be involved in it, that would be foolhardy.

–Well . . . I began, turning to Portia.

–You will need help, she said to Molly, leaning forward. How can we assist?

–Yes, how can we help? I echoed, reluctantly.

But, as it turned out, their request was pretty modest. They wanted me to inquire discreetly among the Nigerian community if anyone knew Juma's whereabouts, if some Nigerian family or organization was hiding him. They felt bad that they had lost him. I didn't know any Nigerian groups in London and I doubted if he'd go to any of them for help, but to cheer them up I promised to ask around.

●

Last night, unable to sleep after our visitors had left, Portia had gone back to her father's diaries and had discovered a forgotten picture tucked in the pages of one of the notebooks. It was her, at age one, the picture was turning yellow at the edges, but the likeness was unmistakably her. She was standing outside in a park or in a yard, it was a spring day, behind her a field of green followed by a row of fir trees overlooking a lake. She was facing the camera, striking a pose, her hand on her hip, laughing.

–I have no recollection of this, she said. She sounded perplexed.

On the back of the picture was a date, and a place. *April 1992, Leeds.*

–My mother never mentioned a visit to Leeds when I was one.

–It is definitely you, I said. The same nose, the same mouth, the eyes confident and beautiful even at that age. On

the back of the picture there was a poem, handwritten, dedicated to her. She read it out, slowly.

SPRING
(for Portia)

It is spring, child
Feel the juices, only last month frozen –
Like the lake outside this window –
Let the juices flow

Stand, totter, fall, then stand again
See, the rabbits are out again
And the leaves on the larch

The colours are here again –
Blue daffodils, yellow dandelions,
And green, evergreen for you.

Rejoice with the vine and the poplar,
Shout viva! for the winter was long,
And the sun is here again!

–It is a beautiful poem, I said.
–He wrote it for me. In Leeds. There was wonder in
her voice. She called her mother, who confirmed that yes,
they had been to Leeds when she was just one, it was a brief
visit, they stayed only one month, March to April. It was her
father's last year at Leeds, the next year he moved to Norway

and they never saw him again till Portia was ten. She read the poem to her mom down the phone.

–I am not sure what to do with the diaries, she said later. So far she had located over twenty poems in the five diaries she had found, not all the poems were complete, some were only fragments, about the weather, the sea. Several were dedicated to May, his mistress. One, titled 'Home Songs', was more complete than the others. In it he talked about his childhood and the first day he left home to go to boarding school. There was, in all, about twenty years' worth of writing, all unpublished. The diary entries were sporadic, going entire years without any entries, but toward the end of his life, from 2009 to 2011, he kept a constant flow of notes with several pages for every single day.

–You should get in touch with his publisher.

–They are all retired by now, or dead.

•

We took the National Rail at Charing Cross. It was after the morning rush hour, and the crush of bodies began to thin out as we went further southward, till there were only about six of us in the carriage. A man seated across the aisle was cackling loudly to himself, his long narrow beard shook and wriggled as he laughed. He looked tired, his eyes were red and he kept sipping at his coffee in between laughs, long noisy sips. Portia glared at him, then turned away to look at the passing scenery outside. Balconies with laundry hanging from the rails, brick walls with unreadable graffiti on them. Next to the laughing man was a young woman trying her best to ignore him. She couldn't be older than fifteen, one hand held on to a stroller with a child in it, the other hand held a phone to her ear. She was dressed in pink sweatpants and a flimsy T-shirt against which her tiny breasts strained.

I watched her hand, the long nails painted red, tapping on the phone with its diamanté-encrusted case, its red colours matching the colours on her nails. The words flew faster now, her fingers tapping a beat on the phone as she emphasized each word in a mash of accents, Caribbean, West African and South London. It was a slow train, stopping at every station on the way. The laughing man stopped at Gillingham. At Crayford the young woman stood up to exit. Then came Abbey Wood. We got down.

That morning, Portia's mother had called to remind her to go see her cousin, who hadn't been back to Zambia since he left to study in England. She had handed the phone to me and said, —My mother, and when I looked at her blankly she had nodded encouragingly. —She wants to say hi, she mouthed.

—Hi, I mumbled. I had never spoken to her mother before, I didn't know how her voice sounded. She asked about the London weather, and whether we had been to Piccadilly Circus. I answered 'yes' and 'no' to the strong, clear voice on the other side. Finally, she asked me to make sure Portia went to visit her cousin, Jonah, because his mother was sick and was worried about him.

—I am sorry, Portia said afterward, I took you unawares.

—It's okay, I replied. I was surprised, and impressed, that the mother was fine with the idea that her daughter was here with me, alone, in London. But then, Portia had always made it clear how close she and her mother were. I wondered what she had told her mother about me. Did the mother worry if I was a responsible person, if I was taking care of her daughter? Of course, she must, what mother wouldn't.

I thought of my mother. When I came back from Italy she had pretended I was not home when friends came to see me, or she'd say I was asleep. One day my father said to me, –Your mother had built so much hope on you. She used to tell her friends one day she'd go visit you in America, to meet your wife and play with your children.

My father looked tired, he sat there, not looking directly at me. –Listen, I don't know what happened to you. I just hope you did nothing illegal. I hope you can go back someday and set your affairs in order.

We exited the station and followed the line of litter by the sidewalk, papers, beer cans, cigarette packets, marking the path like signposts. We passed a Waitrose, a curry shop, a laundromat, Portia taking seemingly random turns as guided by her cousin's voice on the phone, and finally we were facing a cluster of council houses behind tall birch and elm trees somewhere off Abbey Road. The houses looked identical: semi-detached, each with a picket-fenced garden at the back and green plastic trash containers at the front. A line of square flagstones led to the front door. Portia rang the doorbell and the door opened. A man in his thirties stood there, still holding the phone to his ear, dressed in Arsenal FC jersey and shorts, and soccer boots, looking like he was about to step out to the training field. He hugged Portia and shook my hand.

–Come in. You guys are just in time. The match has just started. Ten minutes in.

We followed him into a narrow hallway, stepping over a pile of mail covering the doormat, and into a dark and poky living room illuminated by the light from the big TV screen dominating one wall.

—Sit down, Jonah said, his eyes on the screen.

Now I noticed two kids, a boy and a girl, seated on the floor directly facing the TV, they were also wearing Arsenal jerseys. One said Thierry Henry on the back, the other said Pires, the father was Patrick Vieira.

—Hey, Tom, Sheila, say hi to your auntie Portia. The last time she was here was when? He turned to Portia.

—Four years ago? I was at SOAS then, so about four, five years now.

—Wow, Jonah said. Tom was only four then, and Sheila was two. Look at them now.

Tom and Sheila turned briefly and shouted, —Hi Auntie Portia, in unison, their faces dull and expressionless, then they turned back to the screen. Arsenal was playing Tottenham Hotspur. Jonah sat on the edge of his seat, wrapped up in the game, following every strike, every save, groaning or cheering. Often he'd lean forward and clap his son on the back. The kids were as animated as their father.

—Did you see that, did you see that, Dad? the boy shouted. He ran to the kitchen and we could hear him telling his mom what had just happened. The mother had only briefly stepped into the living room to welcome us and then returned to the kitchen, a small woman with a pinched, fierce face. At half-time Jonah stood up and stretched. He looked hopeful – the game was tied at 1–1. He went to the kitchen and came back with three cans of beer, he handed one to me, one to Portia, and opened one for himself. –To Arsenal, he said, raising his can. I have a good feeling about this one.

His wife came in and sat on the arm of his seat, draping one arm over his shoulder, and it looked to me as if she was restraining him. Jonah waved his beer at her in a salute. She had a half-smile on her face, she refused to meet my eye, or Portia's, she kept her eyes fixed to the TV, but it was obvious she wasn't watching the game. The halftime break was over, the players were coming out of the tunnel, making the sign of the cross as their legs touched the field, some bending down to touch the grass, finding their way to their positions. Things took a downward turn for Arsenal in the first ten minutes, and by the end of the match they were down 3–1.

Jonah crushed his empty beer can and flung it against the wall. He jumped up and rushed to the kitchen, his wife threw an apologetic look at us before she followed him, and soon we heard the sound of a scuffle. I stood up, but Portia shook her head. I sat down. The children were still seated, staring at the screen where the pundits were analysing the just-concluded match. They looked as if they were waiting for the players to come back from the locker room, and the game to restart, and their team to reassert its invincibility.

Jonah came back, a bottle of Smirnoff vodka in his hand. He flopped into his seat with a loud sigh and slapped the bottle on the table, he didn't glance at us, not even once. We watched as he filled a glass to the brim and drained it in one go, and repeated the same twice. Half the bottle was gone in a few minutes. I heard the steps of the wife slowly climbing the stairs, each step squeezing out a loud creak, and then the sound of a door closing and it was like a light switch turned off. The children continued to watch the screen. Portia was looking at her cousin, a sad look on her face. He sat slumped in his seat, his face buried in his hands, shaking his head violently, and soon a muffled cry came out between his fingers. –Goddamn you, Gunners! he sobbed, why, Arsenal, why?

After a while the wife came down, she stood at the door, looking at him.

–We will be going now, Portia said, standing up.

She walked us to the door, her back straight, her head high. –He lost his job, you know, she said, looking directly at Portia, the half-smile on her lips. He had a good job at the factory, then the drinking started. He can't keep a job. Security, deliveryman, waiter, taxi driver, he has tried everything. Now he has stopped trying. He watches football and he drinks.

•

The protesters were gathered again, about a dozen persons on both sides of the road, as usual the nativists were closer to the entrance, bunched together, holding up their placards and shaking them in the air. They jostled us as we passed through them, calling out: 'Go back!' and 'Where is he?' and 'Fucking illegals!' Portia calmly opened the front door while I stood behind her, positioning my back against hurled missiles or words. I pushed the door shut behind me and held her before the stairs where she stood, shaking and unable to climb. I felt the shivers traversing her body and I held her tighter till they ceased. For the first time I began to contemplate the possibility of our moving out to a hotel, we might not be safe here. The hallway leading to our door was dark, and so at first I didn't see the two figures standing in front of a door next to ours, huddled in the dark, dressed in long coats, the taller figure was checking in her bag as if for a key, but as we got closer she looked up and I recognized the face: Molly. At the same time she said, −It is me, Molly.

−Hi Molly, I said.

The other lady remained a step behind Molly, her face in the shadows. Now I saw she was black, and her head was covered in a head scarf that fell to her shoulders like a veil. They followed us inside and sat on the couch and now, in the brighter light of the living room, the second lady's face looked vaguely familiar. I had seen those eyes somewhere. Portia went into the kitchen to make tea, I followed her.

−I wonder what they want, I whispered, and the other lady looks familiar, doesn't she?

−It is not a lady, Portia said, it is a guy, it is *him*. Didn't you see his shoes, and the hands?

Of course. She was right. I returned to the living room, and yes, it was him, the head scarf was off, now lying in a pile next to his feet, next to the muddy, broken, laced-up dress shoes. He sat hunched forward, hands clasped between his knees, his eyes looking out at me, waiting, unsure of his welcome. It was a face used to being turned away, kicked out, a pariah dog. I sat, facing them, waiting for Molly to speak.

−We found him, she said.

Juma had wandered back by himself, disguised in a head scarf. Molly looked sheepish, like she was about to make a request she knew was outrageous, one she shouldn't be making. I steeled myself for it.

−Where is Liam? I asked.

She looked at her phone. −I am expecting his call. He has

gone to meet a pastor at St Luke's. He is one of our supporters, he has promised to put Juma up for a while. It is not safe for him here any more.

I turned to Juma and smiled. —Hello.

He shook my hand, then laid his palm over his heart. The gesture took me by surprise, it was a common part of greeting back home, to put the right palm over the heart after a handshake, but I hadn't seen it done in a long time, and I certainly wasn't expecting to see it here.

—Hello, he said. His voice was hoarse, whistling out of his mouth, the long hunger strike had drained him. He accepted the cup of tea from Portia.

—Thank you. I can drink tea and water only, he said. He seemed careful to explain how scrupulously he was observing the rules of his hunger strike.

Molly said, —I am sorry to surprise you like this. But Liam said you are from the same place as Juma, that you are willing to help.

When I said nothing, she looked at Juma, then at Portia. She lowered her head. —We have nowhere else to go.

Another brick had been thrown into the window last night, and the landlord was threatening to call the police, he wanted them out immediately. Tomorrow, if things worked out with the pastor, they'd move to the church, but tonight they needed a place for Juma to stay. They feared either the police or the nativists outside would come banging on the door at any minute. They couldn't even slip Juma out through the back, the protesters had discovered the back entrance and some of them were stationed there. Molly and Juma had been hiding in the stairwell and in the hallways, waiting for us, since 2 p.m. We had not headed home directly after leaving Portia's cousin's house, we had wandered aimlessly for a while, then we went to the British Museum to view the Egyptian collection, we stopped at a Caribbean restaurant for dinner, and from there, instead of taking the train back, we walked about for almost an hour, then we sat in the park for a while, and all that time they were waiting for us, skulking by the doorway, going up and down the stairs, careful not to be recognized by residents who passed them in the hallway or on the stairs.

–Listen, I began, we don't own this place, like you we are sort of caretakers . . .

–It is okay, Portia said from the kitchen. I smiled and shrugged at Molly. –He can stay. For a night.

After Molly had left, I asked Juma if there was anything he needed. He needed the bathroom. He said he hadn't showered in two days. I showed him the bathroom, and the extra towels in the closet. He took off his broken shoes and walked to the bathroom in the flip-flops I gave him. Portia stood looking at the shoes, the heels were so eaten away I wondered how he was able to walk in them, the socks, stuck into the shoes, were patched and grimy. –These socks need to be aired, she said, they stink.

We debated what to do with them: throw them in the trash and get him new ones tomorrow, or take them to the laundry, which might not be worth the trouble, they were practically coming apart in threads. We decided to take the shoes with the socks out and place them by the door – he would find that least offensive, it was customary back home to leave shoes out by the doormat. And then there was the matter of food: what if we wanted to cook, Portia liked to make omelettes in the morning, would that interfere with his hunger strike? It would be extremely cruel to cook while he struggled with hunger. Fine, we would skip breakfast tomorrow, and if he was still here at lunchtime, we would eat out – it wouldn't kill us to alter our routine for one day. Hopefully Liam would be here to get him before the end of day. Portia hung his boxy jacket in the closet, the scarf she also hung carefully next to the jacket.

He sat in front of the TV, his eyes glued to the news. I wondered if he was waiting for news about himself. I asked him,
–Where did you go to yesterday? They were searching for you.
–I took the bus, he said.
–The bus?
He nodded. –Yes. It is really safe on the bus.
He explained that when he first came to England he used to take the bus at night, in winter it was the warmest and safest place he could be. He'd take the bus plying the longest routes, his favourite was the one going to the airport, and he'd stay on for hours, sometimes as long as three hours on one bus, back and forth, only getting down to look for something to eat.
–I was new in the country, I had only my bag, a very small one, containing just my toothbrush and one change of clothes and a book or two. I was afraid to go anywhere or do anything. The bus seemed the safest place to me.
–And the drivers, didn't they complain?

–No. Sometimes I'd hang around at the airport. I didn't stick out, so many faces coming and going. And there is good food there, in the bins outside. I did that for months before they caught me.

–Who?

–The immigration. A driver must have reported me. He stopped talking abruptly, his eyes glued to the TV. Portia nudged me and whispered, –He needs rest.

She gave him a blanket and asked if he needed anything before we turned in. No, he didn't.

In the bedroom I said, –What if Molly and Liam don't turn up tomorrow?

She seemed less worried than I was. –They will come.

After we turned off the light I stood briefly by the window. The protesters were still out there, standing with their signs, some sitting by the kerb smoking, in the corner the police car waited idly.

He was still sleeping when we woke up. We decided to let him sleep and we went out for a walk. We ate in a little place just opening, the owner looked sleepy as she went from table to table, arranging chairs and laying down the cutlery. When we finished we stopped by a fruit stand and Portia bought a crate of apples. He was awake when we returned, watching TV. Portia first put the apples in a bowl by the window, then, with a guilty look at Juma, she moved the bowl to the kitchen. He noticed and said to her, –You really mustn't worry about me. And, as if to further put her at ease, he broke into a story about fruits. He seemed to have a story for every occasion – it was his way of communicating, with stories of all he had been through. Or perhaps it was his way of trying to forget his hunger, and he did it with unexpected stamina, his hoarse voice droning with no inflection. His English was adequate; the English of a non-native speaker, learned mostly from books, making up his own pronunciations of words he had never heard spoken.

–Once, he said, in Greece, two years after I had left home, a friend and I were attacked by skinheads. They trapped us in a building for two days, with no food.

–How did that happen? I asked.

He looked at me and then at Portia, straight in the eyes as he spoke, pinning us down, making sure we paid attention.

–Well, my friend and I had been picking strawberries for over a month for a farmer who then refused to pay us, and when we complained, he had sent these youths after us. We were passing through Greece, trying to make our way to France and then to London. We never planned to stay long in Greece, we arrived at the harvest season, and my friend, Hassan, I met him in a camp in Italy, he is an Afghan, he said it would make sense to arrive in France with some money to pay the people smugglers, or guides as they preferred to be called, who'd get us to England, and so we worked. Five euros a day, plus food. We worked, and at first the farmer was paying us regularly, he'd send his manager in the evening each day with his little bag of money and we'd line up and he'd hand out our money. And then the pay stopped coming. The first day we thought it was a mistake, we went to work the next day, and the next day, now he was owing us for a few days, and when a whole week passed with no word from him, we went

to his office in a group to protest. But he had been expecting
us. The police were there, he must have had them on standby,
like he had done this before. They told us to leave the farm,
and we did, peacefully. We went back to our tents. We were
camped in a park outside of town. Early the next morning the
skinheads came in their black shirts. They started breaking
our tents and beating us with baseball bats. There were many
of us, a few hundred, including women and children, but we
were no match for this dozen or so young men. They were
full of fury, and now, looking back, I wonder why they were
so angry, they were clubbing children and women, kicking
them, screaming. Well, we ran away in different directions,
my friend and I entered an abandoned building and we were
trapped in this building for two days. The skinheads knew we
were in there, but they didn't come in to get us, they waited
outside, it was a game for them, they wanted to starve us into
submission. Two days, with no food, only a little water in a
bottle, and no heating. They waited in a bar across the road,
taking turns to watch us, and when the bar closed they waited
in the street, they knew we wouldn't be able to slip out, there
was only the front exit. We could see them, occasionally coming out to look up at the building, in their black shirts and
boots. My friend Hassan almost gave up. I told him to hold
on, he was crying and begging me to allow him to surrender,
then miraculously we found a can of preserved apples in a
closet in the kitchen. We opened it and drank the juice, then
we ate. We were able to last a day longer on that can, and that
day the skinheads gave up, they just left, and we were able to
get out. When we opened that can and I took out a piece of
apple, the smell of it brought tears to my eyes. I remembered

all the fruits I ever ate growing up, the mangoes, the bananas, the melons, the pineapples. I wanted to go home. The longing for home was so strong I could feel it in my stomach. It was a moment of weakness I never allow myself to indulge in any more. Hunger is a tool. It is power. By refusing to eat, you are telling your enemy, There is nothing you can do to me any more. If I am willing to starve myself to death to prove a point, what else is there to fear?

—Why did you leave Nigeria? I asked him.

The stories kept coming, discursively, randomly. He sat on the couch, the blanket draped over his lap covering his knobby knees and shrunken calves. The sentences tumbled out and it was nothing short of fascinating that so many words could be coming out of this small frame. In the refugee camp in Calais, he had met a woman who used to be rich back in her country, she had a restaurant and a big house, cars and servants, and then she had to leave to save her life. In the camp, bereft of everything she once possessed, she would put on airs, she would refuse to eat, wouldn't take a bath, she would lie in her tent, on a mattress, calling out the names of her maids, now back in her country, to come and clean up the place, to draw her a bath, she would get angry when she got no response and she would storm out of her tent and stalk the little space before the tent, throwing out curses, waving her hands at the children gathered to watch her tantrums. It was sad to see. He didn't know what happened to her afterward. He was there for just two days, but it was the bleakest place he had ever been, the Jungle, they called it, worse than Niger, or Greece, or Germany. In Germany, he had witnessed a demonstration in Berlin, at the Oranienplatz. A man had stayed up in a tree for three days, defying the police who had come to break up the refugee tents. Juma's voice was full of admiration. The police were flummoxed, they didn't know how to handle the man. He stayed there, in the cold European winter, hugging a tree branch, in the falling rain, shitting and pissing on himself, with no food, and only rainwater to drink, but not coming down.

They came and took him away in the afternoon. The landlord, it appeared, had relented after a call from Josh's uncle, he had given them two more days, and then they had to move out.

–Will he be okay? I asked Liam.

I realized Juma might not be all there, mentally. His travails had taken a toll on his mind and often he appeared to be lost, drifting and sometimes hardly aware of where he was or what he was doing. Liam shrugged. –We have no idea. Our greatest fear now is the authorities. Our contacts told us to expect a raid at any moment. We are trying to mobilize the media, to build up some public pressure to stop them.

The demonstrations began early that afternoon. From our room we could hear the chants, swelling and ebbing, they sounded like soccer fans in a stadium, without the density, without the mass, but there was no mistaking the passion. I kept my ears cocked, expecting to hear the sound of boots marching to door number 12, for a call for them to open up, or for a battering ram breaking down the door. But nothing happened. There was a brief mention of Juma on the news, on Channel 4. The shadow immigration minister was condemning the

Home Office's cruel and inhumane immigration policy, and the promise to create a hostile environment for immigrants. Migrants' rights groups were urging their members to go on hunger strike in solidarity with Juma. Inmates in detention centres all over the country were refusing to eat.

–Something is going on down there.

Portia was by the window, looking out at the demonstrators. I joined her. Today the anti-nativist group was larger, some had Juma's name boldly printed on their placards.

–Well, it seems our friend is winning hearts and minds, I said. I feared that this newfound support might work against him. The government wouldn't like to lose face, and might feel compelled to act quickly. My fears were justified, as it turned out.

The next day the police came. Early in the morning, when the street was still asleep, and the sidewalk was still littered with picket signs and water bottles and cigarette butts from last night's protests, we heard loud banging on a door down the hall and I jumped up and rushed to our door. There were five of them, dressed in riot gear and helmets. The door opened and they walked in. Now Portia had joined me at the door. She slipped her hand into mine and held tight.

–What is happening? she asked. But she knew what was happening. After a while they walked out again, two hefty men holding him by his thin, twig-like arms, his skinny, shoeless legs barely touching the ground. Behind them came Molly, also being led by the arm, and then Liam and Josh, and all the way down the stairs Molly's combative voice rang out clearly, –You can't do this. It is not right. You have no right.

Then the footsteps ceased, and the front door closed. We

rushed to the window and caught a sight of the top of the police van pulling away.

—What should we do? Portia asked. She was close to tears. —Is there nothing we can do?

I watched her face crumble, like a child's sand castle on the beach dissolving before the waves.

—I am sorry, I said, holding her.

—It is not fair, she said, echoing Molly, it is not right.

When I was in secondary school I had witnessed a public execution, when such things were still happening in Nigeria. Three robbers had been brought to the soccer field on the outskirts of town and we had come to watch, children, men, women, some with infants tied to their backs. The robbers, their hands tied behind them, were led out of the military pickup and lashed to sand-filled oil drums. I was surprised at how young they looked, like teenagers, their faces sleepy, dazed. We watched the soldiers line up in front of them, and after a barked order from a captain the soldiers opened fire. It was quick, and brutal, and in a minute the men, who a while ago had been alive and young and maybe even hopeful, were now dead, their heads lolling on their necks, and their lifeless bodies being untied and dumped into the pickup. Later, my friends told me that I kept screaming as the shots rang out, over and over: It is not fair! It is not fair!

—I know, I said, hugging Portia tightly, my cheek against hers, feeling the tears streaming down, and I wasn't sure if they were all her tears or mine, I am so sorry.

It was the last time we ever saw Juma, in the flesh. But his images kept popping up everywhere. The news was a brush-fire roaring the name of Juma. There were debates and hurried justifications for what happened. On every TV channel the red-faced home secretary faced a battery of microphones and tried to give plausible explanations why the government found it necessary to spend all that money to deport the Nigerian, and bungle the whole thing in the process.

That morning, they had taken him straight to Luton Airport and bundled him into a specially chartered plane to fly him straight to Nigeria. I imagined the scared Juma huddled in his seat in the plane, empty but for the two security officials sitting on either side of him, too weak and confused to protest or resist, the night outside the window taxiing past, and then the uplift into the clouds. In Abuja the Nigerian government refused to grant the plane permission to land and it had to turn back to London, with its perplexed passenger, after a brief stop in Malta to refuel.

•

It felt strange to come out of our building and not be met by the protesters, with their placards upraised, faces snarling, and shouting obscenities. Molly and Liam were waiting for us by the entrance, and I remembered how they had waited on the stairs that day, two weeks ago, Molly and Juma, like two undercover characters in a B movie. When Liam called and said he had a letter for us from Juma, we had invited them over, but they said they'd rather meet elsewhere, in a pub nearby, and I didn't blame them, the building must hold unpleasant memories for them.

It had rained overnight and there was still a chill in the air, rooks in a nearby rookery called valiantly to each other, lending some cheer to the dull, damp day. We sat in a crowded café behind a bus stop, there was a match on TV and the excited crowd vociferously cheered and jeered the progress of the match. We sat in the back, away from the screen, and ordered a beer each.

–Where is he kept? Portia asked.

In reply Liam handed me the letter.

–His lawyer gave me this. For you both.

Portia and I opened the letter as soon as Molly and Liam left. As Portia read it out aloud, Juma's voice jumped off the page, and it felt like he was there with us, his impossibly sonorous voice coming out of his scrawny, diminished frame, continuing his narrative thread where he had stopped two weeks ago:

You must have heard on the news by now, or from Liam, how my deportation didn't work, and how I am now back in the UK. Let me just say I never thought I was coming off that plane alive. But I don't want to talk about that ordeal, it is too painful. Instead, I want to tell you why I left home. Remember, you asked me, and I never got a chance to tell you. Well, to answer your question, I have to tell you my whole story. But then, some of it I have already told you, and some you have experienced yourself in the course of your travels. This will be a long letter, but I have time here at the detention centre. I spend the days reading books sent to me by kind charities. Today I am reading The Lonely Londoners. *It is about immigrants from the West Indies. Their English is sometimes hard to understand, but I empathize with their situation. 'Are the streets of London paved with gold?' a reporter asks one of them. Very funny. I guess most of them didn't come for gold, they came for a better life, for a better chance. I imagine their lives in the Bayswater, how they negotiate the streets filled with signs and graffiti telling them, 'Keep the Water White!' Nothing has changed. As I write, I remember that bus with its warning sign driving round and round the block. But to go back to my story, I'll take you to the night I left home. It will take me a few days to finish writing, so you will have to forgive me if in places it feels disjointed or if I become repetitive.*

The school where I taught had been attacked by religious extremists. One of their aims is to stamp out Western education. We had been hearing of them for weeks before they came, how they go from town to town, attacking police stations and taking away guns, and attacking local banks and taking away money, every day we see a steady stream of people fleeing from the killers, they pass through our town in increasing numbers. Some have been walking for two or even three days, mostly women and children. I remember one woman, she must have been over seven months pregnant, and when we advised her to stop in our village and rest, she refused. She wanted to put as much distance as she could between her and the killers. We didn't ask her where her husband and the rest of her family was.

That night our village was attacked. The school where I taught was attacked first. It was located a little outside of town, and from our house we saw the flames rising in the night sky. They went to the principal's house and killed him and his wife and three children. They drove through the town in their pickups, firing into the air and shouting religious slogans. I tell you, I have never known fear like that. Each shot was so loud, imagine someone knocking on your door with a rock in the middle of the night, the sound cutting through your dreams. My old father came to my room and told me to run. He handed me a little package, in it was all his life savings. He is over seventy, he and my mother, and they said they were not run-

ning, they'd stay there and face whatever fate had in store for them. 'The worst they can do to an old man like me,' my father said, 'is to put me against the wall and shoot me. As for your mother, they don't kill women. But you, if you stay they will take you and turn you into a killer.'

My father was trying to make me feel better about going away, and I knew he was right, but it was hard to turn away from them and leave, knowing I might never see them again in this life. Well, that is how I left home, with only the clothes on my back.

Why did I leave my country? Well, I didn't even know I was leaving my country. We ran all night long, we crossed a stream, and in the morning they told us we were in another country, Cameroon. We camped in an open field at a school, sleeping on the grass, men and women and children, still too dazed to know what was happening. But our ordeal was not over yet, in fact, it was just beginning. Two days later the terrorists crossed the stream and attacked that schoolyard, killing over half of the people as they slept in the open, the rest of us, the lucky ones, we had to run again. We ran for a whole day and when we finally stopped, they told us we were in another country, the Federal Republic of Niger. I was a refugee. I had no family, no home, no friends, the people running with me were my new family.

I was in Niger for over six months. We were kept in an open field, over ten thousand of us. There was no town or village around us for miles, in the distance there were nothing but baobab trees and scrublands and a few nomadic settlements. I don't want to bore you with the details, I don't want to say how much I suffered, or what kind of suffering I witnessed, but imagine this: over ten thousand people living in a place the size of a secondary school, how much food would be enough to feed them, how many emergency toilets would be enough to serve them, and just imagine the darkness at night because there was no electricity, and the mosquitoes were everywhere because it was the rainy season and sometimes the tents we were in would be swept away by the storm and we had to sit like that, huddled under the falling rain till morning came. And every day people died like flies. You would see a child today, playing in the dirt, tomorrow they'll tell you he died in the night. Often I'd look around me and ask myself, Where am I? Who am I? How did I get here? I saw how others had already become used to this lifestyle. Strange how life goes on. There were people actually giving birth, and getting married and children going to school, all in our ever-burgeoning camp. But my eyes were always turned toward home, I dreamt every day of my father and my mother, and I wondered what had happened to them that day I left.

Every once in a while, officials from the Nigerian government would visit to assure us things were getting better at home, the war was being won, and that soon we would go back home. Six months. The same story. But instead of shrinking, the camp grew daily with new arrivals. And one day I said to myself, You are never going back home. At night we listened to the radio, mostly BBC and the German Africa radio, and from there we learned that the war was only growing, the killers were taking more towns and villages, and they had already established what they called a caliphate, and soon they would be attacking villages here in Niger. Twice our camp was moved, away from the border region. And that was when I finally accepted that I might not be going back home, not so soon anyway. To stay in the camp would be to die, no doubt about that. I decided to leave. Others had left already, mostly the young and strong and healthy. Every day men came from Libya and Algeria and Morocco to tempt us to leave with them. I gave them the money my father *gave me, we left, there were ten of us, three men and four women and three children, two boys and a girl. I will not bore you with how we sat huddled in the truck, hot and baking in the merciless heat, or how the truck broke down somewhere in the middle of the Sahara Desert, near the town of Agades, and how we joined other groups of travellers to walk the rest of the way, with no food, and little water, and how we refused to look back when those walking alongside us suddenly slumped and fell into the burning sand, never to stand up again. I made it to Libya, only to be arrested by border police. I was in prison for many days, weeks, or even months, who knows? We were kept in a dark room and forgotten, in that room I heard different stories from those who had been there for days and weeks and months: they said we were being kept there to be sold to people who would harvest our kidneys and hearts and other organs. Others said no, we would be sold to rich households to work for ever as slaves. I will not tell you how, to survive, we had to drink our own urine, or that only about six out of the twenty men locked up in that room eventually made it out. I had sworn to myself I was going to make it. I had already started training for hunger. One day we heard the sound of gunfire, and then our door was thrown open by men carrying guns and they told us we were free to go, just like that.*

I was in that hell in Libya for a year.

I worked, when I was able to, I won't tell you what manner of work I did, but I was able to save up a thousand dollars after a year. Why did I leave? How do I know? I knew that to stay alive I had to keep moving. I found myself in a group getting ready to cross the Mediterranean for Europe. They gathered us at gunpoint in a little harbour in the middle of the night, hundreds of us, men and women and children, families mostly. It was a sad sight to stand there with that group, knowing that each one of them had a similar or even a more sad story than mine. I saw a man and his wife and two children, dressed in expensive coats and shoes, the wife was carrying a very fine handbag, as if she was in an airport waiting to fly for a holiday.

Later I discovered why our guides had us at gunpoint. You were not allowed to protest where you were assigned in the boat, regardless of how much money you paid for the crossing. It was tight. It was noisy. Next to me a group of women was singing, Hallelujah! They kept singing. It was like a church revival. I was positioned down below deck, next to the portable toilet that served the over three hundred people in that rickety vessel, and which soon overran with urine and faeces. I will spare you the details.

The boat sank of course, less than an hour after we set out. I don't know what happened, I was down there, next to the toilet. Some said we were shot at by a militia boat, some said it was the same traffickers who wanted to take us back and make us pay all over again, I don't know, and right now it is not that important how or why it happened. All that matters as our boat sank into the water was that I couldn't swim, and that people were clawing their way up to the deck, kicking and screaming and holding on to their children's hands. Most of them, like me, didn't have life jackets and couldn't swim. I was saved by that stinking toilet. One moment I was down there below deck, next moment I was underwater, and then I came up, and in front of me was the blue plastic portable toilet. Some pocket of gas, or maybe all that decomposing shit, was making it float. I held on. I wouldn't float for long, I knew. All around were people struggling, floating, screaming. Children floated past, and their mothers, belly-up before sinking, plastic slippers, bowls, books briefly floated, and soon there wasn't anything at all. There was nothing, no heaven, no earth, no boat, only water and the sound of wind over water. It didn't take too long for the toilet to sink, luckily

*for me at that moment a dinghy came by, and they pulled me in. In
the dinghy were two rescuers and a father and his daughter.*

*The father was the most heartbroken, wretched man I have ever
seen. His wife and his son were out there in the water, and he was
here in the flimsy craft with his daughter. He pulled at his hair, he
strained his eyes looking into the horizon, hoping to catch a glimpse
of them. He was a good swimmer and he jumped into the water and
swam around, searching, and then his daughter, about ten years old,
began to cry and call after him and he quickly came back. He sat, torn
and helpless, and me and the other men held him, scared he was going
to do harm to himself. I said, remembering what my father said to me
the night I left home, 'If it is God's will, you will see them again.'
But he kept looking around, standing up, screaming into the wind till
night fell, till his voice grew hoarse, and then he sat down and held his
daughter in his arm and together they cried and none of us could console them. Often I wonder what happened to them, father and daughter, if they ever reunited with their family. Later, I learned, that of the
over three hundred of us who left Libya that morning, only me, the
man and the girl, and five other people survived.*

*Why did I survive? I often wonder. I am not a very religious man,
but you can't go through the things I went through without realizing
there is a God, somewhere, in the affairs of men. But sometimes,
also you wonder if there is a God, why does He allow such things
to happen. Why are some people born to suffering and heartbreak,
while others from the day they were born till they die know nothing
but happiness and pleasure? Is God biased, what did I do to face
so much suffering? What did that man and that little girl do to be
separated from their family? I mentioned this once to a clergyman
I met in Germany. I had spent the night in an empty church, cold*

and hungry, in the morning the clergyman woke me up, and without saying a word, offered me food and shelter for that night. We got talking and I asked him that same question. Is God partial? He said sometimes our suffering only prepares us for a great destiny. I laughed in his face. How were the men and women who perished in that boat being prepared for a great destiny? They are dead. Dead. Is God having a laugh somewhere in His living room, playing chess, or watching TV, oh, I see, we are the TV, a reality show about survival. I get to thinking like that, sometimes, but then I tell myself, Hey, at least I survived, I made it.

I did mention this was going to be a long letter. But now I am almost at the end. I have already told you some of the story, how we were trapped in a building in Greece for two days without food, I and a friend of mine, Hassan the Afghan. He it was who told me of England, and said we must make that our target. But first, we needed to raise some money, which is why we were working in that farm picking strawberries. I remember those two days in that abandoned building, and I remember the sounds of the skinheads' voices at night, their footfalls as they walked around, waiting for us to come out, I remember the smell of fear and sweat on our bodies. Sometimes we would crawl to the window and look into the square at the restaurant where people sat dining, smell the aroma of food wafting up when the wind blew in our direction, driving us mad with hunger.

We eventually made it to Calais in France, through Germany.

Hassan had some contacts in Calais, and he said from there to England was a very short distance. He made it sound so easy, and so I wasn't prepared for what I met there. They called the place 'the Jungle', and it was a jungle. The day we got there, at the edge of the camp, we witnessed a fight. A man was stabbed with a knife. Just like that. An argument had started when one man accused another of stealing his bicycle, an Indian man, who said no, he just used it to go to the city to buy some grocery and he was returning it. But they started fighting and the other man, an Eritrean, stabbed the other one in the neck. That was our welcome to Calais Jungle. I remember the smell, and the trash, it was everywhere.

Hassan took us to his friends and they started talking in their language, I noticed one of them looking at me suspiciously. They offered him a cup of tea but they did not offer me anything. It is strange, I thought. I said I was going to go out, to ease myself. Now the younger of the men actually talked to me, in English, he said be careful, it is a jungle. He looked as if he was trying to scare me, but I felt grateful for his warning, after all, he was the first person to even notice me. I thanked him, and I walked out. I wanted to see if I could spot a known face, anything. I saw a man, a black man, and I went up to him and asked him where he was from. Why do you want to know? he asked, he looked angry. He looked mad, his eyes were wild and his mouth was so smelly when he came close to me and put his face next to mine. I turned and left. Hey, he shouted after me, hey. I kept on walking. I felt scared looking at him, and I asked myself, was I also like that? Did I smell like that, did I look crazy and I didn't even know it? It had been a while since I took a bath, or ate properly, or changed my clothes.

We were there for only two nights, but the memory of that place will never leave me. I already told you the story of the woman who was once a rich person in her country, Eritrea. She refused to talk to anyone. She would sit in the tent and call out orders, she would call out the names of her maids: Esther, come here right now. Bring me my meal, it is past mealtime, Esther. Or she would tell them to run her bathwater. There she sat, in the doorway of her tent with everyone looking at her curiously, like an empress, surrounded by all the trash and her clothes torn and smelly and the flies all over her. Those who knew her said she had lost everything to the government of her country when she escaped. Houses, cars, and her husband was arrested.

Anyway, we left after two nights, and I was feeling lucky, and thankful, that we had made it. We were led to the trucks where they were camped for the night, far away from the Jungle. What if we were caught, I asked, but the smugglers assured us it had been arranged with the truckers, all we had to do was secure ourselves under the truck and hold tight, and to get off as soon as the trucks entered the UK. But my friend did not make it. He must have fallen asleep, or something must have gone wrong with his harness, all I heard was the scream as the tyre ran over him, and then a wet, squelching noise.

The night before we had stood on the beach in Calais, look-ing across the water at the lights on the other side. My friend said, That is Dover Beach. He knew a lot about England. His father had studied there, and he had gone to an English school in Afghani-stan, it was as if all his life he had been preparing for this moment. 'England,' he said, and there was awe in his voice. He asked me if I knew the famous poem on Dover Beach, and when I said no, he quoted a line, from memory. He said the writer's name is Matthew Arnold. The writer had stood on the opposite shore from where we stood, looking at the French shore. I don't remember all the lines, but there is something about the 'eternal note of sadness'. I know what that means.

Well, that is my story, my friend. That is how I came to England. That is why I left my country. You know the rest. Now I am here, in this remote detention centre, waiting to find out about my fate. Liam and Molly still come to visit me. I still continue with my hun-

*ger strike; I have gone a hundred days now without eating. I have
no illusions about how this is going to end. The government thinks
I am going to relent and give up, I can't. I am tired, actually, and I
know in the end this will not change anything, they will continue to
detain people, long after I am gone and forgotten. A doctor came to
see me. He warned me that my fasting will cause irreparable damage to my body if I continue. He looked worried. He took my blood
pressure and looked into my eyes and my mouth and my ears. He
was trying to scare me, to make me give up my hunger strike, to
break my will. I told him I am fasting not because I want to any
more, all that has lost any meaning to me. The truth is I have lost
all desire for food. I even try to put something in my mouth, but I
always throw up after eating. I can't eat. My teeth are falling out. I
can't find any food to my liking. They gave me everything to tempt
me, meat, fruit, vegetable, trying to entice me to eat, but I can't keep
anything down. I want the perfect food. I tell them I want manna,
or ambrosia, the food of the gods themselves, and they thought I
was joking, but I am serious. I want the perfect food, but where can
I find it here on earth? I want my mother's food, the one I grew
up eating. I want the first food I ever ate in this world. I want my
mother's milk, but by now I am sure my mother is dead.*

The café had quieted down. The game was over; our stay
in London was also over, we had only two days left. Tomorrow Portia was meeting with her father's editor, whom she
had been able to track online, to hand over the notebooks
to her; I had offered to go with her but she said no, this was
something she wanted to do alone.

Now she wanted to know if I was coming to Lusaka with
her. She stood up and said, −I am going to freshen up, and

when I come back I want you to say yes. She leaned over and placed her lips over mine before heading for the restroom. I watched the men's eyes follow her as she made her way across the room. She looked stunning in a knee-length black dress that hugged her hips and emphasized the slenderness of her waist. I felt proud that she was with me, and often I wondered why she chose me when she could have any man she wanted, and why did I hesitate, why couldn't I say yes?

Soon she was back, she sat facing me, she took my hand. –Have you decided?

I imagined her home in Lusaka, and it was as if I had been there, she had talked about it so much that I could see the school, the jacaranda trees, the children in their neat school uniform. And she would be there with me, every day. But how would I fit in, and would it matter, as long as we were together? Things would fall into place. I stared at her and I marvelled at how much she had changed from the young impulsive girl I first met in Berlin. How beautiful and restrained she had become. She had suffered too, that was why.

–What if I am not who you think I am, what if something has shifted and broken in me since you last saw me?

–We will start from somewhere. Plus, you must admit, you don't seem to do well by yourself. Last time I left you, you ended up in a refugee camp.

•

I thought of Juma, he'd be in his tiny cell at Harmondsworth Removal Centre, perhaps reading, drifting in and out of sleep, too weak to stay awake for long. Liam and Molly will keep visiting him, daily, dutifully, not knowing any more what drives them. They talk about the weather, how summer is almost over. Juma's voice has grown hoarser and flimsier, and the visitors have to draw nearer to hear him. Liam asks him if he needs some water and he says, Yes. He takes a tiny sip, wetting his chapped, shaking lips. Then the lucidity leaves his eyes and they leave him. The next time they come the officials deny them entry, they say he has been moved to another facility, no one knows exactly where, Liam and Molly will protest, they will talk to the lawyer, but eventually they stop coming, worn out, they stop making inquiries, for even the kindest and most empathetic of us can get emotionally fatigued. Liam returns to Norwich to focus on his studies, Molly goes with him to take up a new job at the N&N hospital. The din in the media quietens. Juma sits in his cell, thirsting for mother's milk, unable to eat anything else, he shrinks, he regresses, back to childhood, curled up in a corner foetus-like, his flesh withers, his bones become as frail as twigs. One day the guards open the door and he is not there, only a pile of twigs on the floor. The cleaner comes and sweeps up the twigs and bags them and throws them into the dumpster.

I stood up and helped Portia with her jacket, then I put on mine. I said, –Yes. Let's go.

END

Unplayable

Unplayable

An Inside Account of Tiger's Most Tumultuous Season

ROBERT LUSETICH

SIMON &
SCHUSTER

London · New York · Sydney · Toronto

A CBS COMPANY

First published in Great Britain in 2010 by Simon & Schuster UK Ltd
A CBS COMPANY

Copyright © 2010 by Robert Lusetich

The right of Robert Lusetich to be identified as the author of this
work has been asserted by him in accordance with sections 77 and 78
of the Copyright, Designs and Patents Act, 1988.

1 3 5 7 9 10 8 6 4 2

Simon & Schuster UK Ltd
1st Floor
222 Gray's Inn Road
London
WC1X 8HB

www.simonandschuster.co.uk

Simon & Schuster Australia
Sydney

A CIP catalogue copy for this book is available
from the British Library.

ISBN: 978-1-84737-887-3 (hardback)
ISBN: 978-0-85720-042-6 (trade paperback)

Designed by Dana Sloan
Printed in the UK by CPI Mackays, Chatham ME5 8TD

For Colleen, Riley, and Dylan

CONTENTS

INTRODUCTION

The call came on a balmy September evening in 2008 as my wife and I were about to take our sons to a birthday dinner for the older one, who had turned twelve. My editor at *The Australian*, on whose dime I'd traveled the world as a foreign correspondent since the mid-1990s, informed me that a Los Angeles bureau was "a luxury the newspaper can no longer afford." The economy was falling apart, advertisers were deserting, and News Corporation had ordered immediate and penetrating cuts to newspaper budgets. Foreign bureaus were suddenly indulgences; where there were almost twenty Australian newspaper correspondents in the United States in the halcyon days of the early 1990s, only three were left by 2010. And just like that, I was unemployed. A hefty buyout helped soften the blow, but I was on the wrong side of forty and had spent virtually my entire working life as an ink-stained newspaper reporter.

What was I going to do with my life? Newspapers were busily sacking, not hiring, as the insanity of giving away their product online for free took its inevitable toll. Readers were canceling subscriptions and advertisers were looking elsewhere as long-standing media models were no longer relevant. I felt like a blacksmith as the first mass-produced Oldsmobile came chugging down the road; the market for newspaper journalism, just like horseshoes a century before, wouldn't be bouncing back.

Of the many assignments I'd carried out for *The Australian*—

spanning every continent except Africa and Antartica and ranging from World Cup soccer finals to civil unrest in Argentina—those I'd grown to most enjoy involved golf, a maddening pursuit to which I myself had become addicted. Specifically, I looked forward to tournaments that featured Tiger Woods. Woods is one of those sporting supernovas who come along once in a generation, if we're lucky. He transcends his sport, which others had before, but none in quite the same way. Roger Federer, whom I'd watched win Wimbledon from a courtside seat, is just as celestial and more graceful, but he had to grow into the champion he'd become; Woods was twenty years ahead of him in evolution and, by the nature of his sport, could remain relevant for twenty years after Federer had retired. It took a perfect storm—parents, upbringing, the sport he chose, the strength of his mind and determination and, of course, a stratospheric talent—to produce Woods. And what is remarkable about him is that he has generated such widespread global appeal in a sport much of the world's population can never hope to play. Golf isn't like soccer or basketball or even tennis, games that require relatively few props or, more to the point, money. Woods's branding has been a tribute to his excellence and, it has to be said, the omnipotence of the Nike Swoosh. Many of my colleagues were cynical about the way Woods's handlers had manipulated his image, but for whatever reasons—and I hope naïveté wasn't one of them—I found it hard to be cynical when it came to Tiger Woods.

Not that I couldn't see the flaws. The stubborn refusal to give up any control, the temper, the cold way he could have with people, the selfishness, the way he was pampered and indulged by those around him, how he was unable to accept any criticism no matter how well-intentioned, and how his true opinions—expressed only to those he could trust—were constantly being suppressed in favor of carefully inoffensive public views. I knew, for instance, that he feels more Asian than black, despite his skin tone, but he would only hint at it, saying things like it'd be insulting to his mother to be called African American. But, really, he doesn't want to open that can of worms. Most remarkably, Woods really did believe he could arrive at a tournament, bask in the glory of sinking the winning putt, then disappear to live a private life, interrupted only by filming the advertising campaigns that put perhaps $100 million a year in his pocket.

But I've been around many prominent athletes, and their flaws are, by and large, worse. There are a few exceptions, like U.S. Open tennis champion Patrick Rafter, who is a saint—he once told me that he'd "tried to be an arsehole but I just couldn't do it"—but most are more like Pete Sampras and Barry Bonds in that they didn't have to try very hard; it came naturally. And in golf, with its tradition of gentlemanliness, the realities of private lives hardly gell with the cultivated public personae. I ran into a well-known player at an airport once, who told me he'd flown in to work with an instructor on his short game, which I had no reason to disbelieve until an attractive young woman who wasn't his wife embraced him intimately as he'd barely finished saying the words. Greg Norman and Arnold Palmer both had a great appreciation for the beauty of the female form, but they reigned in different times. "The times have changed," even Woods acknowledged in 2010. "With twenty-four-hour news, you're looking for any kind of news to get out there." But it was also true that the media looked the other way in years past. Golf writers back then were friendly with the players they covered, and some of them were even chasing the same women. But Woods, with very few exceptions, was estranged from the media that covers him, and when he needed their restraint at the end of 2009, he instead got their revenge.

My view of Woods—admittedly from observations made at

the distance of press conferences or media scrums after rounds but also interspersed with the occasional brief off-the-record conversation—was that even though he is flawed, he is essentially a good guy. And, beyond that, it is the beauty of his playing that always won the day with me. In 2000 I asked him, not for the first time, how much better he thought he could get. "Why do you always ask me that?" he said. I asked because in him I saw something different. I was fascinated by the way he could make life conform to his wishes, as if the universe's many powerful and complex forces could be made to obey him the way a golf ball obeyed him.

Taking advantage of my newfound freedom to think more deeply about what my future might hold, it occurred to me that this was the perfect opportunity to write a book about Tiger Woods.

If I'd had any doubts how compelling a story Woods is, they were eradicated by five unforgettable days in June 2008 at Torrey Pines in San Diego. That was the last time I'd seen him, hobbling in obvious pain but unable to wipe the smile from his face after leaving the U.S. Open media center on a gorgeous Monday afternoon. Woods had called that playoff win over Rocco Mediate his greatest majors triumph, and he may have undersold what he'd accomplished. Had there ever been a greater one? He'd won the U.S. Open on one leg. He knew each swing would bring a shooting pain up his left leg, but he swung anyway. He is not a man short on courage. Woods had been told by his doctors that he couldn't play after the Masters, not with a ruptured anterior cruciate ligament and two stress fractures of the left shinbone. He told them that not only would he play, but he would win.

Woods's longtime caddie, Steve Williams, a straight-shooting New Zealander who's been carrying golfers' bags all his life, told me later that the tournament meant everything to Woods. Not so much because it represented a fourteenth major, but because he won on a course to which he was spiritually attached. Torrey Pines, the famous municipal track cut into the bluffs overlooking the Pacific Ocean, had been the holy grail for Woods as a boy growing up in Orange County. His father, Earl, had promised him that one day, when he was good enough, he'd take his little Tiger to Torrey and they would play together. The boy dreamed of that day, just as years later the man dreamed of returning to win the U.S. Open on Father's Day 2008, for his "Pops," who'd passed away two years before. Golfers are often asked for their fantasy foursome, the three players—alive or deceased—they'd share one last round with if they could. Woods always had the same reply: it wouldn't be a foursome, but a twosome: just him and Pops, the way they used to be.

"We knew after Augusta that he couldn't go on," said Williams of Woods's busted knee. The knee had been a source of pain and discomfort for more than a decade. Woods had a third surgery after the Masters, to remove floating cartilage from the knee, but his surgeons were merely rearranging deck chairs on the *Titanic*. The ACL, a sort of rubber band that stabilizes the knee, had snapped, probably a year before. Williams could literally hear a crunching sound—bone grinding against bone—when Woods swung. The knee needed to be rebuilt, but it would mean missing the U.S. Open. "The doctors told him 100 percent that he couldn't play, but of course I knew he was going to play. In all the years I've caddied for Tiger, I've never heard him talk about one tournament more than the Open at Torrey Pines. From the day they announced that it was going to be the venue, he talked about it all the time. Every time we played the [Tour stop at Torrey Pines], he was always asking, 'Hey, Stevie, what are they going to do with this hole? Where do you think they'll put the pin here?' I mean, he never stopped. Even away from the tournament, he was always talking about it, which is intriguing to me because when he had the chance to hold all four major championships at one time, so you had from the end of the PGA in August 2000 until Augusta next April, so you've got seven months, he never talked about it. It was never mentioned. Okay, when we got closer to Augusta he started talking about what kinds of shots he needed, but otherwise he never talked about it. But jeez, he never shut up about Torrey Pines. His absolute resolve to win that tournament was just incredible. And [during the tournament] he was hitting it fucking awful, but he had it in his mind that he was going to win and nothing was going to stop him. I could caddie for the rest of my life and there will never be another tournament like that. That'll be the biggest highlight for me, ever."

Woods rode off into the sunset, forced to spend nine months away from golf to recuperate from his surgery, and without him the sport fell into darkness. Ratings were down, interest was waning and, worse, the world was soon left teetering in a deep recession that threatened golf more than any other sport. Wall Street's credit default swaps scam had unraveled by late 2008, triggering a real estate crisis in the United States that soon cast a pall across the global economy. Golf had relied on Detroit and Wall Street for its sponsorship dollars, and those sectors were blowing up; the government had to print money to keep them afloat.

Against this backdrop, I wondered if Woods wouldn't return in 2009 as something like a modern-day Seabiscuit, winning majors against the odds and inspiring a nation down on its luck. And that was to be the tone of my book. I had assumed Woods's agent, Mark Steinberg, would have loved the idea. But, as it turned out, I thought too much like a storyteller and not enough like an agent. "You will be making a profit off an unauthorized book about Tiger," he replied. And in case I wasn't convinced, my colleague John Feinstein recalled Woods's reaction when a bad television movie was made about his life in the late '90s. "To be honest, it pisses me off," the twenty-two-year-old Woods had said at a pre-Masters press conference. Pissed him off because it was bad? No. "It pisses me off that people I don't even know are making money off my life. I wish there was some way to stop them."

For better and for worse, much changed during the year I shadowed Woods. To my benefit and that of this book, FoxSports.com hired me to cover every PGA Tour event he played and—unlike Steinberg—Woods was both kind and generous with me, offering insight into the man beneath the Nike hat. But as he did with everyone in his life except for a select few accomplices—not including Williams—and a handful of famous friends, he drew the line at revealing his dalliances with Las Vegas cocktail waitresses and porn queens. It was difficult for me to reconcile the fact that no one outside a very small group had the slightest clue of the secret life one of the most instantly recognizable men on the planet had been living. "He used to go back to his hotel room very early, leave the golf course early," Padraig Harrington said. "I just assumed he was playing video games, you know? I thought his life was quite boring." Tour caddie Ron "Bambi" Levin, whose finger was always on the pulse of the world of professional golf, admitted, "Dude, I had no idea." "You ever want to know what's going on out here, ask Bambi," said caddie Corby Segal. Yet even when a Tour player tried to tell Levin in September 2009 that Woods had been seen boarding his plane with different women, Levin rationalized that there had to have been an innocent explanation. "I'm thinking it was probably a woman from Nike or someone from Gatorade or something like that because you never heard any stories about that guy," he said. "You hear things about lots of guys out here, but no one even whispered things like that about him."

This book was, obviously, reshaped after the events of Thanksgiving and the subsequent shocking revelations of Woods's reckless sexual exploits. It had to be because he'd gone from a god of the sports pages to a devil of the tabloids. "He's scum," wrote New York gossip columnist Cindy Adams. And on what did she base her conclusion? The same information many did: widespread reporting of often unsubstantiated stories by outlets like the *National Enquirer* and TMZ.com. Woods's camp, Steinberg in particular, bore much responsibility for the way the gossipistas trampled all over Woods. "Mark was in way over his head," said a member of Team Tiger who disagreed with Steinberg's stonewall strategy. With no credible public relations crisis management plan in place, Team Tiger fell back on what had always worked in the past: build higher the walls of the fortress and say nothing. But they were no longer dealing with the domesticated animals of the golf press; they were being mauled every day by the wild animals of the tabloids, who'd stop at nothing. In writing this book, I was determined to not make it a salacious tell-all, but neither could a portrait of Tiger Woods be complete without examining his infidelities, and so they are addressed as I piece together the story behind the story. But, to me, what the adultery most spoke to was a fault Woods himself acknowledged in his televised public apology of February 2010: that he'd felt entitled; that the rules did not apply to him. It turned out the world avoided another depression, and Seabiscuit, Woods wasn't. But he remains a unique and deeply fascinating character and, perhaps a little like Nick Carraway and Gatsby, I've told his story. All of it.

Unplayable

CHAPTER 1

Match Play

Not for the first time, Tiger Woods had beaten the dawn's early light into the parking lot of a golf course. A lifelong difficulty sleeping had turned Woods into both an early riser and, paradoxically, an inveterate night owl. But sleep had been more elusive than usual on this cool, cloudless February 2009 night in the high Sonoran desert. Understandably, perhaps, as he wasn't just literally arriving in the dark at Dove Mountain, site of the Accenture Match Play.

As Steve Williams—always the driver—pulled the courtesy car into a venue so new that the host property, a Ritz-Carlton, hadn't actually yet been built, even he wasn't sure what to expect. The New Zealander had for a decade played the role of the loyal Sherpa Tenzing Norgay to Tiger's Edmund Hillary in the scaling of Mount Nicklaus and Jack's peak of eighteen majors, the only record that matters to Tiger Woods. Williams had seen more than enough otherworldly deeds to believe that, on a golf course, nothing was beyond his boss. But Williams had been carrying golf bags for professionals ever since his father talked five-time British Open champion Peter Thomson into letting a twelve-year-old caddie for him at the 1976 New Zealand Open. He well knew the vagaries of being forced to the sidelines and understood, perhaps uniquely, that not even the great Tiger Woods was completely immune to them.

Williams rolls his steel-blue eyes and shakes his graying temples from side to side at metaphysical talk of a preternatural Woods, of a man who, as the legend goes, may or may not be a god but was almost certainly sent by one. "Most people have this conception that he's different to everybody else but in actual fact he ain't," says Williams. "A lot of people look at him and marvel at how he can execute shots and finish off tournaments and have this incredible ability to win, and they think he's probably got something that nobody else has got when in actual fact he doesn't. He works harder than anybody else and he has that desire to win. His desire to win is incredible. When you're around someone like that, it gives you a whole different perspective. Winning is everything. But away from the course, he's normal. He's doesn't do anything different to anybody else." These words would be interpreted in an entirely different light later in the year as the greatest scandal to hit golf unfolded in the tabloids, but at the time he uttered them, Williams was speaking the truth as he knew it.

And so while all around him expectations of Woods's return were spiraling out of control—among others, that oracle of the ADD generation, ESPN, had already crowned this the greatest comeback in golf history, short-changing Ben Hogan—Williams had taken a much more pragmatic view. "He'd been away from the game for nine weeks before, but this was nine months," he says. "Let's be honest, that's a long time to be gone. I'd be lying if I said I wasn't curious about seeing him swing again. I knew he'd been practicing, but the swing was always going to be different because he'd always been compensating for that left knee. And you can practice at home all you want, running around in a golf cart with your mates, but it's not the same as playing in competition. That's as true for Tiger as it is for anyone else."

After Woods's stirring triumph of the spirit at Torrey Pines, Williams had returned to the sanctuary of his farm outside Auckland, a serenity offset from time to time by the roar and adrenaline of his successful stock car team, Caddyshack Racing, named after the iconic golf comedy that both he and Woods list as their favorite movie. Golf had been far from his thoughts. Williams doesn't pretend to keep up with the game when he's away from the Tour. He wouldn't dream of watching a tournament on television and couldn't tell you who'd won in his off weeks. But he thought often of his friend and employer in Orlando. After regular international phone calls spread over many months to check on his boss's progress, Williams sensed that the surgery had taken other, unforeseen, tolls.

"Those first few months after the operation, talking to him, it wasn't the same Tiger Woods I knew," he says. Immobility, then learning how to walk again, had sapped Woods, who's more shark than tiger in his primal need for constant motion. "I can't imagine to have to sit down for even three or four days," says Williams. Woods, who tended to play his cards close to his chest, would later say only that the months of his rehabilitation were "no fun."

But there was more to the story than merely a demanding rehabilitation. The recovery had not gone well. Compounding his knee problem, when he began to train again in December 2008, Woods tore the Achilles tendon in his right foot. He would re-tear the tendon throughout 2009, and was often unable during his swing to push off his right side. By February 2009, the reconstructed knee was still bothering Woods. The decision was made—though Woods's agents, the ubiquitous International Management Group, would later deny it was theirs—to fly in a controversial Canadian doctor to perform a radical blood-spinning therapy. Dr. Anthony Galea, a pioneer in the field, went to the Woods home in the exclusive Isleworth community of Orlando a handful of times in February and March to try to accelerate the healing of golf's most important knee. Dr. Galea, a Dorian Gray man in his fifties who'd married cutting-edge medicine with the sensibilities of a New Age mystic, performed a procedure called platelet-rich plasma (PRP) therapy on Woods.

The procedure involves extracting blood, spinning it to isolate platelets—an important component of blood that contains large doses of bioactive proteins—then reinjecting a small amount of the platelet-rich blood directly into the injured area. Proponents of the procedure, which is widely used on high-performance athletes, say it has a marked effect on speeding recovery from injury, and after just one session Woods knew it was the answer to his prayers. Later in 2009, Dr. Galea would be charged in Canada over the possession of Actovegin—essentially, calf's blood—and human growth hormone, which is not illegal in Canada and which he claimed was for his personal use. There was never any suggestion that Woods had taken HGH or any performance-enhancing drugs. In 2010, Woods would indignantly deny any wrongdoing, echoing his agent's denial of late 2009. "The treatment Tiger received is a widely accepted therapy, and to suggest some connection with illegality is recklessly irresponsible," said Mark Steinberg, Woods's agent. "That rehabilitation did not involve human growth hormone, a substance that Tiger has never taken." Steinberg, an Illinois lawyer who was usually as circumspect as they came, naïvely e-mailed the *New York Times* in December, when the newspaper caught wind of Dr. Galea's association with Woods, and asked that they kill the story. Steinberg had e-mailed the paper's golf writer, Larry Dorman, whom he knew, but Dorman forwarded the response to his editors.

According to the *Times*, Steinberg, whose favored method of communication was e-mail, asked that "you guys don't write this. If Tiger is NOT implicated, and won't be, let's please give the kid a break." Woods was, of course, at the time in the middle of a nightmare of his own making; his infidelities had turned him into the butt of jokes, and Steinberg felt the *New York Times* was piling on. The éminence grise of American journalism, of course, published the story, complete with Steinberg's plaintive e-mail. For a man who was already paranoid about the media, the incident only confirmed to Steinberg that journalists couldn't be trusted. Woods's physical rehabilitation had been daunting, but like the Special Forces soldier he would've been had it not been for golf—a reminder that we are, for better or worse, in ways both big and small, always and forever our fathers' sons—he was prepared to tolerate the pain and work as hard as was necessary. But commitment, diligence, and a high pain threshold wouldn't necessarily be enough. Doctors, perhaps because they've devolved into a class of pessimists, careful not to overpromise in an age of capricious malpractice lawsuits, had refused to give him guarantees. Woods could faithfully follow their every instruction, but just one misstep in an unguarded moment or reaching for a little too much, a little too soon, and the rebuilt knee could be ruined; nine months of pain and suffering rendered worthless. And the implications of such a worst-case scenario threatened even more. Where would a ruined knee leave his career? What if he was robbed of the opportunity of scaling Mount Nicklaus? These were difficult truths to accept for a man who doesn't like shades of gray in his black-and-white world.

There are those who know Woods who characterize him as

a control freak because of his headstrong insistence that life always go according to his wishes, though what is that, other than an acknowledgment that he is willing—and able—to exert his will onto his environment? But in February 2009, Woods had accepted that there was an element of uncertainty in the equation of his rehabilitation.

If he'd doubted it, he had to look no farther than to the cautionary tale of Ernie Els. The South African had mangled his left knee in a fall from a rubber tube while being towed behind a boat during a 2005 summer vacation in Italy. Els was a laid-back man whose nom de guerre, the Big Easy, so aptly—for better and worse—encapsulated his approach to life and golf. Woods resisted parallels between them because he felt that Els hadn't done the hard yards necessary in rehabilitation, and (uncharacteristically, given his avoidance of uttering anything controversial) publicly said so in Boston later in 2009, calling Els out as "not a big worker." But it wasn't lost on him that his greatest rival had been reduced to a shell of himself after returning too soon from ACL surgery. When a right-handed golfer swings, his weight at impact has shifted onto the left leg, and that knee is absorbing the torque. The left knee must function properly—a nonnegotiable fact. In this context, Woods's long-awaited comeback at the Match Play—which pitted the top sixty-four players in the world in a knockout competition—represented something of a gamble.

In truth, it wasn't a gamble Woods had to take. He would've been better served by waiting another week and coming back to competitive golf at Miami's famous Doral Blue Monster, a low-impact, flat course he knew well, had won on several times, and was conveniently located down the road from his home.

But commercial considerations forced his hand. Woods at the time had a lucrative financial arrangement with the Fortune Global 500 company Accenture, which had based its worldwide marketing campaign around slogans like "We know what it takes to be a Tiger" and "Go on. Be a Tiger." The world's biggest consulting firm also happened to sponsor this event, and so, quid pro quo.

Although Woods had always maintained that he abided by the general philosophy that focusing only on what was best for his golf allowed "everything else to take care of itself," on this occasion Tiger Woods Enterprises won the day. It wasn't ideal—especially given the undulating Jack Nicklaus–designed Dove Mountain course and, it would later be discovered, the most exasperating greens complexes on the PGA Tour—but Woods was determined to make the best of the situation. He may not have thought the expectations surrounding his return were fair, but ever since he gave Bob Hope a putting lesson on the *Mike Douglas Show* at the age of two, Woods had done his best to disabuse us of the notion that he was bound by the limitations of the human condition. And so he knew the score would be as ludicrous as always: anything short of a win was a loss.

What Woods didn't know as he and Williams walked from their Buick SUV toward Dove Mountain's contemporary Southwestern-themed locker room was that Phil Mickelson would be waiting. Oddly for a man who'd made his bones by staring down opponents in the cauldron of Sunday afternoons, Woods didn't like face-to-face confrontation. With the world's cameras trained upon his every move, Mickelson wasn't giving him a choice. Seeing Mickelson in the parking lot, Woods and Williams didn't need to say a word. They knew they were being set up. Mickelson didn't exactly have a history of predawn practice rounds. Yet as the golf world awaited the return of its king, there Mickelson stood, accompanied by his longtime caddie, Jim "Bones" Mackay, and swing coach Butch Harmon, whose estrangement from Woods had been decidedly acrimonious. Woods sensed immediately that Mickelson wanted the last word on an episode dating back to December 2008, when Williams ill-advisedly "had a bit of fun" while speaking at a charity function in New Zealand. Williams was pressed during a question-and-answer session at an event in support of his own foundation to discuss the relationship between Woods and Mickelson. "That's probably the question I get asked the most. What do they really think of each other?" says Williams. Thinking that what happens in the antipodes stays in the antipodes, Williams confirmed what most inside golf's highest circles long knew: Woods didn't like Mickelson. Williams went on to call Mickelson a "prick," hardly the sort of language expected in a sport that prided itself on gentlemanly behavior. Or at least, the outward pretense of such behavior. The caddie also told an amusing story about a spectator shouting "Nice tits" at Mickelson during the U.S. Open at Torrey Pines the year before.

Williams's comments were leaked to a local newspaper, which published them on its Internet site, then were quickly picked up by the *Guardian*'s U.S.-based golf correspondent, Lawrence Donegan, thus guaranteeing they wouldn't quietly disappear into a black hole in the blogosphere. Williams was given the chance to deny the comments by another New Zealand journalist the following day, but in all good conscience he could not. Williams is a straight shooter—indeed, his primary defense would later be that he was only being honest in describing how both he and Woods felt about Mickelson—and so he admitted that he'd been quoted accurately. Williams made the disclaimer that he didn't intend the comments to be made public, but that was, by then, wasted breath.

The typically sleepy golf off-season had been awakened by that rarest of occurrences: a juicy story. Predictably, two quotes from Williams appeared most prominently in reports: "I wouldn't call Mickelson a great player 'cause I hate the prick" and "He pays me no respect at all and hence I don't pay him any respect. It's no secret we don't get along, either." Mickelson was far too proud to let this kind of an outburst slide. And, in fairness, his anger was not misplaced. "Steve's a caddie, and he should remember that," says a player who himself was not particularly fond of Mickelson. "He was out of line saying what he said about another player. He's lucky Tiger's got his back, because not many other caddies would've survived that."

What really riled Mickelson was the anecdote making fun of his breasts. The Californian was especially sensitive to jokes about the "subcutaneous fat," which he blamed for the protruding nature of his breasts. "I will always have fat on me. There's nothing I can do about it, just genetics," he said in 2003. "I've got subcutaneous fat. And most people who are ripped have visceral. There's nothing I can do about it. It just lies underneath the skin as opposed to underneath the muscle. Some people put on weight, but they're still ripped because it's underneath the muscle. I don't have that luxury." Skeptics point out that Mickelson's fondness for eating and disdain for physical exertion didn't help his cause. Mickelson's former coach, Rick Smith, recalled that the left-hander consumed three of Augusta National's enormous club sandwiches before going out and winning his first major in 2004.

But irrespective of Mickelson's weight problems, the kicker was that Williams got his facts wrong. The incident he joked about didn't happen at Torrey Pines but occurred six years earlier at the first Bethpage Black U.S. Open in New York and, further, it didn't even involve Mickelson. That jibe—typical of the raucous Long Island golf crowds, who behave as if they're at a Jets NFL game—was directed at another prominent golfer with an even bigger subcutaneous fat problem—and even thinner skin—Scotland's Colin Montgomerie.

Mickelson had his publicist, former San Diego golf writer T. R. Reinman, issue a statement admonishing Williams for "grossly inaccurate and irresponsible statements." He wanted it known that Monty was the butt of that joke but he also wanted to slap down Williams and, by extension, put pressure on Woods to act. "After seeing Steve Williams's comments, all I could think of was how lucky I am to have a class act like Bones on my bag and representing me," Mickelson said. Mackay, a genial character who—unlike his boss—got along fine with Williams, said that he would never have made such derogatory remarks about Woods and that, if he had, Mickelson wouldn't have had to fire him because he would've resigned. The implication was that if Woods and Williams were men of honor and integrity, Williams would either be fired or fall on his own sword.

Harmon, a man not without substantial ego who had an ax to grind after being fired by Woods after a decade by his side, got into the act, too, calling Williams's remarks "deplorable." "Phil Mickelson is one of the most popular players in the world, every bit as popular as Tiger Woods," he was quoted as saying. "He's a nice guy, all the guys like Phil, so I don't know where Steve was coming from with that comment. Personally, I would assume he would wish he'd never made it. I would have loved to have heard a recording of the conversation between [Williams] and Tiger. I worked with Tiger for ten years and I can tell you he wouldn't have been very happy with that. Golf is a game of honor and integrity, and that was a very uncalled-for remark. I don't think it's any reflection of what Tiger thinks of Phil Mickelson."

Harmon's nose presumably grew after making that last remark. He, perhaps more than anyone, knew that Woods had had worse— much worse—to say about Mickelson, whom Woods considered to be a phony whose public and private personas didn't exactly gel. A prominent golf broadcaster says that Harmon, when he was working with Woods, told him of a confrontation in a hotel elevator between the rivals, which culminated with Mickelson storming out, yelling, "I'm not your bitch!" After Mickelson's ill-fated implosion at the 2006 U.S. Open at Winged Foot, Golf Channel anchor Kelly Tilghman told colleagues that Woods responded to her text message about Lefty's demise by wondering "which tit he tripped on."

Woods, it must be said, was not alone in feeling antipathy toward Mickelson. There was a widespread belief throughout the PGA Tour locker room that Mickelson was an aloof know-it-all who showed very little respect to other players. To his peers, Mickelson often appeared in public as if he were running for office—the perpetual candidate. They called him FIGJAM (Fuck I'm Good, Just Ask Me) and Genius. One veteran player, who asked not to be identified because he was linked to a company with ties to Mickelson, recalled having to play thirty-six holes on a bitingly cold Sunday one year at the old Bell South Atlanta tour stop. "It was fucking freezing, the week before the Masters, and none of us were happy playing thirty-six, including Phil, who was bitching about it in the locker room. Then the next thing I know, I see him doing an interview on TV saying how great it was that we got to experience what it was like in the old days," the player said. "You just shake your head at some of the shit that guy says because you know even he doesn't believe it."

In 2006, Mickelson was the most surprising entry and the only golfer to appear in *GQ* magazine's poll of the top ten most hated athletes by their peers. In *Sports Illustrated*'s 2007 survey of PGA Tour pros, not one listed Mickelson as a favorite playing partner (Woods topped the list) while Mickelson was behind only the universally despised South African boor Rory Sabbatini as the golfer they least want to play with. "Tiger's not the only one who sees straight through that shit-eating grin," says a longtime caddie. "Phil's the least liked player by his competitors and the most liked by the fans. That's hard to do."

A member of Mickelson's inner circle dismissed such claims as "jealousy" stemming from the fact that "Phil doesn't hang out with the [Tour] bottom-feeders." He also said that Mickelson didn't dislike Woods at all but that until Woods got married and started a family, the two had little in common. "One guy was living in California and sleeping with his wife, the other guy was living in Florida and sleeping with Mark O'Meara," he said in a tongue-in-cheek reference to Woods's longtime friend and mentor. The irony was that in recent years Woods had mellowed considerably on the subject of Mickelson, if for no other reason than his adversary had finally joined the club and won three majors. Woods respected achievement. In that sense, he was the ultimate meritocrat. It was interesting that while he didn't particularly like Vijay Singh, or Mickelson, he tipped his hat to the fact that they had both won the big ones. Sergio Garcia, on the other hand, was another kettle of Spanish mackerel. Woods has no respect for Garcia because he thought he hadn't earned the right to strut.

Harmon was right that Woods was not happy with Williams for his outburst, but only because he'd aired dirty laundry in public, which Woods would be forced to clean. But he was never going to fire Williams, whom he respected as both a caddie and a friend. It was Woods who'd called Williams late one night in their Tokyo hotel and encouraged him to marry his girlfriend, Kirsty. He was the best man at their wedding. But Woods understood that he needed to be seen to have acted, so he issued a statement saying that he'd been "disappointed" to read about Williams's comments. He pointedly called Mickelson "a player that I respect." "It was inappropriate," Woods went on. "The matter has been discussed and dealt with." Woods wanted to put an end to the saga.

Mickelson, however, wasn't done. As the two posses came together that morning on the outskirts of Tucson, the media was too far away to hear what was said. The cameras showed Mickelson and Williams shaking hands, and it was assumed the gesture was a public signal that bygones would be bygones. However, the truth was far less amicable. And far more interesting. Mickelson had approached Williams aggressively and said, "Do we have a problem?" Williams could not believe what he'd heard and responded with a few choice words. They would be the last words the two would exchange all year. Williams was furious because he had called Mickelson to apologize in the days after his comments were published. The two spent half an hour on the phone. Most of the conversation involved Mickelson asking Williams why Woods so disliked him and what he could do to improve their relationship. He'd asked Williams to put in a good word for him with his boss. Williams agreed, and in return asked Mickelson to let it be known publicly that they had spoken and had put the issue behind them. Mickelson assured him that he would. But not only did he never make such a statement, when I asked Reinman in Miami a week later about Williams's apology, he replied with an even stonier face than usual. "Apology? Well, he called him, but I don't know that you could categorize that phone call as an apology."

Shortly after 7 a.m., Woods—still chafing that Mickelson had pulled such a stunt—ventured from the clubhouse to the practice range, an army of media in tow. Mickelson had set up on the left side of the range; Woods, predictably, assumed a station as far away as he could on the right. He wore gray slacks and a matching sweater, which was about the right color for his first warm-up session: a mixed bag of crisp irons and rocket drives interspersed with swings best described as indifferent. Woods enjoyed hitting golf balls on a range and could do so all day, but he was on a tight schedule and shortened the session. Once warm, he marched to the first tee. Just after 7:15, with photographers having assumed every vantage spot on the opening hole, Tiger Woods stuck a tee in the ground, hit a serviceable drive, and began walking briskly after his ball. It was just like old times. Woods would later marvel at how it felt as if he'd hardly been gone from the game.

As he often did when on unfamiliar terrain, Woods used the round as reconnaissance, getting acquainted with a course that was hosting the tournament for the first time. He didn't finish any holes, sometimes hit two tee shots, and usually pitched and chipped around the greens to where he thought pins would be placed. He didn't appear very happy, but that may have had more to do with the lack of privacy afforded him by the media circus than the state of his game. Although he looked rusty at times, he did more than enough to suggest that he hadn't lost his game entirely. What was clear from his facial expressions was that he had quickly grown to dislike the greens. They were slow and ponderous, but because of their humps and bumps, couldn't play any faster for fear of becoming unputtable.

Woods took longer than he'd anticipated to finish his round, prompting a tardy start to his news conference from a man to whom watches could usually be set. Woods had entered the back door of the makeshift media center, where a standing-room-only crowd awaited, flanked by his agent and business manager, the always serious Steinberg, wearing his standard uniform of a Nike golf shirt, perfectly pressed trousers, and a frown, and his newly hired publicist, the personable Glenn Greenspan, who'd been poached from Augusta National. Laura Hill, an attractive, friendly blonde who was the equivalent of the White House press secretary in PGA Tour commissioner Tim Finchem's administration, took the reins. Barbara Walters, she was not. "Tiger, it's been about eight and a half months since we last saw you," she said. "You've had knee surgery, welcomed a member of the family, and welcome back. Just a couple comments for us." For Woods, it was just like getting back on a bicycle. He'd been doing these news conferences for so long it was doubtful he even heard opening softball questions. It didn't matter anyway as he was going to say only what he wanted to say. "Yeah, it's great to be back," said Woods. "Sorry I'm late. I forgot how long it takes to play eighteen holes walking. But no, it feels great to be back out and get back out here in a competitive environment again. It feels really good."

This was the motif of a Woods news conference in a nutshell, the way it'd been since he arrived on the scene in 1996. He threw in a touch of humor, often self-deprecating—but never too much so—that illustrated the point he really wanted to stress, and the rest was as meaningful as navel lint. In this case, Woods wanted the world to know that he had not walked a golf course in almost nine months. Put another way, he was saying that he'd been gone a long time and expectations should be adjusted accordingly. Except, of course, he would never directly make such a concession, for Tiger Woods never betrayed weakness. Having made his point—by not making it—Woods then launched into the first of an interminable number of descriptions of how his left leg felt. "I feel a lot stronger in my left leg," he said. "Both legs have been stronger than they ever have been. Stability is something I haven't had in years. So it's nice to make a swing and not have my—as I've said before—my bones move. Since I had a lack of ACL for a number of years, no matter what I did, it was always moving. So I would try and hit into my left side, but the more I did it, the more it would move, so hence one of the reasons why you saw me jumping off the ball is to get off that leg. But it's nice to be able to hit into it for the first time."

Most politicians have to be taught to stay on message; Tiger Woods was born that way. He would repeat the above sentiments, sometimes using the exact same words—but having the gift of delivering them as if they'd only just occurred to him—dozens and dozens of times over the coming weeks. It was a remarkable skill, requiring two of Woods's best attributes: patience and discipline. What it also did, however, was allow Woods to control the message. If he'd decided the message of the day was that the greens were slow and bumpy and that his putter never adjusted but that he hit good putts that just didn't go in, that would be what he gave. This was especially true of the brief electronic media interviews with the PGA Tour's official broadcast partners—either CBS or NBC, the Golf Channel, and Sirius XM Radio—which Woods conducted immediately after signing his scorecard. Woods stuck to his message so faithfully that after a while I'd stopped bothering to take notes while listening in on these interviews. I knew he would say precisely the same thing in his postround news conference, so nothing would be missed.

As the press conference continued, I asked whether he'd missed golf while he was sidelined. I expected him to wax lyrical about how much he had missed that to which he'd devoted his life. Instead, he said he did not, giving an answer that portrayed him as the ultimate family man, an ideal that would take a battering within the year. "I didn't realize how much I loved being home and being around Sam and Elin and now Charlie," he said. "I mean, I'll tell you what, that's something that is just so important to me. I knew family would be, and it has been, but I didn't know it would be to this degree, the closeness that I feel. That's something that as I said was a blessing in disguise. As players you travel so much that I would have missed a lot of that, so I was very lucky there."

Woods could be mischievous at news conferences, often amusingly so. When asked what he most missed while he was away from golf, he broke out a wry smile. "I missed sitting here in front of you guys," he said, "talking, just hanging out here." We all laughed, of course, knowing that Woods would prefer a root canal to having to answer questions he viewed as invasions of his privacy. But then Woods, who'd not long before spoke of not missing golf, decided that he had missed it, after all. Another important lesson to learn about Tiger Woods: he could be all things at once. "I miss that rush of playing and competing, I really do, getting on that first tee and feeling it," he said. "I miss that. As much as you can have money games at home with the guys, it's not the same. This is what I do for a living, and this is what I've always wanted to do my entire life, and not being able to do it at the highest level was frustrating at times." This last sentiment was most telling, for it revealed perhaps the greatest secret to the success of Tiger Woods. There were players who arrived at tournaments knowing that they were not really prepared, especially early in the year. Their poor performances were justified as "rust," but what it really meant was that they didn't do the work necessary to be ready. Not Woods. His preparation was as meticulous as it was exhaustive. He never showed up and slapped it around for four days. He was as serious and committed to winning as any other athlete who'd ever lived. "I care about what I do and I take great pride in what I do," he said when asked if he could've come back earlier. "I didn't feel like I was ready to come out here and embarrass myself. And I had to make sure that I felt my game was good enough and ready to compete and win again." I asked him whether he'd ever showed up not fully prepared and confident that he would win. I knew of only one instance where this was true: in the wake of the death of his father, Earl, in 2006. Woods played the U.S. Open at Winged Foot and missed his first cut at a major as a professional. He had not prepared; not only was his game missing, his heart wasn't in it. "That was the only one, yeah," he said before leaving the media center.

If Woods got a break, it was that his first-round opponent, Australian Brendan Jones, was as undercooked as he was over-awed. After one unsuccessful season on the U.S. Tour, Jones tasted some success playing in Japan, enough to have squeezed into the Match Play field in the sixty-fourth and final spot. But the Japanese Tour was in the middle of its off-season. He had not played competitively since December at the Australian Open, and it would be another two months before he'd resume playing in Japan. Jones had a typically laconic Aussie sense of humor. If he were a betting man, he said, he'd "bet the house" on Woods. He was asked what he'd say to Woods when they met. "Can I have three a side?" He was only half joking. If he was looking for a light in the darkness, it might have been that Woods had faltered three times at the hands of unheralded Aussies in the Match Play. He was felled twice by left-hander Nick O'Hern, a short hitter who lulled opponents to sleep with his steady fairways-and-greens play, and Peter O'Malley, a marvelous ball striker whose recalcitrant putter held him back from greater achievements. Jones had spoken with neither but mischievously said he'd gotten advice from Stephen Ames. It wasn't true, but it made for a good story as Ames notoriously called out Woods before the 2006 Match Play. Though Ames was trying to be funny, Woods wasn't laughing. Ames was pummeled in their match, 9 and 8, and his name became a cautionary tale.

Jones was understandably nervous, and his caddie, PGA Tour veteran Ron "Bambi" Levin, tried to get the butterflies out of his man's stomach and the stars out of his eyes. He and Jones went looking for Woods to get introductions out of the way, but they never found him until their high-noon shootout. Jones was brushing putts with his broomstick putter on the practice green when he first caught sight of Woods. Woods was, as he could be in moments like these, not especially friendly. He'd look elsewhere, pretend he didn't see his opponent. Woods isn't by any stretch a voracious reader, but it was as if he'd been guided by Sun Tzu, who 2,500 years ago wrote, "The Art of War teaches us to rely not on the likelihood of the enemy's not coming, but our own readiness to receive him." Woods would have made the Chinese militarist proud, too, with his choice of positioning: the highest part of the putting green.

Eventually, when Jones bit the bullet and decided to walk over to introduce himself, Woods—perhaps coincidentally, perhaps not—put a foot on his golf bag and bent over to tie a shoelace that wasn't undone. Jones stood there with hand outstretched. Woods left him standing there for a moment before straightening and shaking Jones's hand. But by then the damage had been done: both players knew the natural order of things between them.

On the 1st tee, Woods shut out the circus around him—no one did this better—and struck a perfect 3-wood with a little draw down the right side of the fairway. The swing was smooth and effortless, which was not always the case with Woods, who could be violent. "Walking on the tee, I was just in my own little world, just trying to make sure that I knew what the number was to the bunker, where the wind was coming from, slightly off left, am I going to the hit a flat 3-wood, draw the ball, trying to decide what shot I want to hit," he said later. "And that's basically how I am with every round going to the first tee. So that didn't change. So over the tee shot it was just being able to hold a little draw up there and put it down the right side and give myself an angle at that flag, and I was able to do that." This was vintage Woods: shut out the significance of what it all meant, focus only on the immediate task at hand. Jones, however, was flustered by the attention. He took out his driver and tried to cut one off the left side of the fairway, but his ball finished in the rough, from where his play to the elevated flag would be problematic given the large greenside bunker directly in his line. Woods had a perfect position and brought roars from the galleries with an 8-iron shot that came to rest 5 feet from the hole. Jones's ball found the bunker, but it wouldn't matter as Woods made his putt to take a 1-up lead.

I saw Woods play countless holes in 2009, but he played none better than the 2nd at Dove Mountain. A blistering drive down the right side left a long iron to a green that no one had managed to keep the ball on that day. Every player who reached in 2 was left with a very exacting up and down from gnarly rough over the back of the green to a short-sided pin. It was almost better to lay up and go at that pin with a wedge. Woods, however, hit the most majestic 3-iron shot from 237 yards and watched the ball stop 4 feet beneath the hole. "Those first two holes stunned me as well," said Williams later. "Hit that driver on 2 as good and long as he could hit it and a long iron as good and as long as he could hit it right at it. I think it stunned Brendan Jones, too." Jones's mouth was agape at what he'd seen. He would concede the eagle to Woods after having a longer putt left for par than Woods had for 3. Later, the Aussie would refuse to believe that Woods hit a 3-iron into the green, insisting that it had to have been a 5-iron, given its height and the softness with which the ball landed. "That iron he hit there, I've never hit a shot like that in my life, that high and soft," Jones said. "We're walking up there and his ball's 4 feet short and I said to Stevie, 'Your yardages are out,' and he said, 'Oh, it might take me a bit to get back in the groove.' I mean, he hits shots that other people can't hit. His ball flight's different from pretty much everybody else's, and it was fun to see different trajectories that he hits the ball at. But, yeah, he's Tiger; he does freakish stuff."

If the story ended there, the return of the king couldn't have been scripted better. But it did not. Four perfect swings gave him a 2-up lead, and spiritually if not mathematically, Jones was already defeated. But on the 3rd hole, a slightly downhill par 3 over water, Woods blocked a midiron into the sand trap, short siding himself. It was a bad mistake and, as is his wont, he berated himself. What was different about that swing was that Woods took a 6-iron, flighted it down, and hit it a distance he could easily have covered with a full 8-iron. He aimed right, but the ball didn't draw much. It was a swing he'd often repeat in the coming weeks, with decidedly mixed results. As any good caddie would do, Levin took a peek at Woods's bag when he was on the tee and saw that the 6-iron was missing. He was going to hand Jones a 7-iron but reassessed—this was Tiger Woods, after all—and they, too, settled on the 6. Except that Jones promptly flew the green. Whatever sliver of hope the Aussie had disappeared when he bladed his straightforward chip and could do no better than match the bogey made by Woods. Woods would go on to win the match, 3 and 2, but it wasn't quite the coronation it seemed. In truth, Jones would have beaten only one player in the field that day, Lin Wen-Tang, who was 7 over par through thirteen holes before Anthony Kim finally put him out of his misery, 7 and 5. But the beauty of match play is that all that is required is the defeat of the man opposite. It could cut both ways, of course. Stuart Appleby one year at La Costa would have beaten every player in the field except one, his first-round opponent, Scott Hoch. Woods emerged victorious, and whatever deficiencies were betrayed were washed away in the afterglow that came with winning. Jones seemed like a man who'd always known his fate. What would he do now? a reporter asked. "It's beer o'clock, mate, isn't it?" he responded with a smile.

Awaiting Woods in the second round, however, was stiffer competition. Tim Clark was a dogged little South African who knew and liked Woods and, as it turned out, was not starstruck. "I literally hit every shot where I wanted to hit it today," Clark said, after shocking Woods, 4 and 2. "It's obviously a massive victory for me. He doesn't get beaten very often, and to go out in that sort of atmosphere, it really is a different experience going out with obviously all the media and all the people, there's not too much support for the other guy, so that's big."

Woods lost badly, but that hardly told the story of a match Woods had in his control until Clark made birdies on the 11th, 12th, and 13th holes, and Woods, who should've matched him, started missing shots to the right, and not by small distances. Still hot under the collar, Woods wasn't in the mood for self-criticism afterward when talking to a handful of reporters. "To the airport," he replied pithily when asked where he'd go from there. He was particularly incensed at the suggestion that he missed a lot of shots to the right. Climbing into a van to head to his new $60 million Gulfstream G550 for the long trip back to Florida, Woods wasn't happy. Those around him, Steinberg, Greenspan, Williams, and swing coach Hank Haney, knew that when he was in this mood—"unplayable" was their code word—it was better to stay silent and wait out the storm. "No matter what I do," he said to no one in particular as he sat in the van, "it's never fucking good enough. Nothing I do is ever good enough."

CHAPTER 2

Doral

Tournament directors are, by nature, gregarious creatures. And then there is Eddie Carbone. A Bostonian whose cultural transformation upon moving to Miami became so complete that he warmly embraces friend and stranger alike with an effusive "Bubba!", Carbone ran the CA Championship, the first stroke-play event on the World Golf Championships calendar. Venerable Doral, the tournament venue, had been a mainstay of the PGA Tour since the early 1960s, when New York apartment magnate Alfred Kaskel—the Donald Trump of his day—bought swampland on the cheap and quickly had it fashioned into a high-end golf resort. Kaskel understood that, like in most things in life, money talked in golf, so he immediately offered a purse that was double that of any other in Florida. Like moths to a flame, the best players came to a resort he named by taking the first three letters of his wife's first name, Doris, and adding the first two letters of his. And so a star was born. Of the four courses at Doral, the jewel was the Blue Monster, and luckily for Carbone, Tiger Woods liked it. And when Woods liked a course—and didn't have a conflicting schedule, as he did when Doral was opposite an event in Dubai, where no expense was spared to lure Woods—he invariably dominated the tournament. In six prior visits to the Blue Monster, Woods had lifted the trophy three times. "Certain courses just fit your eye," Woods says. Such words were music to Carbone's ears.

But even Carbone couldn't be sure whether Woods would be in the field for his tournament, set to conclude on the Ides of March. There had been rumors floating after the Match Play that the knee was bothering Woods and that, with his eye on the Masters, he might take the week off. Given the economic uncertainties of early 2009, with the world still on the precipice of a depression, Carbone needed Woods more than ever. Indeed, golf needed him. But there was no making Tiger Woods do anything he didn't want to do. "The difference between him playing and not playing? Are you serious? Where do you want me to start?" Carbone said. Woods had been the proverbial goose that laid the golden egg ever since he turned professional in 1996. Revenues for the PGA Tour—not including the four major championships, which run independently—were at a staggering $981 million in 2008, up from $302.5 million in Woods's rookie season. Prize money in that span grew at an even faster pace, from $70 million to $277 million. It didn't take Milton Friedman to figure out that Woods was single-handedly responsible for the explosion in interest in golf and the money that followed. Indeed, if the impact of Woods on the sport as a whole—from new courses built to exorbitant greens fees to the sale of clubs and apparel to television rights and beyond—were possible to calculate, the figure would surely be in the tens of billions. Woods might just be the single greatest money spinner in sports history. But he had single-handedly raised not only the ante in professional golf but also the cost of doing business. Having Woods in the field would guarantee that cost would be more than covered.

Woods had gotten into the habit of waiting as long as he was allowed—5 p.m. the Friday before a tournament—before committing to play. He adopted the policy in his rookie year when, exhausted after playing the BC Open, he played one practice round before withdrawing from the Buick event at Callaway Gardens, Georgia. A major public relations disaster followed in the wake of his withdrawal, and Buick—a primary sponsor, to the tune of at least $8 million a year—was not amused, given the dinner that had been organized with him as, essentially, the main course. Woods had always been sensitive to criticism. He determined that he'd never again put himself in a situation where he had to pull out of a tournament, and so welcomed the advice of a wise old head, Arnold Palmer, to not commit until the last minute. He'd stuck to the policy steadfastly even if it made life difficult for tournament directors, who could never be quite sure whether they would get the main attraction. It all amounted to an anxious first week of March in Miami for the tournament staff.

Months later, Carbone was able to recall the precise time he'd gotten the call he'd been awaiting the way fathers remember the births of their children. At 2:23 p.m. on Friday, March 6, Woods gave Carbone the good news. Corks popped, drinks flowed, and, as soon as the word got out, the phones rang off the hook at the tournament ticket office. Carbone liked Woods personally, but he loved him professionally. He'd gotten to know Woods well over the years but shrugged when asked to describe what the man beneath the Nike cap was really like. "I have no snippets on 'Stripes,'" he said. "Really, nothing." Perhaps he was masking an unpalatable truth—everyone in golf knew that Woods punished loose tongues—but his disposition suggested that he was not hiding any dark secrets. In the context of events later in the year, it confirmed my suspicions that Woods lived separate lives, which he kept away from each other. I asked Carbone what would most surprise people about Woods. "He is zero maintenance," he said.

During a round of golf on one of Doral's B-list tracks, a pushy lady with a thick Cuban accent who was operating the drinks cart asked if I knew Woods. Before I could answer, and while she mixed Bloody Marys for my playing partners, she unleashed a torrent of abuse. He was a zero in other departments, too, she made clear. "Someone needs to teach that guy to tip," she said irately. "All these years he's coming here and he never leaves a tip for nobody. He's the richest guy but he's a cheap guy." This was a refrain repeated often about Woods, who, the legend goes, was notoriously tight with money, to the point of taking pride in the accusation. He was a bad tipper judged relative to his wealth. Mickelson, for instance, thought nothing of leaving a $100 bill for a $12 breakfast. Woods, who rarely had much cash in his pockets—again, unlike Mickelson—was more likely to leave $15 on his American Express card, which he'd calculated as a 25 percent tip and, therefore, quite generous. Part of the woman's anger, however, was misplaced. Woods didn't stay at the luxurious resort when he played Doral.

On an idyllic day in south Florida, the reigning Masters champion, Trevor Immelman, was standing haplessly by his golf bag. Woods had already come and gone, but Immelman was still on the range. He was so befuddled by his golf swing that he invited virtually anyone walking by to offer an opinion—later in the year, he'd grow so scared of hooking the ball that he addressed every club 45 degrees open—and among those who tried to give a lending hand was Adam Scott. Ironically, the handsome young Australian would, like Immelman, find 2009 to be a horrible year on the course, but in March that nightmare was not yet fully evident as Scott launched long, high draws with his driver at a palm tree on the far right of the range. Scott had known Woods for ten years, since they both were guided by Harmon. On the day Scott, who'd spent a year playing golf on a scholarship at the University of Nevada, Las Vegas, decided to turn professional, he called Harmon to break the news. Harmon suggested he drive over to Rio Secco, on the outskirts of Vegas where the swing guru was based, and he'd have a surprise of his own. Scott found Woods waiting. Harmon told Scott that now that he was a pro, he needed to measure himself against the best. "Tiger likes to play for money but I didn't have any, so we just went and played," Scott remembers. After nine holes, Scott was only one down. "I thought, 'This is pretty sweet.'" Woods presumably didn't. He proceeded to win the next five holes, take a penalty stroke for an unplayable lie on the last, and still set a new course record of 63. The following week, Woods would go on to win the U.S. Open at Pebble Beach by a record-shattering 15 shots, and Scott wasn't surprised. "Even though I was still an amateur, I'd played golf with very good professionals, but the golf I saw that day was like nothing I'd ever seen or could even have imagined. He shoots 63 in thirty-miles-per-hour winds on a course where there's fairway and then there's desert, rocks. You miss the fairways and you've got nothing. It was frightening how good he was." So frightening that Scott wondered about his decision to turn professional. "I went home that night and had a re-think about turning pro," he says with a shake of his head. But that was then, and nine years later Scott was a grizzled veteran. He'd got his own $40 million Gulfstream, begun a relationship with the beautiful Serbian tennis star Ana Ivanovic, and saw Woods in an entirely different light. Scott no longer marvelled at Woods's physical talent. Indeed, he plainly said Woods "isn't as intimidating as he used to be," an opinion echoed by other players.

But Scott waxed lyrical about what he now sees as Woods's greatest strengths.

"Of course he's physically gifted, but mentally, that's where no one's even close to this guy. I mean, none of us out here are even close. He's incredible. He's got everything in here [pointing to his head] under control. He beats us by five shots every time with what he's got going on upstairs." Whether that mental superiority would continue after Woods's private life was torn to shreds remained to be seen. "Can he have the same self-esteem as before?" asks Nick Faldo. What Scott specifically was marveling at on that day was how Woods managed his time. "Days are too long out here," the Australian said. "There's no rest time. Wednesday I came out for nine holes. I was here at 8:30, teed off by 10, played nine, had a little practice, had lunch, and I look at my watch and it's 4 o'clock. And now I've got an hour to get ready [for other commitments]. I mean, this is a joke. That's seven and a half hours and that's meant to be the easy day. I'm quite approachable and I've always been that way, so everyone will come for a chat, and I'm not blaming anyone but myself, because I'll stop for a chat. But probably two of those hours I was gas bagging [chatting]. To make a comparison to Tiger, he ain't going to stop for no one. He gets here at 6 or 7 or whenever he tees off in the morning, plays an 18-hole practice round, does his media commitments, and he's home at 12."

Home for the week of Doral for Woods was his $20 million yacht, permanently docked in nearby North Palm Beach, which was more of a floating palace than a yacht. The six-thousand-five-hundred-square-foot triple-decker had a master suite and six staterooms. According to news reports, it was decorated in dark cherrywood and beige marble, with leather-upholstered furniture, white carpeting, and walls covered in white silk. It had a theater projection system, a gym, and an eight-person Jacuzzi, and it could sleep twenty-one people. Not surprisingly, when Woods bought it in 2004, he christened it *Privacy*. It was his escape from the fishbowl of his life, a place—given his love of snorkeling—from which he could launch himself into the sea, where he could be the one doing the staring at the fish. And he got a deal on the price, too, thanks to a reported $1.6 million settlement from the manufacturer, Christensen Shipyards, which he sued for unauthorized use of his image in promoting its business. This was another window into Tiger Woods: don't try to profit at his expense or you will be made to pay.

Woods had finished his traditional Wednesday dawn-patrol practice round at Doral and, again flanked by Steinberg and Greenspan, marched into the resort for his traditional pretournament media conference. Again, Laura Hill was at the podium, and again, Woods stuck to his message. On this day it was that his knee had recovered better than he'd expected but that he needed to play more tournament rounds to get sharper. "I think it just takes reps, rounds, being in a competitive environment and competing again," he said. "I've only played basically two rounds, or if you could say, two tournaments in—what?—ten months, not a whole lot of golf. So for me, I just need rounds under my belt, and this week will obviously be a very positive week for me: four rounds and no cut, to get four more rounds competitively, which is exactly what I need."

After Dove Mountain, where greens were harder to read and more impenetrable than a James Joyce novel, Woods felt happy to be back on familiar turf. But the first round would prove otherwise. It seemed from a 1-under-par round of 71 that what had left him in his time away were those legendary powers of telekinesis. After playing alongside Woods when he won the 2006 PGA Championship at Chicago's Medinah Country Club, Luke Donald remarked that he felt Woods willed the ball into the hole. Anyone who saw the final putt of regulation in 2008 at the Torrey Pines U.S. Open would have to agree; that putt was missing right on the high side the whole way, before suddenly breaking left and catching the hole to set up that victory for the ages. But on this day, as gentle breezes caressed the palms, Woods could will putts only onto the lips of cups. "Doral might have been the best he hit it all year," Williams said later. "And it wasn't that he putted bad, it's just that the ball wouldn't go in. It was the strangest thing."

Standing in a makeshift interview tent by the 18th green, an exasperated Woods called his 71—which left him 6 shots adrift of first round coleaders Phil Mickelson, Jeev Milka Singh, Retief Goosen, and Prayad Marksaeng—the worst score he could've carded based on his ball striking. "It was a little bit frustrating on those greens today," he said. "I hit so many putts that looked good. I thought I hit my lines and I thought I had the right speed, but they just didn't go in." Woods played with Mike Weir, who'd admitted to being curious about his friend's postsurgery game. "He looked good to me," the Canadian said. "He looked like he was compressing the ball; he looked solid. He wasn't favoring his knee at all, it looked like he was well onto his left side at the finish of his swing. It looked like no hesitation there at all." The third member of the group, Robert Karlsson, was also impressed. He especially noted that Woods hit "a number of really impressive-looking drives that I haven't seen him hit in that way before." Karlsson said Woods tended to favor a fade off the tee in the past and would swing very hard. On this day he marveled at the tight draws Woods was hitting with very smooth passes through the ball. "It is now up to him to put all that together in terms of scoring, but he has definitely not lost anything since his injury," said the tall Swede.

The reliance on a draw was not accidental. Drawing the ball requires less body speed—in fact, it demands less body speed—and Woods knew that he wasn't as explosive through the ball as he'd been in the past. For a player who had every shot shape and trajectory mastered, it was no big deal to stay with one. But apart from a dart he threw to within inches on the 15th hole, Woods wasn't really flag hunting with his irons. Typically, he was setting up to the right and looking to draw the ball, but often it didn't draw enough, leaving him longer putts than he wanted. Indeed, his shortest birdie putt in the first round, aside from the tap-in on 15, was a 10-footer. His average distance to the pin was 24 feet, and those weren't always going to fall, even for Woods, whom five-time British Open champion Peter Thomson called "the best 20-foot putter who's ever lived." Woods said, "It's just one of those things that we all know playing the game of golf: you are going to have days like today. I need to be just a touch sharper." And with that he was escorted by a Tour security official to his courtesy car, where Williams waited to drive him back to *Privacy*. It was interesting to note that both Steinberg and Greenspan were gone by the first day of play. At majors, they would stay for the entire week, but Steinberg had young children and, an IMG source said, made every effort to spend weekends at home in Cleveland. Greenspan also returned to his family in south Florida, leaving Woods with only Williams by his side, though they rarely stayed together and did not socialize much away from the course. "We might go out for dinner once in a week, but pretty much he does his thing and I do mine," the caddie said. It perhaps went some way to understanding the double life Woods was leading.

Friday the 13th brought more of the same nightmares for Woods. Although he bettered his opening round by a single shot, he needed a score in the mid-60s to get back into the tournament. Again, he wasn't able to capitalize on good shots, and when he hit a bad one, he paid the price in full. On the 10th, a par 5, he struck a perfect 3-wood to the corner of the dogleg left, his ball riding a stiff breeze on a midflight trajectory, or "traj," as Woods liked to say. From there, a long-iron should have guaranteed, minimally, a 2-putt birdie. But instead, Woods dumped a 3-iron shot into the greenside bunker, hit too much ball from the sand, then 3-putted for bogey. A Roman barista would've been able to brew an espresso using the steam coming out of Woods's ears as he stomped to the 11th tee. Williams trailed well behind, knowing that silence was his only friend.

Williams had been with Woods since 1999. It was a relationship almost over before it began because when Woods first called him to offer his bag, Williams thought it was another caddie pulling a prank and promptly hung up the phone. And neither, strangely, did he jump at the chance. Although he wasn't yet forty, Williams had already spent more than twenty years looping—for a number of Australians, including Greg Norman, before a decade with the game's ultimate grinder, Raymond Floyd—and felt that "this wasn't the sort of thing you do your whole life." He went on, "I thought I'd settle down, go home to New Zealand and do something else, so when Tiger called, I thought about it for a few days. I really wanted to know what his goals were. In all my years caddying, I've never followed golf. I obviously knew who Tiger was, but I wasn't one of these people thinking, 'Wow, this guy's going to be the greatest player ever.' I couldn't tell you how many tournaments he'd won outside of the ones I'd caddied in. But after talking to him, I was very impressed."

Dealing with Woods's temper wasn't as much of a challenge for Williams as it seemed because he'd become adept at gauging the mood of golfers. "Caddying is a very difficult, complex job to explain to someone, even someone who's a golfer. Anybody can carry a golf bag and give yardages. That's easy. You can teach someone how to measure a golf course in two days. But it's the psychology side of it that makes a good caddie. How do you extract the best out of your player? What to say to get things turned around. What not to say. That's what it takes, and you've got to have a very strong resolve. You've got to be able to stand up and say what you think.

"A good caddie knows how to get a player across the line. It's exactly the same as a jockey. You've got to know how to get that horse across the tape first, and a good caddie knows how to do that. Tiger will tell you, the reason we get along so good, I'm the only person apart from his father who can read his mind. And that's why we've been so successful together, because I know what he's thinking and I know what he's going to do next."

Williams also knows to pick his battles. That day in Miami, he left Woods alone, but later in the year, when the scope of Woods's infidelities became clear, Williams did not shirk in criticizing his boss, prompting many to believe he'd be fired. "I'm the sort of person, I've always got to say what I think. If there's something that needs to be said, I'm going to say it. I'm not worried about getting fired tomorrow. A lot of caddies have seen that it's become a very lucrative job now and they don't want to get fired, so they sit on the fence. I'm never one to sit on the fence."

For most professionals, no matter what they say, those kinds of situations leave them convinced that it just wouldn't be their week. So they go through the motions. A few thousand dollars here or there wouldn't make or break them, especially at an event like the Doral, which had no cut and therefore guaranteed money. I put to Woods that, after 3-putting the 10th, perhaps it just wasn't going to be his week. He looked at me like I was an alien. "I figured if I shot 5 under from there on in, I would be in good shape," he said, without the slightest hint of sarcasm or facetiousness. He genuinely believed that he would just rattle off five birdies.

Greenspan later told me that Woods was always like this, calling him "the most positive and optimistic person I've ever known. . . . What's amazing to me is that you never hear him say anything negative," the publicist said. "He's always positive and willing to do whatever it takes to get the job done. He has a bad round and he's not talking about that; he's talking about how he'll need to go out and shoot 65 the next day."

He did get the 65 the next day, but unfortunately he hadn't yet finished the 18th hole. Woods managed to string together a pair of 68s to backdoor his way into the top ten, finishing tied for ninth. As he patiently waited in the baking sun that Sunday after yet another barren afternoon of missed chances for a television interview to begin, he was asked—off camera—about his final round's highlights. "There weren't any highlights," he muttered. Not only was Woods never in the reckoning, but Doral's champion was his nemesis, Mickelson. The mercurial left-hander could be hit or miss, and his chances didn't look great after he came down with a bad case of food poisoning. Mickelson had taken *New York Post* writer Mark Cannizzaro to a well-known steak house to celebrate Cannizzaro's recovery from a serious illness. Mickelson was in such bad shape he had to go to an emergency room and get an IV just to get through the final round. Nonetheless, he held off Nick Wratney and beat Woods by eight strokes. Coupled with his win two weeks before at Los Angeles's famed Riviera, Mickelson had vaulted himself to second in the world rankings. "You're stretching, come up with a better question," Mickelson told a journalist who'd asked whether he had been keeping an eye on Woods, who began the final round ten shots behind the leaders. "Come on, are you serious?" To the winner, the spoils.

But there was an upside for Woods, and it was sizable: he was back. His scores didn't necessarily show it, but his shot making was impressive. With his left knee providing a strong foundation and sparing him the shooting pain he'd learned to live with for years, Woods showed he could make as full and powerful a golf swing as ever. There were no hitches, no rerouting, no sudden thrusts or flipping of the hands to compensate for weaknesses. And although his rotational speed had yet to return, the 355-yard opening drive in the fourth round—leaving him a little 9-iron into the par 5—was a sight to behold, as was the perfect, boring mid-trajectory bullet he launched into a strong headwind on the 8th. For the pretenders to his throne, a long and straight Woods off the tee had to give them pause. Especially since he was stamping out their attempted coups from the rough and the bunkers and the tree lines in years past. In the end, what betrayed him at Doral was the trusty Scotty Cameron putter, usually the most reliable weapon in his bag. For one of the greatest putters in history, Woods's average distance of putts made during the tournament was less than three feet, a tale of futility that left him tied for seventy-eighth in an eighty-man field. The longest putt he made over four rounds was fifteen feet; in all, he made two 15-footers, an 11-footer, a 10-footer, and the next best was holed from four feet. It's mind-boggling to think that in 72 holes, Tiger Woods made only four putts outside of four feet. He later said that he'd hit twenty lips during the week, perhaps the only time such a statistic had ever been kept. "It's part of playing the game," Woods said before leaving Doral. "What are you going to do? Just hit the putts better or hit the ball closer, one of the two." At his next tournament, Arnold Palmer's Bay Hill Invitational, he would do one of the two, and do it unbelievably well.

CHAPTER 3

Bay Hill

Visit the world's great cities and it is soon obvious why the founding fathers chose to break ground there. The sites are practical or aesthetic or, more often, both. Orlando's raison d'être, while neither aesthetic nor romantic, is nevertheless just as obvious: theme parks. A podunk central Florida orange grove town has grown into a sprawling metropolis of more than two million people—and countless billions of bugs—because Walt Disney was looking for cheap swampland. Upon discovering that only 2 percent of Americans east of the Mississippi visited Disneyland in California, the animation pioneer scoured Florida for a site on which to build the world's biggest theme park. On the day John F. Kennedy was assassinated, November 22, 1963, it could be said that Orlando was born. Or at least born again. That was the day Disney flew over the area and noticed bisecting freeways. He'd already decided against locations in Miami and Tampa because they were too prone to hurricanes. The bisecting freeways literally closed the deal.

How Orlando came to be a modern capital of golf is a more complicated story, and far less interesting, but it's an evolution that owes much to Arnold Palmer. The iconic Palmer ventured amid the lakes and orange groves during a 1965 exhibition against Jack Nicklaus at a new course called Bay Hill. It was love at first sight. Bay Hill had been designed four years earlier by the tortured genius Dick Wilson, an alcoholic whose architecture has nonetheless stood the test of time. Indeed, it is worth noting that Woods had won multiple times on every Wilson course that hosted a regular PGA Tour event: Doral's Blue Monster, La Costa in southern California, Chicago's Cog Hill, and Bay Hill. But Palmer wasn't excited about Orlando simply as a winter headquarters. The entrepreneur in him, thriving since joining forces with the shrewd moneymaker Mark McCormack in 1960, had grander plans. After that match against Nicklaus—which Palmer had won—he excitedly told his wife, Winnie, "Babe, I've just played the best course in Florida and I want to own it." It would take a frustrating decade, but Palmer would finally get his wish.

It may be unkind to note but also undeniably true that by March 2009, like its owner and patron saint—who, although almost eighty, beat balls on the range as if he were just one magical swing away from being golf's king again—Bay Hill Club and Lodge was a few decades removed from its heyday. "If you came to Orlando and you wanted high-end golf course living, no, I wouldn't show you homes at Bay Hill," said Orlando Realtor Scott Taylor. "I mean, there are houses there you could have for two hundred grand. A lot of them haven't been upgraded since the seventies." The shame. But while Bay Hill was a little tired, a little Norma Desmond—the nouveau riche had long since moved to more ostentatious, palatial communities like Woods's stomping grounds of Isleworth—Palmer's course was still one of the strongest on the PGA Tour. And, out of respect for Palmer, touring professionals tended to accept an invitation to play his invitational. For many, Woods included, the tournament served as a final tune-up before the Masters.

One player who rarely visited was Mickelson, an absence that illustrated the surprisingly indifferent relationship between him and Palmer. Although cordial, their lack of closeness was odd, given that many saw Mickelson as Palmer's heir as the People's Golfer, kindred spirits beloved not just for what they won but the swashbuckling way they lost. Maybe the left-hander soured on the tournament after falling victim to Woods in 2001 and 2002. Both were crushing losses. The first, Mickelson was convinced, came because of the kind of luck from which Woods regularly seemed to benefit. Years later, Mickelson recalled that Woods hit his tee shot on the 72nd hole way to the left, where his ball caromed "off the fence from going out-of-bounds. . . . He birdied the last hole to beat me, made about a 25-foot putt, but it was how he got there that was what was interesting," Mickelson said wryly. The following year, however, which Mickelson didn't speak of so readily, Woods didn't need smiling lady luck or heroics. Mickelson led by a stroke with five holes to play, but four bogeys down the home stretch gifted Woods the title, his third in a string of four straight.

According to a tournament official, Mickelson soon after made a complaint about "amenities for his family" being not good enough at Bay Hill. Mickelson's displeasure was relayed to Palmer, who personally ordered it addressed, but Mickelson later said he wouldn't return because he didn't like the course. Palmer was stunned. Mickelson—who did ultimately return in 2007— had won at Bay Hill in 1997. But while some wondered whether Woods's dominance at Bay Hill may have factored into Mickelson's decision, a source close to Palmer had another view. "Mickelson's just another one of the spoiled brats out there," he says.

To be fair, Mickelson was not the only player to have raised eye-brows at Bay Hill's lack of largesse. "It's Arnold's money, I guess, and he sure has the attitude that he didn't get as rich as he is by throwing it away," said one player. That was not news to journalists who arrived at Bay Hill's tennis courts to find a quaint old media tent, inside of which it was always 1976. But it is also true that both players and journalists have become spoiled; amenities aren't expected just to be free but also of a certain standard. Gratis isn't good enough anymore when tournaments seduce the millionaires of the PGA Tour by providing shopping sprees and luxurious spa services for their wives, nannies for their kids, or valet parking and hospitality tents for their caddies. Palmer, along with Nicklaus, who hosted the Memorial tournament in his hometown of Columbus, Ohio, decided long ago that they wouldn't play that game. To them, the prize money should be enough incentive, but the scene elsewhere was yet another reflection of what the Woods factor brought.

Woods never hung around Bay Hill long enough to have formed an opinion either way. If he was pushed to provide one, though, it was a safe bet to say he'd pat Palmer—whom he saw as a mentor—on the back, as they were birds of a feather when it came to holding on to their money. As the revelation of Woods's secret life of illicit affairs showed, he and Palmer had much more in common than golf. Palmer was a womanizer who benefited from living in an era in which celebrity gossip websites didn't exist and a golfer's personal life wasn't discussed in public. His peers kept his secret, though former PGA champion and longtime television analyst Bob Rosburg let the cat out of the bag in a 1988 interview, when he told a humorous story of an irate husband threatening Palmer. Rosburg later regretted telling the story because it "hurt" Winnie Palmer, but he never denied that it was true. "You know, the women loved him," Rosburg said of Palmer, "and he's the same as the rest of us." Indeed, many golfers still refer to the "Winnie Rule," which stipulates that any indiscretions must be kept away from the family home because a wife must never be embarrassed. Greg Norman's flouting of the Winnie Rule eventually cost him upward of $100 million in a divorce settlement when his wife, Laura, drew the line at his affair with her closest friend, former tennis champion Chris Evert.

But such nightmares were far from Woods's mind when he arrived early the Wednesday morning before the Arnold Palmer Invitational in his black Cadillac Escalade, provided to him free of charge by General Motors even though he no longer had a sponsorship agreement with the automaker. Later in the year, that car would become as symbolic a prop as O. J. Simpson's white Ford Bronco had been fifteen years before in the unraveling of a sporting legend. Woods, who lived about a ten-minute drive away, literally arrived with his golf shoes already laced.

He had won at Bay Hill the year before, providing one of those signature victory images in the process. He needed to make birdie on the 72nd and, having virtually the same putt he had made to beat Mickelson in 2001, made it again. Of course he did, because that was what he did. In 2008, Woods was so consumed by the jubilation of the moment that he ripped his hat off and threw it to the ground, which he later did not remember doing. "I was so into the moment," he said after watching himself on television. "I didn't know I went that crazy." That may be true, but it was also true that like many other elite athletes, Woods took a certain pride in watching himself on ESPN. "He likes the dramatic," said Williams. "He loves to make *SportsCenter.*"

Despite Palmer's constant tinkering with the design, Woods knew Bay Hill well enough to need only one practice round. He'd been buoyed by having struck the ball better with each passing round at Doral. Williams gauged Woods's ball striking when a shot was needed under pressure, as it was on the closing hole at Doral, especially with the wind blowing. "That 18th hole is a difficult driving hole and he hit four perfect drives there," Williams said. "He played great at Doral, but he putted average. He didn't putt bad, but it was one of those weeks where he just couldn't make one." And so Woods spent his off week focusing on his putting. As always, he went back to the lessons his father had taught him as a boy. "Dad had everything to do with my putting stroke," he said at Bay Hill. "How I putt now is how I always putted as a kid. I look at the picture, how I get my feel, the drills that I do—everything has been taught by my dad. When I go out there and practice my putting, like I did at Doral, I didn't putt well, I didn't make any putts, I went back to all my basics that my dad taught me. It's good times, good memories going back to all those different things. And even I remember in some of the good years I've had in golf, like '99, 2000, 2001, coming back to southern California I'd take my dad out and we'd go putt, and he'd routinely beat me. Anything he said about putting, I'd always listen. He just had a wonderful feel, a wonderful touch, and I really understood how to make the ball roll consistently each and every time." Could Earl, who was not a healthy man at that time and whom I once saw consume a breakfast of three Bloody Marys and a half dozen menthol cigarettes, really have lowered the colors of the most clutch putter in the history of golf? It was possible, of course, but perhaps what the story most said was that Tiger missed his father. Each year around the anniversary of Earl's death—May 3, 2006—Woods became melancholy. "It's a depressing time for him. He really did love the old man and he misses him a lot," said a member of Woods's inner circle. It was perhaps a silent acknowledgment of regret, too, as in the final years of Earl's life his son lived on the other side of the country, had his own family to tend to, ran his own affairs, and probably didn't spend as much time with his father as he could have. In that sense, Tiger Woods was like any of us who'd lost a father suddenly.

Fresh from work on the practice green, Woods made his way into the humble media tent for his mandated pretournament interview. I'd always wondered how many times Woods would appear before the media if it was not demanded of him by the PGA Tour. Whatever that number was, it most certainly would have shrunk after one of the more revealing news conferences of the season on a hot and humid Orlando afternoon. Woods generally abhorred answering personal questions. "Why do they have to know everything?" he plaintively asked in a *Golf Digest* article when still a teenager. But from time to time, when the mood struck him, he'd answer with something approaching forthrightness. He was asked on this day whether he felt he'd changed more as a player or a person since he'd been on the Tour. "I think a person," Woods replied after a moment's thought. "When I first came out here I was single, now obviously being married with two kids. The brand has certainly grown to where I'm doing golf course design, licensing, just different things that I hadn't done before when I first came out here. It was just all golf. I didn't have the balance in my life at the time that I do now, and I didn't know how to." It was revealing to hear Woods describe himself as a "brand." Certainly others had used the term when speaking of him, and it was not an inaccurate description, but it was nonetheless odd to hear a man use such a cold, impersonal word to describe himself. It was almost as if he thought of Tiger Woods as a creation apart from the person he really was.

Woods was asked whether he felt he made mistakes. He said he had, though he did not elaborate. This again was an important part of the Woods psyche to understand: he didn't ever claim to be perfect, but neither was he about to confess his imperfections. "I'm still going to make mistakes, but I think that understanding responsibilities, understanding a life changes, and it's changed for the better, there's no doubt. . . . To have the stability that I have in my life off the golf course has definitely made me a better person on the golf course." Usually that would be enough man beneath the Nike cap to last months. But it didn't last even minutes because Woods would have to deal with a piercing line of questioning from Mark Schwarz, an ESPN "Outside the Lines" reporter working on a story about blacks in professional golf. "A couple of bigger-picture questions about the Tour, specifically African-American representation on the Tour," Schwarz began. "When you were a year old, there were twelve African Americans on the Tour. Today, depending on how you define demographics, there's one. From a racial diversity standpoint, the Tour seems to have gone backward. What does it mean to you?"

The entire expression on Woods's face changed when he was challenged by questions about his role in society. He could talk golf or any sports with humor and playfulness, but he would get very serious very quickly when he had to address more important issues. Perhaps he was just protecting the brand? Woods, it had to be said, was very sensitive to criticism about his societal re-sponsibilities. There was no doubt he'd wished Earl hadn't gone around telling people his kid would have a bigger impact on the world than Gandhi. Tiger Woods really just wanted to make more birdies than Gandhi did. He was no champion of the oppressed, no rebel with or without a cause, and, in fairness, he shouldn't be forced into such a role. It was either in his DNA or it wasn't. And in Tiger Woods's case, it was not. Nevertheless, Woods gave Schwarz an intelligent answer without implicating himself in any way. "I think it's become harder to play out here," he said. "Play-ing opportunities and development and being able to learn the game and mature in the game has become more difficult. If you look at where a lot of those [black] players started, they started through the caddie ranks. That's now gone. A lot of golf courses have golf carts, mandatory golf carts, and players aren't being introduced to the game how they used to. And then the cost of getting involved in the game, and then the maintenance of a person trying to play day in and day out, it's not easy. You know, you have to get lucky and have people let you on for free at times. Like for instance, I grew up on a par-3 course. That's how I played. And then also I grew up on a military course. Two places where it wasn't very expensive. And then to get the exposure to develop your game, it's just very difficult."

Schwarz, however, was neither satisfied with the soft-shoe shuffle nor finished. "And a follow-up, if I could. I've interviewed some people who are coming up behind you, players on the mini-tours, also Eddie Payton, the golf coach at Jackson State, a historically black school. They look at you and say, 'He could do so much more for this cause. He could be more accessible, he could be more tangible, he could use his resources and be there and reach out to people like us.' What do you say to people like that who criticize?" Now Woods's face really became tense. His lips were pursed and he spoke as if he were making an end-of-year oral presentation in front of his civics teacher. Again, while the content of what he said may have been rehearsed, the sentiment was very much his. Woods was remarkably honest about how he saw his wider role. He truly believed that his greatest contribution was to help children find their way in life, just as he was helped in finding his way. But not necessarily through golf, or sports. "Well, I reach out each and every day with my foundation," he told Schwarz. "That's what we do. We don't focus on golf, because that's not the sole purpose of life. Life is not about hitting a high draw and a high fade. It's about being a better person each and every day and helping others. That's what life is all about. Is golf a part of people's lives? Yes, it's part of my life. But it's not the end of all things in my life. I want kids to be able to have a better life because of their brain and their intelligence and their ability to use that to help others, and if they want to play golf, then sure, we have the means to help them through our foundation. But I'd much rather see them become leaders of tomorrow than see kids just hit a high draw and a high fade." And maybe he was not wrong in believing that tangibly helping one kid was more worthwhile than marching alongside Jesse Jackson. And anyway, it was doubtful whether he and the Reverend Jackson would share many beliefs. Barack Obama was probably the first Democrat for whom Woods had ever voted. He was not a political animal at all. His friend and mentor Michael Jordan taught him well how the brand could be damaged by the kind of controversy that politics invites. "Republicans and Democrats both buy sneakers," Jordan once famously said. And, of course, everyone knew that a black man who threatened white society wouldn't sell as much Gatorade as one seen as friendly. As far as I could tell, Woods had two core political beliefs: first and foremost, he wanted low taxes, and he also wanted the military supported. Though a registered Independent, he was a natural-born Republican in a sport filled with them. I once asked Paul Goydos, the resident wit of the Tour, how many professional golfers were Democrats. "Well, there's me," he said, pausing for a beat. "Did I say me already?"

It was an oversimplification to suggest, as some have done, that Woods supported Obama solely because they both had black fathers and nonblack mothers. But there was no question that he identified with the president on levels that had nothing to do with budgetary policy. Woods had always proudly considered himself of mixed race; he even invented a term to describe his race: Cablinasian (Caucasian, black, Indian, Asian). If he was pushed, he would probably identify more as Thai, an acknowledgment of his mother's influence in shaping him. He was irked at being described as black in large part because he felt it disrespectful to his mother. But the kids he grew up with in the predominantly white neighborhood in Orange County, California, had no interest in his diverse ethnicity. To them he was—as he'd recall in Charles Barkley's 2005 book on race in America, *Who's Afraid of a Large Black Man?*—a "nigger." Woods later acknowledged that he was "hardened" by those who would "use the N word with me numerous times." "I became aware of my racial identity on my first day of school, on my first day of kindergarten," Woods told Barkley. "A group of sixth graders tied me to a tree, spray-painted the word 'nigger' on me, and threw rocks at me. That was my first day of school. And the teacher really didn't do much of anything. I used to live across the street from school and kind of down the way a little bit. The teachers said, 'Okay, just go home.' So I had to outrun all these kids going home, which I was able to do. It was certainly an eye-opening experience, you know, being five years old. We were the only minority family in all of Cypress, California." And so, when Obama was elected, Woods broke his code of silence on political matters—and sacrificed the sale of some sneakers and bottles of Gatorade—to hail the moment as "absolutely incredible. . . . My father was hoping it would happen in his lifetime, but he didn't get to see it. I'm lucky enough to have seen a person of color in the White House."

Barkley had long challenged Woods on race. "Tiger likes to be okay with everybody, to appeal to all people," the former basketball star told *Newsweek* in 2001. "And I tell him, 'That's cool, but the race card is here to stay.' So he knows he's black. Enough has happened to him to see that: the playa hatin' on the all-white PGA Tour and the hate mail and the death threats he gets. I tell him that Thai people don't get hate mail, black people do."

Although Woods left as soon as his news conference was over, the driving range at Bay Hill was still lined with television cam-

eras. As I waited to interview Vijay Singh—the big Fijian enjoyed testing the patience of the media, in the way boys tortured
insects—I noticed the fuss was over the Japanese teen star, Ryo
Ishikawa. A middle-aged Japanese man, whom I assumed was
from one of the Japanese television networks, stood next to me
in the only shade offered on the range, and we exchanged small
talk. He asked me in broken English what I thought of Ishikawa's
swing. I told him I thought it was too much of the reverse-c swing
that ruined the backs of all the great golfers of the seventies. I
told him that I didn't remember Ishikawa flinging his hips and
hanging his upper body back so pronouncedly at Riviera earlier
in the year. He said it was a move taught to him by his new coach.
After about forty minutes, I asked him which television network
he was with. "No TV," he said. "I am his father." I tried to tell
him that my opinion wasn't especially valuable, but he would
hear none of it. He told me that I was a very knowledgeable golf
instructor and left. The young man's coach was soon after fired.
The story illustrated the fickle and faddish world of professional
golf, where relationships could be as lasting as high school ro-
mances. At the other end of the range was Aaron Baddeley, the
young Australian who'd become the poster child for the Stack &
Tilt method of hitting a golf ball. As we exchanged greetings, Baddeley told me that although he'd professed in interviews and an
instructional DVD that the Stack & Tilt method was superior to all
others, he'd given it up and gone back to his boyhood coach, Dale
Lynch, whom he'd originally abandoned for the marketing genius
that was David Leadbetter, before dumping him for Stack & Tilt.

Woods was not immune to the insecurity that comes with
golf. The swing is, really, a mysterious if not mystical thing. One
day it works and the next day it doesn't, yet everything can feel
precisely the same other than the ball veering off in all sorts of
demented vectors. At Doral, Woods's swing was a thing of beauty—

controlled beauty. But all of that counted for nothing at Bay Hill, where he started hitting the ball sideways. When he managed to find the middle of the fairway, he inevitably set up for a draw with an iron and slammed the club into the ground when the ball drew six inches instead of six yards. But, true to the Woods tradition, he applied gauze, in the form of a stellar short game, and stopped the bleeding. Somehow, through three rounds, Woods was at 2 under par for the tournament. On Saturday, he drained a 25-footer for bogey on the last hole to card a 1-over-par 71. He and Williams left the course with many names ahead of them on the leaderboard. Then the wind really kicked up that afternoon and the scores went up, too. Tommy Armor III, normally one of the coolest cats on the Tour, stormed off the course after shooting a 6-over-par 76. "Somebody get me a fucking cigarette," he barked at no one in particular.

Woods and Williams were surprised to find that they'd be in the final group on Sunday. "Tiger played pretty average for two rounds but in windy conditions on Saturday posted a good round, not a great round, but we leave the course two hours ahead of the leaders and all of a sudden they've all come back to the field with the exception of Sean O'Hair," said Williams. The caddie knew his man wasn't hitting the ball very well, but he'd been around too long to discount his chances, even with O'Hair—a beautiful iron player—five shots ahead. "The one thing about Tiger is that come Sunday, he'll find a way to compete even if he's playing poorly. He finds a way on Sunday to stay in there. When you've got a five-shot lead you're not going to play that aggressive. So if he [O'Hair] makes a couple of mistakes early, Tiger makes a couple of birdies, it changes the whole dynamic." How prescient Williams would prove to be. O'Hair, who had a history of being unable to close the deal, was no match for the best closer any sport's ever seen. It was a lamb against a lion. "His five-shot lead was down to one by the turn," says Williams. "That's where you're always going to take your hat off to Tiger. He finds a way to get it done." And in the most dramatic, theatrical way. Woods spent the day willing the ball into the hole; three times he was plugged in bunkers and made heroic pars. Typically, it came down to the last hole. He had 16 feet for birdie to win the tournament in fading light. The final green at Bay Hill was a natural amphitheater. The electricity in the air was palpable. Palmer stood to the side of the green. "It's happened every time," he said. Zach Johnson was being interviewed behind the green when he looked over and rolled his eyes. "I don't think I've ever seen him make a putt when he really needed it," he said. "And that was the epitome of sarcasm." As Woods sized up the putt, someone yelled out, "Playoff!" The light was fading so quickly that the Tour had made contingency plans to return to Bay Hill at 10 a.m. the following morning. Woods later said he'd heard the shout. "I thought, nah," he said. The flashbulbs of cameras gave the scene a surreal aura as Woods's ball fell into the hole and he struck a pose that would lead every newspaper's sports page—if not front page—the next day.

After accepting the trophy from Palmer—a unique sixteenth-century hand-crafted Scottish Highlander Claymore sword—Woods, wearing a too-big blue winner's jacket, wandered over to the media tent. Williams threw Woods's clubs in the back of the Escalade and left the engine running in the lane outside. The role of getaway driver suited him. But his boss wasn't in a hurry to escape. Woods sat politely and almost anonymously at the back of the interview room—clutching his trophy—while O'Hair, still heartbroken over a final-round 73, bristled when I asked whether he'd felt the same awe watching Woods drop the winning putt. "It's not like it's the Tiger Show and I'm just out there to watch him," he said. "We're trying to win golf tournaments and he just happens to be that good." Woods wasn't ever cruel when the battle was over. He liked O'Hair, and by his demeanor it was obvious that he emphathized.

As he sat there in the chair, looking like everyone else, it occurred to me that perhaps this might have been Tiger Woods in his native state. He seemed to me a wide-eyed boy, holding joyously on to his trophy. There was something very sweet, very innocent about him in that moment. Upon taking the podium, he spoke about the importance of winning a tournament so soon after his comeback. "I hadn't been in the mix since the U.S. Open," he said. "So it was neat to feel the heat on the back nine again, and got myself into the hunt and into contention." But while the world gushed that golf's superhero was back and once again ready to dominate his sport, I got the feeling that Woods himself understood that this was a victory made from smoke and mirrors. His putting had masked flaws that needed to be addressed before the Masters. Later in the year, I would ask him how he viewed his sixth title at Bay Hill. Removed from the adrenaline of the moment, he replied with clarity and a shrug of his shoulders. "If you have 102 putts," he said, "you should win the tournament."

CHAPTER 4

The Masters

Maybe because he was a transplanted New Englander and not culturally bound by the genteel mores of the South, four-time Tour winner Billy Andrade said it best about Augusta. If it weren't for a certain golf course, the only reason to veer off Interstate 20 at exit 199 would be to "gas up and grab a donut before getting back on the road." Augusta National's presence about a mile from the Washington Road exit, in the midst of an otherwise unremarkable Southern city of almost two hundred thousand, is the most incongruous of juxtapositions, like surrounding the Taj Mahal with strip malls and a Wal-Mart. For an out-of-towner, it is impossible to conceive of one place sustaining so many fast-food joints and churches; for good measure, there is even a fast-food joint called Church's.

But the oddity of the setting is quickly forgotten, left behind along with the riffraff of Washington Road once the turn is made onto Magnolia Lane, Augusta National's historic entrance. A journey down that boulevard of golfing dreams is like traveling through dimensions, through a crease in time and space. Because nothing inside the gates of Augusta National remotely relates to what is on the outside of the onetime indigo plantation. First-time players at the Masters usually don't fare well because, as Geoff Ogilvy says, "you're like a tourist when you first come here and it's easy to forget you're supposed to be playing in a tournament that happens to be a major." On the inside, it is the place where time stood still. A Coke sets you back a dollar and another buck fifty buys a sandwich, though be sure to stay away from the pimiento cheese, which is, euphemistically speaking, an acquired taste. Those lucky enough to sit on the upstairs veranda of the clubhouse can enjoy the chowder and the peach cobbler à la mode washed down by the finest homemade lemonade for less than the same meal would cost at a dingy diner on Washington Road. And it is not just the prices that never change. "It's such a unique place because you come here and see the same faces and they're sitting in the same seats, year after year," says Greg Norman, who finished fourth in his very first Masters in 1981 and, after a quixotic tilt at the 2008 British Open, where he led with nine holes to play before succumbing to reality and taking third, had qualified for one last hopelessly romantic shot at the elusive green jacket.

An old caddie, when one of us asked how long he'd been walking these acres, pointed to the 18th and remembered that he was coming up the steep fairway when he "heard the news that they bombed Pearl Harbor." Caddies—a predominantly African-American corps with colorful names like Stovepipe, Sweetness, Po Baby, and Daybreak—may not be able to walk anymore, much less schlep golf bags, yet they are still taken out in carts by members because they've been reading those greens since they were boys. For the uninitiated novice, trying to read the putts on Augusta's famous greens—imagine putting on mounded linoleum—is like trying to understand Sanskrit. Stuart Appleby took a local caddie during a practice round one year and got a read on the first green, which was ten feet farther right than where the Australian was looking. "Now this wasn't my first rodeo. I'd already played six or seven of these things at that stage and I thought I knew my way around, so I play half [the break he was given] and it almost goes off the green. Not even close. I drop another ball and putt it to where he told me, and sure as hell I almost make the thing. I suppose that's why they call it local knowledge."

For all the folklore associated with the Masters, it is the course itself that is the star of the show. The National is the most pristine of three-dimensional portraits, a setting for fairy tales. The reverence with which the course is held is evident everywhere, from the ludicrously expensive SP-55 sand in the bunkers, which makes them look like they are filled with brilliant white sugar, to the way the fairways are not so much mowed as manicured. One of my favorite moments during the week of the Masters is to watch the mowers line up at dusk and waltz in synchronization. At three-eighths of an inch and without a single blade of grass out of place, many a municipal course would love to have these fairways as greens. And each hole has a name, not just a number, so the round begins with Tea Olive and ends with Holly. And everywhere there is history.

Designed by the former English surgeon Alister MacKenzie, whom club founder Bobby Jones chose ahead of Donald Ross to create his dream course, Augusta National is arguably the most exclusive golf club in the world. Money alone can't buy membership, much to the chagrin of many wealthy men, including Microsoft founder Bill Gates, who might have been the richest man in the world but was made to cool his heels for years before being invited to join. Among the three hundred or so members are the predictable clusters of aging oil barons and captains of industry and banking; it is a club where the whippersnappers are in their fifties. But while these men—and they are, famously, all men—might literally own the place, Tiger Woods, in a stretch of four days during 1997, made Augusta his realm. That unforgettable victory, by a record-setting twelve strokes, changed the face of golf. For the first time, golf broke the fifty-million-viewer barrier on television in the United States. Thanks to Tiger Woods, golf was no longer the domain of the WASP country club elite. His deeds and, just as crucially, his sponsors' capitalization on those deeds through saturation marketing campaigns, guaranteed that as long as Woods was riding high, golf would, too.

Augusta National was his stage, then, as the Globe was to Shakespeare, the Met to Caruso, La Scala to Verdi. By 2002, Woods had won his third green jacket and it seemed that Jack Nicklaus may have underclubbed with his 1996 prediction to Arnold Palmer that Woods would win the Masters more times than the two of them combined (six and four, respectively). But Woods would have to wait until 2005 to claim a fourth Masters title, and even that was lucky. He closed with two bogeys, allowing the scrappy Chris DiMarco into a playoff. Woods played the 73rd hole perfectly, hitting a 3-wood and an 8-iron to set up the winning birdie, salvaging his reputation as the game's greatest closer. But it had the feeling of papering over cracks, cracks that did not go unnoticed in the locker room.

After hoisting the trophy in seven of eleven majors between August 1999 and June 2002, Woods instilled fear in opponents. If he held the lead on a Sunday, everyone knew how the story would end, including the poor sap who was playing alongside him. "He had that confidence that he knew he was better than you and he was going to go out and prove it," says Hunter Mahan. But after opting to change his swing again, this time in accordance with Hank Haney's idiosyncratic theories, Woods would endure ten straight majors without a win. By April 2005, Woods no longer was the intimidating giant among Lilliputians. "Guys weren't scared anymore," says Mahan. "They figured out he could be beaten." Though some of his victims from the early part of the decade were left with permanent psychological scars—Els, Garcia, Montgomerie, and David Duval, chief among them—other pretenders to his throne saw him as flesh and blood. His swing was prone to misfiring, just like theirs, and there were days when his legendary Scotty Cameron putter couldn't save him.

Among the herculean deeds of 2000, when Woods won the final three majors of the season—then added the 2001 Masters to hold all four of the sport's glittering prizes at once, the so-called Tiger Slam—it was easily forgotten that he'd had his colors lowered by Darren Clarke in the final of the match play at La Costa. Even Clarke's manager, the always colorful English artful dodger Chubby Chandler, gave his man little hope of the upset. "Ah, he's a big baby," Chandler told me when I asked about Clarke's constitution. Hard to imagine an IMG agent being so honest. But Chandler was happily proved wrong. The Ulsterman took some mighty blows from Woods, but he wouldn't go down and ultimately prevailed over thirty-six holes. Woods would unexpectedly fall to others, the little-known Australians O'Malley and O'Hern, Jeff Maggert, Chad Campbell and, in 2002, for the first time at a major when Woods was in contention, the leader didn't fold like a cheap suit. Rich Beem, a gambler from west Texas who knew that real pressure was playing for your own money, held his nerve and provided the ripostes to Woods's string of late birdies to claim the PGA Championship at Minnesota's Hazeltine. "It's like the old four-minute-mile marker: Once somebody [broke] it, then everybody got it in their mind that they can do it," says Woods's former college teammate and good friend, Notah Begay.

Technology, too, had changed golf while at the same time hurting Woods. By the middle of the decade, Woods was no longer thirty yards ahead of the field off the tee. He may have pioneered pumping iron and maximizing the physical advantage, but ironically his stirring deeds brought stud athletes to the Tour. There may have been a handful of touring pros in the gym when Woods was a rookie, but within a decade there were a handful who had not added a personal trainer to their entourage. Advances in ball and shaft technology enabled many competitors to hit as far as Woods and, in many cases, straighter. "The fields are getting deeper," Woods observed. "With the equipment technology, guys' margins of mishits are not going as far off line. The game is getting closer and closer together. It just makes it harder to win." Woods was slow to embrace technological innovations. He preferred steel shafts to graphite and wanted a higher-spinning ball so he could retain the ability to shape shots. Woods once asked Annika Sorenstam—who was also managed by Steinberg—what her "go-to" shot was. The Swede replied that she just hit her normal shot, which was a straight ball. Woods couldn't fathom such an answer because in his mind, a reliable shot hit under the cosh should be shaped to go one way with a consistent flight. But while that may have been the case for many years, it was no longer necessary once the rocket scientists who'd been laid off by defense contractors in the 1990s were hired by golf companies.

After Woods had his way with the ol' southern belle in 1997—hitting a mere half a sand wedge into the last hole to seal his triumph—he had to know that Augusta's green coats, like Confederate generals in the War of Northern Aggression, would not stand idly by and watch their precious treasure be rendered obsolete. The members' rearguard action involved hatching a plan to "Tiger-proof" the course. The redesign, which stretched her tighter than the face of a Beverly Hills dowager, altered the sight lines of many holes. The National had been made by MacKenzie in the image of its patron saint, Bobby Jones, who'd ordered up holes that accommodated his high, hooking draw. Woods, prior to his swing overhaul, was a high right-to-left player, too, so the fit was natural. But by lengthening Augusta to 7,435 yards, it became just another long course. Woods had spent years figuring out where to play into greens so the ball would catch the notorious undulations just right and leave him with a viable birdie putt. It was true that only at Augusta was the best shot sometimes one played twenty feet away from a pin. Those plays were far more difficult to achieve with mid-irons at bad angles than with wedges at good ones. "I just remember being here as an amateur and being able to play practice rounds with so many great champions, guys telling me where to hit it, what angles you want to have," Woods says. "But over the years, that's changed. You don't have those angles anymore because you don't get those locations because the golf course has changed."

Still, Woods was coming off a win at Bay Hill and was once again, in the eyes of many of the savants, the Masters favorite. Perhaps he deserved to be whenever he played, but the truth was that something had soured in the love affair between Tiger Woods and Augusta National. There were hints of a break in the harmonic in 2003 and 2004, when Woods recorded two of only three finishes outside the top eight in twelve Masters appearances as a professional. Although he survived DiMarco in 2005, he was unconvincing. And the estrangement continued over the next three years. In 2006, Woods finished third, followed by a tie for second in 2007 and was runner-up again in 2008. He could easily have won them all, but he uncharacteristically stalled on each Sunday afternoon. Weather was a factor—not only was Augusta National longer, but it was playing longer still because of rain and/or frigid cold—but since when had a long course been anything but an advantage for Woods?

The explanations, then, had to come from within. In the twelve rounds he'd played in those three years, only one—the Saturday of 2008—was in the 60s. His final rounds were marked by misadventure and exasperation, especially at putts that wouldn't fall. In 2006, he lost by three shots to Mickelson when, in perfect scoring conditions, he could only muster a Sunday round of 70. Seven players shot in the 60s that day, including Mickelson. The following year he lost by two shots to Zach Johnson after turning in a disappointing even-par Sunday round of 72 while Johnson, Rory Sabbatini, and Retief Goosen (the later two tied for second with Woods) all had 69s. In retrospect, this day was a watershed moment for Woods. It was easily forgotten, but he had, albeit briefly, the final-round lead. For the first time in his career, Woods couldn't close the deal. Johnson's sharp iron play and unconventional but effective putting style won the day. In 2008, Woods finished three shots behind Trevor Immelman after another final-round 72.

It seemed to me that what had changed was Woods. He was playing not to lose rather than to win. Perhaps this was the hangover of all those majors won by doing not much other than watching opponents implode. Woods was no longer the aggressive Sunday player he had been. When I asked him about his failures at Augusta, it was clear from his disposition that he was both fully aware of and not happy about the turn in his fortunes. "Frustrating," he said through gritted teeth. He would later blame the downfall on putting. "The last couple of years, my putting has been streaky here. I get on rolls where I make everything and I get on rolls where I didn't make anything. Consequently, I didn't win the tournament. You have to be very consistent around this golf course, especially now; there are not too many birdie opportunities. It's not like how it used to be. So given that, you've just got to be, obviously, very patient, and hit the ball well, but make the putts when you have the opportunities, because they are not going to come as frequently as they used to."

Woods made a surprise appearance at Augusta late on Monday afternoon when the course was nearly deserted. A bitingly cold and strong wind had made conditions unbearable and, as players retreated for the comfort of the former plantation homestead that serves as Augusta's iconic clubhouse, the patrons—the quaint term the club likes to use for spectators—left, too. Tim Clark and Jeev Milkha Singh, both looking to impress the International captain Greg Norman in a Presidents Cup year, scheduled a practice round with the Shark and his protégé, Adam Scott, yet when the foursome putted out on the 9th green, Clark and Singh bid their farewells and scampered indoors. Scott was cold, too, but didn't want to leave Norman by himself. It was interesting that Scott would be a surprise captain's pick, and Singh was overlooked.

Woods started his practice round on the 10th hole and made it to 14 before he, too, had had enough of the arctic conditions. He cut across to play the 18th, jumping ahead of Norman and Scott, whom he did not see as they practiced putting from different sections of the 17th green. The Australians both good-naturedly admonished him for his bad etiquette. The triumvirate—not so long ago they might have represented golf's immediate past, its daunting present, and its promising future—then played the 18th together, giving the few remaining spectators something to remember. If Woods thought Augusta had been less than hospitable to him, perhaps he needed to compare scorecards with Norman. Somehow, the larger-than-life Australian never won a Masters despite finishing in the top six nine times. He should've won at least one of those by accident and, of course, infamously choked on a six-shot final-round lead in 1996. Bad things always happened

to him on Sundays in Augusta. Coronations turned into cruci-
fixions. "You know, everyone thinks I hate this place because of
everything that's happened to me here," he told me one day as we
stood beneath the old oak in front of the clubhouse. "But I love
this place." He paused for a moment, those piercing blue eyes
gazing out at the Georgia pines that frame the 10th hole. "The
problem is it never loved me back."

If it was the week of a major and Tuesday afternoon and the
clock struck 1, that could mean only one thing: an announcement
made in the media center that "Tiger Woods is in the interview
room." Woods was a creature of habit. He awoke at 5, ate his
cereal, watched cartoons—some of us never truly grow up—then
did precisely what he did the day before, only he tried to do it
better. Tuesday mornings at majors he'd put a peg in the ground
at the earliest possible time, always first off and often accompanied only by Williams. Woods liked to play quickly and do his
due diligence on the course setup. Once that was done, he did
his media commitments, then left for his rented house. Nothing
meant more to Woods in golf than the majors. After spending the
year watching him at close quarters, it was noticeable just how
his demeanor changed during the week of a major. At Bay Hill
on the practice green before the final round, Woods was laughing
and joking—well, teasing actually—with Sean O'Hair about the
fortunes of their respective basketball teams. This was tough to
do with Woods because he claimed teams from southern California, where he grew up, as well as Orlando, where he lived, plus
all kinds of pull-ins: for instance, despite being a lifelong Raiders
fan, he was also a big Indianapolis Colts fan due to his friendship with Peyton Manning, and while he loved the Dodgers, he
was also a huge New York Yankees fan due to his friendship with
Derek Jeter. O'Hair gets teams only from his native Philadelphia,
so he was usually on the receiving end of Woods's taunts. "I'm

from Philly, I'm naturally a ball breaker," says O'Hair, "but he's just better than I am."

But during the week of a major, Woods would go into shutdown. He wouldn't drink coffee for fear that the caffeine would affect his putting stroke, and he wouldn't pick up his phone. Even to friends like Charles Barkley and Michael Jordan, he was totally out of communication for the week of a major. "I don't know anyone who texts more than him, but you know better than to try to get something out of him during a major," says Fred Couples. "He goes into lockdown mode." At the other three majors, Woods had some level of control at his news conferences. The ever-present Steinberg would sit in the room and had developed a code to make the moderator aware of his feelings about how the interview was progressing. If Steinberg thought his man had done enough talking, he would either brush his cheek with his hand or, if standing, pat the side of his leg. The finger across the throat might be a tad too obvious, but the intent was the same. Once Steinberg gave the cue, journalists invariably were told that Woods would take just one or two more questions.

But at Augusta National, the rules are different. Press conferences last as long as the green coat who's conducting them decides they will last. Within the confines of the club, the green coats are a law unto themselves. I once observed a member of the media committee attempting to drive a golf cart between two large and, it turned out, recalcitrant bushes next to the media center. That the cart got stuck should have been obvious (not to mention predictable). But rather than back out, he floored the gas pedal, causing a commotion as the wheels spun. The cart was jammed. Several security guards came to his assistance, but they knew better than to try to stop him. Instead, they pushed as hard as they could to get the cart through the gap and eventually one of the bushes was rendered roadkill. But at least the green coat was on his way. The green coats don't always get their way. The English peacock Ian Poulter had two very choice words in 2009, for instance, for a security guard sent by a green coat to the practice green to remind Poulter that iPods were not allowed on the grounds. But the general rule is that members are not to be crossed.

And so Woods sat in that room for an hour, answering all sorts of questions, including one about Italian World Cup soccer star Fabio Cannavaro, with whom Woods had shot a television commercial. Woods knew about rugby because Williams was a rugby nut—New Zealanders have to be good at something—and since marrying a Swede, Woods also discovered the beauty of real football, though he still had a lot to learn. Looking back on that news conference, two answers stood out. The first went to a subject I had brought up with him several times: did he not think it was beyond coincidental that so many putts fell when he absolutely had to make them? The winning putts at Torrey Pines and Bay Hill were just two of many. Woods was raised a Buddhist, so I half expected him to talk of karma, but instead he argued that if he had such powers, they would always work. "I don't know if I have telekinesis, but it sure would be nice, some of the shots I've hit before to keep them from going into the water. But that just hasn't happened," he said. "I think it's just the moment. Your concentration, your energy, everything comes down to one moment. It's been a crescendo. For our sport, it takes four days to get to that moment. For some reason, putts have gone in." The other answer he gave seemed very different in light of the string of extramarital affairs he had been conducting. He spoke of the difference he felt in life priorities since starting a family. "Golf has certainly evolved in my life. Having kids is the most important thing in your life. It puts a totally different perspective on your life, and making sure that you raise your kids as best as you possibly can. You know, when you have a bad round and you come home, it puts it in perspective. You have kids, and it's really not that bad. You know, no matter how bad your day was on the course, it's not that bad when you come home."

The seventy-third Masters offered other story lines, too. The Irishman Padraig Harrington came in search of the third leg of a Paddy Slam, having won the past two—albeit Tiger-less—majors. Immelman was the defending champion, but his name seemed to be mentioned—along with that of Johnson—only in debates on whether the Tiger-proofing had opened the gates for a series of good, rather than great, champions, a trend that had not escaped the attention of the green coats. Ogilvy and Nick Watney arrived as the hottest players on the planet while the tournament also signaled the dawning of a new era: the teenage flag bearers of golf's Generation Next, Rory McIlroy, Danny Lee, and Ryo Ishikawa, were all in the field.

Compelling, all of them, but as always the stars stole the show. That which had most tongues wagging was renewal of an old rivalry: Tiger against Phil. The world's two top-ranked players arrived at the year's first major on the top of their games and on a collision course with another green jacket—as well as the world number one ranking—on the line. They had not gone head-to-head at Augusta since 2001, when Woods won by two shots. That was at the height of the antipathy Woods felt toward Mickelson. After Mickelson hit driver on one hole and Woods put a 3-wood past him, Mickelson asked, "Do you always hit your 3-wood that far?" Woods, picking up his tee, didn't even look at Mickelson. "No," he said, walking briskly without turning around, "sometimes I hit it farther."

Mickelson, ever the optimist, was feeling confident. "I feel like right now I'm playing some of the best golf that I've ever played," he said. He had missed the cut at the Shell Houston Open the week before but attributed the poor showing to "dumb mistakes."

It is true that that Mickelson is one of the very few players who look awful in missing the cut one week and bounce back to win the next. "I'm driving the ball better than I ever have. I feel very comfortable and confident in my game and in my equipment, and I feel like I'll be able to in the next five years achieve levels of play that I haven't achieved earlier in my career. I don't want there to be any uncertainties; I want to continue down this path and see how far I can go. I would love to be in the same group as [Woods] on Sunday if we are in the final group. I think he's playing some great golf and I think he's going to be there. I think I'm playing some of the best golf of my career and I believe I'm going to be there, too."

Mickelson could be mischievous. He enjoyed ribbing Woods, perhaps in the mistaken belief that Woods took the jabs good-naturedly. He made sure to mention in his news conference that the memento he most treasures from his two successes at Augusta was from his second—not his breakthrough—Masters, in 2006: a photograph that shows Woods, as is customary for the defending champion, slipping the green jacket onto Mickelson at the presentation ceremony. Woods, when asked about Mickelson being his greatest rival, made sure to note that Ernie Els was "the person I've gone head-to-head against most." Maybe that's just comfort food for Woods, because he knows that the South African will forever be Salieri to his Mozart. Woods, who is a trivia buff, was pleased to learn that no player has spent longer in the top ten of the world rankings without reaching number one than Mickelson. Motivation with Woods comes from all kinds of places, but keeping Mickelson from being number one was almost as satisfying to him as being number one himself.

Ogilvy, one of the refreshingly independent thinkers on the Tour—he devours books, and not just golf books—was forthright when I asked him whether Mickelson held the same intimidation factor as Woods. "If you are fearful, you are less fearful of Phil," the Australian said. "Phil can come with seventy-two holes of the most unbelievable golf anyone in the world can play; when he's on, he's on. But he can also have periods where he's completely off the map. When you are up there in a tournament with Phil, anything can happen. With Tiger, you know he's going to play well. Phil is human, like most other guys on Tour, in that anything can happen sometimes. All of us can hit crazy shots in the last few holes of a tournament, but Tiger doesn't seem to do it quite as frequently. I've never really bought into the intimidation thing. It's not like a boxing match when the other guy is bigger than you and it's scary. But if there is intimidation, it's that you know he's going to make that putt on the last hole. You know coming down the last few holes that he is not going to go away, and he's going to do some good stuff the closer you get to the end. If you let him have a chance, he's going to beat you. Whereas you don't know that about anybody else. Everybody else has their moments and their ups and downs, but you know he's going to be there until the end."

Woods was not alone in lobbying the new regime at Augusta National, led by incoming chairman Billy Payne—the man who'd brought the Olympics to Atlanta—to bring back the thrills to the Masters. Indeed, in Payne he had a fellow traveler. Payne was the leader of the club's young turks, who were quietly and discreetly seeking to modernize the place. Don't be surprised to see a female member there sooner rather than later. Payne had been dismayed that the "toon-a-mint," as they like to call it in Georgia, had become a slog and a grind—a U.S. Open in April. He wanted to return the true flavor of the Masters. But he had to tread lightly. Payne did not want to embarrass his predecessor, Hootie Johnson, whose legacy was the National's Tiger-proofing. And so Payne prayed for good weather and quietly allowed the course to be set up to yield birdies once again. He had decided what kind of history he wanted to make.

After years of muted applause at pars, the cacophonous roars returned to Augusta on a perfect, sunny opening day. The field responded to the benevolence of Mother Nature and Billy Payne by setting a new Masters record for most Thursday rounds in the 60s (19). More records could've fallen. Chad Campbell, the flat-swinging Texan who's not afraid to go low, had it to 9 under par through sixteen holes before stumbling with two bogeys. The tournament record of 63, held by Nick Price and Greg Norman, was very much in danger with soft, receptive greens, generous pin positions, and the field playing what amounted to the forward tees. Even Norman, barely a part-time player given the demands of his business empire, felt he'd left shots out there when he came in with 70. "I had a lot of opportunities, really could have shot a nice, mid-60s score today," he said. Maundy Thursday repre-sented such a sea change from the dour grinds of recent Masters that fifty-year-old Augusta native Larry Mize got in on the act, too, shooting a 5-under-par 67. And this from a player who had man-aged just one top ten finish on golf's senior circuit, the Champions Tour. "I guess it turned the clock back a little bit," said the 1987 Masters winner, "but there were definitely some more chances for birdies than there have been in the recent years. And I think that's a good thing and I think [the tournament committee] do, too, and that's why they did it."

Everyone, it seemed, wore a smile. Except for Woods. The roars on this day were for others; for Woods there were mostly groans and sighs after he missed the chance to post his best-ever first round at a Masters. It was inexplicable that Woods had never bro-ken 70 in the opening round there. He was well on his way until blocking a 6-footer for birdie on 17, then took a bogey on the last after sailing the green. Haney, following Woods from outside the ropes accompanied by a new blond girlfriend—who a few months later would become his next wife—had been impressing upon Woods the need to be more aggressive in the first round. He felt that Woods's historical approach of beginning slowly and building momentum through the four days was flawed. Haney told Woods that he was giving up too much ground in opening rounds. Yet the soft-spoken Texan was shaking his head in dismay when Woods had tried to "take a little bit off" an 8-iron from the middle of the fairway on the last hole. It was a 9-iron distance—143 yards—but Woods didn't want the ball zipping off the back ledge to the front of the green. So he hit a "flighted" shot at the back left pin. He brought the ball in with a draw and overcooked the shot. Haney was craning through the gallery to get a look at where the ball had come to rest, but he soon turned away. He knew there would be no getting up and down from there, even for the great Tiger Woods. He had let slip the chance for his first ever opening round at the Masters in the 60s.

Woods finished at 2 under, his 70 good enough for a tie for twentieth, but it left him 5 shots adrift of Campbell. As we waited in a cattle pen outside the scorer's hut for Woods to emerge, it didn't take a clairvoyant to read his mind. Jim Litke, the Associated Press national sports columnist and one of the more laid-back members of the fourth estate, casually asked Woods "What's up?" with his first rounds at Augusta. If looks could, well, perhaps not kill, but seriously wound, we would've been calling an ambulance for Litke. "Basically I was in position to shoot 4 under par and I just didn't get it done," Woods said later. If there was consolation, it was that Mickelson didn't get it done, either. The two-time Masters champion wasted a perfect opportunity to challenge Woods for the world number one ranking on a day the course played "as easy as I've seen. . . . I drove it terrible," the left-hander said of his anemic 73. "I played terrible. Putted terrible."

If the first round was exasperating, the second only worsened Woods's condition. His ball striking had been on a steady decline, and mistakes were creeping into his game. Once again he found the middle of the fairway on the last hole, and once again he walked away with bogey after missing his approach in the only place—the deep right bunker—from which he couldn't save par. Woods knew from the fairway he was in trouble, throwing his iron at his golf bag in disgust. He berated Williams all the way up to the green, for no real reason other than he was mad at the world. An even-par round of 72 left him 7 shots off the lead with eighteen players ahead of him, including the resurgent Mickelson. It's true that the wind swirled and scoring was tougher on this Good Friday, but it's also true that Anthony Kim, the devil-may-care bon vivant from Los Angeles, set a new Masters record with eleven birdies. Unlike Woods, Kim wasn't walking around with a constipated look, tentative on every green, throwing up grass interminably in order to figure out the winds, which would invariably switch anyway. Though it was also true that Woods had more at stake than Kim. And Woods didn't engage in a vodka-drinking contest as he flew to Augusta or spend his nights at the "ballet." At least not during majors. It was no consolation that Woods led the field in pars. "Tough day?" someone asked Woods as he walked by with his head down. "Yeah," he replied through pursed lips.

After another futile round on Saturday, an irate Woods stormed off to the practice range, located on the other side of the clubhouse, to work on his deteriorating swing. Williams, who'd already been chewed out, went in the other direction, in search of a sandwich. "He didn't play good but he also putted very poorly," the Kiwi said. "I knew how hot he was going to be, so I thought I'd just go away for a few minutes." Haney, however, remained and bore the brunt of a tirade. "Tiger was just livid and Hank had to sit there and take it," said Williams. Williams didn't read anything into the incident because, he said, Woods often "vents" when he's unhappy with the way he played, but the anger passes quickly and there aren't long-lasting ramifications. But a handful of writers, watching from behind the ropes, witnessed the tantrum and thought it was significant. The incident led to stories that angered the admittedly thin-skinned Haney. Haney would over the next week send text messages to several writers admonishing them for stories suggesting he was on thin ice with Woods. Jaime Diaz, of *Golf Digest*, was particularly targeted by Haney, who accused Diaz—who'd known Woods for many years—of stirring the pot.

As always with the tightly controlled Team Tiger, it was hard to decipher what was real and what was imagined. Woods still wasn't playing well in the third round, able to turn in only a 2-under-par round of 70 when he needed a score in the mid-60s. Worse, his 70 was the best he could've hoped for given where he hit the ball. "You don't want to know my thoughts," he said after the round. He was in a particularly foul mood. "I just didn't hit the ball as precise as I needed to today and just fought my ass off to get it back, just shoot a number. As I said, I'm very proud of that. Today is as hard as I've ever fought to get a score out of Augusta." Former Masters champion Nick Faldo thought Woods had gotten in his own way "for one of the very few times in his career. . . . He really has maybe shot himself in the foot."

A fifth green jacket seemed implausible given the situation, but Easter Sunday in all its glory would at least provide Woods with motivation: he was paired with Mickelson. But after a sputtering start, Mickelson found his way while Woods was treading water. They began the final round 7 shots behind the leaders, Angel Cabrera and Kenny Perry. These two might look more like insurance agents than Masters champions, but 7 shots is a lot of elbow room. To boot, there were nine men ahead of Woods and

Mickelson. Yet what a thrilling final round run they made. Mickelson was at his mercurial best; when he's in this mood, he's like D'Artagnan, slicing and dicing holes at his whim. His birdie on the 7th was a sight to behold. Woods's swing was malfunctioning, but on guts alone he kept himself in the conversation. They both stood on the 17th tee high on the wings of roaring galleries. The Masters could be theirs, either one of them, with a strong finish. Woods's tee shot, however, found the left tree line. "I was dead from there," he later bemoaned. He finished, again, bogey-bogey when two birdies would've got him into the three-man playoff, eventually won with a simple par from Cabrera. Mickelson's capitulation was, in a sense, worse. After a sublime front nine in which he tied the Masters' scoring record of 6-under-par 30, he chunked a 9-iron into Rae's Creek on the signature par-3 12th, missed a 4-footer for eagle on the par-5 15th and a 5-footer for birdie on the penultimate green. He needed to shoot just 2 under par on the back nine to get into a playoff but came up short. If it was any consolation, he'd beaten Woods by a single shot, 67 to 68.

But while Mickelson's mistakes were, as they too often are, the result of a sudden rush of blood to the head, Woods's problems seemed rooted much deeper. The errant shot making masked at Bay Hill by a faithful putter was now plainly evident. For the fourth straight day, he'd failed to find the 18th green in regulation. Only once was he able to salvage a par. Woods is savvy enough to know that majors aren't won by playing the last hole at 3 over par. And he is sound enough in fundamental math to understand that a handful of uneventful two-putt pars on the 17th and 18th holes would have brought him a fifth Masters title despite all the problems in his game. Whether Woods's grumpiness was a result of his poor ball striking, or vice versa, only he truly knows. But he appeared to throw Haney under the bus with his remarks immediately after the final round. "I hit it so bad warming up today," he admitted. "I was hitting quick hooks, blocks, you name it. I hit it all on the range, and then on the very first hole I almost hit it into the eighth fairway [two holes left of the first]. It's one of the worst tee shots I've ever hit starting out. I just kind of Band-Aided around and almost won the tournament with a Band-Aid swing."

CHAPTER 5

Quail Hollow

A Woods confidant didn't pause to ponder the question when I asked which member of the inner circle bore the greatest brunt of Woods's anger. "Hank," he said. "Definitely, Hank." Haney came to Woods through Mark O'Meara. O'Meara, also from southern California and himself a U.S. Amateur champion who blossomed into a top-ten-caliber pro, acted as a de facto big brother when Woods turned professional in the summer of 1996, a relationship nurtured by IMG, which represented them both. Golfers invariably would base themselves in a state where they could play year-round and, more important, didn't have to pay state personal income taxes, so it was no surprise when Woods moved from California to Orlando's elite golf enclave, Isleworth, where O'Meara lived. IMG found him a villa, and the wide-eyed twenty-year-old had celebrity neighbors like Orlando Magic basketball stars Shaquille O'Neal and Penny Hardaway, baseball prince Ken Griffey Jr., and actor Wesley Snipes. Woods and Griffey often jumped the back fence to O'Neal's home to shoot hoops.

Not coincidentally, his other neighbor was IMG's head of golf, Alastair Johnston. "I think his move to Isleworth was pretty important," Johnston told the *Dallas Morning News* at the time. "On one hand, the move means he doesn't have as many friends around him. On the other hand, he can get away from it there. It's a community that's used to having stars around. He can orchestrate his life there. Therefore, I think he gets away. He relaxes. I think he has peace of mind when he goes home. He's got a base to go home to, where he's got his own stuff. I think that will be helpful in terms of dealing with all the pressures." IMG also took the liberty of setting up a personal management team around Woods to run his affairs. There was even a full-time employee assigned to look after Woods's home when he wasn't there. Given his prodigious appetite, her job mainly involved restocking the fridge.

In truth, apart from the media room where he could sit for hours playing video games—in 1996, he was addicted to Mortal Kombat—and eating cheeseburgers, his favorite dish, Woods spent so much time at the O'Meara house he was almost part of the family. It was an important relationship for a young man seeking to live an independent life but very much in need of training wheels. The O'Mearas provided an emotional safe harbor by offering friendship with no strings attached; they weren't looking to exploit him. Woods, perhaps understandably given his meteoric rise, was wary of the motives of those who tried to get close.

His fraternal relationship with O'Meara, who was eighteen years older, extended to fishing trips and regular rounds of golf at Isleworth, and continued for almost a decade. Woods learned other lessons, too. Their trips to Ireland included wild nights. Ultimately, Woods married and started finding his own path in life while the O'Meara marriage sadly fell apart, leading to an acrimonious divorce. Woods by then was spending his time with those he felt better understood his fishbowl existence: men like Jordan, Barkley, and Derek Jeter. Besides, as much as he tried to love fishing like O'Meara, he's an action junkie. As he joked to writer John Hawkins, "After half an hour [of fishing], my ADD kicks in."

Haney had long been O'Meara's swing coach and so was very familiar to Woods. He made no direct attempt to indoctrinate Woods, but because they shared a passion for understanding the complexities of the golf swing, they naturally engaged in long conversations about how that mystery was best unraveled. Woods was a sponge when it came to subjects near to his heart, and the golf swing may be atop that list. "He's a real student of the game," says a member of Woods's inner circle. "I think he could easily operate without a coach but he likes to have someone to bounce ideas off and take a look at him." Few, however, expected Woods, whose swing was naturally more upright and conventional, to find much use in Haney's unique ideas. "I've never understood what Woods saw in Haney," says a Tour winner who also lived in Orlando. "If you've ever played with O'Meara, you know that's not a ball flight you want to copy. It's a sort of playable hook, but it's not pretty, not anything to emulate." He made a motion with his right hand, like a pitcher throwing a quick curveball. "It's a ball that sort of falls out of the sky like a wounded duck." O'Meara, though, had the last laugh, winning two majors in middle age on the wings of that wounded duck. He credited Woods for those successes, saying he was driven to greater heights because he simply couldn't stand being pulverized whenever they played. While O'Meara couldn't possibly hit the ball as far or as well as Woods, he learned to putt better to stay in the game. Not coincidentally, at forty-one, O'Meara won the 1998 Masters by holing a speedy 20-footer with a little right-to-left break on the last hole. He led the field on the game's most treacherous greens that week, needing just 105 putts. The cherry on top was that

Woods, the reigning champion, slipped the green jacket onto his shoulders at the presentation ceremony.

Haney's greatest asset may be that he was the antithesis of Butch Harmon. Where Haney was naturally quiet, private, and circumspect, Harmon was loud and gregarious, the life of the party, not afraid to voice his opinions. Neither had the oldest son of the legendary instructor Claude Harmon ever been shy about extolling his own virtues. Woods was never comfortable with the way Harmon paraded up and down the driving ranges of the Tour, telling jokes and offering swing tips to every Ernie, Phil, and Freddie who came along. He began tiring of Harmon's shtick in the early part of the decade when he felt his coach was taking too much credit for his successes. But what sealed Harmon's fate was that Woods felt he had nothing left to learn. Harmon's view was that he wasn't fixing what wasn't broken; therefore, all Woods needed was maintenance. His proof was seven out of eleven majors. But he badly misread Woods, who was driven by the simple need to be better tomorrow than he was today. "You're always tweaking," Woods told me in 2009. "You're always trying to get better. The game is fluid. It's never concrete. That's the beauty and also the most frustrating thing about it." Woods felt that with Harmon his swing was inconsistent. When his timing was off, he'd get "flippy," meaning he had to rely on his fast hands to square the clubface going into the ball. "I feel that my overall plane and my swing and my release and how I play now is just so much more efficient," he told me. "Bad shots aren't what they used to be, and that's what we were trying to get to. Anybody can play when they're hot, but it's how poor are your mishits, can you control them, and more importantly, can you fix it?"

Haney, who learned his craft from the one plane swing guru Jim Hardy in Chicago, was, like Hardy—and every Texan—a great admirer of Ben Hogan and Byron Nelson. These legends had perhaps the two most dependable swings in golf's long history and both were, not coincidentally, long through the hitting zone. Woods was seduced by the promise of achieving such consistency, and others around him agreed that he had not reached his pinnacle. "You look at the video from when he was with Butch and you can see the contact wasn't as consistent back then," says Williams. "Two thousand was a phenomenal year, but if you look back at his putting statistics, and I keep all Tiger's statistics, he putted unbelievably. I mean, yeah, he played good, there's no denying that, but he putted phenomenal and his short game was great. It would be hard to say to somebody that at Pebble Beach he didn't hit it his best, because you can't say that when the guy wins the U.S. Open by 15 shots. It's going to sound derogatory to the rest of the field, but the truth is he played good but he didn't play great. He managed his game well and he putted unbelievably well. He made no mistakes."

Harmon was the last of the Mohicans Earl Woods had hand-picked to form the original Team Tiger. How ironic that while Harmon was telling golf writers that Earl, who had the habit of making outrageous statements about his son's greatness, was "out of control," Tiger Woods had precisely the same concerns about the man he called "Butchy." (Everyone around him, as an aside, was referred to in names ending in "e": Stevie, Steiny, and his wife was just "E.") Woods had already replaced his first caddie, Mike "Fluff" Cowan, after two and a half years in essence because Cowan, a friendly old hippie, liked to talk. Earl liked to talk, too; indeed, nary a thought passed through his head that wasn't expressed. But not his son. Tiger Woods coveted discretion. The kiss of death for Cowan came when Woods, in attempting to play down rumors of a rift, wrote on his website in early 1999 that there was no substance to what he termed "Caddiegate." "There's nothing wrong between us," he wrote. "People are blowing the situation way out of proportion." A week later, Cowan was fired. Woods replaced him with Williams even though his father was again urging him to hire a black caddie. Earl Woods, always looking at the big picture in positioning his son as the Chosen One, thought it was an important gesture. But Tiger's sole interest, as it had always been, was winning golf tournaments. He cared little for making sociopolitical statements. He acted, as he usually did, guided by meritocratic principles. He chose the man he thought would do the best job. Woods saw the world in a very unfiltered way: you want his respect? Earn it.

Cowan was the third member of Earl's team to be removed; or the fourth, if you count San Diego sports psychologist Jay Brunza, who was out of the picture by the time Woods turned professional. Brunza, a retired naval commander befriended by Earl Woods, caddied for Tiger in each of his six USGA championship victories. Earl adapted his Special Forces psychological training and his experiences in the killing fields of Vietnam to make his son's mind strong. He was convinced—and he was right—that his son's mental strength as much as his gift for hitting a golf ball would make him unbeatable. "Talent isn't always the best indicator for an athlete's success," said Begay. "[Tiger] has the mental capacity." Earl came up with many inventive ways to toughen up his boy. He constantly disturbed the young Tiger as he was about to play a shot. Tiger would boil over in anger, telling him that golf etiquette dictated that he had to be quiet, but his father wouldn't stop. After a while, tired of being angry—and seeing that anger didn't help—Tiger resolved not to be bowed and, sure enough, the day came when nothing would distract him on the golf course. While Earl succeeded, the story was at least as much reflective of Tiger. Indeed, it was classic Tiger: whatever the game, he would not stop until he won. "It's extraordinary how competitive he is," says Williams. "You can't explain it to people because no one will believe you." Everyone who'd been close to Woods had a story to tell about his legendary competitiveness. Perhaps the most humorous came from Jaime Diaz, who had predicted in *Golf Digest* that once Woods committed himself to sex addiction therapy in the aftermath of his infidelities, "It's easy to imagine him wanting to leave a road to recovery adorned with rehab records."

Earl, who was involved in self-help methods like EST, also gave his son tapes to listen to with subliminal messages, while his mother, Tida, introduced him to the Buddhist path to enlightenment. Buddhism was the perfect religion for Woods because it taught that salvation came through self, not belief in faraway and nebulous gods. In other words, only he could be in control of his destiny, find his own happiness. Buddhism also fit in nicely with the teachings of Earl Woods, who told his son that he was powered by an internal "nuclear reactor." But just as Earl knew when it was time for his son to see a professional golf instructor—the precocious youngster on his first day told the teacher who asked him to hit balls at a flag on a range that he already knew how to do that but wanted to be taught how to shape shots around trees to the flag—he understood the need for a credentialed psychologist. Brunza arrived on the scene when Woods was thirteen and both hypnotized him and taught the boy how to get himself into a trancelike state, what in sports is generally referred to as the "zone." Woods was such a good pupil, able to shut out all external distractions at will, that soon enough he no longer had need for the teacher. "Brunza went the way of everyone who outlives their usefulness," says a Woods observer. A member of Team Tiger disputed the inherent cold-bloodedness of such a conclusion, however. "Tiger's an excellent student and pretty independent. Once he gets what you're telling him, he absorbs it and he moves on. I don't think it was personal with Jay, or that he used him. He liked him but he didn't need him there anymore."

Lawyer John Merchant, the first African American to serve on the United States Golf Association's powerful Executive Committee, was removed quickly as Woods's business adviser, though Tiger had his father do the deed. "It's weird considering he's this intimidating killer on the golf course, but Tiger doesn't like confrontation," says a source who knows Woods. "He can be very cold and calculating with people, but he won't be the one to tell you you're out." Indeed, after the third round of the BMW Championship at Chicago's Cog Hill in 2009, Woods was whistling through the locker room, very much the king of his domain, when he stopped at a sink to wash his hands. Rory Sabbatini, who had greatly embarrassed Woods by pulling out of Tiger's tournament at Sherwood Country Club in LA with a dubious excuse, moved to the sink next to Woods. I'd expected a tense exchange, but Woods instead made small talk. When I asked later whether he'd buried the hatchet with the South African, Woods looked at me like I was insane.

Next to fall was Hughes Norton, Woods's first agent. Norton was no one's idea of a shrinking violet. According to his view of the world, Greg Norman would have been just another pro had Norton not created the brand of the Great White Shark. Norman repaid Norton, of course, by firing him, just one of many reasons for Norton's bitterness at the world. Norton was another who couldn't keep his mouth shut. He told stories about how he'd regularly peel hundred-dollar bills because Woods never had any cash. "For a rich guy, you sure are poor," Norton was quoted by *Sports Illustrated* in 1996 as telling Woods. Woods failed to see the humor in such statements. Interestingly, O'Meara, who like Woods was notoriously frugal, had already fired Norton as his agent, and when Woods came seeking counsel, advised him to do the same. Norton was paid hush money by IMG to keep quiet about his time with Woods, and maintained his silence despite being legally free to say whatever he wanted. "He will not be interviewed," said an IMG executive. "His IMG buyout is over but not his contempt for the media."

Woods quickly came to understand that he was the one writing the checks. Therefore, he also thought he should write the rules. He wanted those around him to remember who was boss, keep their mouths shut, and make no attempt to profit from their closeness to him without his approval. Neither was he in the habit of handing out money just because he had it in spades; again, it went to his view that in life, you should get what you earn. There were no handouts. Some saw that worldview reflected in the lack of closeness to his three stepsiblings from his father's first marriage. Hideyuki "Rock" Ishii, the mad scientist who designed Woods's golf ball for Nike, had the right answer when *Sports Illustrated* approached him about a story. "My job is to make balls for Tiger, not talk about him," he told the magazine. "I don't forget how lucky I am to work with Tiger. It's an honor to play even the smallest role." When I'd asked to interview Woods's boyhood friends, Bryon Bell and Jerry Chang, I was greeted with silence.

In the summer of 2002, Woods cut off Harmon. Because there was no one else who could do the deed for him, Woods had to be the one to deliver the news and, typically, it was done awkwardly and inconclusively. He simply informed Harmon before the final round of the PGA Championship that August at Hazeltine that he didn't need his help on the range. He wanted to work alone. A jilted Harmon spent his time watching over Justin Leonard while Woods warmed up at the other end of the range. In the soap opera world of professional golf, only everyone noticed. By the middle of 2003, the decade-long marriage between golf's top instructor and greatest player was officially over. "Agent, caddie, lawyer, swing coach, foundation director—they were all gone very soon," says the IMG executive. They were all, he noted, appointed by

Earl Woods. "But Tiger's replacements," he continued, "are still there."

That observation was certainly true when it came to Steinberg, Williams, Tiger Woods Foundation chief executive Greg McLaughlin, and Chris Hubman, the accountant who handled Woods's personal business affairs. Haney, however, seemed forever on shaky ground. Henry, as Woods calls him, knew when he started working with Woods that it was a no-win scenario. There was only one way to go after Woods had tasted such unprecedented success under the tutelage of Harmon. Haney knew how long it would take to learn and master a new swing and that it was unlikely Woods would be winning during the reeducation. But Woods talked him into it and wanted to learn a better swing. He also wanted a swing that would be easier on his body and allow him to play at a high level into middle age. Woods understood that his swing was built on speed and power and that it had caused damage to his left knee. "My philosophy as a teacher," Haney writes, "is to teach my students to become their own best teacher by getting them to understand the flight of the golf ball and how it relates to the swing, with emphasis on swinging the golf club on their own correct swing plane." Innocuous enough, except that virtually every swing guru in golf believed Haney's ideas were wrong. Harmon became the chief antagonist, telling anyone who'd listen that Woods was ruining his career, though he was hardly alone in that belief. A Tour winner, a disciple of 1980s swing guru Jimmy Ballard, told me that Haney had cost Woods countless majors and "should be strung up for what he's done to the kid." Woods had many laudable traits, but they didn't include taking criticism well. The more vocal the opposition to Haney, the more Woods supported him. He was going to be right, even if he wasn't.

Woods arrived in Charlotte for the Quail Hollow Championship—played on a course he liked—knowing that the hornets' nest had been stirred by his tirade at Haney on the practice range at Augusta. Journalists wrote that Haney's position was tenuous, and after a pro-am round played alongside his friend, quarterback Peyton Manning, Woods's first order of business was to defend his coach. "That's complete speculation," he said of reports that Haney was on his way out. "It has nothing to do with Henry. I didn't hit the ball the way I wanted to and I didn't make any putts. I felt like that every day it was 17 and 18 that hurt. I didn't finish off my rounds the last couple days, and it cost me a chance to win the golf tournament." So why, then, did he explode at Haney? "Usually you just leave me alone, let me vent for a while, and then I'll be ready to focus on what I need to do to get ready for the next day," he said. "It's happened before, he's seen it before, Stevie has seen it. You've got to vent. We don't get a chance to do that because we come off the green, we do media right away. You're constantly on, and I just need to vent for just a little bit. Give me five minutes, ten minutes, and once that's over, it's, 'What do we need to do to get ready to win this golf tournament the next day?' "

Woods said he needed to be patient because he felt his body was still in the process of recuperating. "I'm just now starting to get my pop back," he said. "I'm starting to get my speed back, and that's obviously going to take a little time. I've been away from the game for such a long time, and I haven't been able to hit as many balls. So I'm just now starting to get my speed back, which is great." Time was needed, he said, because there was danger in rushing to achieve too much, too soon. "You don't want to stretch out the ligament again. It's still healing. It takes basically two years. But it's still healing, still got to watch out for that, and my muscles are now starting to come around where they're starting to become more explosive." He was asked again about how having children had changed his life and in answering paid homage to his father. "I love to teach, and to be able to teach Sam and as soon as I can start teaching Charlie a few things, that's fun," he said. "I live to be able to do that. Like my dad always told me, each and every day is a way to teach your kids something new. He's always done that. My entire life he always looked at each and every day as that, and I do the same with my kids."

Woods arrived in North Carolina without his family and without Haney and stayed at the high-end Ballantyne resort. He'd seemed more relaxed than he'd been at Augusta two weeks before. As far as Masters hangover cures went, his first-round 65 wasn't bad. He had the lead by 2 strokes. But appearances could be deceiving. Woods's struggles off the tee continued unabated. He hit only five fairways, but his iron play was good enough to find fourteen greens and his short game was off the charts. He got up and down on each of the four greens he missed, none of which was straightforward, and, for good measure, took only eleven putts on his inward nine, turning lemons into a 6-under-par 30. Unfortunately, that opening round was the high-water mark. Woods's play deteriorated markedly throughout the tournament, but as pure testament to his indomitable spirit, he was still in the hunt on Sunday. The opening hole at Quail Hollow was benign; it played downwind and required no more than a bunted 3-wood to set up a short-iron approach. Woods took his driver and hit it at least 80 yards right, into a forest. He somehow escaped with a bogey. After failing to birdie two easy par 5s, his goose was cooked. An even-par round of 72 was good enough for fourth place, a great week for most players, though Tiger Woods didn't play for $312,000 checks.

When David Feherty, the CBS analyst and resident jokester, interviewed Woods after his round, he asked whether Woods felt like a loser. It was the sort of question only a friend would ask,

because it cut awfully close to the bone given Woods's struggles with the long game. But Woods cracked a smile. It was reminiscent of the legendary—if somewhat embellished—exchange between Australian AP writer Andrew Both and Steve Elkington. After a poor round, Both asked the volcanic Elkington if he'd share his thoughts or "should I just go and fuck myself right now?" Elkington, who surely would've sent Both on his way, laughed and stopped to talk to him.

Woods's mood was again noticeably different from Augusta, when he was essentially in the same position, having lost one he should've won. At Augusta, Woods looked like he was about to rip Bill Macatee's head off as the interviewer made small talk by going over his new breakfast regimen while CBS took its sweet time cutting to them. "Well, I was," Woods told Feherty, "and I wasn't even first loser, either." Sean O'Hair, whom Woods had slaughtered in the final round at Bay Hill, won the tournament despite two closing bogeys. Woods finished only 2 shots behind in a tournament no one wanted to win. He was disappointed but waited around for O'Hair to finish and congratulated him on his third Tour win. O'Hair marveled at the way Woods was able to keep such clean lines of distinction between the good friend he was off the course and the coldhearted assassin he was on it. "No matter how friendly you are with him," O'Hair reflected, "he wants to slit your throat on the golf course." But without a reliable swing, he was bringing knives to a gun fight.

CHAPTER 6

The Players

As profitable an enterprise as the legally not-for-profit PGA Tour has become, it burns the suits in Ponte Vedra Beach that they don't own golf's glittering prizes. The majors are independent operators, and the PGA of America rubs a mountain of salt into the Tour's wounds of envy by owning the year's final major and the Ryder Cup, too. These are the five biggest revenue weeks on the golfing calendar, and there's not a red cent in it for Tim Finchem. In any other sport, it would be like owning the regular season but not the playoffs. One of the many inventive ideas that percolated through Mickelson's mind—not limited to golf, because he's circulated a plan to solve the world's gas crisis, too—went as far as suggesting the Tour charge appearance fees in order to squeeze dollars out of Augusta National Golf Club, the USGA, Royal & Ancient, and PGA of America. "If the commissioner were in a position to control when and where players played, as I believe he should be, and if he were able to sell that, he would be able to go to the four majors and the Ryder Cup and say, 'If you want our guys to continue to play in your event, you have to pay the Tour a certain fee,' " Mickelson told *Golf Digest* in 2009. "After all, the players are the product, right?" Even Finchem—perhaps envisioning telling Woods he needed to report for duty at the first tee of the Viking Classic but couldn't play in another major until the Tour got a taste of the action—rolled his eyes, leaving Mickelson bemoaning that, not for the first time, he'd been "totally disregarded" by the commissioner.

And so, given the lack of its own marquee presence, the marketing geniuses at Tour HQ came up with the idea of promoting their in-house championship, The Players, as the year's fifth major. The tournament was even moved to May, the only "golf month" without its own major, to conclude on Mother's Day. The positioning wasn't coincidental. It was intended to echo the U.S. Open's traditional Father's Day finish. Borrowed from the Masters was the idea of keeping the venue the same every year, the Tour-owned TPC Sawgrass. Not that anyone would mistake Pete Dye's "tricky"—Woods's description—layout with Augusta National. It'd be like comparing Kim Kardashian to Sophia Loren; they may have the same kind of humps and bumps, but that's where the similarities ended. Even though Finchem could sell smog to Los Angeles, selling The Players as the fifth major was an uphill battle. Turned out that prestige couldn't be manufactured. Or bought.

The history of the four majors dates back to Bobby Jones, and even though the Grand Slam has been redefined, with the U.S. and British Amateurs dropped as the sport embraced professionalism in favor of the Masters and the PGA, there are still only four. Elevating The Players would also make for some significant changes to golf history: Calvin Peete would've been the first black major champion, Greg Norman would've actually won a major on American soil, and Sergio Garcia and Adam Scott would've gotten the major monkey off their backs. And it would change the elevation of Mount Nicklaus, because Jack won three of them and Tiger just one.

And if it were a major, Woods would've cared much more than he did. His attitude was one of indifference, given that he wasn't especially fond of the course, and for all those years the tournament was held in late March, when he's always got Georgia on his mind. Legend has it that one year he refused to alter his putting stroke on the slower-than-usual Sawgrass greens because he didn't want it ruined for Augusta. Neither was the weather always kind in March, and rain and bog dampen Woods's spirits. It's true that he's become less of a mudder as he's gotten older. "I didn't like playing here when we caught mud balls all the time," he said of the Stadium Course at Sawgrass. "It's not a golf course where you want to have mud balls." Indeed, the prospect of soggy fairways and waterlogged greens with craterlike footprints surrounding the hole—thus making putting a crapshoot—kept Woods more often away from the LA Open and the AT&T Pebble Beach, two tournaments he'd probably play if they were held at a drier time of the year. While Woods generally played golf against history more than his peers, oddly enough it didn't seem to bother him that he'd never won at Riviera in nine tries. Many saw it as a hole in his résumé. Hogan's Alley's was the only place he'd played more than four times without winning. Yet he remained remarkably relaxed about his failures there and was in no hurry to return as long as the tournament was played in February, the only month virtually guaranteed to rain in southern California. Greg McLaughlin, who gave the sixteen-year-old Woods a start at Riviera when he was running the LA Open in 1991 and was rewarded by being made the head of the Tiger Woods Foundation, shrugged when I asked whether Woods would ever play in his hometown event again. "Hard to say," he said.

Woods had been more amenable to The Players since the date

was moved, because it not only didn't interfere with his preparation for majors but represented a better prospect of a hard and fast
setup, which rewarded those who could control their ball and
putt well. "I love a golf course firm and fast, the faster the better,"
he said. "I think it brings back creativity, hitting shots, and especially when the greens get hard and fast, to be able to have to land
a ball in a certain spot and see it roll out, expect it to bounce. I
think that's how golf courses should be played. You can't always
have that because of the weather. But if you can, I think it's great."

A hard-and-fast Sawgrass figured prominently in the Woods
lore. In 1994, at the age of eighteen, he became the youngest
U.S. Amateur champion in history there; his first major if golf's
Tridentines had their way. The tournament was played at the
height of a stifling summer on a course that was rock hard. Five
down with twelve holes to play, the skinny Cablinasian kid in
a goofy Panama hat drew even with Trip Kuehne on the 34th
hole of the final. Kuehne was a member of a Texas golf royal
family—all three siblings, Kelli, Hank, and Trip, would win
USGA championships—and was coached, ironically, by Haney.
In what would become the motif of his career, Woods dramati-
cally took his first lead of the match with an audacious birdie on
the fearsome island green 17th. He dialed back a wedge from 139
yards and fired straight at the tucked pin on the right. His ball
landed in the no-man's-land right of the flag. Given the firmness
of the putting surface, it should've bounced to a watery grave.
And maybe if any other player had hit that shot, that's just how
the story would've gone. But Woods hit it and so the ball stopped
with about nine inches to spare. Because this was how fairy tales
went, he holed out from 14 feet. Later he was unable to remember
anything about the putt or the exuberant fist pump celebration—
the first time he broke out that signature move on the national
stage—which followed. He told reporters he had been "in the

zone." Some found it strange that his memory failed him so soon after the event. But the revelation might just be proof that Woods inhabits an alternate consciousness in such defining moments. Everyone else, however, saw what had happened: Tiger Woods had his first Arthur-and-Excalibur moment. "You don't see too many pros hit it right of that pin," Kuehne, who went on to lose the final hole, too, later ruefully remarked.

Lost in the hurrah of that historic day was that Woods should never even have been in that final; he was 3 down with five holes to play to past champion Buddy Alexander. The accomplished University of Florida golf coach had a 3-footer on the 14th but lipped out. It could be easy to say that Woods smells blood when he senses weakness and goes for the kill, but the truth was more complicated. Opponents had a habit of unraveling in his presence. In his fourteen major championship victories, Woods had a scoring average almost four strokes lower than his playing partner. Alexander, usually steady and composed, couldn't muster a single par over the last five holes. What was just as fascinating as that famous Woods victory—two more Houdini come-from-behind U.S. Amateurs would follow—was that he turned down both David Letterman and Jay Leno, who'd wanted him to appear on their top-rated television shows. Not many eighteen-year-olds would've given up a chance to sit on those couches. It was a decision that spoke clearly about the importance—or lack thereof—of the media to Woods.

Woods was unexpectedly forced to delve into this theme of where the media fit in his worldview at the end of an otherwise by-the-numbers Tuesday morning press conference at The Players. He was talking about changing shafts in his driver and working on his swing—subjects with which he was comfortable, if never always entirely forthcoming—when he was asked, out of the blue, about the impact of two seminal magazine profiles written more than a decade before. The first was crafted in 1996 by Gary Smith, the excellent *Sports Illustrated* writer, and remains perhaps the definitive article on Woods. It asked, prophetically, as it turned out, whether "the machine" of modern fame and celebrity that created heroes only so they could be torn down would ever allow a Tiger Woods to succeed. A year later, another talented wordsmith, Charles Pierce, published a profile in *GQ* that wasn't quite the journey into the soul that Smith delivered—in good part because IMG limited his access—but nonetheless offered insight. In retrospect, Pierce's piece, which unfortunately relied on the betrayal of Woods's confidence for its shock value, proved that Smith was more correct about the insidious omnipotence of "the machine" than he could've known.

Woods took the Pierce experience and used it to build a moat around his castle. Already suspicious of the motives of journalists, he raised the drawbridge and made sure no writer would again penetrate his inner realm. Hughes Norton had at least been willing to consider interview requests and thought positive media placement was important in crafting a public persona for Woods. Once he was replaced by Steinberg, who was at least as suspicious of journalists as Woods—his nom de guerre among the media of "Dr. No" was well earned—the wagons were completely circled. Of the hundred or so media requests that arrived every week, perhaps one was passed on to Steinberg, but invariably Dr. No's answer was the same.

Despite his obsession with secrecy and distrust of the media, Woods was at heart a social creature. One of his inner circle characterized him as "a bit of a loner," which was true, but he was no recluse; he didn't want to lock himself away from humanity, other than the humanity that bothered him at restaurants as his fork was about to touch his lips. Woods enjoyed people and, especially, banter. It was this give and take—though, as one caddie who knew him well noted, "Tiger can pitch but he doesn't catch very well"—that endeared him to his fellow professionals. And while Woods officially kept the media at a distance, there were a handful whom he had allowed to get close. But it was the kind of access that didn't translate to words on a page. It was a source of great comfort to those writers who had either no access to Woods, or were on his shit list, that those on the inside were hardly getting many scoops. There was a reason for that: staying on the inside meant not compromising Woods's confidentiality.

Toward the end of 2009, I'd become one of the handful of writers whom Woods referred to by name at press conferences. It was as if I'd been "made" by Don Corleone himself. In truth, I'd felt conflicted. Although I'd personally grown to like Woods and enjoyed his company, I knew the time would come when I'd write something that he wouldn't like. But I'd decided to cross that bridge when the time came. In the meantime, I got to know him, the real Tiger Woods. Personally, I found him far more likable—and interesting—than the persona he, and those around him, had created.

For instance, one of the misconceptions about him was that he was robotic on the golf course. The image served him, so he perpetuated it, but was a myth. Woods knew precisely what was happening around him and was extremely observant. When an Asian man with a very effeminate voice called his name several times from outside the ropes at a tournament, I'd assumed Woods was too far away to have heard. Later, I'd discovered that he'd not only heard him but described him perfectly. Our exchanges on the golf course ranged from the comedic—after he'd emerged from the Porta-Potty at the PGA Championship and I'd rolled my eyes once again at his lack of bladder control, out of the corner of his mouth he warned me not to "go in there 'cos someone took a huge dump and it's sitting right on top"—to the serious. Things which were raw, sometimes controversial, and almost always peppered with the salty language he favored. It often occurred to me that people would like him more if they knew him in this way: he was, really, very normal. But because he'd said things in confidence, I never wrote about them. But Pierce did.

Pierce essentially made the point that while Smith's piece positioned Woods as some kind of vessel sent by a higher entity, the young man was in actual fact a great golfer, not the reincarnation of Siddhartha. In order to illustrate his thesis, Pierce quoted off-color jokes Woods told during a photo shoot done for *GQ*. His grander theme was that Woods wouldn't be allowed to save the world because too many people would find him not pure enough for the job. Anyone who'd been around Woods knew he loved telling jokes. They also knew the jokes were almost always crudely sexual in nature and, truthfully, not always that funny (though I'd never seen anyone not at least chuckle when Tiger Woods delivered the punch line). His sense of humor lay somewhere between pubescent and undergraduate. A Woods insider agreed: "Not real sophisticated. What you'd expect to hear in a dorm full of college freshmen."

The four offending jokes Pierce made public were an accurate representation of what makes Woods laugh. The first involved St. Peter and Jesus playing golf. St. Peter piped a good drive down the first fairway while Jesus, using a rock tied to a stick, popped his ball straight up, but all kinds of God's creatures assist and, yada, yada, yada, his ball dropped into the hole for a double eagle. St. Peter turned to him and said, "You gonna play golf or you gonna fuck around?" The second featured the Little Rascals. Their teacher wanted them to use various words in sentences. The first word was *love*. Spanky answered, "I love dogs." The second word was *respect*. Alfalfa answered, "I respect how much Spanky loves dogs." The third word was *dictate*. There was a pause in the room. Finally, Buckwheat put up his hand. "Hey, Darla," said Buckwheat. "How my dick ta'te?" The third involved physical comedy, which Woods loves, too. Pierce wrote that the young golfer "puts the tips of his expensive shoes together, and he rubs them up and down against each other. 'What's this?' he asks the women [at the photo shoot], who do not know the answer. 'It's a black guy taking off his condom,' Tiger explains." The other was: Why do two lesbians always get where they're going faster than two gay guys? Because the lesbians are always going sixty-nine. Badda-bing! For good measure, Pierce recounted a conversation between Woods and his limousine driver, who'd played basketball at Memphis State. Woods asked him, "Why do so many good-looking women hang around baseball and basketball?" Woods continued, "Is it because, you know, people always say that, like, black guys have big dicks?"

Woods specifically told Pierce he could not write any of it, a line most writers wouldn't cross. But Pierce, either because he knew he wouldn't need an ongoing relationship with Woods or because he didn't have much else to go with, did so anyway, and Woods was left deeply embarrassed. Perhaps he shouldn't have been, because the teller of crude jokes is a part of who he is. But it's not the only part and, Woods would argue, just a small part. The Smith article featured no such cheap shots, but nonetheless Woods again felt twinges of embarrassment. Smith, who is skilled at divining the inner complexities of those he writes about, focused on Earl Woods. In the short-attention-span world in which we live, an encompassing portrait was reduced to a few rather outlandish statements Earl had made about his son. Evidence again that "the machine" would always win.

"Tiger will do more than any other man in history to change the course of humanity," Earl told Smith. Smith asked him if he meant sports history and rattled off the usual suspects, from

Jackie Robinson to Muhammad Ali and Arthur Ashe. "More than any of them because he's more charismatic, more educated, more prepared for this than anyone," Earl replied. Smith asked whether his son would have more impact than Nelson Mandela, or Gandhi, or even Buddha. "Yes, because he has a larger forum than any of them. Because he's playing a sport that's international. Because he's qualified through his ethnicity to accomplish miracles. He's the bridge between the East and the West. There is no limit because he has the guidance. I don't know yet exactly what form this will take. But he is the Chosen One. He'll have the power to impact nations. Not people. Nations. The world is just getting a taste of his power."

That was the sensational stuff. The rest of the article was a compelling study of Earl Woods's belief that he was on this earth, spared from returning in a body bag from Vietnam, for a very special reason—to nurture and protect and guide his son. "What the hell had I been doing in public information in the Army, posted in Brooklyn? Why, of course, what greater training can there be than three years of dealing with the New York media to prepare me to teach Tiger the importance of public relations and how to handle the media?" Smith says Earl trained Tiger to speak to the media from a young age. Earl would ask him questions reporters asked, like "Where were you born, Tiger?" When the three-year-old replied that he was born on December 30, 1975, in Long Beach, California, his father would correct him. "No, Tiger, only answer the question you were asked. It's important to prepare yourself for this. Try again." Tiger responded with, "I was born in Long Beach, California." The son certainly heeded that lesson well, though too far. Earl told Smith that he believed his "late leap" into the Green Berets was so he could "teach Tiger mental toughness," and that his first marriage was "God saying, 'I want this son of a bitch to really have previous training.' . . . Look at this stuff! Over and over you can see the plan being orchestrated by someone other than me because I'm not this damn good! I tried to get out of that combat assignment to Thailand. But Tida was meant to bring in the influence of the Orient, to introduce Tiger to Buddhism and inner peace, so he would have the best of two different worlds. And so he would have the knowledge that there were two people whose lives were totally committed to him. There can't be this much coincidence in the world. . . . This is a directed scenario, and none of us involved in the scenario has failed to accept the responsibility. This is all destined to be."

Tida didn't back away from her husband's views of their divine duty. She told Smith she took her son's astrological chart to a Buddhist temple in Los Angeles and to another in Bangkok and was told by monks at both places that the child possessed wondrous powers. "If he becomes a politician, he will be either a president or a prime minister," she was told. "If he enters the military, he will be a general." Tida's conclusion, Smith wrote, was that "Tiger has Thai, African, Chinese, American Indian, and European blood. He can hold everyone together. He is the Universal Child." The young Tiger believed, too, or at least he told his parents he did. "I don't see any of this as scary or a burden," Woods told Smith. "I see it as fortunate. I've always known where I wanted to go in life. I've never let anything deter me. This is my purpose. It will unfold."

Years later, Woods bemoaned that Smith's article "went a little too deep. . . . As writers go, you guys try to dig deep into something that is really nothing." A source close to the Woods family at the time says the article at first was well received by them but that soon changed as other media outlets began casting a skeptical eye on the boasts Earl had made about his son's destiny. "There was a lot of focus internally on Earl's quotes and the pressure they put on Tiger, so in a way the Woods family looked at it as

net negative," he says. So how did Woods see those articles almost thirteen years later? Not surprisingly, through rose-colored
glasses. "Let's see, the first part about my father, well, that's a
proud father," he said during his news conference at The Players.
"A father who wants you to do well in life and wants you to give
back and help. And that's what every person should do, not just
me. Every person, every one of these guys in this room and everyone else, should help others; that's what he was trying to convey.
As far as the other piece, obviously you have to be careful who
you say things to and where you say them and trying to be funny,
and obviously [it] didn't come across that way to a lot of people."

With that Woods was out of the media center. He walked up
toward the enormous clubhouse where his wife and children, as
well as their nannies, awaited. It was the first time the entire family had accompanied him to a tournament all season. Elin had
made the ten-minute drive to watch her husband play at Bay
Hill but, as ever, remained in the background. She listened to
her mother-in-law and like her husband wore red on Sundays,
but other than that she favored baseball hats pulled low and sunglasses that hid her in the crowd. She literally disappeared if a
photographer came near her. She was accompanied outside the
ropes at Bay Hill by her husband's full-time Gatorade handler, a
woman whose job it was to make sure that Woods at all time had
an ample supply of the red-and-blue Tiger brand sports drinks.
At one point in the year I asked her whether Woods couldn't just
stop at a 7-Eleven like everyone else and pick up a couple of bottles, and she was mortified. Given that PepsiCo was paying him
around $10 million a year in a five-year deal signed in 2007—as
part of a unique licensing deal that could've been worth well over
$100 million to Tiger if his Gatorade brand had sold better—they
weren't prepared to chance that he'd get thirsty and be photographed drinking a Coca-Cola product. Indeed, in an amusing

bit of corporate mischief, e-mails began circulating during 2009 claiming that a large order of Vitaminwater—the Coca-Cola product that competes with Gatorade—was bought and delivered to Woods's residence in Orlando.

It's true of every golfer on Tour that some weeks just aren't meant to be yours. Mickelson had a chance to supplant Woods as world number one this week and could only limp in with a tie for fifty-fifth. Garcia, the defending champion, was still nursing a broken heart after Greg Norman's daughter, Morgan-Leigh, dumped the Tour's most eligible bachelor earlier in the year. Perhaps she saw what her mother put up with married to a dashing, handsome golf star and thought better of it. The Spaniard's melancholy mood—when someone tried to cheer him up after a poor start to the tournament with "there's always tomorrow," he responded, "and there's always next week, when I'll be home"—manifested itself in a tie for twenty-second. But those rules didn't apply to Woods. He was always in the reckoning, even if he had no business being at the pointy end of a tournament. After three rounds of 71, 69, and 70, Woods somehow found himself in the final pairing on Sunday. His ball striking was awful, but he scrambled and never gave up. "It is what it is, you hit a bad shot and you go play it," he replied after being asked about one especially poor tee shot.

Haney had a standard response to questions about his pupil's ball striking: tell me how many putts he had and I'll tell you where he finished in the tournament. It was a disingenuous argument, because almost any competent ball striker with 100 putts would win a tournament running away. Similarly, 120 putts won't win, no matter how good the play. Tom Weiskopf famously hit 68 greens in regulation in the 1969 Masters, a Hoganesque achievement, yet didn't win. He three-putted eleven times. So extremes in either direction were useless in evaluating a golfer's performance. What was true was that Woods entered The Players ranked ninety-first in greens in regulation, a statistic that he'd traditionally led on the Tour. What was also true was that even his genius couldn't find the putting surface from the wayward resting places of his tee shots. Haney told several writers in e-mails and text messages that Woods didn't win the Masters because he had 122 putts. Only three players who made the cut at Augusta fared worse on the greens. He also was only two out of six in sand saves, chipped inconsistently, and made strategic mistakes. All of that was true, but also true was that Woods had lost his driver swing. It was never more evident than when he arrived at the first tee that Mother's Day in the suburbs of Jacksonville. "The driver was killing him," a Woods confidant later conceded. "There was a real lack of confidence whenever he stepped up to the tee with the driver, not knowing where it's going to go."

No matter how poorly he'd been hitting the ball, there was always the expectation when Woods was in the hunt on Sunday that he would find a way to prevail. But after a wedge to the left flag on the first hole missed so far right that it barely caught the green, I got the feeling this wasn't going to be one of those days. After Augusta, Woods maintained that he'd done the best he could with a "Band-Aid swing." That was Easter Sunday. It was now Mother's Day and his swing was still bleeding. Harmon, who was now Angelo Dundee in Joe Frazier's corner instead of Ali's, was telling people he could "fix" Woods "in five minutes." But Woods was far too proud ever to go back there. "You know how they say someone burned a bridge? Well that bridge wasn't burned, it was nuked," says an insider who remained friendly with both Woods and Harmon. That said, a Callaway Golf source said that in January 2010, Woods called Harmon to talk about his swing. When I asked Woods after his final-round 73—a score that relied on every ounce of fight in him—whether he could repair the broken swing, he was typically unbowed. "We know what it is," he said. "It's just a matter of me doing it. Sometimes, as we all know, playing the game is harder to do on the golf course. I just need to do a little better job of it."

The selling point of Haney's swing model was that it was self-correctable; watch the ball flight and then make adjustments accordingly. It sounded simple and Woods had certainly done well with it in the past. But the aching question to me was that if the best player ever to pick up a club—and the most committed worker in the sport—couldn't do it when he most needed to, who could? Since Doral, there had been a steady regression in ball striking back to the kind of crookedness that characterized his 2004 season, during which he was learning Haney's unique principles. "I just kept hitting those spinners up to the right, and it was frustrating because if I am down the right side, I'd spin it to the right, aim down the left side, spin it to the right. I tried to release it early enough, but it still wasn't right," Woods said. Packing his bags in the locker room was Alex Cejka, the German journeyman who'd had the third-round lead and threw a 79 at Sawgrass that Sunday while playing alongside Woods. "I don't know what he shot, 1 over?" he said of Woods. "It should have been 5 over the way he kind of played. But he's a grinder, you know. He didn't really strike the ball well at all. His short game and his mental strength is phenomenal." But Woods insisted that, with a few weeks off, he would sort himself out. "It's not that bad. I'll fix it. I've got plenty of time." And with that he kept right on whistling past the graveyard.

CHAPTER 7

The Memorial

More than once while under the tutelage of Haney, Woods had lost patience and reconfigured his swing. He was the defending British Open champion at Carnoustie in 2007 when his ball striking betrayed him. Given how well he was putting and executing shots around the greens on the east coast of Scotland—an art form in itself—he could easily have won. But the long game, and especially long irons, on which the stunning victory at Royal Liverpool in 2006 had been built, had become a mystery to him. "It would have been nice if I could have just hit the ball a little better and just given myself a chance," he told reporters before heading back to Orlando to reacquaint himself with his newborn daughter, Sam. "I feel like I putted beautifully all week, but I couldn't get close enough. But when I did, I made them. I wasn't consistent hitting the ball close enough to make birdies, and subsequently I was on the periphery of trying to win a championship." That was a heavily sanitized version of the speech Woods gave Haney.

Woods returned to Isleworth and set about retooling his

swing. "He knows a lot about his swing. He gets in the habit in the wind of standing too far away from the ball. He went home and sorted himself out," remembers Williams. Two weeks later, Woods returned to the stage at Firestone Country Club in Akron, Ohio, which along with Torrey Pines was his favorite course on the Tour rotation. His swing was noticeably less flat and rounded because he was standing much closer to the ball, which had the effect of making for a more upright swing: he'd become more Ferris wheel than merry-go-round. Consequently, his short irons—where the blow was more descending than sweeping—were as sharp as they'd ever been. While the driver issues weren't really solved, he became deadly with the 3- or 5-wood off the tee. Again, the blows were more descending. Even though his radically in-to-out swing path would cause him problems down the track, the changes worked. He won the Bridgestone Invitational at a canter, then salvaged his season with a major, taking the PGA Championship in the sauna that was Tulsa that August. After the triumph at Southern Hills, Woods took second at the Deutsche Bank in Boston, then won both the BMW Championship and the Tour Championship. He was part of the winning U.S. Presidents Cup team at Royal Montreal and finished his year with a 7-shot win against an elite sixteen-man field at his own tournament, then called the Target World Challenge, at Sherwood Country Club. "End of '07, start of '08, that was the best I've ever seen him hit it," says Williams.

In the aftermath of the disaster that was The Players, Woods had little time to devote to working on his swing. He had to go to Las Vegas to host his foundation's Tiger Jam fund-raiser. Tiger Jam, a concert series featuring big-name acts like the Eagles, Prince, Bon Jovi, and Sting, has raised more than $10 million for the Tiger Woods Foundation over its twelve years. It was easily the most high-profile non-golf activity Woods was involved with and the biggest week of the year for his staff. It was interesting to note that other than being photographed courtside at basketball games or on the sidelines at a football game, Tiger Jam was about the only time Woods appeared in the media wearing civilian clothes. It seemed remarkable, in retrospect, that the world's richest athlete attracted so little attention from the mainstream media and less from the tabloids. When Woods's world was turned upside down in late November 2009, photo editors at newspapers and magazines across the world went looking for a file picture of him away from the golf course to better illustrate "sex scandal," and the one they all seemed to settle on—Woods looking vaguely pimpish wearing designer sunglasses indoors with a white T-shirt beneath a P-Diddy-esque cream casual suit—was taken at Tiger Jam five years before.

But in late May, after mingling with celebrities for a few days, he returned to Isleworth and his family and went straight to the practice range with the knowledge that he had only one tournament, the Memorial, to sort himself out before the year's second major. "He went back to something that he'd been working on previously," says Williams. "The movement with his head is the real problem, so he worked on keeping his head a lot more still."

Woods has always dipped his head on his downswing, then sprang up into a posted left leg as he moved through impact. It was a power move employed by many great players. Sam Snead had a pronounced squat as he began the downswing and Hogan incorporated the move, too, so that he would actually increase his spine angle—the degree to which he was bent over—on the downswing. Some savants even saw it as the elusive secret to the golf swing. But Snead and Hogan both released the club differently from Woods and neither violently snapped his left leg, a move that puts intense pressure on the knee. Neither did Snead or Hogan cross over his forearms, as Woods did, right after impact. Their clubfaces didn't rotate through impact but were already square, so all they needed to do was to keep turning. Snead and Hogan were more open to the target as they hit the ball, with their right elbow just behind or touching the right hip, the trait of a straight—though not necessarily long—hitter. Jim Furyk, for instance.

While Woods did a fantastic job of clearing his hips, his chest faced the ball at impact and his arms flew past, extending out toward the target. This allowed him to shape the ball's trajectory and hit it far, but the fact that the clubface was squared by the hands in a nanosecond as it came in contact with the ball made it heavily reliant on timing. The disconnect between the arms and the body—especially at the speeds at which Woods would swing—could lead to inaccuracy. It's easy to see in slo-mo photographs at impact how much room there was between his right elbow and his right hip compared with Snead or Hogan. Compounding these issues for Woods was the fact that as he scrunched his body in the downswing, he tended to get his arms—and therefore the golf club—stuck behind him. The usual result from such a position is a block, especially as the shafts of the clubs got longer. And so it followed that the condition was at its worst with the driver. I wasn't surprised when Woods told me he couldn't swing a forty-six-inch driver at all. When the clubface was open—a foundation of the Haney swing is the fanning of the club on the backswing, meaning tremendous forearm rotation was needed on the way back to the ball—the result was the right-to-right ball flight that had come to plague Woods and was painfully evident in the final round at The Players.

Haney, and Harmon before him, had tried to rid his star pupil of this habit in different ways. Before he began working with Harmon, Woods was typical of elastic juniors who hit the ball impressive distances in spite of their skinny bodies by generating immense clubhead speed through releasing torque with fast-twitch hips. Woods was born with the speed of an elite athlete.

His father used to say that if his son hadn't chosen golf, he'd have been a track star. Woods used to call it his Ole! swing because he'd come into the ball and flip his hands at the bottom to square the club like a matador flicking his cape at the charging bull. The move could be money when it worked properly but had several intrinsic liabilities—inconsistency and loss of distance control. Woods had never had an ego about his weaknesses. He acknowledged them and worked to get rid of them, not hide from them and pretend that the world's greatest golfer was perfect. He knew early on that he needed to make changes because he couldn't perform at a consistent level when a pitching wedge could send a ball 125 or 150 yards. His favorite expression whenever his swing improvements were brought up was that his goal was "pin high." That is, if he were a little left or a little right but had the right distance—had hit his shot pin high—he'd still have a makeable birdie putt. But if he were long or short as well as left or right, his chances at birdie were much more remote.

Harmon tried to fix the Woods dip by getting him to slow his body speed to let his arms catch up. Haney wanted him to always keep the club in front of the torso, a position from which he can't get stuck. Both adjustments were correct, but neither method was guaranteed to work every time. All golfers have days when the timing and rhythm of their swing are off. Nonetheless, Woods arrived in Columbus with the swing thought—he always has one swing thought—of staying taller throughout the swing. Haney, meanwhile, sought to stay taller by sending a string of chiding e-mails to golf writers. "I don't understand why everybody thinks I'm going to get fired," he told Michael Bamberger of *Sports Illustrated.* "Am I going to get fired when he asks me to come to Isleworth? Is he going to fire me when we go to Bethpage? During the Yankees game we're going to afterward? In August when he releases his new video where I'm his teacher? He has a new leg.

He has a new swing because his knee isn't flopping around like it once was. The media give him no slack. It wears me out, and it wears him out as well. I told Tiger about all this crap about me being fired, and he smiled and said, 'Welcome to my world.' "

Many times while in Vegas I'd wondered where all those people in denim shorts sitting at slot machines came from. Not the raggedly cutoff or trendily "distressed" denim shorts, the kind that gorgeous beach girls might wear on the sand at Malibu with their Ugg boots, but the dark blue ones that fall just above the knee and are most often worn by men who could stand to lose both a few pounds and their mullet haircuts. After touching down in Columbus, things were suddenly clearer. Columbus is the most regional of the big stops on the PGA Tour. It's the boyhood home of Jack Nicklaus, and like its hometown hero, it's a blue-collar town without much pretense or an eye for the latest fashions. They love Jack in Columbus, and it isn't an unrequited love, either. Nicklaus has long lived in Florida, but as I stood near him once when he was being announced on the tee, the man doing the introductions asked him quietly which part of Florida Jack was from. "Waddya mean?" Nicklaus responded incredulously. "You say, 'from Columbus, Ohio.' " Once a Buckeye, always a Buckeye.

Woods had the Memorial permanently circled on his playing calendar maybe in part because it was played at Muirfield Village, in nearby Dublin, a course he enjoyed, and in part because it made for good preparation for the upcoming U.S. Open. But really he came because Nicklaus invited him. Woods is at heart a golfer with a tremendous respect for the history of the game. He may have decided as a boy that he would obliterate all of the Nicklaus records, but at every chance, he paid homage to Nicklaus. I've asked him many times if he considers himself the greatest golfer ever, and Woods always gives the same answer: "No. Jack's got eighteen [majors], so he's the greatest."

The global financial crisis of late 2008 and early 2009 wiped out many things, among them the pro-am at the Memorial. Having taken TARP funds from the government, the tournament's presenting sponsor, Morgan Stanley, was gun-shy. The Wall Street colossus paid the estimated $6 million it was contractually obligated to give the tournament but chose not to participate or have its name associated in any way after Northern Trust was publicly mauled earlier in the year for giving the impression of throwing lavish parties at the Los Angeles Open with TARP money. Every spot in the Wednesday pro-am had been bought by Morgan Stanley for its clients, but not wishing to draw attention to the ostentatious wining and dining that financial services firms engaged in as a matter of course, the pro-am boondoggle was scrapped. Tournament organizers instead decided to hold an eight-man nine-hole skins game for charity. The players teed up on a cold and wet Midwestern summer day for $50,000, an amount so pitiful to these multimillionaires that it was obvious they'd gotten out of bed only because Nicklaus asked. Who's going to say no to Jack Nicklaus?

Nicklaus cracked his opening drive and was only half joking when he turned to the galleries almost apologetically and asked if his ball had managed to reach the fairway. The vagaries of advancing years and the miserable weather meant that after the sixty-nine-year-old unleashed a 3-wood for his approach into the uphill 470-yard par 4, he was still 70 yards short of the green. "I had three par 4s I couldn't reach today," he said, sighing. "But that's okay. I know what I am now. That's why I don't play golf anymore." Unlike Palmer, who was still consumed by golf even if he was but a shadow of the shadow of his former self, Nicklaus rarely tees it up anymore. Nicklaus, who has a Midwesterner from Scandanavian stock's distaste for staged sentimentality, told me long ago that he had no interest in being a ceremonial golfer. And he'd been true to his word. But this day was different. It was a chance, perhaps one last chance, for the two greatest golfers in history to share a few moments together on the course.

Woods and Nicklaus had last played alongside one another nine years before at the PGA Championship at Valhalla. It was memorable because it was the last time Nicklaus would play a PGA and because Woods triumphed after an unforgettable Sunday afternoon duel with Bob May. Unbelievably, whoever put together the pairings for this impromptu skins outing decided that Nicklaus should play in the first group with Jim Furyk, Camilo Villegas, and Padraig Harrington. "I said, uh-uh. I said, 'I haven't played with [Woods] for nine years. I'd like to play with Tiger.' So they said okay. I'm really looking forward to it. I told him I'd give him a couple of extra shots if he needed it. I'll throw my ninety-eight-mile-an-hour clubhead speed at him." And with that Vijay Singh was booted from Tiger's group.

Though he was by now an old Bear, every now and again he remembered through the fog of time the Bear of old he used to be. On the par-5 11th hole, where no one risked landing in a winding creek by going for the green with their second shots, Woods, Kenny Perry, and Stewart Cink all laid up to about 100 yards. They were not too far in front of Nicklaus, who needed two mighty blows just to get there. But while their wedges were imprecise, Nicklaus stuffed an 8-iron to a few feet. After being embarrassed on the first hole, Nicklaus was now surveying his chance to take the first two skins. His entire demeanor had changed. He walked across the bridge to that green not like a man almost seventy but like an eighteen-time major champion. After the young bucks failed to convert, Jack Nicklaus was never going to miss. He had the first two skins of the game. He shrugged in his typically self-deprecating way and said, "Blind squirrels" (golfer's shorthand for even blind squirrels find nuts sometimes). But Woods wasn't fooled. "He's a competitor, you can see that," he said later. "Anyone who has ever played the game at the highest level wants to come out and give it their best. You could see on certain holes, certain shots, him kind of revert back to the old Jack. It was neat to see. I hadn't seen it since 2000."

This level of stratospheric athletic achievement—envisioning an improbable goal and having not merely the talent but also the huevos to make it happen—is what excites Woods. He remembered back to that day at Valhalla in Louisville nine years before, when Nicklaus sat near the cut line as the two of them got to their final hole of the second round. "I said, 'Jack, let's finish it up the right way.' He said, 'Definitely.' That means making birdie, and we both made birdie." In the end, a birdie wasn't enough and Nicklaus missed the cut by a single shot. Still, a remarkable feat. But to Woods it didn't matter that he'd missed the cut, because he said he'd make birdie on that hole and, by God, that sixty-year-old man with the bad hip made birdie. "He almost holed it from the fairway," Woods recalled, his eyes twinkling. "I haven't heard a roar that loud in a long time. It was pretty special to see Jack suck it up and hit a shot like that when he absolutely needed it the most."

Even when he's not in the public eye, Woods values most this ability to "suck it up" and deliver. A friend of mine who played against him—well, to be accurate, it was two very good players' best ball against Woods—at Isleworth in 2009 said they'd tag-teamed him back to all square with one hole to play on the 7,500-yard monster—the toughest course in Florida—where Woods at one point, Haney calculated, carried a handicap of plus 10, an absurdity if we were talking about anyone else. It meant he had to average 62 in the ten best previous twenty rounds he'd played. Consider that most Tour players would be somewhere around plus 5 on their home courses, and it would not be inaccurate to say Woods was twice as good. So with one hole to play, Woods, who was over his ball in the fairway, looked back to the cart of the two men he was playing and confirmed that they were all square in the match. He then made a little remark under his breath that they didn't quite catch and proceeded to stuff a long iron to 3 feet. Game, set, and match, Mr. Woods. He would later give them a chance to get their money back shooting hoops inside the grand Isleworth clubhouse. "He's pretty good at basketball, too," my friend lamented.

And so it was, on a rainy Wednesday in Dublin, Ohio, that Woods would hit the shot when he absolutely needed it the most. He chipped in from a ludicrous place on the final hole to add a sixth skin to his haul. Cink had the other. Perry was shut out. Nicklaus was not given to hyperbole, but it was clear as he spoke on the green, wearing just a cashmere pullover as the rain came down while the others were in the latest designer rain suits, that Woods had more than earned his praise. When Nicklaus was asked if it didn't surprise him that Woods chipped in on the last hole, he replied with a more pertinent observation. "Didn't surprise me? It didn't surprise him." This, I thought as I stood on that soggy green, was the ultimate appreciation of one master for another. To the layman, chipping in is a pleasant surprise if not a complete shock; to these men, it's an expectation.

It was also the first time Nicklaus had seen Woods's swing since his return from surgery. Pointedly, Nicklaus thought that from what he'd seen of Woods playing on television—admittedly little because he didn't watch much golf on TV—that he was protecting the lead knee and that caution was probably to blame for the crookedness of recent tournaments. "Do I think he's probably at the level that he wants to be? Probably not. If you look at his golf swing, I don't think he moves out of the way of the ball like he used to. I think that's probably protective, and it's probably a good move on his part." Woods later agreed, saying that the "worst thing you can do is stretch out the ligament right away. . . . The surgery would have been all for naught. That's one of the reasons why it takes athletes a lot longer to come back." But after playing alongside him, Nicklaus noticed a change. "A lot more aggressive than I've seen it in previous tournaments," he said. "I thought he's been babying his leg a little bit, but I didn't see much babying today. I thought he went at it pretty good."

Woods began the opening round at the Memorial, played in far more pleasant conditions, with many question marks. Even though he'd won at Jack's place three times, there was little doubt he needed to make a statement to quiet the chattering classes. Everyone from Lee Trevino to Joe the Golfer on Internet forums the world over was offering Woods swing tips. Though he had many doubters, Nicklaus wasn't among them. I asked him whether he still considered Woods the favorite despite his recent struggles. "Isn't he everybody's pick always to win?" the Golden Bear replied.

Three weeks, it turned out, was a long time in golf. The tentative and exasperated golfer betrayed by an erratic swing at Sawgrass was banished, replaced by, well, Tiger Woods. As he had after Carnoustie, Woods had found himself a weapon he could use off the tee. Where in 2007 it had been the 3-wood—in late summer on hard golf courses, his running 3-wood was plenty long enough—this time it was a driver with a higher loft and shorter shaft. The purists could argue that it was a compensation for a swing flaw—and perhaps they would be right—but Woods was interested in finding only the short grass. And he did. His swing seemed smoother, with a more natural flow, and the result was a breezy 3-under-par 69 on one of the Tour's more exacting tracks. The transformation was so complete that, as he stood on the 18th tee box, Woods was poised to achieve what he had done only five times as a professional and not once in more than six years: hit every fairway in a competitive round. Alas, he missed to the right, caught a fairway bunker, and ultimately misread a short par putt, recording only his second bogey of the round. The other was a 3-putt. "Everything felt pretty good," he said. "Overall, I felt like I controlled the ball well all day. Especially with the wind blowing like this, you have to hit it flush. I did that all day. I didn't miss any shots. The swing is starting to come around."

As ever, Woods wasn't parting with too much information about what he'd altered in his swing, other than conceding that he'd made a breakthrough. "Something turned in the swing but it was, 'If I can do it with the irons, then I can do it with the driver.'" It seemed, though, that Woods's year would be a sort of one step forward, two steps back after he followed up the impressive first round with a 74 on Friday. The strange part was that he missed only two fairways in the second round. "And one of them was by an inch," he bemoaned. But Nicklaus had the greens running somewhere near 14 on the Stimpmeter, which was very spicy even for touring professionals. The winds were gusting and Woods wasn't sharp with his irons, short siding himself too many times, which was never a good idea at the best of times on a Nicklaus design; he gave golfers room off the tees but demanded precise approach shots. To compound matters, Woods missed three short par putts. Still, he seemed strangely upbeat and the following day showed why. He turned in a 4-under-par round of 68 despite three-putting the 17th hole. "I was only 15 feet. You can't 3-putt from 15 feet. Should have been more disciplined on my read and my speed, and I let it get away," he said. Woods often liked to play little mind games with himself. Before the third round, he told Williams that they had to keep the tee box, and he made sure that playing partner K. J. Choi never once got to hit first.

Woods was chasing on Sunday. Six players were ahead of

him on the leaderboard, including major championship winners Furyk, Ogilvy—who'd scored a 63 at Muirfield Village in the third round—and a resurgent Davis Love III. Woods lay four shots adrift of surprise third-round leader, Matt Bettencourt. He knew that there would be no margin for error. And he needed none. Woods did more than return to his stratospheric best in claiming a fourth Memorial Tournament; he made himself the presumptive favorite to win the U.S. Open. "I suspect that major number fifteen will come for Tiger Woods in about two weeks," proclaimed Nicklaus after Woods spectacularly made birdie on the two closing holes to hold off Furyk by a single stroke. "If he hits the ball like that, it won't even be a contest."

Woods was a player transformed, galaxies removed from the uncertain and exasperated man who fought the swing demons in April and May. So thorough was the renaissance that he'd managed in the fourth round what he came achingly close to achieving in the first: hitting every fairway. His closing 7-under-par 65 could've even been a few shots better. Remarkably for a player who had been struggling off the tee, Woods missed only seven fairways over the four rounds, tying his best ever performance as a professional, which came at the 1998 Masters. His iron play wasn't as statistically sharp, but there was no questioning it when he needed it the most: a lunar 9-iron on the 17th hole Sunday to 9 feet set up a rare birdie on the crustiest green on the course, and then there was the 7-iron on the last, which stopped 9 inches from the cup. "I wish you'd all quit pissing him off," Furyk told me only half in jest about the constant stream of media questioning whether Woods had lost his way. "Wish you'd just quit chapping him so much and make him come back and keep proving stuff. Tiger Woods is always Tiger Woods, but I'm sure he answered a lot of questions today."

And therein lay the greater effect of Woods's second—but far more impressive—victory of the season. He had succeeded in restoring order to the empire. The pretenders to his throne were once again aware that it was Tiger's world and that they were just renting space in it. "He's the king," said Bettencourt, who started the day with the lead but could manage only a 73 for a fifth-place finish. "He's the best." Michael Letzig, who had a front-row seat as Woods's playing partner, was like the glee club singer who'd just shared the stage with Pavarotti. He had, he said, a lot of work to do in order to compete at Woodsian heights. "Today was unreal," he told me after being beaten by 10 shots by Woods. "I don't even know how to describe it. It was the best golf I've ever seen." Letzig was a touring professional, and a decent one, but he admitted he just didn't have the game necessary to compete with what he'd seen. He explained that because the greens were so baked, he needed to play away from the pin and hope to catch slopes that funneled toward the hole—always a tricky proposition. Woods hit towering irons and got them to land softly. "I just don't have that shot," he said. "I just don't know how to do that."

Like most ultracompetitive, type A personalities at the top of their game, Woods took a certain pleasure in proving the naysayers wrong. "It was just a matter of time," he said when I asked him how he'd been able to turn his game around. Being able to practice more since not having to ice his knee had helped greatly, but he wasn't giving much away. "I needed to do the reps and do some good practice sessions these past couple of weeks and it came together this week. I knew I could do this. It's just a matter of, 'Give me a little bit of time.' I just came off a pretty extended break, and I was close to winning, but the game wasn't quite there when I really needed it on Sunday. I rectified that. All week, I've been hitting the ball well. I really controlled my flight and felt in control with shaping the ball both ways."

Of course, he wasn't going to resist a chance to give his critics a backhander. He said he was "frustrated"—his favorite verb when he really wanted to curse—by the view that he had not done enough since returning after eight months off. "Coming off of what I came off of, I win one tournament and have four top tens . . . that's not bad, but people said, 'You're not that good anymore.' " He also took the opportunity to defend Haney. The media "jumped the gun on that one. Hank's been just absolutely phenomenal for my game and helped me through a lot." It occurred to me that Haney was safe with Woods not just because Woods enjoyed his company. Woods would rather have pins stuck into his eyeballs than admit that Haney was the wrong choice of coach.

During his postvictory press conference, Woods sat with Nicklaus at the front of the auditorium in the media center taking questions. A young man in his early twenties, casually dressed in cargo shorts and a polo shirt, stood up when called upon by the moderator, Tour media official Mark Stevens, to ask his question. This was unexpected, but given the number of journalism students from Ohio State who'd spent time watching the way the media works at the tournament, I didn't give it much thought. Until the man began to speak. "Jack's gonna hate me for doing this," he said, reaching into his pocket.

The retired FBI agent who was handling security for the Tour that week immediately jumped up from his position against a wall. He was followed by the three plainclothes police officers who'd been assigned to shadow Woods during Sunday's round. I had been near the men for much of the day and knew that they were armed. I saw the guns strapped around their lower legs. One instinctively reached for his weapon, though it was never drawn. It was, to say the least, a tense moment. The man could have pulled anything out of his pocket and, a few feet away from him, were the two greatest figures in the history of golf.

But the man pulled out a grounds pass. He wanted Nicklaus and Woods to sign it for him. The security people began to go after him, but Nicklaus, perhaps wanting to avoid a scene at his tournament, lifted his left hand, calling them off. He told the man that seeing as he'd gone to "all this trouble, the least we could do is give you an autograph." Woods, it was clear, didn't share Jack's goodwill. Although he signed the ticket for the man, who was soon after escorted from the premises, I've always wondered whether he signed his own name. It was a glimpse of the threat that always surrounds Woods and why there are security people in the galleries wherever he plays. Years ago his staff would throw away all the hate mail and death threats Woods received, but Woods wanted to read it; sometimes, he would pin the bigotry on his wall, to remind himself why he needed to be forever vigilant. Strange, dark places, indeed, from whence motivation comes.

After the news conference, Woods did what he hadn't done all year. He hung around. There was no Steinberg or Greenspan there to whisk him away. So he stood for about half an hour "shooting the shit," as he called it, with a handful of writers, myself included. It was, of course, all off the record, not that he said anything earth-shattering. He was relaxed and answered mainly golf-related questions. Nicklaus, meanwhile, was leaning against a doorway, observing. "That used to be you, Jack," I said. He smiled. I told him that if he kept inviting Woods to the Memorial, he'd probably keep winning. "Wouldn't matter to me in the least," he said. "He could win here every year and I'd be a happy man." Then he paused and looked right at me. "I have no ego left when it comes to him," he said. "None."

CHAPTER 8

U.S. Open

Biblical rains had pelted Long Island for almost three weeks before golf's traveling circus moved into Bethpage State Park for the playing of the 109th United States Open. The second wettest—and eighth coldest—June on record had reduced the Black Course to a bog; "Bathpage," players called it as they arrived and, as they are wont to do, immediately complained. It was dueling violins at ten paces: too wet, too long, too cold. Maybe nine-to-five working stiffs teed it up in inclement weather for the love of the game, but not so much professionals. It'd always surprised me just how many Tour players had fallen out of love with golf. The grind of the touring pro's life had reduced the passion of their youth to merely the paycheck of their adulthood. "It's really sweet when you're twenty-one or nineteen; it's just awesome and you can't get enough of it. But ten years in, it's definitely a different mind-set," admits Adam Scott. "To be successful out here is a grind." Scott didn't mean to sound unappreciative, for he understood how lucky he was, but the truth was he'd become so invested in being Adam Scott that his life was no longer his own. And that was before he had to pay for a new $40 million Gulfstream G5. At least Scott still enjoyed teeing it up socially with his friends. There were many professionals who didn't play what they called civilian golf. "Once a year, when I go back to Australia for Christmas, I'll go out and have a hit with my mates down there," says Stuart Appleby. "But that's about it. I've got other hobbies."

As the gallows humor about needing arks and snorkels and wet suits flew all around him in the locker room of New York's most famous—and most difficult—municipal course, Woods had other ideas. The last time the Open was at Bethpage, seven years earlier, he had won, holding off Mickelson. The course was brutally long then, so much so that Bruce Fleisher, the reigning USGA senior champion, gave up his spot in the field because he couldn't reach all the par-4 greens in two. His Champions Tour colleague Hale Irwin realized how astute a move Fleisher had made, when he opened with an 82. In truth, given the rain that soaked that tournament, too, perhaps a half dozen players could hit the ball long enough and high enough and putt well enough to have had a chance. But seven years later, it was longer and the downpours had it playing longer still than its 7,426 yardage. Ogilvy, who'd won his U.S. Open not far away at venerable Winged Foot, couldn't recall ever hitting so many woods on par 4s. "And 3- and 4-irons, we're wearing them out," he said after a practice round. "It's incredibly long." While others moaned, Woods—just like Nicklaus did in his prime—smelled an advantage.

"This is probably the most difficult golf course we've faced from tee to green," he said during his pretournament news conference. "This golf course is all you want. With the weather coming in here this week, it's only going to get longer and it's going to be even more difficult." He took joy from his own grim prognosis because he'd always believed that his advantage was at its greatest on golf's crucibles. Woods was more scared of benign courses where birdies were plentiful than of monsters like the Black. "Because what can I do more than make birdie?" he once told me. "There's nothing that separates you if you make birdie and so does everyone else." He expanded on the theme during his Bethpage news conference. "If you don't shoot 68 [at Tour events], you're losing ground. Here, if you shoot 68, you're moving up the leaderboard. To me, that's fun. Par is rewarded and a birdie is really rewarded. That, to me, is how the game of golf should be played." Of course, that also meant fewer bodies for him to have to climb over in his dogged pursuit of history. "I like my chances in any major," he told me, but "I think I'm still one of the longer hitters on Tour and I'm hitting long irons. A lot of shorter guys are obviously hitting woods into the greens. If it rains, how much are they going to move up the tees is going to be the question." Woods, obviously, was lobbying for a tough setup. He wanted the riffraff out of his way, and even though he knew Mother Nature was going to cooperate, he didn't want the USGA's Mike Davis, who was in charge of setting up the course, leveling the playing field.

The Irish tyro McIlroy, playing in his first U.S. Open, was at least honest when he was asked whether he could challenge Woods. "If he plays the way he did in the final round at Memorial, then no," he admitted. Ogilvy resorted to a little gallows humor. "He doesn't win every one of them [majors]," he said, feigning anger. But then he added with a wry smile, "In fact, he wins less than half. . . . Even when he's had his slumps, if you like, he's always to me looked a week away from winning six of the next eight tournaments." History showed that only six men had won back-to-back U.S. Opens, and none since Curtis Strange two decades before. But Woods was the defending champion of both the tournament and the venue. If the planets could be made out through the rain and clouds, they were probably aligned.

Woods had quietly put an old set of Nike forged blades back into his bag at Memorial, and they served their master so well they were retained for the U.S. Open. Woods has a colorful way of treating clubs, especially wedges and putters that don't behave. He delivers the standard punishments, snapping them into little pieces during fits of anger—always in private—but sometimes he'd get creatively medieval. One of his favorite methods of torture was to tie recalcitrant clubs to the back of his golf cart and drag them along the ground until they saw the error of their ways. Conversely, when they were good, he could be very doting. All equipment companies want professional golfers to use the latest product they're flogging to the public, but in the case of Woods, he chooses and Nike would nod in agreement. A Nike club maker once described Woods to me as "the Holy Grail" when it came to the widespread acceptance of the company's putters. Woods had already single-handedly made Nike Golf a $725-million-a-year enterprise, so I asked whether for their $35 million a year, couldn't Nike just ask him to use one of their putters? He laughed. "I wish, but not how it works," he said. Woods called all the shots, just as he did with IMG, which took only a 5 percent commission from his endorsement deals when the industry standard was 20 percent. A rival agent was shocked to hear that Steinberg agreed to such a small percentage, but upon reflection said that "5 percent of $100 million is still more than 20 percent of what you're getting from most guys." On top of that, IMG had the cachet of having Tiger Woods as a client and Steinberg could keep strutting.

Woods also had retained the Nike driver, shortened in length to 44¼ inches and with 10.5 degrees of loft, which he'd used at Memorial. "As far as my driver is concerned, as we all know, loft is your friend," he explained. "The reason why you hit a 3-wood straighter is because it has more loft, and that helps. My release has changed over the years, and I just need a little bit more loft now. It's working out and I'm driving the ball more efficiently. I still have the same power, but I just need the loft now. When I first came out here on Tour, I used a 6.5-degree driver, and now I'm up to 10.5. Jeez, I'd hate to see what I'm going to hit when I turn forty. I wonder how that's going to be. Maybe a 46-inch driver, with about 15 degrees of loft. But you know, it is what it is and technology has changed and the ball doesn't spin as much as it used to, and you have to have a little bit more loft than you used to play."

It's never a good sign when at the end of the first day of a major championship more meteorologists have been interviewed than golfers. Weather so foul wiped out all but three and a quarter hours of Thursday's play. All 156 contestants spent the day calling airlines and changing their Monday flights home. They were staring down the barrel of the longest U.S. Open in history. "Nature is going to take its course," said a philosophical Padraig Harrington, whose start was suitably leaky, 4 over par after six holes. "We'll get this tournament done and I guarantee you they will have a U.S. Open champion at the end of this week." Looking at the heavens, he reassessed. "Well, at some stage in the next week." Not including playoffs, no U.S. Open in 108 years had stretched past Monday morning, and that had happened only once, in 1983 at Pittsburgh's Oakmont, where the final groups had to return to play just five holes. "We will not determine a national champion until we play seventy-two holes," said Mike Davis. "So if that takes us to Monday or Tuesday, whatever."

Woods made it onto the 7th green but, like the rest of the morning starters, was left wishing that he'd had an afternoon tee time. More than at any major in memory, being on the right side of the draw at Bethpage was of critical importance. A drenched Woods finally left the course with a 7-foot par putt awaiting him the following morning, assuming play was possible. He was ordered back for a 7:30 a.m. resumption of play. "It was a slow day," an unhappy-looking Woods said. "It took two and a half hours to play six holes. It was pretty tough out there. There was a lot of standing water." What contributed to his surly mood was the fact that his game, so crisp at the Memorial, was barely afloat. The tone was set when he began his title defense with a vicious pull hook on the 1st tee. It looked, frankly, frighteningly like the opening drive of the final round at Augusta, so far left it finished marginally this side of Pyongyang. Woods, who always seemed uncomfortable swinging in rain gear—much to the chagrin of Nike's apparel designers who had tried their best to keep him dry and comfortable—appeared to lose sight of the ball. "Way left," said Williams, who'd already strapped the bag on his broad shoulder and begun walking toward the merchandising tent. At Bethpage, missing by fifty yards in places was better than missing by five, and Woods benefited from an inviting lie when he got to his ball: the grass had been trampled by shoppers who were either looking for refuge from the rain or thought $32 was a reasonable price to pay for a hat.

Woods had a look at the pin but found a greenside bunker. From there, he did what he does best and got up and down to salvage par. He settled down and gave himself chances at birdie on the next three holes, but at the 5th came another foul ball, this time to the right. Way right. He was lucky that his ball had caromed off a tree and settled in the rough. But he had no chance at the green and ultimately missed the bogey putt on the low side of the hole. He bounced back, however, with a 15-foot birdie on the next hole. "That tells you right there what he's about," says Williams. "A lot of guys in those sorts of conditions, they make a double and they know it's a miserable day and they're just trying to survive." Indeed, Justin Leonard later said he'd abandoned the ideal of par and "just tried to do the best I could." Many of those sent out Thursday thought they should've been spared, and maybe they were right. Ground staff were squeegeeing the greens in between groups. J. P. Hayes had a 45-footer and even after his line was cleared of standing water, his putt rooster-tailed and finished 15 feet short. But Woods was stoic. "It was a good decision to play today," he said. "We had to get in as many holes as we could. We probably played more holes than we thought." Harrington, playing alongside Woods and Masters champion Angel Cabrera, said the only winners on this most miserable of days were those with afternoon tee times. "I don't think there's a guy who hasn't teed off today that is not sitting very happy right now in their hotel room or maybe at the cinema watching a movie."

Woods was up at 4:30 on Friday morning, not having had a restful night's sleep. He didn't dare take Ambien, a controversial sleeping pill that has caused users to do strange things, because he couldn't afford to be groggy. But though he may have been awake, the tournament was quickly descending into a waking nightmare. Far from thinking about winning, Woods left himself in need of heavy lifting just to make the halfway cut after a disastrous second day. He had serious history to overcome. He'd never shot an opening round as high as 74 and gone on to win a major. And he had to try to create history stuck on the wrong side of the draw, which now carried its own metrics. The scoring average of the unfortunate seventy-eight who had to brave the torrential rains and strong winds of Thursday was two shots higher and dragged the first-round scoring average up to nearly five strokes over par. "I know one guy who is seething, and that's Tiger Woods," said Strange. "He knows he's behind the eight ball, got the raw end of the deal."

Compounding matters was that the other half of the draw got much easier conditions. Of the thirteen players who shot in the

60s in the opening round, which was belatedly completed on Friday afternoon, only two teed off, like Woods, on Thursday morning. And neither of them—amateur Drew Weaver and Northern Irishman Graeme McDowell, who both had 1-under-par rounds of 69—could muscle their way into the top six. While Woods was watching on television, Mike Weir took advantage of the benign, soft conditions to card a flawless 64. Rubbing salt into a festering wound, the players on Weir's side of the draw went straight back out to begin their second rounds on Friday afternoon in even better conditions. With the sun bursting through the clouds, the winds calm, and the greens soft as sponges, it was like throwing Velcro balls from the fairway and having them stick next to the flag, a far cry from the usual modus operandi of a U.S. Open. "Our side of the draw got an advantage," Weir said. "For us to be able to play in nice conditions all day like this is huge."

There's no doubt Woods—who finally finished his opening round almost twenty-seven hours later—didn't get any favors, but neither did he much help himself. He was at a respectable even par with four holes to play and the worst of the weather for the day gone. But the beastly 15th, the most difficult hole on the course, was his undoing. The drive was poor, blocked to the right, followed by a risky approach at the flag when the middle of the green would've been a wiser choice. His second shot plugged into gnarled greenside rough, forcing Woods to take a drop. Off balance, he then played a lamentable chip that ran almost back down to the front of the green. The ignomy was such that Johnny Miller even quipped on air that "he's chipping like me right now." It didn't help that a 3 putt followed, his second double bogey of the round. He closed with preventable bogeys on 16 and 18, too. "I wasn't playing poorly," he later said. "I was even par with four to go, and I was right there where I needed to be, and two bad shots and a mud ball later, here we go and I'm at 4 over par."

Woods complained about mud, which was prevalent throughout the day as the fairways began to dry and mud started sticking
to balls, sending them in unpredictable directions. An argument
could be made that playing the ball down didn't necessarily identify the nation's best golfer, because there was an element of luck
to how much mud stuck to balls. But the USGA wasn't the PGA
Tour, which routinely gave players a break at rain-affected tournaments by letting them clean their balls and replace them. "Lift,
clean, and cheat," Tom Meeks, who was Davis's predecessor, once
said of the rule, making his view quite clear. The USGA, it must
be said, is hardly a favorite of the players. They tend to think
that country club amateurs shouldn't be trying to run a professional tournament because they almost always drop the ball in
ways both big and small. While there's some truth to the USGA's
stuffy blue blazer stereotype, and a lot of truth to the many disas-
ters presided over by what is a dysfunctional organization, it is
also true that the USGA is old school: the ball must be played as
it lies, Mr. Woods.

As blue skies began to break through the Friday afternoon
clouds, Woods's disposition wasn't getting much sunnier. When
he was asked whether he wished he could get back on the course,
he shook his head. "The way I feel right now, no. I don't want
to go back out there right now. Probably would be a few clubs
light." Later, I told Williams that he was unlucky to have gotten on the wrong side of the draw. To my surprise, he refused to
use it as an excuse. "I don't buy into the wrong-end-of-the-draw
argument," he said. "Conditions are hard or easy; whatever it is,
it's still the same par. The thing about it was the final five or six
holes was when the weather was at its best. That took him out of
the tournament, no question about it. A good finish there, those
last four holes, and he was right in the tournament. Okay, if it had
been different, if we had dropped those four shots during the bad

weather, the rain and the wind, it would've been different, but we actually got through all those tough holes good but just made a poor finish."

Four-over-par rounds aren't good harbingers for Woods. He watched ESPN that night, as he usually did, and had to hear how his opening round continued the misery he'd experienced in the New York area since his famous victory at Bethpage in 2002. He was a cumulative 19 over par in the opening rounds of his past four majors played in the shadows of the Big Apple. His 74 was his worst start at a major since he carded 76 at Winged Foot three years before. In 2004 at Shinnecock, on the eastern end of Long Island, he opened with a 6-over-par 76, and shot a 5-over 75 at the 2004 PGA Championship at Baltusrol, in northern New Jersey. Williams recalled it not being a happy night in the Tiger camp but that, as always with Woods, hope springs eternal. He needed something under par, hopefully in the mid-60s, to thrust himself back into the picture.

Saturday, however, wasn't to be his day, either. If there ever was a picture worth a thousand words, it was the one taken of a forlorn Woods and Williams, huddled under an umbrella, soaked yet forced to remain in position on the 11th hole as the rain pelted down. It was a portrait as metaphor, insult added to the injury of an Open title defense slipping away in the deluge. Woods and Williams were made to stand in the rain for more than ten minutes even though play had been halted, even though it was already beyond 7 p.m. and the light had all but faded, and, more to the point, even though the heaviest downpour of the week had turned large portions of the golf course into a frog habitat. It was obvious to everyone except the USGA that no more golf was possible after the third round's belated late-afternoon start. Woods finally was allowed to return to the clubhouse after one of the longest days—almost twelve hours of play—in major championship history. Worse, even though he rebounded with a second-round 69—a fine score given the conditions—he actually lost ground to the leader, who by Saturday night was Ricky Barnes, the former U.S. Amateur champion who'd found the professional life anything but smooth sailing. Once more, the chimera that was the 15th haunted Woods. The only reason he didn't make double bogey again in the second round was that he converted a slippery 6-footer for bogey. "It is what it is," Woods said with resignation. He was still upset about his first round. "Yesterday was the day that did it. On my half of the draw I had to finish at even par, 1 over par at the worst, because I think 1 under par is the best my side of the draw did. That would have been a really good score. But instead I ended up at 4 over par and that was about the mean for the day on my side [of the draw], which is not what it's going to take to win a U.S. Open."

It's truly one of nature's wonders that Woods could never be counted out. To any reasonable, intelligent follower of golf, there was no way he could win the tournament. Yet when another of the longest days in Open history finally ended Sunday night, the eyes of those who should know better all had that familiar look. Logic told them Woods was done, but he had so often defied the rules. Who could be sure? Woods had made the halfway cut by only a single stroke and was 11 back of the leader. But with eleven holes to play in his final round, only seven men were above him on the leaderboard, all of them from the other half of the draw and none of them sure things: Barnes, untested young Englishman Ross Fisher, Lucas Glover, who'd never even made a cut at a U.S. Open before, and, of all people, David Duval, the former world number one who'd won the 2001 British Open, then literally fell off the map, dropping all the way to 882 in the world rankings when he arrived at Bethpage.

Mickelson was in the mix, too, but it was hard to know whether his heart was in the game. He'd just returned from a hiatus from playing after his wife, Amy, had been diagnosed with breast cancer. Luckily, the cancer had been caught in its very early stages and she would recover, but Mickelson that week on Long Island didn't know anything for sure. He was playing just to play and perhaps because it was here in 2002 that he became a favorite of the brash New York galleries. Woods put aside his differences with Mickelson when he'd heard about Amy's cancer and sent a series of text messages wishing them both well. Mickelson thanked his rival, but when Woods said he hoped "they find a cure," Mickelson jokingly texted back that he hoped "they find a cure for your hook."

With a birdie on the exacting 7th late on Sunday, Woods had clawed his way back to even par. Improbable as it was, he could still win, but he needed capitulations from those ahead. "Obviously, it's not totally in my control," he said before leaving for the night. "It's one of those where you have to play a great round of golf and get some help."

One of the gifts Woods had since childhood was an uncanny ability to predict what score would win a tournament. As he and Williams warmed up on the range for a Monday finish, he told his caddie that 4 under par would get into a playoff and 5 under would win outright. Freshening northerly winds wouldn't make it easy for anyone, much less for the man who needed five birdies and had eleven holes in which to find them. The campaign did not begin well. Woods never looked like making birdie all week on the par-3 8th and that didn't change Monday. He could not birdie the 9th, either, and then made bogey on the 10th. It truly should have been the ultimate message that it was over, but he's so stubborn, he played like he was still in the hunt. And sure enough, he breathed life into a quixotic tilt with consecutive birdies, a 2 putt for 4 on the par-5 13th from about 20 feet and a 7-footer downhill on the next, a short par 3. That success was even greeted with a fist pump, the first time all week that he'd shown any positive emotion. Woods was at 1 under par, and even his playing partner, the impressive young Australian Michael Sim, playing in his first major, started to believe in fairy tales. "I was kind of hoping there was going to be history there for a while," he said. "Tiger made two birdies in a row and I tell you he hit a great iron shot on 15. I thought it was going to be about 6 feet."

Ah, the 15th. The 458-yard par 4 sloped gently to the left, its fairways guarded by fescue grass on either side. The green was elevated some fifty feet above the fairway and well bunkered, defending a two-tiered green. A back right pin, as it was for the final round, presented one of the hardest targets in golf. Over the green amounted to an automatic bogey—or worse—and finding the front of the green left a treacherous 2 putt. Woods had hit a beautiful tee shot. Too beautiful, Williams thought. "That's where it's tough sometimes when you're a caddie," he told me. "I mean, he doesn't know he's pumped up but I know he is. That 3-wood off the tee went like 290 into the wind. Fuck, you think he's pumped up?" Williams had been down this road many times in their decade together and each time it was like a tightrope walk. Woods, the scent of victory in his nostrils, becomes filled with adrenaline. More times than he can remember, Williams had deliberately given the wrong yardages to pins because he wanted Woods to take less club and didn't want to get into an argument. Williams was a firm believer in the power of adrenaline. He convinced Woods to hit a lob wedge from 101 yards into the 72nd hole at Torrey Pines the year before when Woods wanted to take a sand iron, insisting that he couldn't hit a lob wedge that far. But he needed a birdie and Williams felt it was the only way to get the ball close. As it happened, he was right and Woods famously rolled in the 12-foot putt to get into a playoff with Mediate.

"Golf's such a weird game because as I'm walking up the fairway there, I know he's pumped up," Williams said. "I thought we can still win this tournament with a good finish, but this was going to be the pivotal hole. I knew exactly what the yardage was because there was a little sprinkler there and with the pin in the back I knew it was a little cut 5-iron and it's the shot he's going to hit, but if he's pumped up he could hit it three or four yards farther than he wants to hit it. When I gave him the yardage, I knew straightaway which club he was going to pick, I knew straightaway which shot he was going to hit, and in my head I'm thinking, it is the club, it was a 5-iron all day, but he's pumped up. But I knew we had to make birdie or else, so you've got to get over the ridge [in the green] and I'm thinking to myself, 'If I tell him 6-iron and he hits a good shot and it hits into that ridge and it comes all the way off the green and he 3 putts or something . . . ' That's the hardest thing when you're a caddie. I'm trying to tell him he's got to hit that ball left of the pin and use the slope to come down. If he had hit that ball six feet left of the pin, it would've been absolutely stiff, but he landed it right at the hole and it took one bounce and there's only a few feet to the edge and it's gone. And you crucify yourself. But in that situation, the cardinal sin if you're trying to win the tournament is to be short. You had to get the ball past the ridge on the left side and let it come down. Unfortunately, he hit the best shot he'd hit all week, but as soon as it left the club I knew it was six feet too long. I could hear it in the contact he made."

The U.S. Open was over after the inevitable bogey that followed. Woods had good looks at birdies on the three closing holes, but befitting his tournament, none fell. It would've been too little, too late, anyway. He finished at even par, four shots back of Glover, who kept his head when Barnes, Mickelson, and Duval lost theirs. Woods finished in a tie for sixth, mirroring his

Augusta finish. Four shots. The four he'd thrown away at the end of the first round? The four he'd thrown away on the 15th hole? Instead, Woods later blamed his putter for the loss. "My good ones were not going in and my bad ones were not even close." He never looked at home on the slow, bumpy greens, but neither did his short game show up. Nor, it must be said, his attitude. Again, it looked like the moment got the better of him, that the great Tiger Woods looked too far ahead, wanted to win so much that he played not to lose. Williams was philosophical. "We didn't play eighteen holes on any one day and we started on a different hole every day. It was a bizarre week. It was like playing in a member-guest shotgun tournament."

It was no consolation to Woods that on the "Mudders" U.S. Open he was the only man not over par on his half of the draw. And that he was the only player in the field to shoot under par for the last three rounds. And certainly no consolation that he'd correctly predicted the winning score. As Woods moved briskly toward the outside interview area to fulfill his media obligations, the funereal look on Steinberg's face said it all: Woods was unplayable. I stood in front of the podium, a foot or so beneath Woods, and had barely gotten out the first part of my question, "Do you beat yourself up over this one, or—" when he snapped back without looking at me. "Yes." He had nothing to add and just stared straight ahead, not bothering to hide his disgust.

Our exchange was the lead-in to *SportsCenter* that night not only because Woods had failed to deliver on the golf course but also because he'd let his guard down in public, with the cameras rolling. Earl had taught his son to control his emotions, but the discipline of his younger years had been waning for some time. Some looked at the angry Woods on the podium that afternoon, dark clouds gathering in the sky behind him, and saw a spoiled man who felt entitled and became petulant when he didn't get what he wanted. There may have been some truth to that—after all, he was conducting simultaneous adulterous affairs—but to me he seemed then like he always had but without the social veneer. Conditioned to seize victory, Woods was the most tenacious of competitors, and he couldn't accept that he had let slip the Masters and now the U.S. Open, too.

CHAPTER 9

AT&T National

About a mile down the River Road exit from the Capital Belt-way lies the most beautiful of country clubs. Congressional, with its landmark six-level, 110,000-square-foot blue-and-gray stone Mediterranean-styled clubhouse, is maybe a twenty-five-minute drive from the Capitol, depending on the vagaries of Washington traffic. But it's a scenic drive, across the river from Georgetown through the canopied forest of George Washington Memorial Parkway to the sylvan sanctuary of suburban Bethesda, Maryland. In 1921, two U.S. congressmen from Indiana, Oscar Bland and O. R. Lubring, saw this picturesque farmland and conceived of turning it into a gathering place to foster closer relationships between the political and the business sectors. Golf, they thought, would be their Esperanto.

Within thirty months, after Commerce Secretary Herbert Hoover gave the idea his blessing and agreed to become the first club president, Congressional Country Club was opened to much pomp and ceremony: the Marines marching band welcoming guests, which included the president, Calvin Coolidge, and first lady. Among the membership were all the storied names of Corporate America—John D. Rockefeller, Pierre S. du Pont, Walter Chrysler, William Randolph Hearst, William Carnegie, Harvey Firestone, to name but a few—as well as the political movers and shakers of the day. Seven presidents would become members and the club became known as a hub of the power elite without the old-boy hijinx found nearby at Burning Tree, where women are still to this day banned.

With many of its members beneficiaries of the illusion that was Coolidge prosperity, Congressional for years lived beyond its means. It was not alone, of course, as the moneyed classes of the Roaring Twenties were sure they'd always be rich and the aspiring classes were sure they'd get rich quick. Greed was such a corrupting influence that people were climbing over each other in order to give con men like the formerly penniless Italian immigrant Charles Ponzi $15 million for the promise of instant fabulous wealth. But it turned out that money didn't grow on trees, Ponzi went to jail, and, like the nation, Congressional fell on hard times. The club never fully recovered and was forced into bankruptcy in 1940. Soon after, it was seconded as a spy training base for the Central Intelligence Agency's precursor, the nebulously named Office of Strategic Services, before ultimately becoming solvent again and, as real, rather than paper, prosperity returned in the postwar years, growing into a Washington institution.

Congressional's cachet isn't simply as an exclusive club in which golf stories are told through the smoke of expensive cigars. Prospective members wait for up to a decade for the privilege of paying a six-figure initiation fee because they also want to play what is by any measure a magnificent test of golf. Congressional's Blue Course, designed by Devereux Emmet and given an extensive face-lift by Robert Trent Jones in 1957, hosted the 1964 and 1997 U.S. Opens and is scheduled to hold the nation's championship again in 2011. It also was the venue for the 1976 PGA Championship and, by hosting four majors, joined an elite conversation of its own, mentioned in the same breath as national treasures like Oakmont, Oakland Hills, Baltusrol, Winged Foot, Riviera, and Olympic Club.

When the PGA Tour lost its Washington stop after the withdrawal of the unfortunately named title sponsor Booz Allen—a consultancy firm based in the greater DC area, not a liquor store as many joked—Finchem was left with little time to fill the void. The capital's simply too large a market to be left untapped, and Finchem lucked out when Woods—who had tremendous leverage with AT&T—saw the chance to realize a dream he and his father had long shared. "I remember back when I first came on Tour and was able to play events and we started our foundation in 1997, my focus and my goal one day with my father was to be able to host an event on the PGA Tour," Woods said in 2007. "This is a pretty momentous day for us because we are lucky enough to have the opportunity to do that. I just wish my father could have been here to see it. It was a dream that he wanted to have for us at that foundation. It was something that we tried and worked so hard to build, to be able to help as many kids as we possibly can. It's basically a no-brainer for us to say yes, that we would love to come here to our nation's capital. With my father's history being in the military and serving in Special Forces, to come here during the nation's birthday."

Woods knew immediately he wanted Congressional as the venue for his tournament, the AT&T National, which would take the form of a limited-field invitational along the lines of the ones hosted by Nicklaus and Palmer. "I would love to have it played there," he said before the club had officially accepted. "Obviously, it's one of the greatest golf courses, not just in the United

States, but around the world. You won't have events like [majors] that come to your golf course unless you are premier caliber. The time I played there in '97 during the U.S. Open, it thoroughly was a test, and it was a test that kicked my butt pretty good."

At the official announcement that at thirty-one, Woods would be getting his own event on the Tour, he was flanked by Finchem and then AT&T chief Ed Whitacre, two men whose styles couldn't be more different. Where Finchem was forever the lawyer, careful and maddeningly indirect with his language, Whitacre, who rose from humble beginnings as a phone company engineer to run the world's largest telco, was a plain-speaking Texan. Finchem as a matter of course would begin news conferences by offering a few brief opening remarks. Of course, they inevitably were neither few nor brief. Bored writers sometimes bet on the length of Finchem's rambling opening remarks, and no one ever won with sub-ten-minute guesses. By comparison, Whitacre, who would go on to run the reimagined General Motors in 2009, was direct and to the point and even threw in a humorous story, in contrast to Finchem, who didn't know any. "I've been called to Washington many times to speak," Whitacre said. "This is one of the few I've actually looked forward to, so it's a good thing. If you ever have to choose between announcing a golf tournament sponsorship or testifying before Congress, my advice to you is to take the golf tournament."

Woods was justifiably proud of his elevation to tournament host and spoke—as he rarely would—of the bigger picture. "We thought it was the best platform in order for us to gain awareness of what we're trying to do with our foundation," he said. "We believe that it was a springboard for us to go global and reach what we are trying to and the kids we are trying to impact around the world." He again went to the core of his beliefs and his passion: that directly helping a child become a valuable member of society was the greatest contribution he could make. To coincide with the debut of the AT&T National, the Tiger Woods Foundation was building a Learning Center in the DC area, mirroring the one in California, which had been a runaway success. The tournament also allowed him to pursue his secondary goal, to salute the contributions made by the military. All active-duty military got free admission to the tournament because "they have put their lives on the line so that we are able to enjoy the lives that we have today and freedoms that we are able to enjoy." Whether or not everyone agreed with Woods that the quagmire in Iraq was doing anything to guarantee the freedoms of Americans, no one would deny his acknowledgment of the commitment and bravery of the American soldier. Woods also decreed that all kids under the age of twelve should get in for free, too, so going to the golf course could be "a family-oriented affair." It spoke to his belief in the sanctity of the family unit, a belief he was himself secretly betraying.

At the end of the news conference, he was asked about a remark his friend Charles Barkley had made, urging Woods to become more politically active now that he had a foothold in Washington. "Well, I don't know," Woods said. "I've had experience, you know, of meeting influential people in the political arena. Right now my main focus is with the foundation and all of my energy is directed to that. I don't know what the future lies for me beyond that and beyond my playing days. But as of right now, I have my hands full with trying to put that little white ball in the hole, and obviously with the birth of our first child and expanding our Learning Center to the East Coast and hopefully our foundation around the world. I've got my plate full for right now." In case he wasn't clear: Tiger doesn't do politics.

Woods played in the first AT&T National, in front of an all-star gallery that included the golf enthusiast Secretary of State Condoleezza Rice. But his putter was cold and he couldn't beat the hot-putting Korean K. J. Choi. "Don't worry," he was told, "not even Jack won the first Memorial." But Nicklaus did win the second, and don't think Woods didn't know that. "Tiger loves trivia," says Williams. "He's a real buff for that stuff." Woods couldn't play in 2008 because of his knee surgery, and Anthony Kim finally lived up to expectations, keeping his head down the stretch to win. Woods, then, was playing for the second time in 2009 and, he joked, he would "love being the greedy host" and presenting the trophy to himself.

When Woods entered a tournament, his sole focus was on playing well and, of course, winning. But the AT&T National was always going to be different because of his added responsibilities as tournament host. He presided over a board meeting of his foundation, followed by a dinner, conducted a junior clinic, visited the veterans' Walter Reed Memorial Hospital, hosted the opening ceremony for the tournament, then had to sit in on countless staff meetings as well as hobnob at events set up by AT&T, which was picking up the tab and expected its pound of flesh. Woods's first order of business, though, was a press conference. It was noticeable, on this front, just how more welcoming he was when he was the host. There was no sign of Steinberg rubbing his cheek or tapping the side of his leg. Woods was happy to let this press conference drag on; indeed, he was happy to help the media. There was none of the attitude that legendary golf writer Dan Jenkins, who'd been close to all the giants of the sport over the years, got when he asked Steinberg about having dinner with Woods: "We have nothing to gain."

Woods was so accommodating to the media that he even took seriously USA Today's Jerry Potter when the pear-shaped Southerner complained about traffic. "Forty-five minutes for me from the Beltway to the parking lot," Potter announced in his slow drawl, perhaps thinking his newspaper's readers would care. In the end, with no pertinent questions left to be asked, a first for a Tiger press conference, veteran radio man Bob Bubka, who rarely asked questions in open forums, put up his hand. He asked Woods whether he was a Michael Jackson fan and whether he had any thoughts on the singer's sudden death a few days before. The answer was vintage Woods: nothing Off The Wall.

"I think everyone here was a Michael Jackson fan," Woods said. That was, strictly speaking, not true because I had covered both of Jackson's pedophile cases in California and found it impossible to look past the truth of his relationships with boys to his musical genius. Woods, however, like many others who knew just the music, waxed lyrical. "One of, probably if not the greatest entertainer that's ever lived. I know my entire generation was influenced by his music. . . . It was always happy. You always wanted to listen to his songs. And his legacy is one as the greatest entertainer. . . . You watch these guys [who followed Jackson] in how they pay tribute, how they perform, how they dance and how they sing, their mannerisms, look at Usher, Justin Timberlake, their moves, they're Michael's moves." He could have easily been talking about basketball players who borrowed from Michael Jordan, and that's the beauty of Woods—he knows how to stay between the lines. A skill he borrowed from Michael. Jordan, not Jackson.

Jordan didn't escape the news conference, either, when Woods was asked about his friend's upcoming induction into the Basketball Hall of Fame. "Michael going into the Hall of Fame, that was a given. That was a no-brainer, wasn't it? Greatest basketball player to ever live. You know, getting to know Michael over the years has been a lot of fun. I call him my big brother. To be able to call him and pick his brain on anything at any time and we've done that, you know, and he doesn't sleep, like me. So he may give me a call or text and I may give him a call or text at odd hours and we're both up and we'll talk for a while, and that's just something that it's been very special to get to know him. Especially when he was playing, see how hard he worked, you know, off the court, away from the cameras, away from the game time. You can't believe how hard this guy worked. People think he just showed up and scored 45. That's not what happened. It is what happened, but to get him to that point, I mean, God, this guy worked hard: the countless hours in the gym, shooting and shooting and shooting. I'm like, Mike, it's one in the morning, you know. 'I'm not ready yet.' He kept shooting and shooting and shooting. I'd feed him the ball or watch him go over drill after drill after drill and watch him in game time, he made that look pretty easy. It was just like what he did in practice. He just rehearsed it again and again and again until he had it. And it was fun to watch, watch him dissect games. It's been a lot of fun to get to know him over the years [as] a player but also [as] a person."

As he spoke those words I wondered just how much Woods really was like Jordan. In their work ethic, they were amazingly alike. Both understand that sporting genius comes as the result of hard work and never short-change themselves. In my admittedly limited dealings with Jordan over the years, I found him to be friendly, courteous, and remarkably accessible. He was also perpetually in a good mood, which was generally contrary to what I'd seen in other celebrities, either in the fields of sports or entertainment. It is very hard not to like Michael Jordan. It always struck me that while Scottie Pippen was not especially smart or gracious with his time and Phil Jackson was aloof beyond words, the star of the Chicago Bulls show would patiently wait at his locker until the last question was asked and till the Japanese television crew got everything they could possibly need. I used to think that Jordan did this because he understood that it was his duty. Some of my colleagues, however, were convinced that he just couldn't stand passing up the chance to have himself deified by one more media outlet.

For all his allure, Michael Jordan is flawed. He conducted numerous affairs throughout his marriage, gambled incessantly—his losses on the tables are well chronicled but his beatings on the golf course are the stuff of legend—and carried grudges to the point of meanness. Yet aided by his agent, David Falk, and that billion-dollar smile, Jordan maintained an image that sold hamburgers and sneakers and underwear and sports drinks and anything else that came his way. Even a decade removed from his retirement, he was earning perhaps $40 million a year and had an estimated worth of $600 million. But what was it all built on? Sublime basketball skills, for sure, and the idea that he was the greatest of all time. But when I heard Jordan's Hall of Fame induction speech, it was a revelation into his character. Rather than take the high road and humbly bow as the world deemed him the greatest to pull on a high-top, Jordan focused on the petty grievances and slights with fringe figures that drove him to that greatness. It was as if he felt he still had battles to fight when he'd in fact long ago already won. "M.J. was introduced as the greatest player ever and he's still standing there trying to settle scores," a Hall of Famer told reporters after the awkward ceremony. Basketball writer Adrian Wojnarowski quoted a high-ranking NBA executive as saying, "That's who Michael is. It wasn't like he was out of character. There's no one else who could've gotten away with what he did tonight. But it was Michael, and everyone just goes along." I wondered if that's who Tiger was, too.

"You want to know why Tiger always plays well in Chicago?" Williams once asked me. "Yeah, he loves Cog Hill and it suits his eye, but it's also because Michael comes out to watch when we're in Chicago. Tiger's not going to give him any opportunity to make a joke at his expense. It's just like if M.J. was playing basketball and he knew Tiger was watching, he'd put up some big numbers because that's the kind of relationship they have. They have a tremendous amount of respect for one another but there's no two ways about it, they're very competitive with each other."

An expanding Jessica Simpson performed a rendition of "The Star-Spangled Banner" only the tone-deaf could love to open the AT&T National. She showed up because her boyfriend, Dallas Cowboys quarterback Tony Romo, had ventured into Redskins territory to play in the pro-am alongside Woods. He dumped her soon afterward. Meanwhile, Kim went out early in the first round and took advantage of soft, receptive greens and set a new course record, an 8-under-par 62. Heavy overnight rains had turned Congressional into a shooting duck gallery; it was playing so easy that Kim wasn't even sure he'd be the first-round leader after setting the course record. Especially with Woods lurking. "I did play very well, but that man can go out there and shoot 60," the Korean American said. He was not far wrong. Woods kept in touch with Kim, firing a 64 to leave himself in a three-way tie for second. What he'd have given for that kind of round—twelve of fourteen fairways hit, fifteen greens in regulation, and twenty-seven putts—two weeks before in Long Island. "No, it's just part of golf," he said philosophically of his U.S. Open disappointment. "Sometimes you just have those weeks, and unfortunately, I had that week at the wrong time. But it's golf. You have days, you have weeks, and you have stretches where you putt well and you putt poorly. But the whole idea is to make sure you have consistent speed. As long as your speed is good, day in and day out, you can turn it around pretty quickly." Williams said Woods was remarkably good at putting defeats behind him, though 2009 would test that attribute.

What Woods appeared to have turned around quickly was that

old "Fore, right!" block. Certainly, he hit the ball well enough to win at Bethpage, but at critical times that old pestilence crept into his play. At Congressional, however, he looked more like the flawless player who'd shot 65 in the final round to win at Muirfield Village. Woods explained that the conditions had a lot to do with the swings he'd made. "You can be so aggressive out there," he said. "You can fire at a lot of flags. The fairways got wide because [the ball's] not going to run out. If you get aggressive and get it going, you can post a number out there." Even though he benefited from the conditions, as the tournament host it was obvious Woods wasn't happy with the ease of scoring. "It's not the way I want it. I'd like to get the greens faster, but you can't do it when you get half an inch of rain overnight. If we get no more rain and this place starts drying out a little bit, we can get these things up in speed. Come Sunday, they won't be springy but at least they'll have a little more rollout to them and you have to think about how you're going to go into some of these flags. You can't just always fire the ball up there. If you leave it 10, 15 feet past the flag, you've got a hell of a putt because it's going to roll out."

Woods felt he'd lost his swing in the second round but got lucky because he played early, before the wind kicked up, and threw in a handful of good shots to offset the forgettable ones. For all his hand-wringing, he still turned in a 66. In four rounds of golf, Woods understood that there would always be one that was the runt of the litter and the trick was to still post a good score for that round. "Absolutely, absolutely," he told me. "Even the tournaments where I've gone pretty low . . . where I've shot 25 under, there's always that one day where you didn't really feel as good as the others. But sometimes those days you actually may score lower. It's just weird how today I hit the ball a little bit scratchy at times, but I putted better. I felt better with the putter today, hit a lot of good putts, easy tap-ins or I was making them. The game is kind of weird that way. Yesterday I didn't really miss a shot, and I shot 6 under, but today, even though I was at 4 under, it could have been just a little bit lower, I guess." It reminded me of what a friend, Mike Miller, who played at UCLA when Woods was at Stanford, told me about playing alongside him when he decimated collegiate records in the spring of '96 at Big Canyon during the Pac-10 tournament. Woods started with a 61, then shot 65 in the afternoon, but Miller says the second round was much better than the first.

After a topsy-turvy even-par round on Saturday—a steamy Fourth of July—Woods had played himself into the final group on Sunday, tied at 10 under par with Kim. Kim told us stories of being a boy in Los Angeles and, while he waited for his father to pick him up at the golf course where he practiced, imagined having a putt to beat Tiger Woods. He was always a cocky kid, so of course the putts found the bottom of the cup. What did the story mean to Woods, who had his own imaginary childhood opponents, named Nicklaus and Palmer and Hogan? "I'm aging, that's what that means." Kim may have been physically aging, he was twenty-four, but growing up was another matter. He had publicly admitted that his rookie year was spent in a vodka-induced haze, stumbling from one strip joint to the next. But Kim saw the error of his ways and reformed, dedicating himself to golf and winning twice in 2008. At least that was the shore story.

The truth, by early 2009, was a little more complicated. Kim is one of these young men who could have a come-to-Jesus moment with an older player—O'Meara was one of them—and be completely convinced that they're turning over a new leaf—right before they jump into a Hummer stretch limousine on the way to party. I was standing with a Tour player one day as Kim arrived late at a golf course, jumping out of his courtesy car with his shirt untucked and his hat on sideways, like some kind of Korean golfing rapper. "He's such a punk," the player said. The consensus on Tour was that Kim wasn't so much the next Tiger Woods as the next John Daly, a belief reinforced by Kim's bragging about racking up a $66,000 alcohol bill with his entourage in Vegas.

"The one thing I will say about Tiger is that . . . he never drinks when he has got a tournament," said Charles Barkley. "Maybe Tony [Kim] can learn that, okay, that there is certain things that I got to do when I play and everything else has got to be second. You can have fun when you are off." Kim also got into trouble during the 2008 Ryder Cup in Kentucky, causing friction within the American team when the wife of a teammate walked in on him with a woman who wasn't his girlfriend, Lisa Pruett. Australian Robert Allenby, who tends to speak first and think later, was so annoyed at having been beaten by Kim later in 2009 in the Presidents Cup singles matches that he launched into a stunning tirade in front of me and three other writers. He said a friend of his staying at the Fairmont in San Francisco, the official team hotel, had witnessed Kim stumbling in "sideways" at 4 a.m., just hours before their match. He, too, called Kim "the next John Daly." Kim denied all charges, and a few days later, after the Tour had gotten to him, Allenby issued an apology with all the usual ramblings and even had the gall to throw in that old chestnut about having his comments taken out of context.

One of those whom Jordan chided in his Hall of Fame induction speech was Jeff Van Gundy, the basketball coach whose crime was to call Jordan a "con man" for befriending competitors only to then shred them to pieces on the court. Woods, in this sense, was just like Jordan. Kim wasn't smart enough to figure that out. Kim likes to kid around with Woods—they are both huge Lakers fans—and thought their locker room banter meant something more. That it would somehow translate to goodwill on the golf course in the heat of battle. One of Earl Woods's attributes, which his son greatly admired, and proudly told Smith about for the *Sports Illustrated* profile, was that he could "slit your throat and then sit down to eat his dinner." Thirteen years later, the son's cold-bloodedness exceeded the father's.

About ten minutes before his tee time, Woods was on the putting green near the end of his usual warm-up routine—it never varied in either time or content—when he'd had enough and began the minute-long trek to the first tee. He was too early, as the previous group had yet to tee off, so he stopped at the secluded short-game practice area to the left and behind the first hole. Williams collected balls with TIGER stamped across them and gave them to Woods, who began chipping out of gnarled lies. Whereas golf balls are usually numbered from 1 to 4, all of the TIGER balls carry the same number. What else but 1? Woods is the only player who has his personal game balls shipped to tournaments for practice, where they are carefully sorted, counted, and guarded like the crown jewels by the range staff. Although Nike's balls are made by Bridgestone, competitors in the golf ball market are always interested in knowing just what Woods plays—it's a much higher-spin ball than most—and so there's a cat-and-mouse game played to get their hands on his balls. In 2003 at Chicago's Olympia Fields, all of Woods's practice balls were stolen, prompting Nike to vow to prosecute anyone found trying to sell them. One former Nike staff player told me he'd long been suspicious that Woods was getting a better ball than was being offered to the company's other Tour players. "Every ball I tested was better than the crap they were making then and you expect me to believe Tiger's playing the same shitty ball they're giving me? I don't think so."

As the tee cleared, Woods walked over to the tent set up behind the tee box, which offered shade, shelter from prying eyes, and food. Woods has an astonishing metabolism and is forever hungry. During every round, he devours Williams's homemade peanut butter, jelly, and banana sandwiches. Williams, meanwhile, was lagging behind, asking me whether I'd heard the result of the rugby match between the British and Irish Lions and the South African Springboks the night before. As we spoke, Kim playfully whacked Williams on the buttocks with a wedge. They laughed and exchanged pleasantries for a moment. Kim got to the tee and tried to joke around with Woods. He was greeted with a stone face. Kim tried again, but Woods offered only his standard Sunday handshake and "Good luck." Kim seemed unsure what to do next. The grasshopper had a lot to learn. There are very few players not intimidated by Woods in this element. One of them was Singh, who once famously responded "Titleist 2"—coldly identifying the ball he was playing—after Woods wished him luck. "There's no reason to make small talk," Singh told me. "It's not like we're friends."

Before he'd arrived at Congressional, Woods was, like many of us, in his hotel room glued to the television. He was watching his friend Roger Federer win another Wimbledon championship. Had the roles been reversed, be sure Woods would've sent "Fed," as he calls the Swiss champion, a text message reading, 15–14. This, again, was classic Michael Jordan behavior: always got to get one-up. But Federer, who'd just taken the lead in their personal battle over career majors, wasn't that kind of driven beast. He's inordinately humble and travels with the smallest of entourages and manages to live a remarkably normal life. He's so unaffected by his fame that he once stood back to let me fill my cup first at the Gatorade machine in the men's locker room at Flushing Meadows. "Great job," Woods wrote in his text to Federer. "Now it's my turn." Woods had won the Memorial just hours after Federer's breakthrough on the clay of Paris, and on this day there was cross-Atlantic symmetry at work again. "His are a hell of a lot bigger than mine, though," Woods said. "He won two Slams."

I asked Woods later about his obvious snub of Kim. Typically, on-the-record, he betrayed nothing. "I was just kind of getting into my own little world. I tend to do that when the situation gets that way . . . you tend to get wrapped up in that and you forget what's going on around you." He made light of his legendary capacity to intimidate opponents. "Well, I'm six five, 250 pounds, you know," he joked. "The great thing about golf is you just play your own game. You can't physically intimidate anybody. You can't physically influence somebody like what happened to [Federer] today. In that sport, you can. In our sport, you can't."

Kim got the hint the second time and didn't speak to Woods again till the third green when he asked if he was away. "Yep," Woods replied. Apart from sotto voce acknowledgments like "good shot" or "nice bird," that was the only conversation they had until the 18th green. Kim seemed hurt by Woods's coldness and initially looked like he was going to make him pay. Where Woods couldn't take advantage of a good opening drive, Kim bombed a 350-yard drive, then flipped a little pitch onto the green and watched it spin back to about 4 inches. A kick-in birdie doubled as a warning shot. Kim was the more impressive player throughout the opening four holes, but Woods kept his cool and waited for his chance. It came when Kim suddenly unleashed a wild drive off the 5th, which sailed left of left. He was fortunate to come up with a relatively clean shot to the green but flubbed a low wedge and, from the front of the green, 3-putted while Woods made par. "What did I learn today?" Kim later asked. "I learned that when you have a birdie putt, you better make it."

Woods split the sixth fairway. Then, as he often did at this point in a round, headed off to the Porta-Potty about thirty yards behind the tee box. He didn't watch Kim hit but gave a quick glance back when Kim's caddie shouted, "Fore, left!" The knowing look on Woods's face told that the tide had turned and that it was time to put his foot on his rival's throat. And so it was when Woods drained a 14-footer for birdie on the 6th, one of Congressional's unfriendliest holes. Kim scrambled his way to par but was now behind on more than just the leaderboard. Woods was suddenly in full flight. He unleashed a gorgeous little draw into the 174-yard par-3 7th, the ball spinning back to about 3 feet. Kim answered in kind, but then missed the putt from 4 feet. Woods knew about looking gift horses in the mouth, and his lead had grown to two when they left the green.

The remainder of the round was a study in winning. Not in excellence, because Woods long ago abandoned the idea of victory as an aesthetic. Or winning by large margins. If leading by six, unlike Jordan, who never relented, he felt no particular need to stretch it to seven. He'd grown conservative over the years in such situations because he'd gotten used to watching his competitors melt in his presence. "Why take risks?" asked Williams. Kim pegged the Woods lead back with an improbable birdie on the par-5 9th, but Woods simply birdied the next, dropping a long putt on a long par 3 over water. The long par-4 11th had been Woods's undoing all week. After misses to the left on the converted par 5, this time he found the right hazard. It was, to be fair, bad luck because the drive wasn't grossly inaccurate and the stream he found wasn't very wide. A telltale sign of Woods's temper is the positioning of Williams. He walked far away from his boss for a reason. An irate Woods muttered unprintable words under his breath as he walked by me to survey the damage. It was remarkable how well he could swear under his breath without anyone more than a few feet away hearing. And he'd learned to drop his chin so the TV cameras couldn't catch him. He was forced to take a penalty drop in the rough, and played his third shot 210 yards from the hole. He understood that a bogey was inevitable and avoided the double that would've endangered the tournament. "I found a way to make 5 or worse four different ways. Beautiful, isn't it?" a rueful Woods said later about a hole he'd played in 5 over par for the tournament.

By now, however, his focus had turned away from Kim and onto Hunter Mahan. Mahan had tied Kim's course record with a 62 to take the clubhouse lead at 12 under par. Woods pays attention to the leaderboard so he immediately set about recalibrating what he needed. "I don't know what golf course Hunter was playing today, but I didn't see a 62 out there," Woods later said. "He went out there and put so much pressure on both A.K. and I. He was done when we were on 12, so six holes to go and at the time I was tied for the lead. It was just like, you can go either way. You can win the tournament or you can lose the tournament from here."

Woods isn't given to panic. He knew that he had an ace up his sleeve: the par-5 16th. "I was hoping I could get one more [birdie] before I got to 16, and then 16 would be my cush," he said. But he missed three putts that would've provided that cushion and so arrived at the 16th tied with Mahan. After hitting a 5-wood short and right of the green, Woods left himself a relatively routine pitch shot to the back left flag. But he played an awful shot up the hill, drawing gasps. What should have been a straightforward birdie was now a 20-footer. "Bad pitch," he said, shaking his head. Other golfers often remark that Woods never hits a shot until he is ready. He never rushes himself. He knew what was at stake and surveyed the uphill putt. He finally set himself over the ball but backed off after a photographer lying by the green got an itchy finger. Williams, true to his reputation, shook his head, and the photographer, a veteran who knew better, apologized. Woods seemed galvanized by the distraction; he gathered himself and the putt found the bottom of the cup.

"It went in, and from there, I said, 'Okay, now if I can just play the last two holes fairways-and-greens, let's just get the win.'" And he did, lagging birdie putts to inside a foot. When he tapped in on the 72nd hole to claim a 1-shot win—the third time he'd won in his last start before a major, and each by the slimmest of margins—he raised his arms in relief more than jubilation. "It was a long week," he told me, "but I got the W."

Elin, dressed in Tiger Sunday red, and the children waited well away from the madding crowds. Woods shook many hands before seeing his family. He hugged his wife and embraced his kids, but he didn't linger. As we walked from the postround interview area, I jokingly asked him when the kids would be old enough to run onto the green as his winning putt dropped. It was a gentle poke at Mickelson, whose three children were released onto the green when he won the PGA at Baltusrol, on the cue of a CBS Sports producer, as if they were doves at the Vatican. I was smirking, but he was not amused. "That's not how we do things in my family," he said sternly. "We celebrate in our own way." It seemed that I had touched a nerve. Little did I know how raw that nerve was.

CHAPTER 10

British Open

The Open Championship, as they like to call it across the pond—mainly for the benefit of heathen Americans who refer to golf's oldest major as "the British"—had not been staged at Turnberry on Scotland's rugged South Ayrshire coast since 1994, when Nick Price won. The other two winners of the famed Claret Jug at Turnberry were Greg Norman (1986) and Tom Watson, who in 1977 bested Jack Nicklaus in an epic battle that became forever enshrined in golf folklore as the Duel in the Sun. The two were in a class of their own that week and, in a mesmerizing climax, Watson made birdie on the last green to beat Nicklaus, who had just made a long birdie putt himself to draw level, by a single stroke. What all four of those players had in common was that they were not just the best golfers in the world at the time they played their Turnberry Opens, but also the best ball strikers.

Woods didn't know the place at all, but he knew who'd won there before and immediately understood what that meant and liked his chances. Williams knew the course well. He'd seen Norman 3-putt the last to shoot 63 in foul weather and he knew a pure ball striker could do well, no matter the conditions. He felt that after the close calls of Augusta and Bethpage, his man would finally get his fifteenth major on the Ailsa, as the championship course is known, named after the enormous rock on the Firth of Clyde that serves as Turnberry's backdrop.

While many of the game's better-heeled players stayed at the famous old resort—and complained bitterly about the Fawlty Towers service that came with the exorbitant room rates—Woods rented a house nearby. There's little at Turnberry other than the hotel and the golf course; it's a remote place on the coast, one road in and one road out. Woods had never liked that kind of scrutiny at any time, much less during a major. So he'd brought his own cook and wouldn't be dining out, anyway. It was perhaps not significant that he chose to leave his family in Orlando—there was, after all, not much for children so young to do—but for the first time Haney did not travel with Woods to a major. Haney had gone to Bethpage but left after the practice rounds, which in itself was a significant development.

Williams shrugged when I asked whether anything should be read into the decision to leave Haney at home. "Generally, when Tiger goes to a major championship, he feels he's ready to play. He's certainly not going there searching for his game. He never makes major adjustments going into a major championship. He knows what he's got and he's going to play with what he's got. He just knows what he's trying to accomplish and he's just going to go there and try to keep it simple. He knows his swing well enough to be able to do that." It may have made sense that Woods wanted to keep his mind uncluttered—and it was also true that Haney was going through a messy divorce at the time—but Woods didn't make such decisions lightly. He was the ultimate creature of routine and so it had to mean *something*.

Woods liked Turnberry from the moment he stepped foot on the course late on Sunday afternoon, the first of three straight days in which he would play practice rounds looking for sight lines, or where to aim. "Just a fabulous golf course," he enthused. He'd always enjoyed links golf, which allowed players to get to the same place in many different ways. Links golf, in that sense, was an ideal outlet for his innate creativity. "I fell in love with it right away," he said. "I played Carnoustie and St. Andrews, my first two true links golf courses, right out of the gate. It doesn't get much better than that. I just fell in love with being able to use the ground as a friend, as an ally. . . . You hit a shot that's from 150 yards, whatever it is, you have so many options of how you could play it. Back home in the States you play pretty much everything up in the air."

But he astutely noted that the wind had yet to blow at Turnberry. This was an admission to be underscored; I'd come to understand that what Tiger Woods feared most on a golf course wasn't another player but the wind. A strong crosswind that blows from left to right was his worst nightmare. It was not a coincidence that his three Open championships came on relatively calm weeks and his poorest performances came when the elements had been at their worst. But in the placid conditions of his Turnberry practice rounds—the Scots get at least a few days of something approaching summer each year—Woods felt very comfortable with his game and good about his chances. He could see why Watson, Norman, and Price had won on Ailsa; the course rewarded the superior player. "You really do have to hit your ball well here," he said. "You just can't fake it around this golf course. You just have to hit good golf shots."

Malcolm Booth, the young public relations official at the Open, took charge of the Woods pretournament press conference. It was lengthy but not especially revelatory, as Woods recycled most of the stories he'd been telling the media all year. He did provide an interesting answer when asked whether with all the hoopla that surrounded him he wished on some days that he were someone else. "Wish I was someone else? No," he said. "Wish I had a little more anonymity is different." After it was over and I saw the extra-stern look on the face of Steinberg, who'd been sitting at the back of a crowded room, I told Booth that he was probably in trouble for letting the interview go on too long. "Did you not see Steiny's cues?" I asked mischievously. Now, I was, of course, ribbing him, but Booth became suddenly pale. "Oh, God, I was looking for him but I couldn't see him in the crowd."

A quick perusal of the Fleet Street papers, which had sent their B team to Turnberry—the heavy artillery was following cricket, as the English were miraculously winning the Ashes, the sport's holiest matches, against the Australians—revealed that Woods was the logical choice to win a fifteenth major. And then the strangest thing happened. Along came Watson, an old man by the Irish Sea, dreaming of an improbable ninth major at the tender age of fifty-nine. The writers went to him like moths to a light. "I think there was some spirituality out there," said Watson, who'd won the Open championship five times and had become something of an adopted Scottish hero. An age-defying 5-under-par round of 65 gave him the clubhouse first-round lead on a course he'd won at twice before, a Senior British Open to go with his 1977 triumph. "Just the serenity of it was pretty neat." There had always been something very boyish about Watson; even in advancing years when he smiled, he had a Tom Sawyer/Huckleberry Finn quality about him. Maybe because he and Mark Twain were both Missourians.

Firm fairways meant that Watson didn't need to carry the ball as far to get himself into scoring positions. With short irons in his hand, whatever physical attributes he may have lacked two months short of his sixtieth birthday weren't important. Indeed, looking at the first-round scores, the case could've been made that youth and power and athleticism were no substitute for guile and experience and wisdom. "The older guys have an advantage," Watson said, pointing to past champions O'Meara and Mark Calcavecchia, who'd also turned back the clock with matching 67s. "We've played under these conditions and we kind of get a feel for it and that feel is worth its weight in gold when you're playing. Experience wins." A graying Bjorn Borg may not have been able to take six games from Federer in 2009, much less beat him, just as Wayne Gretzky couldn't lay a glove on Sidney Crosby or Michael Jordan guard Kobe Bryant, but, on a gorgeously placid day on the coast, there was Old Tom Watson besting Tiger Woods by six strokes.

"If Watson plays the way he played today, he can beat Tiger Woods and everyone else," said Sergio Garcia, who marveled at what he'd seen alongside Watson. There are days when a 1-over-par round of 71 would be a fine score at Turnberry, but the opening Thursday of the 138th Open Championship wasn't one of them. "I certainly made a few mistakes out there today," Woods bemoaned later. "I hit a couple of shots to the right today, and 3-ripped a hole from about 15 feet and I didn't take advantage of [the par-5] 17, so there you have it." Not quite all of it. It was evident that Woods hadn't learned the obvious lessons of the year's first two majors.

Once more he'd played far too cautiously. He tried to keep himself in the tournament by being conservative when in fact it was a time to be aggressive and post a low score. It was the ninth round I'd watched Woods play at a major, and it was clear by his body language and the constipated look on his face that again he just wasn't the same player who'd won three Tour events. Whereas he seemed relaxed and calm and confident at Tour events—like the Tiger Woods the world had grown to know—he seemed to be always fighting something at the majors. Himself, perhaps? At Bethpage, maybe he had reason to be grumpy given his cursed luck, but what was his excuse at Turnberry? The clue may have come on the range that Thursday morning. Whereas he was hitting the ball beautifully in practice rounds, he suddenly began losing shots to the right. It was, of course, an old pestilence, but why was it returning to haunt him at majors?

Could it be that now that he'd gotten within four of Nicklaus's mark, he was pressing too much? Perhaps Woods had it right; he didn't need Haney or any other swing doctor as much as he needed to get out of his own way. In that, he could have taken a leaf out of Watson's book. Watson was at peace—with himself, with his game, and with his surroundings. "I feel inspired playing here," he said. "It doesn't feel a whole lot out of the ordinary from thirty-two years ago except that I don't have the confidence in my putting as I had thirty-two years ago. But, again, a few of them might go in." In 2008, it was Greg Norman who'd sipped from the fountain of youth, taking a 1-shot lead into the back nine on Sunday at windswept Birkdale before ultimately succumbing to the heroic deeds of the younger Harrington. But Watson's bid seemed even more audacious. "Will I be able to handle the pressure? I don't know," he said. "I don't know." But for one day, at the very least, he'd found the young lion he used to be.

In his forty-eight majors as a professional, Woods had missed the cut just once, at Winged Foot in 2006, when he'd tried to play with a broken heart after his father had passed. It was a mistake and he knew it, but it was the U.S. Open, so he showed up. And that's all he could do—show up. One missed cut against thirty-one top tens and fourteen victories. Truly staggering numbers. No one was thinking about a second missed cut after Woods made a safe birdie at the par-5 7th in his second round at Turnberry. The weather had deteriorated quickly, and angry winds were whipping off the ocean. Woods thought that if he could stay at 1 under for the day—leaving him at even par for the tournament—he'd be within a few shots of the lead by Friday night.

He was right, as usual. As it eventuated, even par at the midway point would've had him at the head of the peloton, right behind the leaders and waiting to pounce. Except that he didn't foresee what would be the biggest majors meltdown of his career. Once before I remember Woods totally falling apart on the golf course, as clueless as any Sunday morning hacker. In the final round of the 2007 Arnold Palmer Invitational, he shot 8 over par on the back nine after being in the race when making the turn. Two doubles and a triple. It was windy that day, too. The Turnberry nightmare began for Woods on the 8th; the worst six-hole stretch of his career would follow. He played those six holes at 7 over par. It was shocking to watch. The most controlled of golfers had lost total control of his swing, and of his mind. He was in a free fall, making error after error. To the audience it was so surreal that we kept believing that somehow Woods would birdie the last four holes to save the day—because he always saved the day. Those were our articles of faith, after all. But he could birdie only two of the last four. The shock was so great that otherwise intelligent people were trying to convince me that the cut line would move higher. It did, but I knew it would never go high enough. And so did Tiger Woods. He wasn't even holding on to the slim hope of a small "m" miracle. As soon as he'd signed his scorecard, he was ready to leave Britain, though not before eating. "I'm hungry," he said as he walked by me.

A few weeks later, I sat down with Williams and was surprised to learn that the nightmare of Turnberry was still haunting him. "In all honesty, I don't often blame myself, but I blame myself for his bad play at Turnberry," he told me. "It was one of the real lowlights of my career. I didn't sleep for two or three days because I felt I played a big part in him missing that cut. I play a part in him winning tournaments, but I was as much to blame as he was for missing that cut." Williams said the trouble began when he and Woods were driving to the course that Friday morning. "We've driven halfway to the course and he said, 'Stevie, what do you think about taking that stronger 3-wood just to make it a little bit easier on those left-to-right holes?' While I thought it was a good idea that he's thinking positively because we were going to need that shot, I'm thinking in my head, 'We didn't actually hit that club very good in practice.'" Woods had not used the stronger 3-wood since The Players, and it hardly had been his friend in those crosswinds. The rationale was that the stronger club would make it easier to hit the hard draw that a left-to-right wind requires. It was a shot Woods used to hit at will, but since changing his swing with Haney it didn't come as easily.

"We just made a series of bad decisions," Williams recalled. "It's difficult to explain. I knew in my head if we played those holes, 8 through 11, in 1 or 2 over and made a couple of birdies coming in, we'd be even par and we were going to be right there. But it's very hard to try to play just 1 or 2 over. And we got on that 8th hole and my thought was to take those bunkers out of play. Okay, we're going to have a 3- or a 4-iron into the green, but we can manage it. But instead we take the 3-wood there and it shot into the rough; bad lie, bad second shot, and we made the first 5 there. And then the next hole, used that same club again and the confidence wasn't great after what had happened on the last hole. We should've been hitting the 5-wood off the tee and I should've known that. Now [after another bogey] his confidence was rocked. The next hole, he obviously hit the worst tee shot you could imagine with that left-to-right wind."

The shot was so bad, so far away from the hard draw that the crosswind and the left-to-right sloping fairway demanded, that Ishikawa, who was playing alongside Woods, literally dropped his mouth open in shock as the ball sailed farther and farther right. He would join Lee Westwood and dozens of spectators trying to find the ball, but Williams knew its fate and immediately unzipped the bag and handed Woods another ball. "I knew straightaway we weren't ever going to find that ball." The second tee shot wasn't great, but it was at least in play. "I took a knock on my own confidence after that," said Williams. Woods managed to get up and down from 50 yards to save double bogey, then made a good par on the next, a par 3, which temporarily righted the ship. But the worst calamity still lay ahead. Woods had found a fairway pot bunker on the 12th and, in Scotland, unlike in the United States, bunkers are a real hazard. Usually, a one-shot penalty, and that's the price Woods paid. But his real undoing came on the 13th, which played straight downwind. He found the first cut of rough and had just 159 yards to the hole. "I gave him real bad advice on that second shot," said Williams. "There was oodles of green to the left of that flag and it was probably a little bit softer over there, but I gave him bad advice and he went at it and we ended up over that green." It was the worst possible miss given the circumstances. Woods looked like a beaten man after he flubbed a chip shot and went on to miss a 5-footer for bogey. "He would never say that I had anything to do with it, but I know in my own heart that I contributed to that," said Williams. "I blamed myself. He didn't play good but my advice was poor. I caddied poorly."

Woods, to his credit, didn't run and hide after his 74 but faced the music. "Yeah, I just made mistakes," he admitted. "And obviously you can't make mistakes and expect to not only make the cut but also try and win a championship. You have to play clean rounds of golf, and I didn't. I made my share of mistakes out there today and didn't play a very clean card.

"The wind was blowing pretty good. It was coming off the left pretty hard. You just had to hit good shots, and I didn't do that. It was a crosswind with holes that go from left to right and it was coming over your shoulder. You've got to hit some good draws in there and hold it against that wind, and I didn't do it." Ishikawa, who seemed so stunned by Woods's meltdown that he had one himself, later told Japanese journalists off the record that he couldn't believe how many bad shots Woods, his hero, had played. Westwood, the third member of the group, couldn't disagree. "You don't often see him play shots like that, some of the shots he played. But everybody is entitled to a bad day every now and again. It happens to all of us. It's difficult out there."

What a body blow Westwood inadvertently delivered to the image of the Invincible Tiger. Of course Woods could have a bad day, but the greater point was that, unlike his peers, he'd never cashed in on that entitlement. Bad days were for others, not Tiger Woods.

Meanwhile, back in the United States, a well-known golf instructor who worked with several Tour professionals watched Woods unravel on television and had his suspicions confirmed about the world's most influential swing. Like almost everyone who agreed to talk with me in the writing of this book, he asked that his name not be used. He said he didn't want to seem unprofessional in criticizing Haney but also admitted that neither did he "want to piss Tiger off . . . [because] that guy's got a long memory." In examining swing data from a Danish-based technology company called TrackMan, the instructor came across an interesting if little-known fact. "There are only two golfers on Tour who hit down on their drivers. Tiger and Charles Howell III. Tiger's five degrees down, which is incredible. It's like he's hitting an iron. When you see the long drivers, they're hitting up on their drives, about five or six degrees. To give you a comparison, Tiger's ball speed is very close to that of Bubba Watson's. But Watson's motion is more efficient and he's hitting up on the ball five degrees so he's hitting it much longer. Tiger swings way faster than most of the guys out there, but he launches it a lot lower with a lot of spin and even plays a softer, spinnier ball. He's doing this because he wants to work the ball. Fair enough, but it's not efficient and it's the direct cause of the problems he's been having.

"[Instructor] Chuck Cook played with Tiger in '99 in Ireland in a scramble. He said Tiger drove it phenomenally well. Every tee shot they used Tiger's drive. But Chuck noticed that Tiger's irons didn't have good distance control. What I think's happened is that he worked so hard to fix the distance control in his irons that now he's a really, really good iron player. But he's a so-so driver of the ball because he's using the same swing. It's interesting that players are usually either really good with their irons or with their driver, so it's not just Tiger, but none of them hit down on the driver like he does. And I think this is where the problems he's having are coming from. Why does he need a shorter-shafted driver with a lot more loft? Because he's hitting down and launching it so low. He has no choice. He needs that loft to make it more efficient so he can get the ball up higher.

"The other problem I see is with what Haney's teaching him. Haney professes a lot of forearm rotation. Tiger's got a weakish grip and a lot of forearm rotation. That adds so much extra timing to a golf swing. Not only does he have to keep the club in front of him but now you're adding a lot of rotation to get back to square. The third thing is he's got too much of an inside-to-out swing path. Haney talks about the club being on plane, but that's not all that matters. You need the correct swing path, which is only slightly from the inside. The chances of Tiger's inside-to-out swing path launching it on line are less. When he played badly at Carnoustie [in 2006], I'd heard that he'd basically said, 'Shove it,' and was a bit derogatory toward Hank. And I think he was on the right track because teachers get too caught up in swing plane when there are other factors to consider. At Turnberry, Tiger's problem was making a downward strike and coming too much from the inside. When you do that, the ball is going to start right and it will spin more, not less, and in a left-to-right wind that's going to mean that it goes even more to the right. And you can add to that the fact that you don't want the body moving too rapidly through the hit. The Texan guys like Hank are so in love with Hogan, but it's not a technique you can take a few weeks off and then go back to. I don't know if Tiger's aware of what he's doing or not, but I just don't think he can trust his tee shots the way he's swinging."

Haney, meanwhile, was doing damage control from his base in Texas. Again, he pointed to sloppiness in Woods's putting and short game, including two "two chips," as he termed them. "It was six holes," he told *Forbes* magazine. "It wasn't even really one tournament. I always look and think that you have to pick the low-hanging fruit first, and I think the 3-putt from 10 feet would be the lowest-hanging fruit that there was in those thirty-six holes. But, somehow, everybody had it figured out that all of a sudden his swing is no good. He's human, and it happens, and you have bad days, you have six bad holes, and he finished no worse than eleventh in any stroke play event except for one, and in that one, he had a bad six-hole stretch." They sound very much like the words of a man in denial, but if the accusation could be leveled at Haney, then it also pertained to Woods. They were both in denial by Haney's own definition. He said that which he was "most proud of with Tiger is that he's gotten better at understanding his game and fixing himself when something goes wrong."

But the truth was that Woods couldn't fix the right-to-right shot. The proof of the pudding is always in the eating.

Haney said there wouldn't be any major overhauls in Woods's swing as a result of the disaster at Turnberry. "He just sticks to what he's doing. Tiger is good at sticking to his plan, sticking to what he's working on. He doesn't let highs and lows bother him, and that's one of the things that he's good at.

"We work on his ability to hit all the different shots that he wants to hit. Tiger wants to hit nine shots: the ball starting straight, low, medium, high; the ball starting right, drawn to the target, low, medium, high; the ball starting left, fading to the target, low, medium, high. If he's not hitting one of those shots well, or feels uncomfortable with one of them, we work on it. Tiger wants to have his complete game in order, and his complete game means the ability to hit those nine shots." When asked how he dealt with the criticism, Haney was stoic. "It's part of the deal. Tiger told me, 'Hank, we don't have to like it, we just have to deal with it.' He's held to a standard that's often a little bit unrealistic. But I only have to please one person in my relationship with Tiger and that's Tiger. I just try to do the best I can do." Woods, for his part, wasn't about to abandon his coach. "People thought my career was over when I started working with Hank," he said. "They said I was done then. After my knee surgery, they said I was done then. When I got married, I was done then. After we had our first kid, I was done then. After our second kid, I was done then. I've been done a lot."

There was a sense that the air had been sucked out of the Open once Woods departed for Florida. He was, after all, the headliner. But it turned out that nothing could have been farther from the truth. Tom Watson was not finished. Not by any measure. He'd been golf's Quixote, tilting at windmills, for three days, but when two birdies late on Saturday had given him a 1-shot lead going into the final round, he was no longer just a feel-good story. He was on the verge of the single greatest triumph in golf's long history. Did he need to pinch himself? "I don't need to," he said with a smile. "I'm awake." But were we awake? How could it not have been a dream? Were we really to believe that a man could win the 2009 British Open when he was born in the 1940s, in the same year Harry Truman was inaugurated, the NATO alliance was formed, Mao turned China red, George Orwell's *1984* was published, and *Hopalong Cassidy* had made its debut on an exciting new medium called television?

Maybe that was the difference between us and Watson. We were hoping for a fairy tale ending where he actually thought he could author one. In fact, he'd said it all along. "The first day here, yeah, let the old geezer have his day in the sun, you know, [shoot] 65," he told the media. "The second day you said, well, that's okay, and then now today you kind of perk up your ears and say, this old geezer might have a chance to win the tournament." As he left the media center with his wife, Hilary, to cross the road and return to the hotel, I wondered what kind of night he'd have, sleeping—if he could even sleep—on the lead. Two other things crept into my mind. Could Watson's putter really be trusted to stay loyal in his hour of greatest need? I thought of Hogan, at the end of his career frozen for an eternity over putts, unable to pull the trigger because he knew he was firing blanks. And I wondered, too, if Watson's sentimentality would derail him. Could he keep his eyes dry for eighteen holes? He couldn't do it on that Saturday. On the 18th fairway, after hitting onto the green, he turned to his caddie, the Democratic political consultant Neil Oxman, and brought up their friend, Watson's longtime caddie, Bruce Edwards, who had passed away from complications associated with Lou Gehrig's disease. "Bruce is with us today," Watson told Oxman. "He said, 'Don't make me cry.' So he started crying and I started crying." Before he left the media compound, I asked Watson whether he'd be nervous. "I feel like my nerves are too well fried to feel them. I mean, come on. Let's just go with what I've got."

The ink-stained life of a newspaperman had been good to me, but never more so than on that Sunday. My eyes had seen many wondrous deeds on the fields of play for which I could rarely find the words. I was courtside to see Federer win Wimbledon, ringside when Evander Holyfield stood up to a bully who bit his ear in petulance, on the sidelines at Super Bowls, trackside as Usain Bolt sprinted into history on a steamy Beijing night, watched in horror as the great Zidane lost his mind and the World Cup final for France in Berlin, and courtside as Jordan defied gravity and all odds. I'm sure I've forgotten many others, but it matters little: none could come close to what it was like to be at Turnberry on that fateful Sunday. There are days in my business when it's work. This wasn't one of them. I could recount it all, with the benefit of many months of hindsight, but instead I think the words I wrote that evening for FoxSports.com communicate the swirling emotions of that day much better.

It was with heavy heart and moist eyes that I watched the playoff for the 138th Open Championship. It might have been one of the saddest things I've ever seen in sports. By the time Tom Watson, his legs shot, butchered the third playoff hole—handing the Claret Jug to Stewart Cink—and then sent his tee shot on the final hole sailing into the stands, I wanted to run out onto the Turnberry links, throw down a white towel, and whisk him away. It was over and everyone knew it and Tom Watson didn't deserve to have to endure another moment of humiliation. Those four holes will rank in the annals of sporting cruelty along with leaving Willie Mays in center field when he could no longer shag a fly ball, letting Joe

Namath heave interceptions for the Rams or, worst of all, standing by while the great Ali was pummeled by unworthy hacks like
Trevor Berbick.

This was, of course, not the way it was supposed to end.
Thomas Sturges Watson was to author a real-life fairy tale, the
greatest story in golf, a fifty-nine-year-old winning a sixth British
Open and a first since 1983. 1983! A story so immense it has no
equal. And in doing so he was to single-handedly prove to us that
the years cannot always weary our heroes. That despite the weath-
ered brows and sagging skin, the failing eyesight and the atrophy
of those once-toned muscles, it's the heart of the champion that
beats within that truly separates him.

And so when Watson strode to the 72nd green through the
wind and sunshine of a pleasant Sunday on the Scottish coast,
standing on the precipice of sporting immortality, by God, he was
walking for all of us. For he was refusing to agree with the natural
laws of this universe. He had fought with the heart of a lion to
be there, holding a 1-stroke lead with a hole to play and needing
just a par to make history. Throughout this most unforgettable of
weeks, he'd remembered the man he used to be, resurrecting the
champion who'd won the famous Duel in the Sun on these beautiful acres thirty-two years ago against the mighty Jack Nicklaus.
When his 8-iron hit the 72nd green, immortality was to have become a formality. Two putts to win.

And then, the angel that had been on Watson's shoulder for four
days suddenly deserted him. Somehow, Watson's ball, which had
pitched on the front of the green, kept rolling. And rolling. His
playing partner, Australian Mathew Goggin, said later he thought
Watson had hit "a perfect shot." But had he, for once, misjudged
the weight? He'd been so good for four days, relying on guile
and wisdom and memories, playing a style of golf that can be so
treacherous. His ball wouldn't stop. It scurried past the hole, then

trickled over the bank at the back of the green. It came to rest in a clump of grass. A few inches closer and he could've comfortably 2-putted, Goggin guessed. A few inches longer and Watson could've chipped it close from a better lie.

And that's when Tom Watson lost his nerve. That's when he betrayed his age and the long years it's been since he'd been a golfer winning majors. Watson chose to putt the ball. Once the greatest of chippers in his heyday, in his moment of truth he put his trust in the one club that brought his golden years to a premature end. As it was, he hit the putter too firmly. The ball went eight feet by, to the left of the hole. Everyone gasped. Eight feet to immortality. Eight feet too much. "Made a lousy putt," Watson later bemoaned.

The playoff against Cink, who through no fault of his own was the villain of the piece, was a nightmare. With Cink—who'd made a remarkable birdie on the last hole to get to 2 under par—in the greenside bunker on the first playoff hole, Watson from the middle of the fairway hit a fat 5-iron into another trap. Cink saved par while Watson couldn't. On the next, Watson made a miraculous up and down after the most wayward shot he'd hit all day, but Cink retained his 1-shot advantage. The 3rd hole was an unmitigated disaster; Watson's legs had given out. He made a double bogey on a par 5 he'd birdied an hour or so before. Cink made a 2-putt 4, then birdied the last for good measure as Watson flailed around, scraping a bogey. "The playoff was just one bad shot after another," Watson said. "I didn't give [Cink] much competition."

It was obvious from the polite but lukewarm reception given Cink that everyone had come here to see Watson achieve this most impossible of dreams. And while it was a great disappointment for us, spare a thought for Watson himself. We will return to our lives, but he will be haunted by the myriad ways it could've been different for the rest of his. "In retrospect I probably would have hit a 9-iron rather than an 8-iron [into the last hole]," he said during an emotional news conference. "I was thinking 9 but I said, 'I'll hit 8,' and I caught it just the way I wanted to, and sure enough, it went too far. I chose to putt it from the short rough there. I just felt like I had a better chance to get it close, and I looked at that upslope, looked like there was some grain in there, so I decided I was going to make sure I wasn't going to leave it short and sure, I gunned it on by and made a lousy putt."

During a news conference that ended with a standing ovation to the man they once dubbed the King of Scotland, Watson struggled to maintain his composure. "It would've been a hell of a story, wouldn't it? It wasn't to be and, yes, it's a great disappointment. It tears at your gut, as it always has torn at my gut. It's not easy to take."

I won't soon forget what happened here this week. And I won't soon forget the dignity with which Tom Watson accepted this cruelest of fates. And I want to assure him that his last wish as he left Turnberry will, without a shadow of a doubt, be fulfilled. "When all is said and done," he said, "one of the things I hope that will come out of my life is that my peers will say, you know, that Watson, he was a hell of a golfer."

CHAPTER 11

Buick Open

Although he habitually refused to enter tournaments until the last moment, Woods's schedule was generally easy to predict. He played, by and large, the same events each year; either they were held on courses he liked, or his appearance was sponsor driven. He might play overseas—typically the Middle East, Germany, Japan or, as happened in 2009, China and Australia—but only if his appearance fee of $3 million was met. He was not one for delivering surprises. After a long year of traveling and with the prospect of many more weeks on the road ahead, I'd scheduled a family summer vacation the week of the Buick Open because, I'd figured, there was no reason for Woods to show up at Warwick Hills.

After the Turnberry trauma, those of us who shadowed him for a living assumed he would spend two weeks on the range in Orlando with Haney to iron out his swing and then arrive at one of his favorite tracks, Akron's Firestone Country Club, where he'd been so successful he could probably win a Bridgestone

Invitational playing left-handed and with a blindfold. No one—
including the organizers of the Buick Open—believed Woods was
going to Michigan the week before Akron and two weeks before
the PGA. Woods didn't like playing two straight weeks, much less
three in a row. To boot, Flint had fallen so far off the golf map that
Jim Furyk was the only player of any note in the field for an event
on its deathbed.

Beyond that, Woods had never gone out of his way to do corporate favors, and he and Buick had ended their nine-year association at the end of 2008, in what the automaker's spokesman,
Larry Peck, had characterized as "a mutual and amicable separa-
tion." Peck could find work in Hollywood crafting those kinds
of statements, but the strange part was that he wasn't spinning;
both parties really had decided to walk away with no hard feelings. Not only that, but it was Woods who initiated the divorce,
not GM as had been widely reported. Of course, GM eventually
would've had no choice given its insolvency and subsequent pan-
handling in Washington. But Woods was happy to bring an end
to a contract that still had a year at a little less than $10 million
left to pay him. Maybe some of his motivation came from wisely
assessing that, with a reeling GM taking government handouts, it
wouldn't look good if he was collecting taxpayers' money. But at
least as much, an IMG source disclosed, it came because Woods
had grown tired of the pound of flesh he was expected to deliver in return for the money. "I can't overemphasize how much
he'd grown to hate doing what he has to do for his sponsors," the
source said. Ten million bucks a year just wasn't worth the hassle
to a man who was closing in on becoming the first billionaire athlete, a status he told me he hadn't yet achieved in 2009, despite
Forbes magazine's proclamation.

Within GM there was disquiet, too, about the first big deal
Steinberg had brokered as Woods's agent. Internally, execu-

tives quarreled almost from the outset over the worth of Woods to the brand. "I remember back in '99 when we had the initial discussions with Mark Steinberg at the NEC in Akron, we wondered even then if the relationship would sell a single car," Jim McGovern, who ran Buick's golf sponsorship program at the time, wrote after the deal had ended. "Would anyone believe a young, wealthy, famous black athlete would be caught dead in a Park Avenue unless he actually was dead and the Park Avenue was a hearse?" The auto giant understood, however, that it needed to give its poor-selling luxury line a makeover; it needed to do something to make Buicks appealing not just to traditional buyers— who were, literally, a dying breed—but also to a younger, hipper market. Steinberg sold GM on the idea that Woods was the perfect vehicle for the campaign because Buick was the biggest sponsor of golf—the favorite pastime of Buick customers—and his client was golf's biggest star. It may have made sense on some level, but the truth was that the marriage never really worked.

Sources inside GM concede that the failure was probably more the fault of Buick, which was unable to produce a car anyone wanted to buy, than a reflection on Woods's appeal as a corporate spokesman. He wasn't Michael Jordan, but he could move product. That said, the harsh reality was that Buick sales fell during the Tiger decade and the heavy hitters at GM, always quick to point fingers of blame away from themselves, sought to make Woods the scapegoat. Bob Lutz, GM's flamboyant vice chairman, was surprisingly publicly critical of Woods in early 2010 at a car convention in Orlando. After thanking his lucky stars GM didn't have to deal with the repercussions of Woods's sex scandal, he said that "we weren't too lucky with Tiger Woods for Buick. He wasn't a spokesman. You would just see him in the ads. Maybe we didn't have him say the right things at the time, either." Lutz was echoing what factions within the dysfunctional GM family, and Buick dealers especially, had long held: Woods somehow wasn't earning his keep. The irony was that Woods actually liked Buicks and, even though he drove the free Escalade GM shipped to him, his wife drove a Buick SUV; it was free, too, of course, but it was still the vehicle she drove. Throughout the 2009 golf season, more often than not Woods's loyalty to the brand was such that the only Buick in the players' parking lot would be his. But dealers complained to the head office that Woods didn't play in every Buick-sponsored event, didn't hold forth on behalf of the company enough, and wasn't accessible enough. Which is to say, he didn't play enough golf with them.

A few days before the deadline to enter the Buick Open, I received a call warning me that Woods had decided to play in Michigan. Family summer vacation was duly canceled, and a flight arranged to Detroit, which I'd found to be just as I'd left it: still America's most depressing city. From Detroit, I drove the seventy miles north to Flint, past the Silverdome, the abandoned old home of the Lions and, for a decade, the Pistons. There was a forlorn For Sale sign outside the dilapidated property, where weeds had grown through cracks in the cement. I wondered just who was in the market for a dome these days. Revealing just how bad things had become in Michigan, a Canadian developer bought the Pontiac dome in late 2009 for just $583,000 at an auction with no minimum bid. Only four bidders bothered to show up. The dome was built in 1975 for $55.7 million, or more than $200 million in 2009 dollars. Its demise was emblematic of the fall from grace of the car industry and all those jobs lost at the Big Three. In 2009, the financial crisis hit hard everywhere, but nowhere harder than Michigan. Unemployment in Flint, the birthplace of General Motors, which had lost almost half its population since 1970, had reached 24 percent in August.

Warwick Hills, it turned out, wasn't in Flint but in nearby

Grand Blanc, where there was no need to attempt a faux French pronounciation. "It's Grand, as in, 'Ain't that grand,' and Blanc, as in, 'You can write me a blank check anytime, honey!' " said a jovial woman, much to her own amusement, at a convenience store. Buick owned the tournament, which had a warm, small-town feel to it, easily the least corporate stop on the Tour. As John Daly once famously described it, "a beer drinkers' tournament." Amid the blue-collar crowd, it wasn't difficult to spot Peck with his expensive haircut, tailored pink shirt, and off-white pants. I asked the personable marketing man why Woods had agreed to one last hurrah for the company that had thrown upward of $70 million his way. "You'll have to ask him," he said, "but I can tell you this: he owes us nothing and we expected nothing. We really had no idea he was coming. And there's no contract in place between Buick and Tiger Woods." Some speculated that Woods was so distraught after the British Open that he wanted to get back on the horse and sort out his game as soon as he could. Peck wasn't buying that theory. "You want to know what I think it says? It tells you what this guy's really about. I've been around a lot of athletes, and he's special. That he came here when he had no reason to is a testament to his character and the kind of man he is."

At the Courtyard Marriott in Flint, I ran into Steve Williams and his wife, Kirsty, a friendly woman with an even thicker New Zealand accent than her husband. Their four-year-old son, Jett, who loves golf much more than his dad—who doesn't play much anymore—was asleep. The family spends northern summers in Oregon's lush Sunriver region, which Williams says reminds him of home, and often travels together to tournaments. Williams told me that Woods was staying at the hotel, too. I was shocked that the world's most recognizable sports star would be in a Courtyard Marriott—surely the only guest in the chain's history to check out and jump into a $60 million jet—but, in retrospect, what was more surprising was that during that entire week I never once saw Woods at the hotel. In fact, I never saw him off the golf course. Flint is not that big a town, and there are only so many dining options. It occurred to me as I struggled to digest the magnitude of his illicit affairs later in the year that in all the time I had known Woods, I'd never once run into him outside a golf setting.

Williams isn't anyone's idea of a night owl. Having dinner with him during a tournament week means food on the plate by six o'clock. One beer, maybe two if his arm's twisted sufficiently, then he's off to bed. It's hardly the caddie lifestyle of lore, where men like Lance Ten Broeck, a former Tour player who had since turned to caddying, thoroughly earned noms de guerre like "Last Call Lance." In an outdoor bar in Flint, I ran into a group of caddies on the prowl, meeting women who'd tried to hook players that day at Warwick Hills but had to settle for their caddies. "It's like they're the rock stars and we're the roadies, except most of these guys [Tour players] are so straight they don't party at all, so that means there's more for us," said one antipodean caddie. I offered to buy a round of beers but was intercepted before I'd made it to the bar. "No beer," one of the caddies told me. "Vodka and cranberry juice, 'cos you can't smell it the next day." Although most players know their caddies hardly live a monastic life, free of sins of the flesh, there exists an unwritten rule that a caddie cannot arrive to work drunk or even smelling of a time well spent at the bar. Many a relationship came to an end when that line was crossed.

Williams was already in REM sleep as his peers were just getting started at the Redwood Lodge, not far from the Courtyard Marriott. In the bar's cigar room, the CBS Sports crew was holding court, led by the charismatic master storyteller Gary McCord. Ian Baker-Finch was there, too, as was David Feherty, who'd make news he wished he hadn't later in the week. Among his fellow caddies, Williams was considered somewhat distant and some say a little full of himself. Having gotten to know him, I found him to be the most misunderstood figure in golf. While he was protective of his boss—and unapologetically so—he was far from mean; a man more likely to laugh than growl. The next morning, Williams was in the gym at the crack of dawn, had gone for a run—Woods can beat him over shorter distances but the forty-five-year-old proudly notes his superiority over longer stretches—and spent the rest of the morning with his family. He had the motor of the Buick Rendezvous courtesy car running by the hotel's side entrance as Woods emerged, ready to make the ten-minute journey to Warwick Hills and an afternoon tee time.

The day before, in the pro-am, Woods was paired with Mr. Old Time Rock 'n' Roll himself, Bob Seger, a Michigan native and avowed golf nut. At first glance, I'd thought a homeless man had wandered onto the course and joined the Woods group, but I reconsidered only because a homeless man would probably not be wearing a golf glove on each hand. Certainly Seger had set a record of sorts: it had to have been the first time anyone had played with Woods in a pro-am wearing raggedy black shorts and mismatched socks. The sixty-four-year-old later spoke in awe at the way Woods had played. "It was so extraordinary. He hit every fairway, hit every par 3, made every putt the first nine holes." And that's about what it takes to win at Warwick Hills, a lovely old tree-lined classic design that has been ravaged by technology, so much so that with its short par 4s and all its 5 pars reachable in two, par is realistically around 68, not the 72 it says on the scorecard.

Steve Lowery, less than two years away from the easy money of the Champions Tour, shot a 9-under-par 63 in the first round of the Buick Open. Woods limped in with a flaccid 71. "Probably one of the worst putting days I've ever had," he lamented as he languished in a tie for ninety-fifth. Probably he didn't need to use the qualifier. Woods had 32 putts, which should've been 33 given that the bomb he made to save par on the short 4th hole was pulled but he misread the break and it went in anyway. Woods had won at Warwick Hills twice in eight visits and hadn't finished below the top four in nine years. His worst finish ever in the event was a tie for eleventh, but there he was, on a sticky summer afternoon in the heartland, being asked whether he worried about missing the cut. The irony was that he "drove it on a string" off the tee, was so-so with his irons, but the short game was MIA and the putter was DOA. He 3-putted from no more than 10 feet on the 2nd.

While Woods put on a brave face in public, he wasn't so stoic on the ride back to the hotel. "I was a little bit hot," he later admitted. He decided not to work much on his game after the round but instead "just go home and get away from it for a little bit." Williams was worried. "I had a bad week after the British Open," he told me. "I take great pride in what I do and probably more pride than anyone will ever know. A lot of people look at me as a bit of a hardhead, which I am because you've got to be, but I take a lot of pride in my racing and I take a lot of pride in my caddying and I think about it a lot. I grade myself each week, and I know if I do the best job I can when he's playing, he's going to be hard to beat. But [at the Buick] a bit of that insecurity from Turnberry showed. I know I didn't do a great job the first round."

When he returned to the Courtyard Marriott that Thursday evening, Kirsty sensed all was not well with her husband. Williams told her that he wasn't sure of himself. "My wife actually gave me a real chewing out that night because I told her that I was lacking a bit of confidence. The next three rounds of that tournament I did not make one mistake. And I think Tiger fed off that. I got into his ear a little bit more than I normally do because I was trying to turn it around. Usually when he gets on the green I don't say anything unless it's something glaring, but I said something to him before every putt, before every shot, and it was just to try and turn things around. And we got some good breaks. We turned it around."

Although I see little point to going through the birdies and bogeys of Woods's mistresses scorecard, one particular dalliance resonated with me and is worth recounting. As much as it would deflate Williams to think so, Woods seems to have had another source of inspiration at the Buick Open. The sometimes pornographic actor, Josyln James, whose real name is Veronica Daniels, alleged that she had been having a three-year affair with Woods. Perhaps that was true, perhaps it wasn't. But after reading text messages she said were from Woods, I had no doubt that she'd spent that Thursday night a few doors down from my room at that Flint Courtyard. Woods was indeed in room 201, as her text messages alleged. He'd flown her in, as he often did with women during tournament weeks, for a brief rendezvous, most of them lasting two or three nights. James said Woods warned her he needed to get up at 4:15 a.m. for the following day's round, yet she said after they'd had sex earlier in the evening, he'd had trouble falling asleep and called her back to his room for another tryst just a few hours before he had to wake up. She estimated that he'd had perhaps two hours of sleep by the time the unsuspecting Williams drove their car to the hotel's side entrance. Given the activities of that night, Woods's start to that second round was simply astounding. He was 7 under par through seven holes.

Woods should, in truth, have done even better than the 63 he turned in, even though it was his lowest score anywhere in four years. His good mood wasn't dented even when a journalist asked again whether he'd worried about missing the cut. Woods bit his tongue. "No," he said. The third round was a study not in great ball striking but in scoring. "There's a lot of guys out here who can turn a 65 into a 69, but there's not many who can turn a 69 into a 65, and that's what Tiger did today," said Williams. When Michael Letzig made a careless double bogey on the last hole Saturday, Woods had the third-round lead at 17 under par.

For a brief moment that Sunday, Letzig allowed himself to dream of an upset. The old swing demons were back, haunting Woods. He was spraying his tee shots to the right and, for good measure, missing his irons to the right, too. His body was fast through the shot and his clubface was open. Letzig had last played with Woods in the final round at Memorial, where he'd seen the world number one at his stratospheric best. The man playing alongside him at Warwick Hills, however, was a far cry from the one who'd won at Jack's place. Letzig even thought he smelled vulnerability. "I thought, 'Maybe.' You could tell he wasn't on his game early and I kind of thought if I could get it going he would be beatable," said the twenty-nine-year-old from Kansas City. Yet it is a measure of Woods on Sundays that he finds a way. After eight holes, with smoke, mirrors, and guts, Woods, who really is golf's ultimate grinder, was at 2 under par for the day while Letzig, who drove it beautifully only to miss birdie putt after birdie putt, made just one mistake—albeit a costly one, a double bogey—and found himself at 2 over. Far from being in a position to win, he was five shots adrift of Woods's lead. "He just doesn't make mistakes," said Letzig. "When he does make mistakes he recovers and then makes the birdies on the easy holes that you're supposed to. He's just laughing at all of us. He's so good."

By the time the final group had made the turn, the result seemed beyond doubt. Woods hadn't coughed up a third-round lead since his rookie year, at the Quad Cities Classic, and the streak looked very much like extending to 37–0. Woods was usually a self-contained fortress on Sundays, but he seemed to know that he was safe and so was relaxed. Indeed, as Nathan Green, the easygoing Australian who routinely introduced himself to playing partners as "the worst ball striker on Tour," ventured onto Woods's fairway on the 9th, Woods took time to congratulate him on his breakthrough victory the week before at the Canadian Open. "Blind squirrel," said the self-deprecating Aussie.

Feherty, meanwhile, was in the shade of the tree line, providing his colorful brand of course commentary. "No way he's losing this one, not to these guys," the genial Irishman told me. I agreed. Feherty then gave me the news that he'd eaten beans for lunch and that his stomach was grumbling. "I've got one locked and loaded in the chamber," he said, like a proud parent. Feherty and Woods had long engaged in farting contests on the course. "My stomach's killing me, but I've got to hold this one in and really give it to him good today." He sought revenge, he told me, for what Woods had done to him at Warwick Hills in 2006. "It was his fiftieth Tour win and I just got lost in all the hoopla associated with that, and after we do our postround interview, I stupidly put out my hand to congratulate him, and what does he do? He pulls my finger and lets out this enormous fart. The bastard got me good."

Though it appeared a formality, there were still nine holes to play and Woods at least made it interesting on the par-5 13th. He'd been playing safely but decided to diverge from the blueprint in trying to slice a 3-wood around a tree on the right of the fairway despite a left-to-right wind and water to the right of the green. His squirter of a shot landed in the middle of the lake, prompting Woods to pull his hat over his face and have a few stern words with himself, in private. Woods said, "I was a little angry." I later asked Williams why Woods risked playing the shot that was, at best, a fifty-fifty proposition. "You think it was fifty-fifty? It was ninety-nine to one. I couldn't talk him out of it. I knew that was a stupid play. It was just a 5-iron punch down the fairway and he would've had the same pitch that he had after hitting it in the water. But I knew he was going to win the tournament. I don't know what he was thinking, but he wanted to hit that shot. I tried to explain to him it's no snack out of that [left greenside] bunker, and if you miss the bunker left it's not an easy pitch, but if you hit a 5-iron down there, seven out of ten balls you'll get up and down. But sometimes he likes the dramatic. Now if he was one shot ahead or one behind, it would've been different, but he knows if he knocks that ball in the water he's probably going to get it up and down for par, and he did. But if it was important, I never would've let him get the 3-wood out of the bag."

Woods had a safe cushion going into the last hole, where he waited for the group ahead to finish. Feherty sensed that it was his moment to pounce. While Woods bent over to stretch, Feherty launched a sick-sounding fart from nearby, so long and loud that both Woods and Williams immediately looked over to him and began laughing. Unfortunately, Feherty had forgotten to turn his microphone off, and the fart, plus the reaction of Woods and Williams, was not only part of the broadcast but became a cult favorite on YouTube in no time. It triggered a controversy dubbed "Fartgate" and led CBS to issue a statement exonerating Woods as the perpetrator—though not naming Feherty—and YouTube was ordered to take down the clip.

Woods, meanwhile, was oblivious to the implications of Fartgate. He'd won the tournament by 3 strokes and felt heartened about his chances at Hazeltine. "I'm starting to feel better than I did the last time I played," he said. "I can use this as maybe a little bit of momentum going into the next two weeks." For all the hand-wringing about his failures, he'd won four times in 2009, and no other player had won more than twice. Meanwhile, Letzig offered a glimpse into how comfortable life had gotten on the Tour when he spoke of his happiness in securing his playing

privileges for the 2010 season. Wasn't he devastated at not winning? "I wasn't really here to win the tournament today. It was
just kind of a battle with myself out there. You try and match him,
it ain't gonna happen." Steinberg acknowledged as much when
he called that night to congratulate Woods on winning "the first
Nationwide Tour event of your career."

When Woods had finished with his media obligations and Williams waited outside, Peck and a handful of Buick Open officials
came to say their good-byes. It was to be the last Buick Open,
ending a streak that began in 1958. "It was quite an emotional
moment for us," Peck later told me. "He's really become a great
friend and for me it was a really special relationship. I wanted
to say good-bye to him one last time. He's just a great guy. He's
amazing. It was an emotional good-bye. He said we'd see each
other again, but . . ." I was touched by Peck's genuine affection
for Woods and asked him to write an appreciation of sorts for this
book. He agreed, but when the news broke of Woods's adulter-
ies, Peck changed his mind. "Given the latest developments," he
wrote to me in an e-mail, "I think it would be best if I made no
comments."

CHAPTER 12

Bridgestone Invitational

After the stink of Fartgate spread in the days after the Buick Open, it became clear just how odious it could be to be Tiger Woods. The target was forever painted on his back. In Michigan, I had asked him whether he wanted to respond publicly to an article by Rick Reilly berating his on-course temper tantrums at Turnberry. Reilly wrote that "in every other case, I think Tiger Woods has been an A-plus role model. Never shows up in the back of a squad car with a black eye. Never gets busted in a sleazy motel with three 'freelance models.' Never gets so much as a parking ticket. But this punk act on the golf course has got to stop. If it were my son, I'd tell him the same thing: 'Either behave or get off the course.' " It turned out Reilly was wrong on a few scores; at the time I had thought he'd been overly dramatic in his condemnation of Woods. Perhaps it's columnists' wont to poke and prod for a reaction, and Reilly's certainly been adept at drawing blood since shape-shifting from one of the finest magazine writers in the game at *Sports Illustrated* to an oracle at ESPN. Woods mulled over my offer for a moment, then simply shrugged. "Either way," he eventually said, "I can't win."

"One of his greatest assets but also the thing that people have the most disrespect for with Tiger is that he does get pissed off and he does show his emotions," says Williams. "He can throw a club, rip a glove, kick the bag, swear, whatever it might be, but his great asset is that once he's done that, it's over. And then he's the same person he was prior to hitting that shot. A lot of people don't like that, a lot of people think that he shouldn't show any anger, but that's his makeup, that's the way he does it. It's always going to be the same; that's the way it is. I think it's one of his great strengths because he can get that out. Now if that was Greg [Norman], that'd be his downfall because he could never let it go. He'd still talk about shots or bad breaks weeks later, sometimes a year later; he couldn't ever let it go. But with Tiger, I know as soon as that's gone, there's no need to wonder if he's still pissed off because we're back on it, thinking about the next shot."

The evolution of the Woods temper is revelatory. When he was young, a bad shot, unlucky bounce, or missed putt could put him in a foul mood for a few holes, a few hours, or even a few days. Slowly, Earl Woods—who'd remind his son that golf was meant to be fun only to hear back that winning was what was fun—allowed him to get angry but challenged Tiger to shorten the duration of the tantrums. Eventually, he got to the point where the dark clouds would be lifted by the time he was ready to play the next shot. There is, too, an element of survival in such a philosophy, which appealed to the young Tiger. He understood that he needed to have his wits about him and not cloud his judgment with needless negativity. Was the whole exercise really necessary? Did he really need to throw clubs and have tantrums? Probably not, and Woods deep down knew that, at least on an intellectual level, and worked hard throughout 2009 to tone down the puerile behavior. But I'd come to see that he relied on anger to keep him sharp on an emotional level.

It's not an uncommon tactic for athletes who depend on a me-against-the-world mind-set to rise to a challenge when they otherwise don't feel particularly motivated. Again, Woods learned well at Jordan's knee. Jordan was the king of digging up slights, real or imagined, to help him find an extra gear when he felt flat. When Colin Montgomerie questioned whether Woods was experienced enough to win the '97 Masters against seasoned professionals, did that provide extra motivation? "Big time," Woods acknowledged. When the 2000 Presidents Cup singles meant virtually nothing, the Americans sure to win, Woods played as if his life depended on beating Vijay Singh when the Fijian's caddie, Paul Tesori, wore a hat with TIGER WHO? emblazoned across the back. "I certainly didn't appreciate it," Woods admitted five years later. "I thought it wasn't real respectful. He tried to do it in fun, but I didn't take it that way. I went out there and beat him two and one. So that's my response to it." Stephen Ames became a cautionary tale after shooting off his mouth about Woods's crookedness before the Match Play. When asked what he thought of Ames's comments—which were admittedly said tongue-in-cheek—Woods said "9 and 8," the margin of the shellacking he delivered to the Trinidadian. "Rory [Sabbatini] popping off was good for him," Haney told *Golf Digest* in 2007. "Phil and Butch working together is good for him."

A source who knew the Woods family said it had always been so with Tiger. "Part of what makes him tick is that his whole life growing up he was an outsider, an idea reinforced by his parents. Golf wasn't a sport for kids with his skin color or background, and I think that's part of why he never liked Mickelson, because Mickelson represents the country-club brats Tiger had to go against

as a kid. And he wouldn't ever let himself lose to those kids because he wanted to show them that they weren't better than him,
despite their advantages. So was some of that motivation negative and probably unhealthy? I'm sure it was. Did it work? Absolutely." Woods once said that he got "no fulfillment with fame"
and would "much rather have anonymity but still go out and kick
everybody's butt. That would be fun. As long as everyone I com-
peted against knew I beat them, and for me to know as well, that
would be enough."

By the time the traveling circus had arrived in Akron, there
was still no end to Fartgate. The story was clearly unimportant
in the scheme of things, but it gnawed at me that the media was
awash with discussion of what the incident said about Woods.
In truth, it said much more about how as a society we naïvely
believe whatever we read on the Web; how lazy bloggers operating from their couches had hijacked an entire profession and redefined what news was and how it was gathered. It spoke also to
the abdication of the responsibility for news by traditional media
outlets, which having missed the boat in the Internet's infancy
decided that if they couldn't beat the Matt Drudges and Perez Hil-
tons and Harvey Levins of the world, then they'd join them. In the
process, time-honored news-gathering methods were discarded
in the haste to get a story up on the website. Journalists had no
time to flesh out stories because they had to produce blogs or
other content for websites, so it was a vicious circle. Not that journalists looking to find out if the perpetrator of the fart really was
Tiger Woods were going to find any joy by asking either Greenspan or Steinberg. The fatal flaw of the Woods media strategy—
say nothing—would be exposed later in the year.

TMZ, the celebrity gossip website that would play a major role
in the undoing of Woods at the end of 2009, was not constrained
by old-school journalistic ethics. "Whoever Smelt It Dealt It," read

the headline on the Fartgate story. The accompanying photograph had Woods, who'd turned awkwardly on his right ankle earlier in the fourth round at Warwick Hills, shaking out his right foot. "Take a close look at Tiger's reaction. Is that the face of a guilty, gassy man?" There was no stopping the machine. The story was that Tiger Woods had farted on national television, whether it was true or not. And judgment, like gas, had to be passed.

In response, I wrote a column on FoxSports.com that was really an accumulation of a year's worth of thoughts about Woods. I had been stunned throughout the season at the vitriolic nature of e-mails and posts generated by any column I wrote sympathetic to him. Woods always seemed to me to be such a vanilla kind of character: talented and successful and likable but, at heart, not especially interesting away from golf. But there were those who hated him. Deeply. By the crude metrics I had at my disposal, I'd calculated this number to be around 30 percent of those who'd written to me or responded to a column. It was a mystifying hatred. Was it because he was good? Because he was successful? Or because he was those things *and* had a dark complexion? The Fartgate column drew several thousand comments, by far the most I'd received up to that point, and was clicked on by more than one million readers within a day. The column, excerpted below, had touched a nerve that I hadn't known existed.

David Feherty passes gas and Tiger Woods gets the blame. That's the way it is when your life is lived inside a giant fishbowl. Although relatively innocuous—and humorous—the incident nonetheless illustrates that when you're Tiger Woods, there is no such thing as privacy; no moments are ever allowed to go unguarded. Is it any wonder, then, that his gloves are always up when he's in public? My colleagues often bemoan the fact that on the rare occasions that Woods speaks—has any sporting superstar, by the way, granted fewer man-behind-the-mask interviews?—he rarely says anything of note. But the truth is that if he did, if he really spoke his mind, Woods believes he'd be lambasted. It's a classic lose-lose scenario for him and it's hard to argue against his reasoning.

What he's also acutely aware of is that, for whatever reasons—and I believe one of them to be racism—there exists a small but noisy group of naysayers for whom Woods can do no right. These Tiger haters peddle whatever argument they can dream up to belittle his achievements. And it takes some serious mental gymnastics to sell Tiger Woods short. With his victory Sunday at the last Buick Open in Michigan, Woods has now sixty-nine Tour titles. He's third on the all-time list and wins at a pace years ahead of both second-placed Jack Nicklaus—whom he now trails by only four—and Sam Snead, the all-time leader, with eighty-two Tour wins. But to those who seek to diminish Woods, it's not good enough. It's never good enough. They babble on endlessly about technology being better and fields being weaker. They whisper that Woods is on the juice without the slightest iota of proof (as if the Tour doesn't drug-test him), that he wins at the same courses (as if other players don't play at their favorite courses each year), and that he doesn't have worthwhile rivals, as Nicklaus did in Palmer, Watson, Trevino, Player, et al.

This last one really is a peach. Ever pause to wonder why Woods doesn't have any real rivals? I've been watching him at close range since he arrived on the scene thirteen years ago and here's what I see: one by one, he's vanquished all the pretenders to his throne. He's a rivals serial killer. Ernie Els, let's face it, is a shell of the player he once was and, in a quiet moment, he'd probably admit that losing over and over to Woods in the early part of this decade took its toll. David Duval's certainly had to face adversity on and off the course, but the fact remains that once he got to the top of the world, he discovered it was a lot tougher staying there than it was getting there. Sergio Garcia? A wondrous prodigy, but he's never been able to beat Woods, and do you think it eats at him? To quote Jack Nicholson in *Chinatown*, only when he breathes. Padraig Harrington? What happened to him after three majors in thirteen months? And let's not forget Colin Montgomerie's pomposity in suggesting that the young Tiger cub might not be able to handle the pressure of the moment when the two were paired in the third round of the 1997 Masters. How'd that one turn out, Monty? Phil Mickelson's the only one who at least has fought back after being pummeled by Woods for years, but the fact remains that he's spent longer inside the world top ten without making it to number one than anyone in history. Vijay Singh gave Woods a run for his money for a while, but now he's just another who's fallen by the wayside. I tend to defer to the Golden Bear himself when it comes to evaluating Woods. He calls Woods the greatest golfer ever.

When Woods wins, as he's done four times this year, setting himself up as the front-runner for yet another Player of the Year award, his detractors turn the focus to his behavior. He is, to be sure, passionate and emotional, no more so than athletes in other sports, but golf is, of course, a more gentlemanly pursuit. His emotions can spill out sometimes in unfortunate ways, and I'm not going to justify his choice of words and throwing of clubs, but I will say that I believe he knows it's not the message he needs to be sending and is trying to change. Sunday at the Buick Open, when he sent an ill-advised shot into the pond on the 13th hole, he pulled his cap over his face and unloaded on himself for making what could've been a game-altering error. Many times this year he has walked by me and sotto voce has berated himself, but without anyone more than a few feet away hearing. Indeed, he's gotten so good at this that his lips barely move. Some call it petulant, but I believe it's a mechanism Woods has long used to sharpen his focus after a mistake. It's been ingrained for a long time as part of his mental strategy and it's not easy to suddenly stop. Does he go too far at times? Yes. But I have witnessed many golfers do worse but never have to pay the price because the cameras weren't trained on their every move.

It's not my job to be an apologist for Tiger Woods—I have certainly criticized him in the past when it's been warranted—but I'm paid to call it as I see it, and I think he too often gets the short end of the stick. The bottom line is that we live in an era where we have the chance of bearing witness to one of the greats, not just of golf but any athletic endeavor, and that should be hard to hate.

A sheepish Feherty rolled his eyes as he walked by me on the practice range on Thursday at Firestone. "I'm not looking forward to this. I don't think he's going to be happy with me," he said. I'd tried to sound hopeful, but in truth I was thinking, "dead man walking," as Feherty wandered over to face the music. Williams stood, as he often did, like a sentry posted next to Woods's black golf bag. He meticulously cleaned each club after its use with a damp towel, then returned it to its proper place. Woods was hitting fairway woods, shaping them as he liked to do, altering their trajectories, then briefly analyzing each before bending over to put another ball on a tee just barely sticking out of the ground. Woods could get into a trancelike state when hitting balls, oblivious to all that was going on around him. But his concentration was broken by the arrival of Feherty. Woods turned to the Irishman and just stared blankly for a beat. Williams remained silent, too. Without saying anything, Woods reached into a pocket of his golf bag, pulled out something I couldn't distinguish, and handed it to Feherty, at which point all three began laughing hysterically. Later I asked Woods what he'd given Feherty. "Beano," he said with a smirk. Feherty was as relieved as a man who'd been spared from the gallows. "He's got a great sense of humor, that man," he said of Woods.

First rounds didn't typically mean too much to Woods. He went about his business, building into a tournament much like a distance runner settled into his race. He didn't want to use up too much energy too early, though Haney had been telling him that he'd find it easier on Sundays if he felt a little more urgency on Thursdays. But that particular first round was different; Woods was motivated as if it were a Sunday. On that sticky morning, Woods was paired with Sergio Garcia. It would be an understatement to say the two didn't like each other. "They can't stand each other," said a source close to Woods. "He's a kid and he's very insecure. He and Tiger have had words before, really pretty strong stuff, but it's not like he's in the same fucking ballpark [as Woods]." Part of Anthony Kim's motivation in drumming Garcia at the 2008 Ryder Cup came from knowing how much Woods would have enjoyed watching. In broad strokes, Garcia believes Woods to be arrogant while Woods thinks the Spaniard was a petulant whiner who hadn't done enough in his career to strut around like a peacock. But, as always with Woods, nothing was ever betrayed in public. On the 2nd hole, after Garcia was forced to lay up to the par 5 and hit an exquisite third shot to a right back flag, which sat on a plateau, Woods, who was on the green in two, quickly acknowledged his foe: "Good shot, Serge." To the bystander, none of the animus of their relationship was remotely obvious. But what was obvious to those who understood the backstory was the way both were grinding. It was a fascinating game within a game. I don't think Woods would so much have minded shooting 75 that day as long as Garcia had shot 76.

Garcia, as he often does given his impressive, effortless swing, hit the ball well all day. He's naturally left-handed, and some savants hold that a stronger lead arm makes for a better golfer.

Mickelson, for instance, is right-handed in all things other than golf. Hogan was also a natural lefty and, like Garcia, not very tall, exceedingly flexible, and double-jointed in the wrists, so creating a lot of clubhead lag came easily. But whereas the young Garcia was, like many kids, a confident and successful putter, by his midtwenties he'd devolved into the worst putter on golf's top shelf. Even the hapless Vijay Singh—who'd won the 1995 Phoenix Open putting with his eyes closed—had kept it together on the greens enough to win three majors. But Garcia, who suffers from the double whammy of a Latin temper and the belief that he's unlucky and gets bad breaks others don't, had become too robotic on the greens, ironically the opposite of his carefree and loose approach to ball striking. As a result of futility on the putting surfaces, Garcia's career had been regressing. He'd won only seven times on the PGA Tour and five of those victories came between May 2001 and June 2004. Since 2005, there was only one win, and although he'd finished in the top ten fifteen times at majors, Garcia hadn't been able to close the deal on Sunday afternoons despite ample opportunities. Appleby recalled seeing the Spaniard in the locker room at the Southern Hills U.S. Open in 2001, standing in front of a full-length mirror "admiring himself" before he went out to play. Garcia was 1 shot behind the leaders and ready for his close-up. An even-par round would have put him into the next day's playoff, ultimately won by Retief Goosen, but on a day the aging Tom Kite shot 64—a score matched by Singh—Garcia could turn in only a miserable 77. And don't think Woods hadn't noticed Garcia's Sunday stumbles. "He knows everything," says Williams.

Garcia, however, had not only hit the ball better than Woods in the first round at Firestone but also appeared comfortable on the greens. Yet though his mistakes were few, they were costly. Woods managed his game better. He didn't do much of note—and again lost the ball to the right as his head dipped too much in the downswing—but came away with a 2-under-par round of 68 with just a solitary bogey. With Woods safely on the last green, it was Garcia's 2-under-par round that seemed in jeopardy. He'd missed the fairway far to the left, then hit a pitching wedge over the trees that ran too far and settled near a tree trunk, 90 yards from the green, in the right rough. "It seemed like nothing good wanted to happen for me on that hole," Garcia later bemoaned. "I have no idea how that ball ended up there against that tree." As he stood by the tree, assessing his rotten luck and shaking his head in disgust, he seemed so different from the nineteen-year-old swashbuckler the world had first encountered at Medinah at the 1999 PGA. There he made his name with a brave shot played from next to a tree. As he ran up the sloping fairway, skipping to see where his ball had finished, he was the picture of the exuberance and optimism of youth. Ten years, though, is a lifetime on the Tour. Woods won that PGA, his second major. But it seemed to be only a matter of time before Garcia would break through, too. He looked that week for all the world a natural rival to Woods. But Garcia's time in the sun never came. If you wanted to be unkind, you'd answer "fourteen majors" if someone asked the difference between the two. But Garcia still had enough fire in his belly to somehow scramble a par on that last hole in Akron. "I hit a great third shot and made the putt," he later proudly said. For once, at least, he hadn't had his colors lowered by Tiger Woods. Garcia, a rabid fan of Real Madrid, knows that some days a draw can be closer to a win than to a loss.

"Perfect par, wasn't it?" said Woods with raised eyebrows when I asked him about Garcia's last-hole dramatics. "Four shots." After emerging from the scoring tent, Garcia smiled when I asked him to remember back to Medinah. "I've been out here eleven years but it feels like it's been about four. It's amazing how fast time goes. I know some people say it could've been better, but I'm happy with my career so far. I mean, it could've been worse, too. Taking Tiger away, I'm only twenty-nine and I think it's been pretty good." And then Garcia betrayed what lies between the two men, noting that it was "always good" to play with Woods because "you see how he can get it around even without hitting it very good." It was a little slap, not unlike Mickelson's famous backhanded compliment to Woods in 2003: "Tiger is the only player who is good enough to overcome the equipment he is stuck with." But don't think Woods took the high road. He knew full well the last time he and Garcia had been paired had been in the final round at Hoylake three years before. The day Garcia dressed all in lemon, or was it banana? The day Woods won the British Open and, of course, Garcia did not. "I think the last time was at Hoylake, was that the last time?" Woods said with a straight face when I asked him during his postround interview. "I think that was the last time that I played with him." Neither did Woods resist temptation when he was asked whether he thought Garcia would've won a major by now. "Yeah, I would think so. You would've thought. He's been so close. He's been in the final group a few times and he's been right there with a chance. Hasn't gotten over the hurdle yet. It's just a matter of time. Sergio certainly has the talent to do it." Left unsaid was Woods's long-held conviction that talent alone is never enough.

Woods is blessed with a tremendous appetite for work. He rises by 5:30, eats breakfast, and by 6:30 is in the gym, where he has no ego. No golfer is more knowledgeable than Woods when it comes to working out, and none is more committed. He can bench-press three hundred pounds, but because he wants a golf-specific body, he works instead with less weight and more reps. It's pertinent to note that Woods appears much larger on television that he actually is; he's maybe a shade under six one and weighs about 185

pounds, though if he plays a lot of golf in the summer he struggles keeping his weight up. Because he has maintained a thirty-
inch waist into his midthirties, has worked hard to broaden his
shoulders, and has a small head, Woods can appear on television
like an NFL linebacker; he's probably built more like a light free
safety. After a rigorous ninety-minute workout, Woods begins his
golf practice. He hits balls for about an hour, then putts for about
thirty minutes before nine holes on the Isleworth course. Rein-
forcing the idea of a day at work, he allows himself a one-hour
lunch break. After that comes two more hours on the practice
range followed by an hour of chipping and putting and then another nine holes. The day is rounded out with an hour more on
the putting green. Woods firmly believes that in order to be the
best, he has to work the hardest. Corey Carroll, a junior whom
Woods gravitated to in 2004 after watching his eight-hour days on
the practice tee at Isleworth, told *Golf Digest* that "as gifted as he
is, I know that every piece of swing that works the way he wants
it to work, he's had to fight for. He basically tells me, 'You know
how to work hard, so you've got the toughest part down. Keep
learning and keep grinding. And see how far it will take you.'"

In Akron, I asked Woods whether he had more respect for
the toiler who worked hard over the dilettante with natural talent. "Absolutely. I mean, I think that they always ask me who
are the guys you should go watch play, who are the guys you
think you should model yourself after, and I always say Paddy
and Jim Furyk and Vijay. Those guys work so hard on their games.
A guy like Paddy and a guy like Jim, they don't have the length
that Vijay does, but how they manage themselves around the golf
course, I think everyone can learn from that, especially kids. And
the work ethic for Paddy, you know what he's done with [coach]
Bob [Torrance] over the years, countless hours, in the snow, it
doesn't matter, he's going to get it done. I've seen him miss cuts

and he's out there all weekend long practicing and getting ready for the next week. I admire guys like that because that's how you become better. You have to go earn it. And I think Paddy is a great example of a guy who goes out there and earns it each and every day."

It was no surprise that Woods found much to admire in Harrington, golf's most blue-collar champion. The Irishman is just as obsessive as Woods, though less talented, which perhaps makes his determination even greater given his three major wins. Harrington isn't a natural at the game but he possesses a huge heart and a single-minded desire. This is the stuff of Woods's dreams. And perhaps only Woods could truly comprehend what Harrington had done after winning those three majors: taken apart his golf swing and rebuilt it entirely. The rebuilding process was a disaster, at least in the short term, as Harrington labored through the no-man's-land between the old swing and the new. After two rounds at the Bridgestone, though, Harrington had the lead on his own at 7 under par. He revealed he'd finally done enough thinking about his swing and began to concentrate on scoring again. It was interesting that while many of his peers thought Harrington had been out of his mind to change anything after winning those majors, Woods not only understood but also applauded him. "You have to make changes in order to get better, but a lot of times you're going to get worse before you do get better. It's a matter of other parts of your game trying to pick you up and understanding how to score when you don't have your best stuff. You have to believe what you're doing is right even though people tell you what you're doing is wrong. I've been through that twice, and I think I've turned out on the good side both times. It's just that you're going to get a lot of bombardment, not just from the media but from fans, from friends, family, whatever it may be; they're going to always doubt and question you. But you've got to have the internal resolve to stick with what you believe is going to be right and that you're going to get better. Paddy has always done things according to his own accord. He's worked extremely hard. We've all admired him for that, because I don't know how many second-place finishes he had [30], but he really didn't win that much. But then he kept progressing and kept getting better and better and more consistent, and then all of a sudden, boom, he's a three-time major championship winner. That's the thing you have to admire about some guys, when they are able to do that."

Harrington doesn't dislike Woods at all, but he's like Woods in that he recognizes that there can be only one winner, and therefore, friendships can go only so far. Harrington says that he is his father's son. His father was an Irish cop who boxed and kept a single-digit golf handicap. Among the many traits he passed on to his son was stubbornness. "That's my nature; I'd be the very stubborn one who if I was told to do something," Harrington said, "I'd want to do it my way. I'm not interested in standing still. I want to get better as a player. If I thought I was standing still, you know, there's no incentive for me to get out there. . . . The improvement is what I enjoy in the game: feeling like I'm going to be a better player tomorrow, next week, next month, next year."

And so these birds of a feather, who'd first stared each other down in the 1995 Walker Cup—where the heavily favored Americans were beaten by Great Britain and Ireland—arrived at the 1st tee Sunday afternoon with the tournament at stake. No quarter asked for, and none given. Woods began the final round 3 shots behind. He plays differently depending on his positioning. Given the fact that Harrington's not one to crumble, Woods decided to come out swinging. An exquisite eagle at the 2nd hole put the Irishman on his heels. Woods was at his celestial best on the front nine, not missing a green. He had putts of 14, 23, 10, 13, 27, 19,

14, 16, and 7 feet, and the real surprise was that he made only three birdies to go with the eagle. Nonetheless, already 5 under by the turn, Woods had given himself a 2-shot cushion in what was a two-man race. No one ever hunts down Tiger Woods when he's got a lead with nine holes to play on a Sunday afternoon. But golf's pugnacious Cinderella Man wouldn't go away. Like James Braddock, the Irish-American underdog with granite in his right hand and in his chin who shocked Max Baer to win the heavyweight championship of the world in 1935, Harrington refused to go to the canvas.

In other circumstances, Woods would have not felt threatened. But he sensed the tournament wasn't over. "I told Stevie, we need at least two birdies on this back nine to win the tournament. I figured Paddy . . . he's just a grinder. Considering that he's won three major championships of late, and I believe the last two he shot 32 on the back nine, so you know he's not going to go anywhere." Harrington kept his head, making steady pars, and on the 11th hole it was Woods who blinked first. After hardly missing a shot all day, Woods found himself under a tree. He recovered well but not close enough to the hole to have a legitimate birdie chance. Harrington, seizing the moment, stepped on a pitching wedge and made the 10-footer for birdie. There was no question that Woods felt the pressure. He hit another poor iron onto the next hole, a par 3, missing the green for the first time all day; he was lucky to escape with a par, sinking a long putt. But the swing, as it had at crucial times already throughout the year, was becoming erratic. Woods's short game couldn't save him from consecutive bogeys on the 13th and 14th holes. Harrington had a 1-shot lead but had done nothing especially spectacular. It was Woods who was falling apart.

With three holes to play, Woods was desperate. He needed birdies. Or an implosion from Harrington. But the Woods radar malfunctioned again on the 16th, shooting his tee shot left on the downhill par 5. He had no choice but to pitch out and leave himself 178 yards for a third shot onto a green that players weren't able to hold with lob wedges. Harrington, meanwhile, missed the fairway to the right and also faced a lay up. But the Irishman, who is meticulous and never rushes his shot, was flustered—and it had nothing to do with winning the tournament or Tiger Woods. A rules official had placed him and Woods on the clock, meaning they had been warned for the second time for falling behind the group ahead of them. Harrington had long had a reputation as one of the slowest players in golf. Such reputations are hard to shake, but the truth was that he'd become much faster. "Paddy's a pleasure to play with nowadays," says Williams. Feeling the heat of the stopwatch, Harrington rushed his punch shot. Instead of leaving himself 80 or 90 yards, his pulled effort left him in the rough above a fairway bunker, 164 yards to the hole and with an awkward stance. It got worse for Harrington when Woods played what Williams later called "the best shot he'd hit all year." Woods threw an 8-iron high, high into the air, taking dead aim at a pin cut near the water on a hard green. Not only did the shot hold, it spun back to within 9 inches. Harrington sent his third over the green, then made the cardinal error, putting a flop shot into the water.

"That's what Tiger's about in moments like that," says Williams. "He forced Paddy's hand on that fourth shot. If he doesn't stuff it in there, do you think Paddy's going to play such a risky fourth?" By the time the shots were counted, Harrington finished with an eight, golf's dreaded snowman. And with that, the tournament was over. Woods put a cherry on top with a birdie on the last. He had now held the trophy aloft in twenty-two of his previous forty starts since the 2006 British Open. "Imagine if you weren't in a slump," I said to him in jest as he was congratulated by his family, again in a quiet corner, away from the crowds and cameras.

Afterward, in his victory press conference, perhaps because he could afford to be magnanimous, Woods seemed more annoyed than Harrington with the slow-play ruling. After all, did the executives at CBS Sports care that they might have to run three minutes late given the drama of that final round? And the irony was that even after all the misadventures on that 16th hole, Woods and Harrington were back in position by the 17th. "I'm sorry that [rules official] John [Paramor] got in the way of such a great battle for sixteen holes, and we're going at it head-to-head and unfortunately that happened," Woods said. For a man who'd rather have his teeth pulled than be dragged into a public controversy, Woods wasn't pulling his punches. He later told me he was so thoroughly enjoying the heat of the battle that he felt cheated. I got the impression that Woods was more upset with Paramor for what he'd denied him than for throwing off Harrington. "This is why I play," he said. He really had wanted to see if he had it in him to win with his back to the wall. Harrington chose not to make excuses—that is the sort of man he is—and though the ruling bothered him, he was more annoyed with himself. But lost in the headlines of yet another Woods win was the vulnerability he'd shown on the back nine. It was not lost on Harrington. After they shook hands on the final green, he looked Woods squarely in the eye. "We'll do battle again."

CHAPTER 13

PGA Championship

Y ou betcha that Minnesotans are the friendliest, most welcoming of Americans. And, ya darn tootin' they love their golf Up North. More golf is played, on a per capita basis, in the land of 10,000 lakes than in any other state. Minnesotans are also imbued with a sense of civic responsibility, so it's not uncommon to find them marrying these passions in organizations like the USGA. The backstory of Minnesota's influence in the game is key to understanding how Tiger Woods found himself for the second time in seven years at Hazeltine National Golf Club contesting the year's final major. The Twin Cities boast some wonderful courses; unfortunately, Hazeltine National isn't among them. The PGA of America owns Valhalla, in the boonies of Louisville, so following the money explains how that most uninspiring of courses came to host two PGA Championships and a Ryder Cup. But how was Hazeltine awarded two U.S. Opens, two PGA Championships, two U.S. Women's Opens, one U.S. Senior Open, a U.S. Amateur, and the 2016 Ryder Cup? Surely, such honors should be reserved for one of the game's grand stages? The short story was that Totton Heffelfinger, who in 1952 became the USGA's youngest president, founded the club with the idea of creating a venue on which to bring major championships back to his home state. Gems like Interlachen—where Bobby Jones won the U.S. Open in his grand slam year of 1930—or A. W. Tillinghast's Rochester Golf and Country Club or the Donald Ross classic Minikahda with its stunning views of the downtown skyline simply weren't long enough; they'd been made obsolete by technology like so many other beauties from the golden age of course design. It didn't hurt Hazeltine's cause, either, that one of its most prominent members, Minneapolis personal injury attorney Reed Mackenzie, eventually followed Heffelfinger as USGA president.

The candid Dave Hill lacked only tact when he replied "eighty acres of corn and a few cows" upon being asked what the course needed after his second-place finish at 1970 U.S. Open. "They ruined a good farm when they built this course. Plow it up and start over. Just because you cut the grass doesn't mean you have a golf course." Hill later claimed that he'd been ready to drive a tractor to the presentation ceremony if he'd won the tournament. Almost half the field didn't break 80 on the first day of that U.S. Open and the other half didn't have anything very nice to say, either. It was not a fair test of golf, merely punitive. Designer Robert Trent Jones had crossed the line: brawn was fine, but it hadn't been counterbalanced. There was too much yin, not enough yang (though the lack of Yang at Hazeltine would be soon remedied). And, to make it worse, Jones's layout lacked any aesthetic to offset its arduousness. Hazeltine serves to remind that greatness can't ever be manufactured.

The club's members were, predictably, aghast at Hill's bluntness and set about reshaping the design; doglegs at three hundred yards from the tee weren't ever necessary and neither were fairways that sloped with the dogleg, rolling balls into the rough no matter where they landed. Hazletine would in the ensuing years receive more face-lifts than a Palm Springs socialite. The most prominent came in the late eighties, at the hands of Robert Trent Jones's son, Rees, which launched his career as "the Open Doctor," the man to call if a course wanted to pass muster with the USGA. Much to the chagrin, by the way, of his estranged brother, fellow designer Bobby Jones Jr., with whom Rees had a poisonous sibling rivalry. But, in the end, no matter its shortcomings, Hazeltine ultimately offered space for corporate tents, parking, merchandising pavilions, and television compounds; somewhere along the way that became the most important criterion when it came to choosing major championship venues.

Woods and his family had boarded his 2008 Gulfstream G550 at the Canton/Akron airport and flown directly to the Twin Cities, where Woods had rented a beautiful home on Lake Minnewashta in Chanhassen—next door to former baseball pitcher Rick Helling—for the week. Woods was so relaxed that the day before the tournament began, he didn't even bother going to Hazeltine, instead spending the day with his family on the lake and then taking them to see the Disney 3-D movie, *G-Force*, about guinea pig secret agents. The day before, at his pretournament Tuesday afternoon press conference, Woods acknowledged that length and brute force would probably win the day at this championship. At 7,674 yards, Hazeltine was the longest course in majors history by 138 yards, which as good as eliminated much of the field. "It's a heck of a lot longer than what we played in 2002," Woods said. "It's going to be just a great test all week. It's playing a little bit soft right now. I don't know how much it's going to dry out with all of the rain they had, but . . . you're going to have to hit the ball pretty good out there, especially if they play it all the way back." The news conference was notable, too, because Woods disputed a story by the AP's Doug Ferguson, the rare writer with whom he's close, saying that Woods was to be fined by the PGA Tour for his verbal attack on John Paramor in the aftermath of the Bridgestone Invitational. Slugger White, the PGA Tour's chief rules official, had made no secret in Akron of his belief that his British colleague had acted correctly in putting Woods and Harrington on the clock and, further, that Woods had gone too far with his criticism. Ferguson had a well-earned reputation for reliability, and Woods had often complained that he'd been the most fined golfer in Tour history, so there was no reason to doubt the story. But Woods took great pleasure in not only denying that he'd been fined—which the Tour soon after confirmed was true—but also stepping up his attack on Paramor. It was Woods flexing his muscle; he'd called Finchem's bluff and won. Woods always paid his conduct-unbecoming fines without complaint, but he felt he was right and Finchem knew he needed Tiger Woods more than Woods needed him.

Attending a Woods press conference, especially at a major when questions are posed by those who hadn't heard them answered in spades before, could be best likened to panning for gold; there's mostly just plain rocks, a little fool's gold, but every now and again an unexpected nugget emerges to wake you from your slumber. Woods was asked whether he could beat the Tiger Woods of 2000. It was a question that cut to the heart of everything Woods believed about having gotten better every day of his life. But was he really better now than he was in 2000? Many didn't believe so, from Harmon to those players victimized by the force of nature that was Tiger Woods at the turn of the millennium. Woods, perhaps because it was necessary for his own sanity, held to the belief that he was a better player in 2009. "I would win now. I know how to manage my game a hell of a lot better than I did back then. Just understanding how to get the ball around; I have so many more golf shots now to get me around the golf course. And that's just experience. That's nine more years of learning how to play and how to manage my game around a golf course. And I'll probably say the same thing in nine more years, because I'll have that much more understanding mentally. Physically, I don't know if I'll be able to hit the ball quite as far, but understanding how to play, that's just years of experience." Five days after he uttered these words, I came to seriously doubt whether the Tiger Woods of 2000, a young man who if up by seven shots wanted to win by eight, and if up by eight, then tried to make it nine, would've lost to the conservative strategist at the 2009 PGA. Certainly, the Tiger Woods of 2000 never missed a putt he had to make.

On a humid Thursday morning, Woods arrived at the 10th tee, his first hole of the championship, feeling good about settling an old score with the PGA and Hazeltine: seven years before, Rich Beem hadn't buckled under the pressure of four closing birdies from Woods. It was the first time Woods had finished runner-up at a major, ending a streak of sorts, and the man has an elephant's memory and a vigilante's capacity for retribution. By 1:14 p.m., Woods took the lead by himself at the ninety-first PGA Championship. If it were a horse race, I thought, I'd have lowered my binoculars. He was Secretariat in a swoosh. "Kinda ominous," said Beem, who for old times' sake played alongside Woods and watched him shoot an impressive 5-under 67. "He's got a pretty good track record from the front." Only once when Woods had started a major that well—the 1998 British Open when he was only twenty-two and still hadn't quite deciphered the vagaries of links golf—had he not gone on to lift the trophy. In 2000, at both the U.S. Open and PGA, he began with 6-under-par 66s and went on to win, while at the 2000 and 2006 British Opens, he fired 67s and won those, too.

It wasn't just his score that separated Woods from everyone

else. This performance had none of the smoke and mirrors he'd relied on for other low rounds during the comeback season. "Just how efficient he played today," said Beem when asked what impressed him. "It wasn't anything crazy. No big tee shots way right or way left or anything like that. It was easy." The score could've been lower because several putts burned the lip of the cup. "I played really well today," agreed Woods. "I hit just a bunch of good shots. And this round could have been really low. I missed a bunch of putts out there, so it was just a very positive start." What was obvious, too, was that his demeanor was very different from what it had been in the year's first three majors. He was neither grumpy nor overly serious nor particularly concerned. He was relaxed, talking more than he usually did and even joking throughout the round with Harrington, who'd somehow become a permanent playing partner. Those who have played with Woods away from the cameras say he's impossible to beat when he's carefree and relaxed. No thinking gets between him and his play. He just, as Nike likes to say, does it. "I felt pretty comfortable," he told me. Not that he was awarding himself the tournament, but Woods's answer when he was asked whether he'd ever played as well as he could and lost a major was telling. "There are times I've put it together and I've had some pretty good margins of victory. When I'm playing well, I usually don't make that many mistakes." Woods gave away his plan for the next three days when he said he'd "just keep plodding along . . . The whole idea is not to make that many mistakes. All the majors that I've won, I've made very few mistakes for the week."

The wind began to blow on the prairies on the second day, playing havoc with golf balls and putting more squares than circles on scorecards. Woods began with a bogey and for good measure finished with one, too, but such was his control on the tournament that with a round of 70 he'd managed to increase his lead to 4 shots at the midway point. Woods's Friday round was a salient lesson in what separated him from the Lilliputians. Those who teed off in the morning, both on Thursday and Friday, got the better conditions. But the Friday afternoon crowd, Woods's side of the draw, got hot, blustery winds and greens that had already become bumpy and treacherous. Woods, however, was the only player in the top sixteen after the opening round to break par on the second day. "It was tough out there, you had to play the wind on putts today . . . I had to kind of grind it out," he said. "I could have easily shot a couple over par today, but I turned it into an under-par round." Because he so often plays brilliantly, Woods's ability to grind is too often overlooked. The 2003 PGA at Oak Hill was at that stage his worst finish as a professional at a major, a tie for thirty-ninth, but I recall that every day of that tournament he should've shot 80. He hit twenty greens in regulation the entire week and shot only 12 over par. I thought it was a feat just this side of a small-*m* miracle. When I told Adam Scott of Woods's scrambling prowess, he shook his head. "Five greens [in regulation] a day around this place and he's only shooting a couple over each round? How many times do you think I got up and down this week?" I had no idea, I told him. Scott said it was "simple to figure out." He didn't once save par after missing a green. He'd missed only twenty greens for the week and made twenty bogeys, to finish 4 shots better than Woods at 8 over par. "That guy's a freak," said Scott as he left.

Woods with a 4-shot lead after 36 holes was money in the bank. He'd won all eight times in majors where he'd held the halfway lead and had won his last twelve events with the halfway lead. "Just because I'm twelve for twelve doesn't mean anything tomorrow. You've got to go out there and play and those shots, those things I did twelve times doesn't do a damn bit of good to-morrow. You have to place your golf ball around the golf course, you've got to play and execute, and tomorrow is supposed to be just as windy, so again, another day of executing and being very patient." Even if Woods was not yet ready to start celebrating, a fifteenth major and a record-tying fifth PGA—joining Nicklaus and Walter Hagen—seemed to the rest of us just a formality. Indeed, the sages in the press tent had already all but awarded him the championship. So bored and bereft of anything to write were the assembled scribes that Barker Davis of the *Washington Times* even felt emboldened enough to throw out the *c*-word during Woods's second-round press conference. "We know there's been some instances where it just didn't happen for you at majors," he said to Woods. "But in your opinion, has there ever been a single instance in a major where you've done what you consider to be choking?" Woods seemed stunned by the question, appearing to briefly shake his head but said nothing, leading to what was a very awkward silence. The PGA media official moderating the press conference, Kelly Elbin, finally broke the silence with a statement: "We'll take that to be a no." Davis had regretted his phrasing, which Woods felt was inappropriate, but by Sunday night the question could've been revisited. It would've taken a brave soul to dare.

Although much would be written about the final round at Hazeltine, Woods's greatest mistake was the major miscalculation he made in the third round. With the winds whipping up again Saturday afternoon, Woods thought there was little chance that any of his rivals would post a good score. Woods, like Nicklaus before him, prided himself on knowing just what number he needed to shoot to keep the pack at bay, but he got that number wrong that Saturday. He figured that aiming conservatively to the fat of greens and safely 2 putting while throwing in a few birdies on the par 5s and keeping bogeys off his card would be enough to maintain his advantage. It was not. His round of 71 had in fact caused his cushion atop the leaderboard to shrink from four shots to just two when the Korean Y. E. Yang, who'd battled to make the cut, threw a 67 at Woods. "I thought it was going to be playing a little bit more difficult today, but it wasn't. They gave us a lot of room on a lot of these pins, so you could be fairly aggressive. I just felt that with my lead, I erred on the side of caution most of the time. If I did have a good look at it, a good number at it, I took aim right at it; otherwise I was just dumping the ball on the green and 2 putting." He could have gotten away with his conservatism had he capitalized on the par 5s. Instead, a man who has built his career on mauling par 5s, averaging birdie on better than half of the par 5s he played, could muster only four pars. More important, the cutting of the Woods's lead had a psychological impact on his competitors. "We have nothing to lose," said Harrington, who was the defending champion and remained in the hunt. "Everybody expects it's going to be him, so we get a free run at it."

The last time Woods had lost a third-round lead that he held alone on the PGA Tour was the first time he'd been in that situation: the 1996 Quad Cities Classic, making Ed Fiori the answer to a trivia question. Twice after that, both times at Eastlake in Atlanta, Woods had failed to win while holding a share of the third-round lead. But never had he lost a major when he'd started the final round with the lead. Indeed, each of his fourteen majors was won from the front, making him, unequivocally, the greatest closer in sports. This single statistic, more than any other, formed the foundation of the Tiger Woods mystique. If it crumbled, the entire edifice would suddenly seem wobbly. But Woods had an ace up his sleeve. "Tiger closes great because he knows the other guys are going to struggle," Nicklaus once said. "All he needs to do is play good, solid golf. I did the same."

But what constituted good, solid golf? Increasingly, what it meant to Woods was to make pars and watch his opponents implode. His final-round scoring average in the fourteen majors he'd won was 69.5. His playing partners in those rounds averaged 73.14, almost four strokes worse. Only two, Bob May at the 2000 PGA and Chris DiMarco at the 2005 Masters, bettered his score. So the lesson Woods learned over the years was to do no more than sit back and make pars. Harrington had told me in Akron that he didn't mind losing to Woods as long as he didn't "hand it to him and let him just make pars to beat me." The Irishman had won the 2006 Dunlop-Phoenix tournament in Japan against Woods because he sensed Woods wasn't paying attention. "Tiger was cruising home. I could see he was in cruise control. He was playing lovely golf and was settling for pars. In that situation I saw an opportunity for myself, even though I hadn't played particularly well up to that, that if I could start making birdies, maybe he's just taken the foot off the pedal a bit early. That worked out well for me. We had a playoff that day and I came out on top."

Woods's playing partner in that final round, however, wasn't Harrington but Yang, whose only real claim to fame prior to 2009 was beating a field that included Woods in Shanghai three years earlier. Yang found his way onto the U.S. Tour in 2008 but never got any traction, finishing outside the top 150, and had to return to Q-school. He barely made it out of the second stage but went on to earn his playing privileges back and responded by winning his first event of 2009, the Honda Classic. But there wasn't much follow-up to that success, and Yang, it had to be said, didn't seem to have the pedigree to outlast Woods; this was, at best, Chuck Wepner, "the Bayonne Bleeder," going up against Muhammad Ali. Yang had grown up working on his parents' farm on the island of Jeju, dreaming of becoming a bodybuilder and someday opening his own gym. He was drawn to golf only after an injury ended his bodybuilding dreams and he landed a job picking up balls at a driving range. Yang taught himself how to swing and was good enough to break par at the age of twenty-two, but he was already a year older than Woods was when he'd won his first Masters and still faced compulsory military service. But he persevered with his golf ambitions, moving to New Zealand to try and eke out a career as a professional. He'd had a smattering of success but nothing at this altitude. Prior to arriving at Hazeltine, Yang had played in only seven majors and made just two cuts. His best-ever finish was a tie for thirtieth at the 2007 Masters. But he seemed to me to be a wild card.

As I spoke to him, through his interpreter, that Saturday afternoon on the putting green, he seemed oddly at peace and not especially intimidated. He also seemed to have faith in himself, which might just be half the battle. "I believe in luck," he said through his agent. "And it's certainly been a lucky year so far. I think it all started from the second stage of Q-school and it was the last day, last putt, and I made a 7-foot uphill putt and I think the confidence just took a turn and ever since then it's been sort of, I wouldn't say downhill, in an easy way, but it's been easy and that's why I have one win under my belt now. So, yeah, it's a lot of luck. I mean, apart from working on my game, it's been a lot of luck and also, yes, that helps a lot with your confidence as well." He admitted that he would be nervous playing alongside Woods, "but I've been looking forward to it. And I've thought about this, playing with Tiger recently, and it came true so fast. If I could concentrate and keep my flow, you know, not get caught up in all the rhythm and just keep playing the game, I think I'll be fine." What stayed with me, too, was Yang's assertion that he would try to "not go over par." What a strange and very small goal, I'd thought. Genius, as it turned out.

Fred Couples sent Woods a text message wishing him luck that Saturday night and was surprised when Woods responded immediately. Woods rarely communicated with friends during the week of a major, so Couples interpreted the text as an indication that all was well. Certainly it was true that neither Woods nor Williams felt anything different about that Sunday from the fourteen that had come before. "Everything was normal," says Williams. And so it seemed, after two penetrating, precise blows on the difficult opening hole—mercifully playing downwind for the first time all week—left Woods with a 6-footer for birdie. He stalked the putt, looked at it from every angle, then called over Williams. They huddled over the putt and settled on a line. The ball didn't touch the hole, missing low the whole way. "That was disappointing," Williams said afterward. "We both misread that putt." If it were just that one putt, Woods would've won the tournament. But he was abysmal on the greens, needing 33 putts. After Yang birdied the 3rd hole, Woods 3-putted the 4th for bogey for the second straight day and, suddenly, they were tied. Twice more Woods took the lead back, but both times he threw it away with bogeys. Yang, meanwhile, was parring Woods to death. "To me, the pivotal hole was 13," Williams said later of the exacting 240-yard par 3. "Yang's in that left-hand bunker. The odds of getting up and down from there are slim. Tiger hit that 3-iron real close, 6 or 7 feet, best shot he hit all week. As we're walking to the green, I'm thinking if Tiger makes that putt, it's probably going to be a 2-shot swing. But Yang gets it up and down and Tiger misses. Then he chips it in on the next hole." Yang's eagle chip from just short of the 14th green got him the lead—Woods had to make a long birdie putt just to stay only 1 back—and the Korean celebrated with a fist pump that he later called "my best Tiger imitation." Woods was not amused.

It should be said that Woods has never been above playing mind games with opponents. If they like to play quickly, he'll throw out the anchor. He'll dawdle to his ball, take an eternity on the greens, and do whatever he has to do to throw an opponent off his rhythm. Conversely, with slow players—like, for instance, Letzig on the last day at Warwick Hills—he ups the tempo and forces them out of their comfort zone. If he is in the penultimate group on a Sunday, he'll purposely take his time to putt until the leaders are in sight because he wants them to see him make the putt and hear the gallery's roar. If an opponent has a 3- or 4-footer for par, Woods always finishes putting out first, then stands to the side of the green because he knows the galleries have come to see him and moves to the next hole, creating a commotion that only adds to the distractions his opponent faces. "He uses every trick in the book," acknowledges a member of the Woods camp, which was why it was amusing to see Yang crowding Woods while he was over putts on the back nine at Hazeltine. It visibly annoyed Woods, who twice backed off and stared at Yang. But Yang didn't flinch.

It's difficult to say exactly where Woods lost that championship, but failing to birdie the par-5 15th—he'd made only one birdie on his final eight par 5s—didn't help. If there was a hole when I'd begun to wonder if the game was up, it was at the signature 16th. Seven years before, Beem hit an approach into the par 4 that should've kicked into the reeds on the right of the green. Somehow, the ball stayed up and, from off the green, Beem drained a bomb for an improbable birdie that would ultimately deny Woods the win. Yang had a 1-shot lead going into the 16th and there was no way he would venture anywhere right of the flag. But he pushed his iron shot badly. Like Beem, his ball somehow stayed up after flirting with the hazard. He safely made par to match Woods. On the next, a 190-yard par 3, Yang hit a 6-iron to the front of the green, leaving a long putt. Williams thought a 6-iron was the right play. Anthony Kim's caddie later told him Kim had hit a 5-iron that barely made it onto the front of the green. But Williams felt that because Woods was "pumped up," a 7-iron might be the more prudent club. "I thought he could hit that as hard as he wanted and no way was he hitting a 7-iron over that green," he said. And yet there was a way. "I got the downwind gust," Woods later said. "I couldn't ask for a better golf swing, just hit it right over the top of the flag." Woods sailed the flag and finished over the green, his ball resting in gnarled rough. "It was one of those spots that I don't think anyone had walked in all week so it wasn't flattened at all," said Williams. "We had a shit lie, just a shit lie." Woods couldn't get up and down but was dealt a lifeline when Yang left his approach putt short and yipped his par attempt. He'd betrayed nerves for the first time.

It seemed the aura of Tiger Woods still had a bit of kick to it. Woods unleashed a gorgeous drive on the last, finding the right side of the fairway, from which he had a perfect view of the back left flag. Yang finished down the left and had a tree in his way. As the players walked up the sloping fairway, it was very conceivable that Yang would make a bogey and Woods would birdie and author yet another incredible comeback. But from 207 yards, Yang played the shot of his life, a hybrid into the elevated green that bounced just onto the putting surface and came to rest well within birdie range. Woods appeared stunned. He had 197 yards and was left with no choice but to hunt that flag. He hit a lovely draw, but he was too aggressive and the ball kicked into the rough. Yang stood impassively to the side of the green as Woods stalked his chip. "I think only, 'Tiger chipping, miss the chipping, just please,'" Yang later said. Woods did miss, leading to the most surreal and anticlimactic of finishes. Woods marked his ball, then Yang made his putt, leaving Tiger Woods with the last putt of a major on a Sunday, which meant absolutely nothing.

The shock reverberating throughout the golf world was palpable as Yang lifted his golf bag above his head in celebration. How did a five nine journeyman who considered himself "lower than

average" among Tour professionals slay this Goliath? I asked him
how he managed to do what Mickelson and Els and Garcia and
Singh and Goosen and Duval and Westwood et al. hadn't been
able to do? "The great names you've mentioned, when they tee off
with Tiger, their competitive juices sort of flow out and they go
head-to-head and try to win," said Yang, through his agent. "For
me, I don't consider myself as a great golfer. So my goal today
was just hit at least even [par], not go over par. I think that's probably the mind-set that I had." Later, he expanded on the reasons
behind his success. "I always dreamed about this. Try to visual-
ize and try to bring up a mock strategy on how to win, if I ever
played against Tiger. When the chance came, I sort of thought,
'Hey, I could always play a good round of golf and Tiger could
always . . . Tiger's good, but he could always have a bad day.' And
I guess today was one of those days."

Woods, it must be said, handled the loss with complete professionalism. He knew that this was the equivalent of Michael
Jordan hitting the rim on the buzzer in game seven, Muhammad
Ali walking into a Butterbean roundhouse, or Joe Montana over-
throwing Jerry Rice with a Super Bowl ring on the line.

"Y. E. played great all day, I don't think he really missed a shot
all day," Woods said. Of course, he bemoaned his putting, which
really cost him the championship. "I was in control of the tournament most of the day. I was playing well, hitting the ball well.
I was making nothing, but still either tied for the lead or ahead.
Unfortunately, I just didn't make the putts when I needed to make
them."

With that, Woods left the media center and headed to his car,
where his daughter, Sam, awaited. He changed his shoes in the
car while she hugged him, an embrace that lasted quite a while.
She had no idea what had happened to her daddy, only that she
was back in his arms, and there seemed comfort in that for both

of them. Greenspan had packed his suitcase and brought it to the media center that day, saying he hoped to get one of the twenty seats on the G550 for the flight back to Florida. I'd wondered if he might not have wanted to fly commercial, given that the mood on that flight wasn't going to be very pleasant.

Yang, meanwhile, basked in the glory of becoming Asia's first major champion. He and his wife and three children lingered in a state of disbelief outside the media center as the light faded on what he called "the best day of my life." "Rematch?" Yang said when asked about meeting up with Woods again. "Never again. I would like to stay as the guy who won over Tiger at the PGA Championship and that's it. No redos." No one knew better than Woods that in major championship golf, there could be no mulligans. His mother, meanwhile, wanted the names of any writers who'd called her son a "choker." Woods had long maintained that his mother was the far more "brutal" of his parents.

CHAPTER 14

The Playoffs

New York is America's last great newspaper town. Newspapers are on the road to consolidation, if not extinction, elsewhere, but in the Big Apple, they have yet to go the way of the dinosaurs. Three newspapers are still alive and kicking in the city while many more remain relevant in the outlying sprawl of New Jersey, Westchester, and Connecticut. Perhaps their survival is merely a function of New York City being a commuter city where wireless signals can't penetrate into subways, but, whatever the reason, journalists remain gainfully employed. And the competition of America's most cutthroat newspaper market keeps editors and reporters on their toes. The city's two feisty tabloids, the *Post* and the *Daily News*, live to scoop each other— the *Post*'s combative Australian editor, Col Allan, delights in any opportunity to denounce his rival as the "Daily Snooze"—and together the tabs take great joy in mocking as ponderous and out-of-touch the éminence grise, the *Times*. Theirs is a dynamic pointedly portrayed in the film *The Paper*, starring Michael Keaton, who, after being haughtily told that he's missed his chance of "covering the world" by turning down a job at a paper modeled after the *Times*, declares, "I don't live in the world, I live in New York City!" That is the attitude of the tabs: they cover the world's most important city. Once Tiger Woods committed to playing the Barclays, the first time he'd entered a regular PGA Tour event in the metropolitan area in six years, he was squarely in their sights.

Editors demanded to know where Woods was staying and what he would be doing away from the course during the first week of the FedEx Cup playoffs. Three years before, while competing at the U.S. Open at Winged Foot after the death of his father, Woods moored his 155-foot yacht at the out-of-the-way Derecktor Shipyards, where *Privacy* was carefully hidden behind a large shed. But not carefully enough for the newspapers, which duly reported its whereabouts, much to the chagrin of the Woods camp. Woods, however, brought neither the yacht nor his family to Bethpage for the Open. It was perhaps not coincidental, given that he had renewed his friendship in June with the thirty-four-year-old New York nightclub hostess Rachel Uchitel, whose taste in paramours extended from the famous all the way down to the merely rich. Upon returning to New York in August, Woods again traveled alone and would stay in a hotel. Despite the best efforts of the *Post* and *Daily News*, his life once he left Liberty National was his own. To their eternal regret, they had missed the story to launch a thousand splash headlines.

Woods seemed in good spirits on a warm Wednesday on the Jersey side of the Hudson River despite the miseries of the FedEx Cup playoffs, which would mean four tournaments in five weeks, and the ostentatious $250 million Liberty National, a quirky layout built on a former toxic waste dump. Given the gimmickiness of the Tom Kite design, it could be safely concluded that Liberty National was hosting the first playoff event because it offered CBS the backdrop of the Manhattan skyline and the Statue of Liberty. As I waited in the piercing sun for Woods to finish yet another interminably long pro-am, a veteran caddie confirmed the poor early reviews. "I've never heard so much bitching about a course," he said. Another, who caddied for a majors winner, laughed and said that "to call it a goat track's being diplomatic." Woods was so underwhelmed he wondered aloud whether Kite designed the course before he had surgery to repair his eyesight. The remark was intended only for the amusement of his pro-am partners but, of course, one of them told a reporter, who wrote it the next day and reaffirmed Woods's conviction that when it came to him, no one could ever be trusted. Not that those familiar with Woods-speak were left with any doubts about his opinions when he finally arrived in the colossal glass-and-steel clubhouse. "It's interesting," Woods said with a barely suppressed smirk when asked his opinion of the course. "In a good way?" a journalist asked. "It's interesting," Woods repeated.

Woods was there because the reengineered formula for the FedEx Cup playoffs had forced his hand. He and Mickelson were both against having four events in the playoffs. Neither had historically played much after the PGA and were far too wealthy to be influenced by just money. But they understood that the Tour needed to give fans, and sponsors, a reason to focus on golf beyond mid-August and therefore the idea of a season-long playoff series, similar to the model used in NASCAR, was created. But when the FedEx playoffs were born in 2007, both Woods and Mickelson wanted to have to play only three events. Finchem agreed, but then in selling the idea to the four sponsors—the Barclays, Deutsche Bank, BMW, and Coca-Cola—he promised to deliver the A-list to each event. So the appearance of Woods and Mickelson became a crucial element to sealing a lucrative deal. Mickelson was so incensed at Finchem's two-faced dealings that he promptly skipped the BMW Championship in 2007 after winning the week before in Boston and publicly admonished the commissioner. Woods, meanwhile, had milked plenty of concessions from Finchem over the years and rolled with the punches. But he didn't show up until he had to. Which in 2007 meant that he could pass on the first event in New York. Finchem was nothing if not persistent and changed the model so that a player could not afford to skip any of the playoff events in order to claim the $10 million prize, which Woods had won in the inaugural year. With Woods on crutches in 2008, Vijay Singh won the FedEx Cup, though it was anticlimactic, as all he needed to do was put a ball in play at the Tour Championship to claim the loot.

Like the majority of his peers, Woods had no real clue how the point system worked. He shot a Tour media official a strange look upon winning at the Buick Open and being told that he'd earned five hundred FedEx Cup points. "I'll be honest with you, I don't really know. I don't think anyone knows. You come in there and you go, 'How many points did I make today?' and no one has a clue." Woods started paying attention, however, when he discovered that majors were worth six hundred points, yet the Barclays was worth two thousand five hundred to the winner. Therefore, a player could win the Grand Slam and ludicrously have fewer points than the winner at Liberty National heading into the second playoff tournament in Boston. It was Finchem's way of making sure players were at every event and that the winner of the FedEx Cup wouldn't be known until the final putt fell at the Tour Championship.

"The points structure is different, no doubt, and on top of that, you're playing for a position in the Tour Championship, which is different," Woods said in New York of the redrawn rules. "It's not cumulative. So that's a bit of a change from the last time I played. I haven't played under this system, so I guess no one else has, either. It will be interesting to see how that works going into the Tour Championship." When asked how he liked the system, Woods again threw out his word du jour. "I think it's just interesting. You keep resetting. The entire year, you work hard, say you won twenty-five tournaments this year, it doesn't really matter. You come here, you don't play well, you're not getting in the Tour Championship. It is different. You want to put more weight at the end of the season, which they are trying to do, trying to make it a little more interesting. They have changed the system twice and now it's the third time changing. Hopefully this will work. We'll see what happens." Hardly a ringing endorsement.

In a wide-ranging interview with a crowded press room— New York had by far the the largest contingent of sports media in America—Woods also said that he'd learned his lesson from losing the PGA. I wondered what that lesson was. Make more putts? Instead, Woods said that he wouldn't again be playing two straight weeks before a major. "That's the thing, [playing] three weeks is fine, but being in contention just about every day, it puts a toll on you. It was a long three weeks." Losing his umblemished Sunday record with the lead put a toll on him, too. "That night was tough, no doubt. I went home and took a few days off, away from golf. I was a little tired of it."

Woods had skipped the Barclays for many years—even when it was sponsored by Buick—because it was played at Westchester, a course he didn't like and where he'd never had a top-ten finish. But he reported for duty that Thursday at a course he liked even less. The tournament had hired a ferry to bring players, caddies, and guests across the Hudson from Battery Park to Jersey City, a beautiful fifteen-minute commute that passed Lady Liberty and Ellis Island. The ferry was mostly the domain of merchant bankers, whose boorish behavior served to remind everyone that it

wasn't an accident that the London Cockneys chose their profession as rhyming slang for *wanker.* Of all the strange sights
I'd witnessed on that ferry during that week, none was more incongruous than the forlorn figure of Mark Calcavecchia, having
missed the cut, schlepping his golf bag off the ferry and walking
with it slung across his shoulder like a Sunday morning hacker
into Manhattan. Mickelson, who was sponsored by Barclays and
had to earn his keep, took the ferry, but Woods did not. Williams
picked him up every day from his hotel and returned him there.
The element of celebrity that bothered Woods most was not being
left alone in public, and to this end, he made the right choice in
not taking the ferry.

After a heavy Wednesday night rainstorm had cleared the
skies, Liberty National was easier to play than a wide-eyed Mid-
western sucker with a fat wallet in Times Square. For everyone,
it appeared, except Woods. He could manage only a 1-under-par
round of 70, and for the first time all year declined to be interviewed after play. So even on a day in which he made no news,
Woods made news. The conspiracy theorists among the New York
media immediately speculated that it proved he just didn't like
Gotham. Maybe it was the way New Yorkers—or at least loud-
mouthed goombahs on Long Island—had embraced Mickelson at
his expense in 2002. The answer wasn't filled with much intrigue:
he was simply annoyed at his play, especially on the greens, and
wanted to work on his putting stroke, not feign politeness in front
of the cameras. The Tour's media officials, who tended to walk on
eggshells around Woods because nothing compelled him to speak
to the media after each round, knew to pick their battles, and that
wasn't one they'd win.

Woods even brushed off a request for an interview with the
Golf Channel, a Woods booster network that was invariably reverential toward him. In the cloistered world of the golf media, much

was read into the fact that he refused to stop for the Golf Channel cameras. Woods is a television junkie, plasma-screen TVs covering the walls of his home, including the bathroom. But while he enjoyed cartoons and edgy survivalist shows on networks like Discovery, he spent most of his time watching the Golf Channel and ESPN. The talking heads on the Golf Channel were always minding their p's and q's so as to avoid his wrath. The network's executives knew that Woods could be vindictive, as when he blackballed CBS analyst Peter Kostis when he criticized Woods's swing. Critical commentary also got Nick Faldo on the Woods shit list, which was perennially topped by NBC's Johnny Miller.

The Golf Channel, however, was the minor leagues of tournament coverage in every sense—a coverage led by Kelly Tilghman, whose loyalty was rewarded after her texting buddy intervened to save her career. Incredibly, she'd said on the air in 2008 that if Woods's younger rivals wanted to stop him, they needed to "lynch him in a back alley." Woods issued a statement through Steinberg in support of Tilghman, who escaped with a two-week suspension. *Golfweek* editor Dave Seanor lost his job for putting a noose on the cover of his magazine in response to the furor Tilghman's comments sparked, but, significantly, Woods didn't go to bat for him. *Sports Illustrated* writer Farrell Evans thought the incident said as much about Woods as it did about Tilghman. "The more pertinent question is: Why didn't Woods take offense? Maybe it was because last week also brought news that Woods made an estimated $100 million in endorsements in 2007, an income derived from his stature as the brightest star in the largely white, corporate-friendly world of golf and not as a minority agitating for social justice. . . . Woods doesn't have to become a civil rights spokesman, but he could have at least acknowledged that he understands the meaning of the word, and how powerful and hurtful it remains. In other words, wouldn't it be nice if for once

Woods saw himself as the heir not only to Jack Nicklaus but also to Jackie Robinson?"

If there were Woods agitators on the Golf Channel, they were former players Frank Nobilo and Brandel Chamblee, both astute and articulate, though ironically they might also be Woods's truest fans. Woods believed that Chamblee, especially, had it in for him, though in truth Chamblee was like many savants who wished Woods would abandon Haney's unorthodox swing theory. Chamblee, who once took lessons from Haney, often got into heated exchanges with the swing coach over his belief that Woods's swing was betraying him, particularly with the driver. Chamblee believed that Woods's arms moved too far away from his body in the backswing, a position from which only Lee Trevino had ever been able to recover. He liked to say that there was only one player on any golf tour in the world who'd actually lost distance during the technology boom of 2000 to 2009: Tiger Woods.

Woods, as it turned out, had no beef with the Golf Channel. He simply was not in the mood to talk and left Liberty National in the early afternoon after his police escort walked him to his courtesy car, a Buick in a parking lot filled with BMWs. It should not go left unsaid that Woods crossed paths with Yang and failed to acknowledge him. "I just passed by him," the Korean told me. "We never even made eye contact." At first I thought that Woods was being petulant but, really, what was there for him to say? He had been gracious in defeat at Hazeltine and that was clearly all Yang was going to get.

The trick of the trade when Woods isn't talking is to find someone to talk about him. Garcia, the thoughts of Hazeltine still fresh in his mind, was happy to oblige. He'd long believed the day would come when Woods would lose a third-round lead at a major. "But was I surprised? Yeah, I mean, I'm not going to lie to you. I was surprised that he didn't win that tournament. It felt like he was in control the whole week." Garcia gave credit to Yang. "He probably did something that most of the people haven't done when Tiger is up there. He just stayed there all day long. You know, he never went away." I asked the Spaniard whether he felt inspired by Yang and whether the day that particular bell might toll for him drew nearer as a result. "I'm not thinking any different than I thought three weeks ago. We all think that he can be beaten. It's just difficult. But obviously if you play well and he doesn't play his best, you can beat him."

If Woods was unhappy with the first-round 70, then a second-round 72 surely didn't improve his mood. Again, he blew off the media afterward. "He's not real happy," Williams told me. Woods had grown exasperated with the greens complexes. He couldn't read his putts and seemed perpetually perplexed as the ball broke one way, then the other, or broke uphill. Putting has always been an endeavor for the confident, and they come no more confident than Woods. But his confidence had been dented. By Saturday, Woods arrived at the conclusion all players in putting slumps eventually come to: hit it closer to the hole. After another soaking rain allowed players to play with ball-in-hand, Woods took full advantage with a third-round 67. He went from an also-ran to propelling himself into the hunt.

I'd always had the feeling that Woods sometimes won tournaments he had no business winning, though my evidence wasn't entirely empirical. It was an instinct validated, however, by Professors Richard Rendleman of Dartmouth and Robert Connolly of the University of North Carolina, who concluded in a 2010 study that Woods was the only golfer who could win by just playing "average." Using data from 83,823 Tour rounds between 2004 and 2008, the academics built a statistical model factoring in scoring difficulty, which showed that Woods could have won thirteen of the seventy-two events he'd played during that span with nothing more special than his normal game. So about half the time in those years—which weren't his best years—he'd won by just playing okay, a statistic made all the more remarkable when contrasted with the fact that no other player could've won even once by playing "average."

Could Woods win the Barclays with something even less than his average game? The tournament would have a surprise ending, all right, just not the one Woods expected. An ending that was to provide yet another clue that the legend of Tiger Woods was slowly being dismantled. Williams had told me a few months earlier that what left him most in awe of Woods was his uncanny ability to make the big putts in his hour of greatest need. "If you ask me what's the most amazing thing about caddying for this guy in all the years I've been with him, it's that in all these years, he's only ever missed one putt that he had to hole to either win the tournament or get into a playoff, and that's unbelievable. And that putt was at a Ryder Cup, so it doesn't really count. But it's incredible. He's holed putts from 3 feet to 80 feet. It's staggering."

Not as staggering, though, as that which transpired on the seventy-second green at Liberty National. Woods missed a 7-footer for birdie, which would've at worst forced a playoff and at best piled more pressure on Heath Slocum, who would go on to sink a 22-footer for the victory. Worse, the putt Woods hit didn't even scare the cup. "Neither of us saw the break on that putt, which was disappointing," said Williams. I expected Woods to be unplayable when he arrived for a brief post-tournament interview after having watched Slocum's putt fall on a television inside the scorer's room. Instead, he was strangely accepting of his fate, almost nonchalant. "If I would've hit a poor putt, I would've been pissed, but I didn't. We read it either right center with a little pace, or inside right. We misread it by almost a cup. That's frustrating when you misread a putt that bad. Kind of the nature of these greens, a little bit tricky to read." For good measure, Woods added that he could never recall bringing in Williams to navigate so often. "I don't ever call Stevie in on this many reads. They were tricky putts, double-breaking putts, 10-, 12-footers, just tricky greens. Not too many golf courses that you misread putts that badly." In other words, Woods wanted to remind us that he was still money on the greens and if he hit a good putt that didn't go in, then it was surely not his fault. At that moment, I flashed on Greg Norman at his peak, when every missed putt would be followed by a tapping down with the putter on his line; as if to say, "The Shark couldn't miss from six feet, so it had to be a spike mark." The great putters, I'd come to understand, have to cling to their infallibility. What else is there? And so Woods left New York with his cup half full. "To miss as many putts as I did this week, to still have a chance on the last green with a putt, it goes to show you how good I am hitting it. That's a great sign."

With the runt of the FedEx Cup playoffs litter out of the way, Woods moved to the suburbs of Boston and the Deutsche Bank Championship, where he'd won once in five tries, to go along with two second-place finishes. Beyond his liking for the course, Woods had ties to the tournament because his foundation was a beneficiary. When he was asked prior to the tournament beginning about kids emulating him, Woods said that it was "pretty flattering. You always want to do the right thing and you always try. You don't always do it, but you always try." It was a week he needed to try harder. Not only did he spend his nights sexting porn queen Josyln James, whom he would fly to Chicago the following week for a rendezvous, but he threw his driver in disgust following one of many errant tee shots, touching off yet another round of debate on whether Woods needed to learn to control his temper.

"I didn't really do much of anything positively today," he

said after an opening round of 70. "I didn't feel good over any shot today and didn't drive it very good, hit my irons worse, and didn't make any putts. Other than that, it was a good day." Woods flirted with the cut line in the second round but ultimately saw a few putts finally drop to shoot a second-round 67 and survive to play the long weekend. "Is grinding on a cut line any different from grinding in contention? Is there any philosophical and emotional difference?" Woods was asked. "Yeah," he replied. "If you're grinding on the lead, you're playing a lot better than if you are grinding on the cut line." Worrying about cuts was for the bottom feeders, not for Woods. He most prided himself on his consistency, which was best reflected in the fact that he'd missed only six cuts in fourteen seasons as a professional. Woods needed two low rounds to have a sniff at the TPC Boston but imploded in the third round with a 72, after which there was, predictably, no post-round interview. He had an early final-round tee time for the first time since Doral, the last time—putting aside Turnberry—that he knew that he had no realistic chance of winning.

Those who have played casual rounds of golf with Woods swear that he is even more impressive a player zipping around a course in a cart with his hat on back to front and wearing shorts. McLaughlin had been the victim of so many beatings, all bets that seemed enticing on the first tee, that he'd lost count. Woods would routinely take on three good amateur players, let them play from the white tees while he teed off from the tips, and still get into their wallets. At tournaments, though, Woods is less gung-ho. At tournaments, he plays one of nine shots into greens. This is his gospel: if a shot is played correctly, it will begin at the middle of the green and work toward the flag. Once at Torrey Pines I'd noted what a good shot he'd hit on the first hole, an iron that almost flew into the flagstick in the back left of the green. He laughed. "I pulled the shit out of that." When he is playing at the peak of his powers, Woods crafts the shot a flag demands. A front left pin brings a high draw, starting at the middle of the green and working left. A back right flag calls for a lower-trajectory cut that lands short and releases. Middle flags bring either slight cuts or slight draws, but Woods loathes hearing a player speak of straight shots.

No golf shot is ever, factually, straight, even if it gives the appearance to the untrained eye. To the layman, straight in golf is good, and I often wondered whether Woods wasn't handicapping himself by introducing unnecessary complexities. It is almost as if he were golf's answer to Bobby Fischer, rebelling against memorization techniques that make chess more straightforward because they dilute the value of true genius. In golf, balls that don't spin much and advances in club design have made it possible for shots that are mishit to lead to birdies, infuriating a purist like Woods. He believes golf shots are meant to be shaped in the way traditionalist Catholics believe in the Latin Mass and my Italian mother believes that pasta should be lovingly made by hand.

When I asked him about his strategy, Woods reasoned that if the ball didn't turn as much as he wanted, the worst he'd be left with was a putt pin high and near the center of the green; all things being equal, a 20-footer for birdie, a range at which he is perhaps the best ever. But on that Monday at the Deutsche Bank, Woods made an adjustment at the range, standing closer to the ball at address, and began, as he liked to say, "puring" his shots. He had no reason to play safe, so he went after every flag and was truly a sight to behold. He was 6 under par through seven holes, having converted birdies of 14 inches, 4 feet, 3 feet, and 4 feet, and holing a 9-iron for eagle on the 465-yard par-4 6th hole. There would be four more birdies to come as Woods hunted every flag, though he also threw in two careless bogeys on his way to a 63, which catapulted him from thirtieth to a tie for eleventh. "It probably could've been a couple less than that," he said of the round, "but still wouldn't have been good enough. The whole idea was to try and shoot something in the low 60s and that would probably get me in the top ten. Certainly, from where I was at, I couldn't win the tournament, even if I shot 60 or something like that."

Woods's friend Steve Stricker, who'd lost his Tour card in 2004 and reinvented himself, won the tournament and took the lead in the FedEx Cup race. But Stricker wasn't under any illusions. "He's the man still," he told me when I asked about Woods. "We're just taking up space in his world. We all know who the guy is out here. I'm just happy to be in the position I'm at and with the opportunity to do something special for myself. He's done enough other special things, maybe let somebody else do something special. We all know what he's about and how great a player he is, but this format adds a lot of excitement for a guy like myself or anybody else to kind of challenge him. Whoever is going to win this, whether it be him or me or anybody else, you're going to have to play some pretty good golf for two more events, and it's going to lead to a lot of excitement."

As the seventy players who remained in the FedEx Cup race arrived in Chicago, I asked Padraig Harrington what he thought about Stricker's chances of causing an upset. "What's great about Steve Stricker is he's trying to be Steve Stricker. He's going to try and beat Tiger Woods by playing Steve Stricker's golf. He's not going to go out there and try and play Tiger's game, and that's very important to distinguish those two things. He doesn't try to do anything that he can't do. He plays well within himself, and when you add those numbers up at the end of the week, it's very impressive, and that's the only way any player can compete with Tiger. The best way of beating him is doing your own thing and making Tiger perform better. And if he does, you'll say, 'Well done.' But the key is not to have a situation where you've played [poorly] and Tiger can get away with not playing his very best and still win."

Woods would play his very best at Cog Hill. Even though Rees Jones had tinkered with the design—it had been lengthened to 7,600 yards—with a view to securing a U.S. Open, Cog Hill was still like home cookin' to Woods. He opened with a 68, took the outright lead with a second-round 67, and then killed the tournament with a Saturday 62. As Brandt Snedeker, who'd play alongside Woods and Australian rookie Marc Leishman in the final round, joked before he left the course Saturday night, Woods would need to have a heart attack to lose a 7-shot third-round lead. The porn star James would in 2010 claim some of the credit for Woods's great play on weeks she visited him. Woods was so relaxed the following day that he walked up to me after Leishman had expertly putted to a few inches from 50 feet up two tiers and said, "Is it just me, or can everyone from Melbourne putt?" Woods had long been in awe of Melbourne's famous sandbelt courses that collectively boast the toughest greens complexes in the world. Neither was it a coincidence that many of the finest Australian putters, from Geoff Ogilvy to Aaron Baddeley, cut their teeth on those greens. But it was odd to have this exchange on a Sunday at a tournament.

If there was any drama on that pleasant Sunday afternoon in the west of Chicago, it came on the 9th hole after Leishman unleashed a furious drive, emasculating the 600-yard par 5, then struck a flawless 4-iron that left a makeable eagle putt. Woods, meanwhile, was in jail. He'd blocked his drive about 60 yards to the right of the tree-lined fairway into a barbeque pit. From there, he somehow threaded a low 3-iron through the trees, only to see his ball roll too far, stopping beneath a tree on the left of the fairway. "I thought I might be able to get 1 or 2 up on him here, maybe put a little bit of pressure on him," said Leishman. "Maybe this could get back to four [shots]." From 109 yards, Woods hooked a low 9-iron shot that stayed under the tree, landed 50 yards short of the green, and scurried up the slope before settling 15 feet behind the pin. "When he hit that shot, I actually just started laughing, it was such a good shot," said Leishman. "He didn't really need it, but he needed it to keep a big lead." The Australian missed his eagle putt, tapping in for birdie, then watched as Woods made his putt.

"Nice halve," Woods said with a mischievous smile as he walked by me. That was what the afternoon had come to: little games to play to keep his interest because the big game was over. Woods's seventy-first victory on the Tour came by 8 shots. It was just like the old days. "To play as well as I have of late and not get the Ws has been a little bit frustrating, no doubt, because I've been so close. It's just been a matter of making a couple putts here and there . . . and, lo and behold, boom! I hit the ball just as well, just as consistent this week, and I made a few putts. That's how it happens." Having won for a sixth time in 2009, Woods declared the comeback season among the best of his career. "Absolutely it's one of my best years, there's no doubt about that. I haven't won as many times as I did in 2000, didn't win any majors this year, but I've never had a year where I've been this consistent. To have, as I said, an opportunity just about every time I tee it up to win the championship on the back nine, I can't tell you how proud I am."

He'd always judged success or failure in terms of majors, but now he wanted to move the goalposts. Perhaps it was disingenuous, but the fact remained that he was the best player in the world in 2009. Only Stricker, with three, had more than two wins to that point. And Woods left Chicago with an adjusted scoring average of 68.06, three shots better than the Tour average—which translated to 12 shots a tournament—and 1.26 shots ahead of Stricker, who was in second place. So Woods was statistically five shots better per tournament than the next-best player. And apart from the missed cut at Turnberry, Woods hadn't finished lower than a tie for eleventh. Stricker finished in a tie for fifty-third at Cog Hill, 25 shots behind Woods. He beat Y. E. Yang by 32 strokes, an average of 8 per round. Woods left for the Tour Championship, at historic East Lake in Atlanta, just two wins behind Jack Nicklaus on the all-time list. After that there was only Sam Snead's 82 left to chase. But Snead and Nicklaus were both forty-two when they won their seventy-first tournaments, nine years older than Woods. "It feels good," Woods said. "Winning, that's the ultimate goal."

Although he toed the company line when he had to, Woods was generally an independent thinker and a traditionalist, so while winning the FedEx Cup would have been nice, it wasn't the Super Bowl. "No, it's not," Woods said after playing nine holes on the Wednesday at a still soggy East Lake. "The nature of our sport is a little bit different in that regard. You try and have this season-ending championship be our big event, but there's four other ones that are pretty big, too." Not that the $10 million prize money wouldn't pay for some jet fuel. A year before, Woods would have already had one hand on the Cup, but under Finchem's new system, points were reset going into Atlanta, which meant that instead of a 1,500-plus point lead, Woods led Stricker by only 250 points. Any of the top five players—Zach Johnson, Jim Furyk, and Heath Slocum were the others—could take the Cup with a victory at East Lake while everyone in the field had at least a mathematical chance of winning if the planets aligned correctly. There were many fanciful scenarios, such as Furyk, who hadn't won a tournament in two years, finishing second to any player not in the top eight and hijacking the Cup with Woods finishing fourth. It could happen. Even Furyk thought the system was flawed, not that he'd have given the money back. "It could happen, but at the end I'd have to sit here and look at y'all and say, 'It's not my damned fault.' I'd be like Sylvester—I just swallowed a Tweety Bird and that would put a big smile on my face."

An enterprising writer, looking for something different to write, asked Woods whether he felt the pressure if he stood over a putt Sunday to win both the Tour Championship and the FedEx Cup, a putt worth $11.35 million. The answer provided insight into the way Woods's mind is wired. "When you hit a putt like I did in 2000 [at the PGA] to get into a playoff for the opportunity to win three straight majors and do something that hadn't been done since Hogan, when you're over that putt, all you think about is where you're playing that ball. All the other stuff takes care of itself. It's nothing else but starting that ball on that line with the correct speed. That's it. When I had that putt last year at the U.S. Open to get into a playoff, again, it was all about starting the ball on that line and making that putt." He thought only about the process, stayed only in the moment, never allowed himself to think about the consequences. "Why? You have plenty of time after."

Sean O'Hair prepared for the Tour Championship by playing money games with his buddies in Philadelphia for six straight days. And having his wallet emptied. "I was giving them too many shots. They were winning the bets on the first tee." The truth was that the twenty-seven-year-old was suffering from an old complaint: his putter wasn't cashing in on his ball striking. Woods gave him a tip on the Wednesday, and O'Hair responded with a 66, one shot better than Woods, which took him to the top of the leaderboard after the first round. "I'm not even close to doing exactly what he told me to do. But I truly believe in what he said, and I think it's the key for me to kind of take my putting to another level because, let's face it, that's kind of what's held me back for a long time." O'Hair had 28 putts—1 fewer than Woods on the day—including a 56-footer and six others longer than 6 feet. What impressed O'Hair was Woods's generosity. He might be the best putter in history, but O'Hair said that "the thing that impresses me more is the quality of guy he is. I mean, I'm his competition, and for him to help me out like he did was very classy." Woods, who rebounded from a sluggish start to finish at 3 under par, 1 shot back of O'Hair, said his motivation was "very simple; you always help your friends. Sean is a friend of mine, and like all my friends, you always try to make their life better somehow. That's the whole idea of having friends in your life. Sean has been struggling a little bit on the greens this year and I thought I could offer a little bit of help and insight into how he could change that, and now, as I said, I'm going to go chew him out."

Although Woods would follow with rounds of 68 and 69 to get him into the last group on Sunday, he seemed to be losing sharpness, as if the long year had taken its toll. As he warmed up on the range before the final round, Johnny Miller approached. He stood next to me and watched as Woods hit shots. "I love the way his right shoulder's moving," Miller said. He truly deep down appreciated the genius of Woods, but I'd always wondered whether Miller ever really believed anyone was better than he was. He was, certainly, one of the great ball strikers, but a lousy putter who had to give the game away after brushing them in from two feet became a task fraught with danger. Eventually, Miller moved toward Woods, who knew he was there the entire time but never once acknowledged him. "Hey, Tiger," said Miller. "Hey, Johnny," Woods responded, with the most forced smile I'd ever seen him make. Miller complimented Woods on his good swings and soon launched into a dissertation on the role of the rear shoulder and how important it was to his swing. Woods just listened and said nothing. Miller got the hint and said his good-byes as Woods returned to hitting balls. It was clear to me that once crossed, Woods wasn't a man to quickly forgive. Whatever goodwill Miller may have earned—or perhaps of his failed détente with Woods—their estrangement would be guaranteed a few short hours later when Miller predicted that Mickelson in 2010 would finally supplant Woods as the world number one.

Mickelson, fresh from rehabilitating his putting stroke under the watchful eye of the old sage Dave Stockton, was flawless on a difficult Sunday. With his hands pressed forward as he addressed putts, the left-hander couldn't miss on the greens. Woods, meanwhile, was frustrated into shooting a 70, which won him the FedEx Cup, though not the tournament. I'm not sure if there was a stranger sight in golf than Woods and Mickelson posing for photographs at the presentation ceremony, Woods with the big check and Mickelson with the small one. Yet it was Mickelson who wore the car-to-ear smile. "It was a strange feeling, a little bit deflating," Woods later admitted. "It feels certainly not like it did a couple years ago when I won the tournament by 7, 8 shots, whatever it was. I think it's just one of those things where obviously, I'm a little disappointed. I'm sure I'll probably be more happy tomorrow than I am right now." Mickelson, on the other hand, couldn't resist a jab at his rival. "I like the way today went. I was 2 back of him, I beat him by 3, he gets the $10 million check and I get $1 million." Miller couldn't wait for 2010. "When Phil's on, he is not afraid of Tiger Woods, I can assure you of that."

CHAPTER 15

Presidents Cup

Twin forces combined to create the Presidents Cup, a biennial match play competition pitting the United States against a disparate team made up of players from anywhere other than Europe. In the early '90s, a number of leading players, including the world number one, Greg Norman, as well as Nick Price, Ernie Els, and Vijay Singh, were from countries that weren't eligible for the Ryder Cup; that competition, which dates back to 1927, was restricted to Americans against Europeans. Well, it was the United States against Great Britain and Ireland until it became so boringly one-sided that they decided to let Seve Ballesteros, who combined great skill with Latin passion and a penchant for gamesmanship, play, and it was, thankfully, never the same again. Norman, in particular, thought it a good idea to introduce a third team into the mix for the global growth of the game and, even if under the dubious and vague banner of Internationals, it'd be as close as he'd come to representing his native Australia in a team event. The other driving force was, as always, money. The PGA

Tour did not own the Ryder Cup and, more to the point, didn't get any of the $50 million or so in profits the event generated.

With the growth of golf in Asia, incoming Tour commissioner Tim Finchem, who'd been involved in the development of the Presidents Cup as chief operating officer, hoped to build the matches into a global event that rivaled the Ryder Cup. But the exercise got off to a rocky beginning. First, there was an uprising within the ranks of the Internationals because the Tour had installed David Graham as their captain for the first matches in 1994, at Robert Trent Jones Golf Club on the outskirts of Washington, DC. Graham seemed a good fit because he was Australian, lived in Texas—and would therefore be available for organizational and promotional work—and had the pedigree, having won the 1979 PGA and the 1981 U.S. Open. But what Finchem didn't know was that Graham could be cantankerous—"not a good people person," as countryman Craig Parry told writer Jaime Diaz. Graham managed to rub his entire team the wrong way, especially another prickly Aussie, Steve Elkington, who could bear grudges with the best of them. Even the easygoing Nick Price, who was then the hottest player on the planet, had his feathers ruffled by Graham's my-way-or-the-highway despotism.

Neither, it must be said, were the players as invested as they could have been in the event itself. Ernie Els, who had just won his first major, the U.S. Open at Oakland Hills, did not play due to "a prior commitment." This ranked alongside the one about dogs eating homework on the Mount Rushmore of lame excuses. Els blew off the Presidents Cup to play the British Masters, where he cashed a check for £25,000. Norman mysteriously withdrew on the Monday before the matches began, citing, of all things, the flu. He did fly up on Sunday to act as a sort of overqualified cheerleader, though when CBS asked to put Norman on air throughout the singles' matches, Graham curtly refused. "This isn't going to be the fucking Greg Norman show," he said in the presence of several shocked witnesses. Bradley Hughes, a journeyman Australian, had to be flown in from Japan, where he'd been playing, to make up the numbers. Not surprisingly, the Internationals were trounced, 20–12.

Before the next matches, the mutiny that had been brewing among the Internationals was completed and Graham's blood was spilled. Finchem, fearing that players would boycott the event after a player meeting at the British Open had voted to ax Graham, had no choice but to remove him. Norman had called Graham to say he had not been the ringleader of the cabal, but Graham didn't believe him and said so in very direct language. He was replaced as captain by another Australian, five-time British Open winner Peter Thomson, who was urbane and delightful company. The second matches, again held at RTJ—a bone of contention for the Internationals, who'd wanted the competition to go to their countries—began as the first had finished, the Americans leading 7½ to 2½ after Friday's play. But the Internationals fought back, and if Singh had been able to find a way to beat Fred Couples in the final singles' match, the Americans would've lost. They did lose the next Cup, though, as they were dragged kicking and screaming to venerable Royal Melbourne two weeks before Christmas and enjoyed neither the heat of an Aussie summer nor the flies that come with it. Their lack of spirit embarrassed captain Jack Nicklaus, who had to endure his players whining their way to a 9-point loss.

"They're like a bucket of prawns on a hot day," announced local boy Stuart Appleby of his American counterparts. "They don't travel well." By Sunday, when there was no real doubt as to the outcome, Woods, who'd gotten only one point in four matches, asked Nicklaus for a favor. The young Tiger wanted a piece of the Shark in Norman's backyard, and it was always

Jack's style to let his players run the show. Norman, still relevant as a golfer, though not in his prime at almost forty-four, was
up for the challenge. Maybe it didn't hurt that Norman had fired
Harmon—to whom Woods was then close—as his coach, ostensibly over a business deal, though some wondered whether Norman had been jealous of Harmon's devotion to Woods. Woods
won the spirited match 1 up, and while Norman celebrated with
his teammates into the wee hours drinking his beloved VB beer, it
struck me over the years as telling that he was the only major figure in golf to constantly refer to his conqueror as "Woods" instead
of "Tiger," as everyone else did.

The United States exacted revenge two years later, back at
RTJ, in a drubbing memorable only because Singh's caddie, Paul
Tesori, infamously wore the TIGER WHO? hat during the Sunday
singles' match against Woods. Woods won what wasn't a very
gentlemanly match. And he was front and center in the best of
the Presidents Cups, held in South Africa two years later, when
he and the local favorite Els went mano a mano in an unforgettable duel that ended when the sun set with the scores all square.
The Americans retained the Cup, though they shouldn't have.
"We were ready to come back the next day and play, for sure. We
weren't happy they were going to retain it like that," said Adam
Scott. The Americans, however, were ready to board their charter
that night and head back Stateside. It revealed much about what
team competitions really mean to the top players and especially
the Americans, who face one of these every year: they are exhibitions, nothing more.

A very large elephant sat in the middle of the room when it
came to team competitions. No American player would dare not
represent his country, because the damage would be untold—to
them, their sponsors, and the sport—but it was an open secret
how unhappy most were with the structure. When Hunter Mahan

spoke in 2008 of being a "slave" during the week of the Ryder Cup, he was merely continuing a tradition begun a decade earlier by Mark O'Meara. O'Meara had never been one to leave a dollar lying on the table. He'd noted that the Ryder Cup started turning a profit in the mid-1980s, when the British and Irish were reinforced by the Europeans, who breathed fire into the matches, making them once again competitive. But the players shared in none of those profits and received only a small amount of money that they could donate to the charity of their choice. O'Meara became the unofficial spokesman for the discontented players, chiefly Woods and David Duval, who believed they were being exploited. O'Meara made his point to journalists by telling them to "come and donate your salary to a charity that week, too. You guys don't mind doing that, do you? Either that or they shouldn't charge the spectators to come and watch." O'Meara took matters into his own hands by donating to the "charity" that was his kids' exclusive private school in Orlando. Look no farther as to why O'Meara, a natural fit with his Irish ancestry, was overlooked by the PGA of America in favor of Tom Lehman as the U.S. captain when the matches went to the Emerald Isle in 2006. Woods was privately just as militant as O'Meara, but he was guarded in public. Yet he let slip his true feelings in 2002, when he said he'd rather win the American Express Championship that was played the week before the Ryder Cup. "Why? I can think of a million reasons," he said, referring to the winner's check. It should be noted that the Europeans didn't complain about money and looked forward to Ryder Cups.

Fred Couples's casual, carefree approach to life can be misinterpreted. Couples has a lazy, smooth swing, but he is much sharper than he is given credit for and cared deeply about being made captain of the U.S. team for the 2009 Presidents Cup in San Francisco. He knew precisely what he was doing by selecting

Michael Jordan as one of his assistant captains at Harding Park, a decision met with derision by the golf orthodoxy. And it was even questioned by golf's maverick thinkers, like the dry-witted Paul Goydos. "I don't get the Michael Jordan thing. He's a nice guy, but I don't know what he has to do with golf other than he's tall." Jordan had been an unofficial cheerleader at many Ryder and Presidents Cups, but Couples, who'd himself grown close to the retired basketball star—both men shared a love for a bet—wanted to formalize the arrangement. He'd given myriad reasons why he thought it would help his team, but it wasn't until the Cup had been successfully defended, before he was to leave for a night of celebration at the Fairmont Hotel, that Couples came clean on his real rationale. "I felt like he was going to make Tiger show up," he told a few of us in the parking lot.

Couples knew how competitive the alpha dogs were; indeed, they were like two brothers whose dynamic was altering as the younger sibling began to threaten eclipsing the older. Jordan could no longer boast that he was the richest athlete in American sports history, a title of great importance to him. And don't think Woods missed any opportunity to rub it in; the "needle," as Woods referred to trash talking, was the language they spoke to one another. In a 2006 interview with News Corporation's gamer website IGN to promote his EA Sports game, Woods said of Jordan, "Oh, we have friendly wagers [on the golf course]. But we compete in everything. We play golf, we shoot hoops together, we play table tennis, pool, cards. We play anything and everything, trying to beat each other."

Of course Woods was competitive, chiefly with Mickelson. It was largely viewed as a thawing of their cold war when Woods agreed at the 2004 Ryder Cup—when Hal Sutton disastrously paired them twice; both matches lost—to play table tennis against Mickelson. It was Ping-Pong diplomacy. The general view at the time was that Woods, who because of his youth had never before considered himself a leader on U.S. teams, had realized that he needed to set a good example of sportsmanship and be a team player. But not everyone viewed the invitation to Mickelson as an olive branch. "Maybe it was, but maybe it was just another thing he wanted to kick Phil's ass at," one of Mickelson's inner circle told me. "Man, they go at it," said Kenny Perry, whom Woods nominated as the best of the Americans at table tennis. "There's a lot of paddle throwing, tantrums, balls pounded into each other. I love all the barbs between them. Their language, whoa, it's unbelievable." He had declined to provide me with a transcript other than, "Just say it's X-rated."

Though Woods and Mickelson have each at various stages claimed superiority over the other, at Ping-Pong, I was told by a neutral party that Woods had prevailed in 2004. Mickelson, who favored slices and heavy spin shots against Woods's power game, wanted a chance at revenge, and he got it at the following year's Presidents Cup. "They went out and played the first game, and Tiger won; they played the second game, and Tiger won," Nicklaus recalled. "And Phil said, 'I've got this buffet behind me, and I can't swing. Tiger, switch sides with me.' He said, 'Sure.' So they switch sides and Phil wins. Phil says, 'Let's play another one,' and Tiger says, 'Uh-uh, two to one.' And they never played again. But they were giggling about it and had fun."

Woods, though, was predictably irked when Mickelson made a throwaway comment to the Golf Channel about his supremacy and had payback on his mind when the two met for a rematch at Royal Montreal during the 2007 Presidents Cup. Mickelson won the first match, which prompted an irate Woods to put his hat on backward and remove his shirt. "I couldn't believe he took his shirt off. He was pissed and he meant business, man," said a caddie for one of the Americans who witnessed the match. Woods

won a close second match, then ran away with the deciding rubber, 21–9. That same year Woods received a miniature Ping-Pong
table when Elin gave birth to Sam. The gift came with a note:
"Our kids have had a little head start on Sam Alexis and expect
them to continue the Mickelson domination over the Woods in
pong. But we thought we should give Sam Alexis a chance to
jump-start her own game." Jim Furyk goaded Woods when I asked
him about Mickelson's Ping-Pong game. "Why don't you just call
Phil out?" Furyk said. When Woods declined, Furyk revealed that
Mickelson had "brought his own paddle this year, his own kit,
little bag. They're having fun, and people don't think they do,"
Furyk said. "I'm not trying to say that they're the best of friends,
but when you watch them play, listen to them talking a little
smack, they're having fun."

Fun was the name of the game at the Presidents Cup. It was
a friendly competition for bragging rights—there is obviously no
money at stake—between one group of golfers who lived in Florida against their neighbors. "It can still get a little bit chippy, but
for the most part, the guys who play on the International team, a
good percentage of them live in the United States," said Furyk.
"I see Vijay weekly at home. I realize he's on the other team, but
he lives in my backyard." Couples, too, acknowledged the chum-
miness of the competition, which is very distinct from the Ryder
Cup. "It's a fun event, not so grueling. You know, [not] five days of
saying some word to someone and it gets blown out of proportion
and they hate you. And then you go to Europe and they hate you.
That's not going to happen." Adding to the relaxed atmosphere
was the fact that the Internationals were mostly Australians and
South Africans, men who understood that having a good time
involves beers. After the 2005 competition, none of the Internationals showed up at the final press conference. I had to talk Ian
Baker-Finch, who was the assistant captain, into taking me back

to the team chalet, because I needed to interview at least a couple of my countrymen. He fished out Peter Lonard and Stuart Appleby, neither of them particularly sober. "These are the best two I could get from that mob," Baker-Finch said. Lonard, who'd earlier in the week told me he couldn't understand why the Americans "got their knickers in a twist" over perceived slights at team competitions, provided me with a quote I've never forgotten. "We finished second in a two-horse race. Some people would say that was like finishing last."

Everyone had a theory on why the Internationals had won only once in the competition's history, but Singh's made most sense to me: "Really, we have a better time than the other team, I guess. That's what everybody says." He actually believed the Internationals had a better chance at Harding Park because "there are a lot more younger players [Ryo Ishikawa and Camilo Villegas] on the team this year, and they are a little bit more into it. Obviously, they don't drink as much, and they don't party as much. They are more into winning the tournament." Sean O'Hair later disputed Singh's assertion. "We have bevvies, too," he told me. "I had a few myself last night." But to illustrate the cultural difference between the teams, Hunter Mahan's jaw dropped when he heard O'Hair talking of drinking, smoking cigars, and gambling— Jordan's influence was immediate—in the team room. "He actually told you about that?"

Norman, serving as captain for the first time, had made the point to his players that all their losses in the past could be traced back to poor starts. And after the first day finished 3½ to 2½ in their favor, Norman felt confident. The matches were mostly close, except for Woods and Stricker's 6 and 4 walloping an out-of-form Geoff Ogilvy, who never was much help to his impressive partner, Ishikawa. Woods had seventeen different partners during these competitions but never really gelled with any of them. "In the past, they've paired Tiger with the wrong players a lot," said International player Robert Allenby. The exception was Furyk, a bulldog of a competitor, who was every bit as tough as Woods even if not as talented. But his general discomfort with team play was reflected in Woods's underwhelming records in both the Ryder (10-13-2) and Presidents (13-11-1) Cups.

Ironically, it wasn't Woods who usually played poorly in his partner matches, which had been even more exasperating for him. His partners tended not to perform at their best. Who could forget the look on Woods's face when Mickelson sliced a 3-wood 50 yards left on the 18th, costing them the match at the Ryder Cup in Detroit? "We didn't have a perfect record, but it was fun to play with him," said Davis Love III. "I hope I'm playing with him at the [2010] Ryder Cup because I'd love to go back into the battle over there again with a guy like that, who you know is going to be driven to win. I'll never forget him telling me at the Belfry. I said, 'What do you want me to hit off the tee?' He said, 'I don't care, hit it in the fairway.' I said, 'Well, how far down there do you want it?' He said, 'I don't care, just put it in the fairway and I'll put it on the green.' That's the way he thinks: 'I don't care if I'm hitting a 3-iron in or a 7-iron in, I'm going to hit it close.' Of course, the 1st hole I missed the fairway, and then the 3rd hole I missed the fairway, and we were 2 up quick because he was so determined to win, and it was amazing. That was the first match I had ever played with him, and it was just incredible to watch him play." Unfortunately, Woods felt too often his partners did just that: watch him play rather than play well themselves.

But in Stricker, whom Woods had been paired with for much of the playoffs, Couples had unearthed a gem of a partner. Woods declared at a team dinner that Stricker was "the best putter I've ever seen." But although Stricker more than held his own, it was of course Woods who delivered the killer blow at Harding Park—"the defining moment," Norman said. Woods and Stricker were 1 down with two holes to play in the morning alternate-shot session against the tenacious duo of Mike Weir and Tim Clark. Woods hit a birdie putt on the 17th from 20 feet, which labored up the slope like a caboose out of steam. Yet it somehow found the energy to collapse into the cup, prompting Woods to go into full fist-pump mode; it was the most excited he'd been on a putting green since draining the championship-winning putt at Bay Hill. The theatrics should have mattered little, except that Weir missed a 4-footer for birdie to end the match.

Woods has always found motivation from the most unlikely of sources. It was not lost on him that it was Weir—with whom he was very friendly—who had defeated him in the Presidents Cup singles two years before in Canada, and Clark who had put a damper on his comeback tournament, the Accenture Match Play. Who didn't know how the story would end? Stricker found the fairway and Woods unleashed one of those majestic long irons in the par-5 closing hole; he stared at it, took a step and, for dramatic touch, punctuated it with an admiring twirl of his club. He knew it would be a *SportsCenter* moment. Stricker didn't even need to convert the short eagle putt, which was conceded after Weir and Clark couldn't muster a birdie. The Americans had been handed an improbable point. The only win to date by an American team that had been down on the 17th turned the tide, Norman said, facing a 3-point Sunday deficit. "If Tiger doesn't make that putt on 17 and Weir makes the putt, it's all over, and we go into tomorrow behind 1 point," said Norman on Saturday night. "Don't over-analyze this whole thing. It was just great golf by Tiger Woods." Woods said that he'd been "part of losing Ryder Cup teams and winning Presidents Cup teams, and it's basically who wins the

18th hole more that week. It's amazing how it can turn an entire Cup around just by having a guy win one match going into 18 or halve a match."

Couples knew that when he and Norman paired the singles, Woods would play Yang. There was a score to settle, and wasn't Yang right when he said in the immediate aftermath of the PGA that he wanted no redo? Woods became only the third player in Presidents Cup history to go 5-0 when he exacted his revenge on the South Korean in the singles and, for good measure, for the first time in eleven Ryder and Presidents Cups delivered his country's winning point. "For me, yeah, obviously it's one of my better Cup experiences; we won," he said. "That's the name of the game, whether you go 0-5 or 5-0. The fact that we won, that's the number one thing. We came here to win as a team and we did it." Norman was left to tip his hat to Woods. "That's what you expect out of your number one player in the world. You need him to step up to the plate, and sometimes he hasn't done that, and this time he stepped up to the plate, big-time." Woods never likes gloating in public, but there was a certain sense of satisfaction in downing Yang comprehensively, 6 and 5. "He got me there, and I figured I could get him here. I actually played pretty good."

CHAPTER 16

The Reckoning

My instincts have never lied to me.
—TIGER WOODS, August 2001

It was noticeable just how much Tiger Woods's mood had changed by the third round of the Australian Masters, the last tournament he would play in 2009. With the championship in his control, he brooded his way through an even-par round of 72, dropping him back into a tie for the lead. The motif of the round was a driver thrown into the ground in a fit of pique, which bounced into the gallery; it was conduct unbecoming and prompted a new round of hand-wringing about Woods's temper. He later bemoaned "terrible shots"—he'd once more failed to master crosswinds—but his bad mood that Saturday had little to do with golf. He'd arrived at Kingston Heath with a lot on his mind. His life was about to descend into the darkest pit of tabloid hell.

Woods had been greatly enjoying his mid-November sojourn Down Under. He'd always felt a kinship with antipodeans. Aussies, Kiwis, and South Africans were mischievous iconoclasts, a by-product of rejecting at every chance the implied superiority of their English colonial masters. During the wars, their men didn't salute enough, drank and gambled too much, and chased women whenever they could. But when the moment of truth came, they fought like lionhearts, never surrendered, and would die before abandoning a "mate." Woods, who'd grown up feeling like an outsider despite his great talent, related to and admired such a cultural identity. He loved that antipodeans respected him but never treated him reverentially. After mentors O'Meara and John Cook had gone to the Champions Tour, and with his old friends Begay and Chris Riley on golf's peripheries, Woods most enjoyed playing practice rounds with two laid-back Aussies, Rod Pampling and Richard Green, Williams said. He went on, "When you're from our part of the world, you learn to take shit and you learn to give it as well. That's kind of an antipodean thing. That's how you grow up as kids. It's the guys who can't take it that don't last. Ninety-nine percent of kids in New Zealand grow up playing rugby, and it's a brutal sport; you've got to learn to take some hits and take some shit and get up, keep playing, and give it straight back, or you won't last. Tiger likes that kind of attitude. It fits right in with him."

Woods held a 3-shot lead after two rounds at Kingston Heath, maybe the jewel of the Melbourne sandbelt. While St. Andrews was his favorite course, the cluster of courses in the suburbs of Australia's southern capital, which included the legendary Royal Melbourne as well as classics like Metropolitan and Commonwealth, had long held a mystical allure for Woods. He'd jumped at the chance to play at Kingston Heath and was encouraged when Williams told him to bring his camera because Alister MacKenzie had created there "the best bunkering in the world." But Woods was not about to set a bad precedent and play for free; it was bad enough that the PGA Tour banned appearance fees. The deal to play in Australia for the first time since the 1998 Presidents Cup was sealed only after the state government in Victoria kicked in the remaining half of his standard $3 million appearance fee. His wife stayed in Orlando with the children, but Woods's mother wanted to see kangaroos, so he flew her out and dined with her each night at one of the Crown Casino's excellent restaurants. But after she retired for the night, he spent his time with Rachel Uchitel, whom he'd also flown to Melbourne. This decision would trigger his downfall.

Uchitel was a cocksure child of Manhattan privilege. She was thirty-four years old, smart, attractive in a surgically enhanced way, socially ambitious, and with expensive tastes and very sharp elbows. She enjoyed the power of giving a thumbs-up or -down from behind velvet ropes at swank nightclubs from the Hamptons to Manhattan to Las Vegas. Uchitel was different from the parade of mostly blond, vacuous bimbos who typically caught Woods's eye, but she was a magnet for drama and couldn't keep secrets. And neither could her friends.

Woods was careful to keep Uchitel hidden, especially from his mother. Uchitel had been accompanied on the long flight to Australia by Bryon Bell, Woods's childhood friend who headed his golf course design business. Woods had long trusted Bell with organizing the logistics of his dalliances. It was Bell, along with another school friend, Jerry Chang, who most often accompanied Woods to nightclubs, where the golfer had grown ever more confident—and less discreet—about picking up women. "The thing is, Bryon and Jerry aren't, you know, these cool hipster guys or anything," said a Las Vegas nightclub hostess who'd served Woods's entourage. "But, yeah, he partied with them a lot."

Uchitel had known Woods for two years—they met when she was dating his friend Derek Jeter—and was on the rebound from a high-profile tabloid relationship with the married actor David Boreanaz. She had started an affair with Woods in early October. She was to accompany him the following week to Dubai, where the billion-dollar Tiger Woods Dubai development was in deep trouble. His first golf course was to have been completed in September 2009, but Dubai had run dry of money. By March 2010, sales at the development were at a standstill, and only eight holes were finished. But that crisis was a headache for another day; Woods had more pressing concerns that Saturday.

Uchitel was confronted by a reporter for the *National Enquirer* when she arrived in Australia on Thursday, November 12. The supermarket tabloid photographed her checking into Crown Towers and at Melbourne airport. Uchitel had not checked into the hotel under her name; in fact, there was no record of her having been there, not even a room key issued in her name, yet she had a key to the sumptuous thirty-fifth floor. There were only two suites occupied on the casino's marquee floor that week, one by Woods and the other by "people from his management group," according to an executive at Crown. Steinberg was with Woods in Melbourne. When Uchitel tried to take the elevator to Woods's floor—he'd long before left for the golf course—a reporter for the *Enquirer* confronted her. She was caught off-guard but instinctively denied she'd gone there to see Woods. The incident put a damper on a brilliant opening-round 66 for Woods. Uchitel tried to talk her way out of the story. In phone call conversations with the *Enquirer*'s executive editor, Barry Levine, over the ensuing days, Uchitel made several plaintive denials, but Levine wasn't buying what she was selling. Ultimately, Woods decided that she needed to return to Las Vegas while a plan was hatched to deal with the *Enquirer*.

That Woods went on to win the Australian Masters by 2 strokes, earning a modest $250,000 to go with his appearance fee

plus a garish yellow jacket—an idea knocked off from Augusta—
and also giving him a victory on every continent, he joked, except
Antarctica, was a testament to his indomitable will. It spoke, too,
to his rare and frankly astonishing ability to compartmentalize
life. Woods, I had come to see, lived his life in boxes, which,
like an expert juggler, he made sure never came into contact with
one another. The "golf" box was separate from the "family" box,
which was separate from the "business" box, separate again from
the "adulterer" box. And it was almost as if he assumed a different personality for each box. Certainly the thorough, disciplined
golfer who left nothing to chance bore little resemblance to the
party animal who indiscriminately hit on cocktail waitresses. "I
think he's good at playing the person that you want [him to be],"
one of Woods's mistresses, Jaimee Grubbs, said in an interview
with KTLA in Los Angeles. "There's so many sides to him I didn't
know. I couldn't even tell you the person that he is."

Woods was worried but took solace in the fact that he'd been
in the same pickle two years before, when the *Enquirer* had evidence of his adultery. He immediately brought back into the fold
Jay Lavely Jr., the pit bull Hollywood lawyer who'd gotten him off
the hook last time. Lavely's expertise was extricating celebrities
from scandals and stiff-arming the tabloids. According to both the
Wall Street Journal and former *Men's Fitness* editor in chief Neal
Boulton, the *Enquirer* in 2007 had photographs of Woods making a sexual rendezvous in an Orlando parking lot with a plain-
looking pancake house waitress, Mindy Lawton. The tabloid kept
hidden from Woods's camp the fact that the photographs were
of poor quality. The *Enquirer*, according to the *Journal*, Boulton,
and Lawton—who claims Steinberg told her he'd take care of it—
agreed to a proposal from Woods's advisers to spike the story in
return for the golfer's appearance on the cover of its American
Media Inc. stablemate, *Men's Fitness*. The three-thousand-five-

hundred-word cover story was a coup for the magazine but raised red flags throughout the golf world, where it was well known that Woods loathed doing media interviews and certainly would never do one for free. "[Steinberg] wouldn't have thought twice about turning down the cover of *Time*," a former IMG executive told me by way of comparison. Further, Woods had a financial agreement with *Golf Digest*, which wasn't happy about the arrangement with *Men's Fitness* but had little choice other than to accept his decision. Questions about the magazine cover eventually faded, and soon it was back to business as usual. The truth about Woods's secret life had been buried, but rather than scare him straight, the incident emboldened Woods. If he'd merely thought he was bulletproof before, he now believed he was untouchable.

Lavely, whose list of clients included the heavy-hitting celebrities like Arnold Schwarzenegger, John Travolta, Jennifer Aniston, Brad Pitt, and Jennifer Lopez, got to work quickly. He had identified the *Enquirer*'s sources. Uchitel, in the late summer of 2009, had renewed an old friendship in Vegas with Jennifer Lee Madden. Like Uchitel, Madden had worked as a nightclub VIP hostess and had also been a *Playboy* model. Madden in turn introduced Uchitel to Ashley Samson, whose latest marriage had fallen apart and whose affair with Mötley Crüe front man Vince Neill had led to a public altercation with his wife. In October 2009, Uchitel had offered to fly both women on an all-expenses-paid holiday with her and another woman to Marbella, Spain, for three days. Samson and Madden claimed they had no idea they were expected to "entertain" four men who'd flown in from London. The trip ended disastrously, but during their time in Spain, Samson and Madden overheard Uchitel on her phone speaking with Woods, who was in Vegas. They claimed in numerous media interviews that Uchitel had told them graphic details of her affair with the golfer. Soon after arriving back in the United States, the two went to the *Enquirer* in search of easy money. Samson, who gave the tabloid a photograph of her and Uchitel in a suggestive pose at a Marbella nightclub as proof of their friendship, passed a polygraph test. She was paid $25,000, while Madden, who was not identified in the story—she would later appear, in disguise, on NBC's *Dateline* exposé of Woods's secret life—was paid about half as much for corroborating Samson's story.

The Woods camp developed a two-pronged strategy to combat the story. First, Uchitel would continue denying it to the *Enquirer*—claiming Samson and Madden were lying to get even with her—in the hope of buying time to silence both women. Samson wanted a large amount of money—"just preposterous," according to a source involved in the negotiations—but was ultimately offered $200,000 by the Woods camp. She had to sign a contract in which she admitted that she'd lied to the *Enquirer*. But Samson procrastinated. It was almost comedic in the undoing of Woods that Samson might have been more willing to take the hush money had she not been upset at Uchitel for giving her the cold shoulder during a night out at Yellowtail, the exquisite Japanese restaurant at the Bellagio. Uchitel left Samson and another woman to sit with *Entourage* star Jeremy Piven. Samson was so miffed that she determined to sell out Uchitel, whom she described to the *New York Daily News* as "a celebrity whore." Uchitel, however, talked a good game, and when she, too, offered to take a lie detector test for the *Enquirer*, the tabloid's editors decided to wait a week before publishing.

Woods ran into a fellow Tour player at Isleworth upon his return to Florida. The player, who'd known Woods for some time, sensed his friend was preoccupied. "I think I'm about to come out on the wrong side of a big media story," Woods confided. By Monday, November 23, Woods knew the *Enquirer* would be publishing that Thursday. The story had already started to go viral on the

Internet, though no mainstream news outlet—fearing the mother of all defamation lawsuits—dared rely on the *Enquirer*'s reporting. Uchitel, who'd worked at Bloomberg News in New York before getting into the nightclub business, was already talking to reporters, trashing Samson as unreliable and a woman with a vendetta against her. She repeatedly denied having an affair with Woods, saying she'd met him only a few times in the course of her duties at the clubs where she worked. The plan was for Woods to eventually issue a statement echoing Uchitel's denials in the hope that his credibility as a family man and sporting icon with a spotless character would outweigh the claims of women his team would portray as troubled Las Vegas party girls. Woods told his wife about the story that Monday. He denied he'd been unfaithful and on Wednesday persuaded Elin to speak with Uchitel. The two women spoke for half an hour until Elin was satisfied that her husband was telling the truth. She still, however, wanted to see his phone, prompting some quick maneuvering on Woods's part.

All was going according to plan until Thanksgiving. Woods had not been around the house much of the day and went to play poker with friends at Isleworth's clubhouse after dinner. He returned home late and called Uchitel, whose number was saved under another name in his phone. At around midnight he told her he was going to bed and took an Ambien, a potent sleeping pill that he often needed. About an hour later, Uchitel received a text message from Woods's phone. She replied that she thought he'd gone to sleep. Her phone then rang and, as it was Woods's number on her screen, she answered. It was, however, his wife, who'd gone through her husband's cell phone after he fell asleep and found incriminating evidence. "I knew it," Elin told Uchitel, whose voice she immediately recognized from their conversation the day before. "I knew it." Elin then confronted her groggy husband. An argument ensued. What happened over the next ninety minutes is truly known only by the two of them, but several sources close to the situation denied that she struck him with a golf club, as was widely rumored. Miami-based journalist Gerald Posner, who reported a similar version of the Thanksgiving happenings on the Daily Beast website in January 2010, quoted two sources close to Elin as saying she'd chased her husband through the house with one of his golf clubs.

What is known was that at about 2:25 a.m., Woods, dressed in a T-shirt and shorts, pulled his Cadillac Escalade out of the driveway and crashed into a fire hydrant and a tree. The Escalade's headlights shone into the home of his neighbor, Orlando physician Jerome Adams, waking his family. His wife, Linda, and two adults sons, Jarius and Jerome Jr., immediately ran outside and found Woods on the ground and his grief-stricken wife hovering over him, "freaking out," according to Jarius. One of the Adamses, a religious family, began reciting the Lord's Prayer as Woods drifted in and out of consciousness. Woods had a split lip, and blood was in his mouth. Jarius Adams made the 911 call, and in the background Woods's mother could be heard yelling, "What happened?" The Adamses brought out a blanket and pillow for Woods, who was soon snoring. When the authorities arrived, Elin told them she'd heard the accident and ran outside and, using a golf club, had smashed the back side windows in order to rescue her husband. She also told them that he'd been drinking earlier in the day and that he'd taken the powerful painkiller Vicodin— which he'd been taking since his knee surgery—as well as Ambien. Significantly, the paramedics would not let Elin ride with her husband to the hospital as a precaution in the event that a domestic dispute had led to Woods's injuries. As he was loaded into the back of the ambulance, his distraught wife began to cry again. "I love you," she said.

Woods had been traveling at very low speed—the car's air bags had not deployed—and it was conceivable that he'd hit his mouth on the steering wheel when he crashed. And it was conceivable that his wife had smashed the rear driver's side window in order to unlock the front door and rescue him. But alternate scenarios were just as likely. Investigators wanted to know, for instance, why both side rear windows had been shattered and exactly how Woods's lip had been split open. But when Woods was released from Health Central hospital early the following morning, he did not return home. His overarching priority was to deflect any attention from his wife. "Protecting Elin was his number one priority," said a source close to Woods. His lip was in bad shape and needed to be fixed. On the recommendation of an Orlando doctor, Woods would fly to Arizona to have it repaired by a plastic surgeon. The thinking was that he needed to lie low for a few days, anyway. It was a fateful decision, because the Woods camp had completely underestimated the media firestorm the story would touch off. Lavely and Steinberg thought like lawyers, but their client needed a public relations crisis management expert. "Mark was in way over his head," said a Woods insider who'd disagreed with Steinberg. It could get no worse for Steinberg than hearing that human train wreck John Daly say, "I love his agent, but I think he did a horrible job."

Within hours of the clarification of the first erroneous report—that Woods was in "serious condition" after a car accident—TV helicopters buzzed over Isleworth as the networks' satellite trucks were parking across the road. The three-ring circus that followed the Big Story had come to town. I'd been part of that circus, stretching back to O. J. Simpson through to Columbine and Michael Jackson's trial, and knew how it worked. The media was not unlike a three-year-old child transfixed by a glowing ball, acting as if there were nothing else in the world other than that ball, which got its whole and undivided attention . . . until the next shiny ball came along. But, unfortunately for Woods, December and January are the deadest of months in the news business. In the absence of anything better to report—Iraq, Afghanistan, and health-care reform weren't sexy enough—Woods had become the Big Story. The story could have evolved very differently had Elin not turned away the Florida Highway Patrol investigators that Friday afternoon, but of course she had no choice: her husband was in Arizona having emergency plastic surgery. But turning the troopers away with the excuse that Woods was sleeping only deepened the intrigue and mystery of the story. When the FHP was turned away again the following day, it seemed that Woods had something to hide. Woods did not leave Phoenix until 8 a.m. the morning of the 29th. When he finally met with the FHP later that day, the troopers who interviewed him reported that his only visible injury was "a fat lip." At the 2010 Masters, Woods revealed that the injury required five stitches.

The swollen lip made it difficult for Woods to speak properly. He didn't want to be seen in public and took to issuing statements on his website in an attempt to dampen speculation. Seeking to protect his wife, he said she'd "acted courageously when she saw I was hurt and in trouble. She was the first person to help me. Any other assertion is absolutely false." The statement said that the "situation is my fault and it's obviously embarrassing to my family and me." He vaguely hinted at something more by saying, "I'm human and I'm not perfect." Woods asserted that "my family and I deserve some privacy no matter how intrusive some people can be," but hiding behind the right to privacy wasn't going to make the satellite trucks and helicopters go away. Even with a fat lip, which he could have joked about, Woods needed to step in front of the cameras and, as they say, get in front of the story. Instead, he announced that he would be pulling out of his own tournament, the Chevron World Challenge outside Los Angeles, the following week. That enabled him to hide the injury and escape a barrage of uncomfortable questions about his marriage but only deepened the resolve of the media to get to the bottom of the story.

Once his lawyers got Woods off the hook for the crash with just a $164 fine for careless driving, it was back to tracking down women with whom he'd had affairs and buying their silence. But either they weren't fast enough or the list was too long. Even though Uchitel was still maintaining that she and Woods hadn't been having an affair, the game was up when Grubbs, a Los Angeles cocktail waitress with a checkered past whom Woods had been seeing for thirty-one months, sold him out to *US* magazine for $100,000. Any further attempts at plausible deniability were destroyed when Grubbs released a voice mail from Woods, which she said he'd left on November 24: "Can you please, uh, take your name off your phone [message]. My wife went through my phone and, uh, may be calling you. If you can, please take your name off that and, um, and what do you call it, just have it as a number on the voice mail; just have it as your telephone number. That's it, okay. You gotta do this for me. Huge. Quickly. All right. Bye." Anyone who knew Woods and his speech patterns immediately recognized his voice. Grubbs also released sexually themed text messages from a trove of three hundred she alleged she'd kept from their affair, which began when she was a twenty-one-year-old slinging drinks in Vegas. In response, Woods released another statement on his website, regretting "transgressions"—a word only a lawyer could love—and admitting that he had let his family down.

The savvy Uchitel quickly changed teams. She dropped her denials and retained the Los Angeles "victim's rights" attorney Gloria Allred, whose speciality was generating publicity for her clients and for herself, not usually in that order. Uchitel wanted Lavely to know she meant business. After flying to LA from her home in New York, harried by paparazzi at both ends of the trip, Uchitel called a news conference to discuss her "relationship" with Woods, the first time she'd used the word. It was widely reported that she would spill the beans on their affair. The news conference, however, was canceled at the last moment, and it was well known that Allred didn't cancel news conferences without good reason. Or millions of good reasons. Allred's daughter, television legal analyst Lisa Bloom, estimated that Woods had paid "at least a million" to keep Uchitel quiet. In fact, the figure was higher.

Woods, meanwhile, sank to his lowest ebb. His wife, whose financial security had been sweetened in the immediate wake of the scandal in a desperate attempt to keep her from leaving then and there, was devastated by his betrayal. She consulted divorce lawyers and didn't want him under the same roof. All of her husband's golf trophies, which had filled the family home, were removed. Woods moved into another home at Isleworth and changed his phone number. He was in "the fetal position," according to one source, and didn't want to talk to anyone. Long-standing friends, including Charles Barkley and Mark O'Meara, publicly lamented the fact that they could not reach Woods. Steinberg drew much fire from many of Woods's friends who were unable to get through to him. "He became very reclusive, he was depressed, devastated, and most of all, I think, embarrassed," said a source close to Woods. A member of Team Tiger told me at the time that Woods "wasn't reading anything, wasn't watching TV" because it was "too depressing." If he had been, he would've known that tabloid allegations of mistresses spread by Internet celebrity gossip sites were now being reported in the mainstream media.

A key member of his team often bemoaned to me the lack of "ethics" of the mainstream media during the feeding frenzy but failed to see his and his colleagues' responsibility in the way the story was reported. It was a game, but they refused to play and so lost by default. They thought silence and demanding privacy would make the story go away, when in fact it only gave the merchants of gossip a louder, more commanding voice. The *Enquirer* had to be right only once—as it was with Uchitel—and that scoop had given the tabloid a newfound credibility. When one of Uchitel's friends leaked her travel itinerary to Australia, which implicated Bell, to TMZ.com, it gave respectability to that dubious website. When the New York tabloids were breaking fresh angles almost daily, reputable news outlets felt left behind and began to parrot their stories. In a vacuum, anything gets sucked in, including lies, and Tiger's team helped create that vacuum by not countering the fabrications—even off the record, with leaks. A source with some knowledge of the media strategy defended the handling as the by-product of a bunker mentality coupled with the fact that they didn't know how many women would come forward with claims. "They got a lot of criticism, but you've got to understand that they didn't know the scope of the problem. It was a wait-and-see game to see who else would come out of the woodwork."

The scope of the problem turned out to be beyond their worst nightmares. Sponsors, all of whom had standard morality clauses in their endorsement contracts, began abandoning ship. Accenture, AT&T, and Gatorade took about $30 million a year off the table, while Gillette and Tag Heuer suspended campaigns featuring Woods. Fund-raising for his foundation became nearly impossible. Pettily, General Motors made a song and dance from the fact that Woods would no longer be provided with free cars and that the world's most famous Escalade would be returned. Only Nike, which had built a $750-million-a-year golf business on his shoulders, and EA Sports, which made the profitable Tiger Woods video game, stuck by him.

Woods wanted to save his marriage. The only light at the end of that particular tunnel, however, was that his wife had yet to file for divorce. Elin had her own reasons for waiting, and none had to do with salvaging her husband's image. She was the child of divorce, and knew how difficult it was for the children. In December, a Woods insider who liked Elin told me that there was "no way that marriage is going to survive." But another source said it was not as cut-and-dried. "If it wasn't for Sam and Charlie, she'd have been out of there, but she's thinking of them. She's not going to be rushed into anything. Maybe in the back of her mind she thinks he'll be different?" To that end, Woods convinced his wife to attend therapy sessions with him in California and spend a family Christmas at their home in Newport Beach, south of Los Angeles. It wasn't lost on Elin that Jamie Jungers, one of Woods's paramours, had said she'd had sex with Woods at that house, filled with family photographs and wedding pictures, the night his father died in 2006. These ghosts will haunt him for the rest of his life.

But both Elin and Tiger were devoted parents and determined to keep their children's lives as normal as possible. And so, as the media stalked them in Orlando the family opened presents under a large tree and celebrated Christmas in California. For a brief moment, it seemed all could be right again, but the unpalatable reality of his life dawned on Woods when his wife took their kids—to whom she speaks Swedish—on his jet and flew to Europe for the rest of the holidays. Woods stayed behind to contemplate his next step. He no longer wanted to hide under a rock but needed to show his wife—and, one would hope, himself—that he was serious about reformation. He spent the week with his mother and reconnected with the Buddhist philosophy he'd strayed from since his teenage years. "Just before his 34th birthday on December 30th, [Tida] accompanied Tiger on their annual visit with a Buddhist monk," wrote Jaime Diaz in *Golf Digest*. "Afterward, her son confided that he was struggling with all the upheaval. 'I tell him, Tiger, right now you are in a dark hole, and I know it's hard, but you can do it,' Tida says. 'You know Mom is strong, and you have my blood. You are strong, too. You made a big mistake, but now you know the cost. So you are going to be much better and stronger, a good husband and a good father. Just go to work like you do.'"

With that, Woods bit the bullet, and after his birthday checked himself into Pine Grove, an out-of-the-way rehabilitation facility in Hattiesburg, Mississippi. Woods remained for forty-five days of inpatient care, which by all accounts was grueling and at the very least helped him confront the person he'd become. Even if experts were doubtful that sex addiction even existed, Woods was made to examine his behavior as part of a twelve-step program similar to Alcoholics Anonymous. Midway through Woods's rehab, word leaked that he was at the facility, which quickly built a higher fence to keep the paparazzi out. But eventually he was snapped and the photograph sold, fittingly enough, to the *Enquirer*. A few days later, a black man, bearing a resemblance to a local police officer, was seen wandering around the facility wearing the exact same clothes Woods had been wearing when photographed, right down to the hoodie. The juvenile attempt at misdirection didn't fool anyone.

A contrite Woods emerged from therapy—which his wife had been part of—and on February 19 at the PGA Tour headquarters in the suburbs of Jacksonville, he assembled several dozen family members, friends, and business acquaintances to offer an apology. His wife was not there, and it was perhaps just as well, for America had already seen too many clichéd apologies from adulterous politicians whose wives stood next to them like props. Woods allowed a television camera to film him, but only a few reporters were present as observers. He did not take any questions. Woods, who was clearly nervous, wrote the thirteen-and-a-half-minute speech himself, which was cleaned up only for grammatical errors, an insider told me. It was delivered in a funereal atmosphere, with Woods emerging from behind a dark blue curtain dressed somberly in a blue button-down shirt and a dark blazer. He was a very different man from the red Tiger of Sundays on the golf course. He apologized for "selfish and irresponsible behavior." Again, he was at pains to absolve his wife of any blame. "The issue here is that I cheated, I am the only person to blame." Significantly, Woods seemed to acknowledge the underlying causes of his infidelities. He may have been "very highly sexed," as Jungers and other women maintained, but more to the point, his real downfall was that he'd felt he could act on his whims with impunity; the sex was symptomatic of a greater problem. "I stopped living according to my core values. I knew what I was doing was wrong but thought only about myself and thought I could get away with whatever I wanted to. I felt I was entitled. I had worked hard. Money and fame made me believe I was entitled. I was wrong and foolish. I don't get to live by different rules. The same boundaries that apply to everyone apply to me. I hurt my mother, my wife, kids, friends, my foundation. This has made me look at myself in a way I never wanted to again."

Even after the apology and the subsequent five-minute mini-interviews he gave to ESPN and the Golf Channel ahead of his return to competitive golf at the 2010 Masters, the question that lingered most was, Why? Why had he thrown it all away? Theories abounded. His high school sweetheart, Dina Gravell-Parr, offered insights in a round of media interviews. She recalled Woods calling her when he was at Stanford, crying that his father, a serial philanderer, was with another woman and how it was devastating his mother. "He loved his father. And I know that was the one thing about his dad that he could never get over. So yeah, it's interesting that it's turning out that he's doing the same thing." But she also felt there was another factor in Woods's childhood that might have contributed. "Tiger's biggest setback was he didn't have an example of a normal family life. He was close to both parents, but they just weren't a family unit. Everything was golf and school. He doesn't have the know-how to make a family work."

Neither were Woods's friends living monastic lives. Woods might not feel black, but he gravitated to famous black athletes for guidance after his breakthrough Masters. According to a 2001 story in *Newsweek*, Woods went to see Jordan in 1997 after a game at Chicago's United Center and "the two sped away in Jordan's black Porsche to Lake Michigan, where they boarded a luxury casino boat to relax away from the glare of the spotlight. The two men, who had previously chatted only in passing, talked into the wee hours about the pressures of fame, the strain of competition and what it means to be in the select group of people known as the 'greatest ever.' A friendship was struck that night, and soon Tiger found himself part of Jordan's inner-inner circle, along with former basketball player Charles Barkley and pro-football star turned announcer Ahmad Rashad. The Brothers, they like to call themselves. 'Our bond is that we're black, famous and rich, and living in a fishbowl,' says Barkley. 'Tiger is our younger brother— that's the best way to describe him,' says Jordan." But these brothers weren't exactly good influences; when they were in Las Vegas, they managed to avoid the gossip pages by bringing the party upstairs, positioning burly bodyguards in the corridors to ensure discretion. Years before, *Vanity Fair* reported that John Merchant, Woods's then lawyer, warned him to "stay away from that son of a bitch, because he doesn't have anything to offer to the fucking world in which he lives except playing basketball." Well before the truth about Woods's secret life broke, Jordan received a text message from Woods and, according to a source who was there, shook his head, saying Woods had gotten "out of control." Jordan tried to talk Woods into being more discreet, but his warnings fell on deaf ears. Woods had become even more reckless. His trysts were no longer limited to Las Vegas or conducted while he was "traveling," as he told his wife, either at tournaments or on business. Woods had taken to partying in bars in Orlando. "I tried to stop, and I couldn't stop," Woods told Kelly Tilghman during a March 2010 interview. "It was just . . . it was horrific."

It was almost as if Woods, knowing he couldn't stop himself, found another way to bring an end to his destructive pattern of behavior. "She gave him a long leash, but I just figured maybe that's because Swedes are a little more relaxed about these things than American women would be," said a source. "But in a sick, sad way, I have to think he knew he would get caught. These women [he'd had affairs with] weren't rocket scientists, they were basically glorified call girls. He had to know it was only a matter of time before they'd sell him out. Personally, I think he was self-destructing. There's no question he was under a lot of pressure, being Tiger Woods. He's had a lot of pressure on his shoulders for a very long time. There's all these people who are always counting on him, plus he's got to win. No one else has to win every time they play except him. I think it got to him." But the friend also offered another view, one echoed by others I'd spoken with about Woods's marriage: that it was never the idyllic union it seemed. "He was a late bloomer. Even when he was at Stanford, he was kind of nerdy. Then suddenly his body changed and he matured into this confident guy and he made up for lost time. What I've always wondered is, Did he get married too early? I think he just got caught up in the idea of getting married. I think he jumped into it too soon."

When Tom Rinaldi asked Woods why he'd gotten married if he

wanted to keeping playing the field, Woods responded earnestly, "Because I loved her." Elin Nordegren was by many measures a great catch. Woods noticed her immediately when he saw her looking after the children of golfer Jesper Parnevik, whose wife, Mia, met Elin in a Stockholm boutique and thought she'd make a great nanny. Nordegren was stunningly beautiful, level-headed, independent, smart, sporty and, very important to Woods, had no desire to be in the limelight. The daughter of a veteran radio journalist father and a politician mother did not give interviews and would turn down even *Vanity Fair*. The only person who had ever spoken publicly about her was Bingo Rimér, the Swedish photographer who'd used her as a model. "Elin doesn't care about modeling," he told *Sports Illustrated*. "She never has. Even the few things I got her to do, I had to drag her into the studio. Being famous, the whole celebrity thing, she really and truly does not care about that." A member of Team Tiger said that Nordegren "knew her role, which was to stay out of the public eye. If you noticed, she was never there when he finished a round. If she'd been watching him, she was gone by the time he finished." He shrugged when I asked whether the couple had simply fallen out of love. "I don't know."

But it's worth remembering that Woods didn't just decide one day that he was unhappily married and begin affairs; he'd been having these rendezvous for years. He just didn't stop when he got married in 2004. I'm not even sure what that says other than in his compartmentalized mind these women represented merely a recreation, much like the scuba diving he enjoys. "Let's get one thing straight, these weren't relationships," says a source close to Woods. "He wasn't ever leaving [Elin] for one of these women."

The grander question, the one that cuts to the heart of everything and can't yet be answered, will be how this most tumultuous of seasons will shape his career. How will history judge

Eldrick Tiger Woods? Where will "serial philanderer" feature when his obituary's written? Will the revelations of 2009 define him, overshadowing all else? Is that fair? But is it any less an incomplete picture of the man than the one offered by the moral relativists and the simply hedonistic who see his adultery as irrelevant? It would've been less relevant if he hadn't wanted to be a role model—thus betraying his own ideals—and hadn't taken all that money from sponsors who needed him as the wholesome all-American hero to move product. Many others will look at Woods and see a flawed genius: a victim of, as Smith wrote, "the machine" of fame and celebrity, which says just as much about us as it does about him.

But maybe in the end, even if he won't alter the course of human history as his father believed, he'll just be the world's greatest golfer. Nike chairman Phil Knight—who admittedly has a vested interest in thinking so—says that "when his career is over, you'll look back on these indiscretions as a minor blip." And perhaps he's right. People are, by and large, forgiving and nothing succeeds in effecting selective amnesia like success; the fuel on which America runs. F. Scott Fitzgerald may have believed that there were no second acts in American life, but Tiger Woods may yet author one.

He begins the next act of his career as a 35-year-old with fourteen majors and a marriage in limbo. Because he'd never concede defeat at anything, he was determined to make the up-and-down of his life in saving that marriage. But even if he fails, even if his cheating destroyed his marriage, can he still be golf's greatest player? He needs five majors to realize the dreams he'd dreamed as a boy. He has less time than he thinks to win them. Nicklaus won only four after he'd turned 36, including a hopelessly romantic sixth green jacket at the age of 46. Byron Nelson won his last major at 33, as did Tom Watson, Gary Player won only one of his nine majors after the age of 38, Walter Hagen was 36 when he stopped winning them, and Palmer never won one after turning 34. Bobby Jones retired at 28 after winning his Grand Slam. Certainly, Woods has the talent and the drive to make it happen. But the next act of his life will depend entirely not so much upon how we see him, but how he sees himself. "I remember he always used to say to me, 'I just can't sleep. I can't get any sleep,' " a friend of Woods told me. And if he is to succeed, maybe that's how he'll know. He'll be able to sleep again.

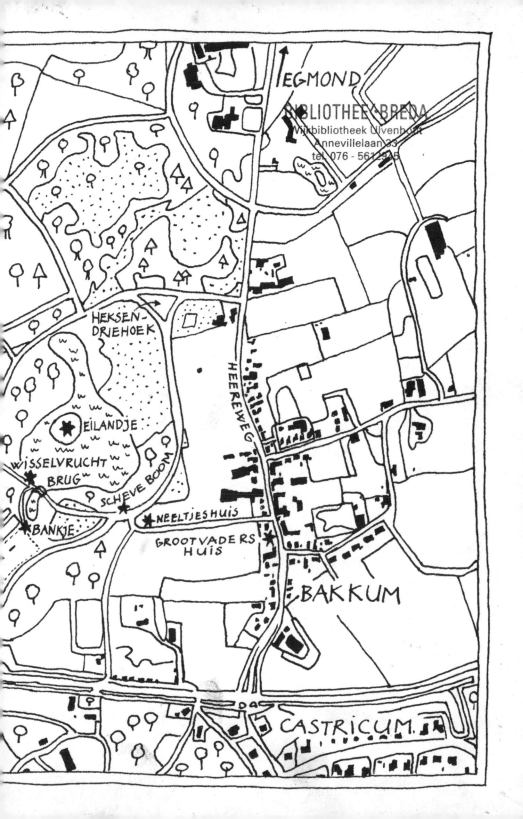

EGMOND

HEKSEN-
DRIEHOEK

HEEREWEG

EILANDJE

WISSELVRUCHT
BRUG

SCHEVE BOOM

BANKJE

NEELTJESHUIS

GROOTVADERS
HUIS

BAKKUM

CASTRICUM